C0068 90335

D0335701

Praise for the Rhona MacLeod series

'Forensic scientist Rhona MacLeod has become one of the most satisfying characters in modern crime fiction – honourable, inquisitive and yet plagued by doubts and, sometimes, fears . . . As ever, the landscape is stunningly evoked and MacLeod's decency and humanity shine through on every page' *Daily Mail*

'Lin Anderson is one of Scotland's national treasures . . . her writing is unique, bringing warmth and depth to even the seediest parts of Glasgow. Rhona MacLeod is a complex and compelling heroine who just gets better with every outing' Stuart MacBride

'Vivid and atmospheric . . . enthralling' *Guardian*

'The bleak landscape is beautifully described, giving this popular series a new lease of life' *Sunday Times*

'Greenock-born Anderson's work is sharper than a pathologist's scalpel. One of the best Scottish crime series since Rebus' *Daily Record*

'Inventive, compelling, genuinely scary and beautifully written, as always' Denzil Meyrick

'Hugely imaginative and exciting'
  James Grieve (Emeritus Professor of Forensic Pathology)

The Killing Tide

Lin Anderson is a Scottish author and screenwriter known for her bestselling crime series featuring forensic scientist Dr Rhona MacLeod. Four of her novels have been longlisted for the Scottish Crime Book of the Year, with *Follow the Dead* being a 2018 finalist. Her short film *River Child* won both a Scottish BAFTA for Best Fiction and the Celtic Film Festival's Best Drama Award and has now been viewed more than one million times on YouTube. Lin is also the co-founder of the international crime-writing festival Bloody Scotland, which takes place annually in Stirling.

Paths of the Dead
When a body is found inside a Neolithic stone circle, Rhona is called in to investigate.

The Special Dead
Rhona and DS Michael McNab look into the ancient practice of Wicca following a ritualistic killing.

None but the Dead
Rhona heads to the remote island of Sanday when human remains are discovered beneath an old school.

Follow the Dead
A killer stalks the Cairngorms in the Scottish Highlands after a mysterious plane crashes on a nearby loch.

Sins of the Dead
Rhona is being targeted by a terrifying killer whose methods echo the ancient religious practice of sin-eating.

Time for the Dead
Rhona investigates a series of brutal deaths on Scotland's Isle of Skye.

The Innocent Dead
A decades-old cold case is reopened when a body is discovered in a peat bog south of Glasgow.

The Killing Tide
When three bodies are found on a wrecked ship in the Orkney isles, forensic scientist Rhona MacLeod is brought in to investigate.

The Killing Tide

Dark water. Darker deeds.

LIN ANDERSON

PAN BOOKS

First published 2021 by Macmillan

This paperback edition published 2022 by Pan Books
an imprint of Pan Macmillan
The Smithson, 6 Briset Street, London EC1M 5NR
EU representative: Macmillan Publishers Ireland Ltd, 1st Floor,
The Liffey Trust Centre, 117–126 Sheriff Street Upper,
Dublin 1, D01 YC43
Associated companies throughout the world
www.panmacmillan.com

ISBN 978-1-5290-3369-4

Copyright © Lin Anderson 2021

The right of Lin Anderson to be identified as the
author of this work has been asserted by her in accordance
with the Copyright, Designs and Patents Act 1988.

All rights reserved. No part of this publication may be reproduced,
stored in a retrieval system, or transmitted, in any form, or by any means
(electronic, mechanical, photocopying, recording or otherwise)
without the prior written permission of the publisher.

Pan Macmillan does not have any control over, or any responsibility for,
any author or third-party websites referred to in or on this book.

3 5 7 9 8 6 4 2

A CIP catalogue record for this book is available from the British Library.

Map artwork by Hemesh Alles

Typeset in Meridien by Palimpsest Book Production Ltd, Falkirk, Stirlingshire
Printed and bound by CPI Group (UK) Ltd, Croydon, CR0 4YY

This book is sold subject to the condition that it shall not, by way of
trade or otherwise, be lent, hired out, or otherwise circulated without
the publisher's prior consent in any form of binding or cover other than
that in which it is published and without a similar condition including
this condition being imposed on the subsequent purchaser.

Visit **www.panmacmillan.com** to read more about all our books
and to buy them. You will also find features, author interviews and
news of any author events, and you can sign up for e-newsletters
so that you're always first to hear about our new releases.

For
Vina and Geordie Pirie
Who gave us our first home in Orkney

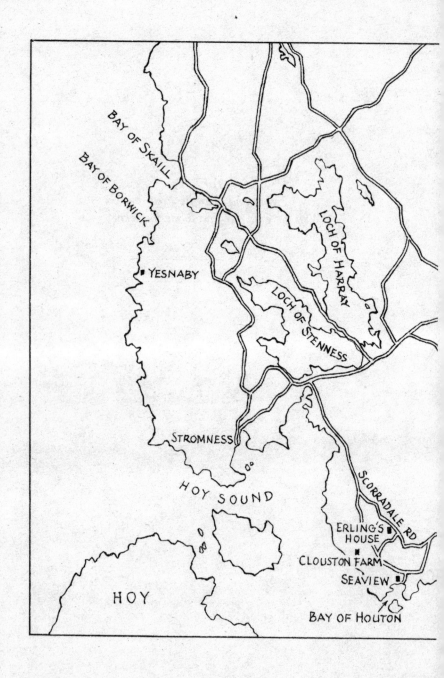

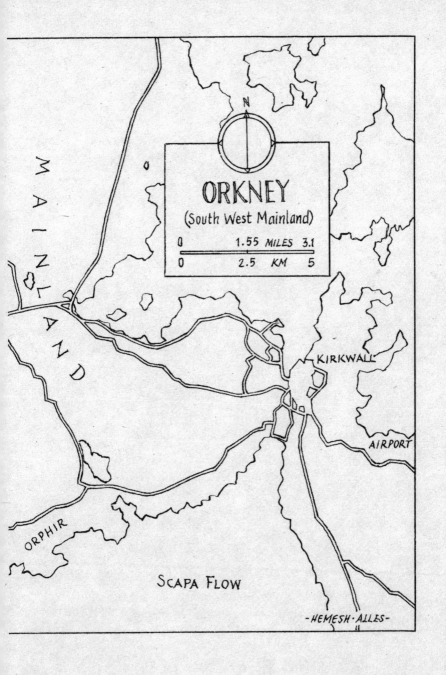

1

The latest storm was female.

Birka had swept in from the Atlantic like the Viking shield maiden she was named after, sharpened sword at the ready to attack the northern isles of Scotland.

Orkney, used to high winds and seas, was weathering the late April storm, just as the archipelago had done over the centuries, its low houses and sheltered towns built to survive the worst that the weather might throw at it.

Towards daybreak, as the wind began to diminish in strength, a few folk ventured out to check that their barns, housing the wintering kye, still had their roofs, and the sheep in the fields hadn't been blown away.

Geordie Findlater was one of them. His farm, being on the western side of the Orkney mainland, often took the brunt of the cross-Atlantic weather, with the fields closest to the Yesnaby cliffs soaked by salt spray.

Having satisfied himself that his barn and cattle were unharmed, Geordie now headed for a knot of sheep huddled in the shelter of a dyke. At that moment the clouds parted and the dawn light lit up the frothing sea beyond the cliffs . . . and something else.

Geordie, brushing the driving rain from his eyes, tried to focus on what he thought might be the outline of a ship.

As the moon peeked out again, he saw that he was right.

What looked like an unlit cargo ship was being driven towards the cliff face. Geordie decided to try and get closer. Already on his knees, he dropped to a crawl and managed to get near enough to the cliff edge to see it properly.

Taking out his mobile, he did his best to capture some shots, thinking all the time that if anyone was still aboard that ship, they were in serious trouble.

Mission accomplished, he began his retreat only to be confronted by what all fishermen knew as the seventh wave. He noted the outsize wave as it came rushing towards him, felt the ground beneath him shudder as it crashed against the cliff face, deluging him in its spray, and knew what would happen next.

Grabbing at the nearest rock, Geordie hung grimly on as the sucking backflow threatened to drag him with it.

Eventually released, he got to his feet and, with the wind now thankfully at his back, headed for the lights of the farmhouse. Throwing open the door, he staggered into the warmth of the kitchen, where Bella, his wife, cried out in relief.

'I was about to come and look for you, Geordie. What is it?' she said, seeing his expression. 'What's wrong?'

Still choked by wind and water, Geordie handed her the mobile. 'Look,' he managed.

Bella stared at the fuzzy photograph unblinkingly for a moment before her face registered what she was seeing.

'Take off your wet things, Geordie, and sit by the range. I'll make you a hot drink after I call the coastguard.'

2

Rhona surveyed her cleared plate with satisfaction. Not much of a cook herself, she usually settled for a takeaway after work, especially if she'd been at a crime scene.

Once at a locus, she could be there for up to twelve hours, meticulously processing the victim and their immediate surroundings. That didn't stop her getting hungry, of course, plus her forensic assistant Chrissy McInsh was famous for the size of her appetite. There had been plenty of times when a 'starving' Chrissy had felt the need to send a uniform off to the nearest chippy while still working a scene.

If Rhona arrived home hungry from a long day at the lab, she went straight for the menu cards in the kitchen and ordered whatever would arrive the quickest.

Not tonight, however.

Tonight she'd come home to the scent of slow-cooked venison in red wine with mushrooms, garlic, onions, carrots and potatoes prepared by the man opposite . . . Sean Maguire, the dark-haired, blue-eyed saxophonist who, although they weren't actually living together, did on occasion both feed and bed her.

This evening the sex had come first.

Sean indicated her almost empty wine glass, offering to top it up. Rhona nodded as another blast of rain hit the kitchen window.

'Jeez,' Sean said, 'that's one serious wind.'

According to the radio update, Glasgow wasn't in the direct line of the storm sweeping in from the Atlantic, although the forecaster did mention the great gale of '68 when many of the tenement buildings, similar to Rhona's, had had their roofs torn off by the strength of the wind.

On this occasion it seemed the worst of the storm was hitting Orkney, where gusts of over ninety miles an hour had been recorded. At this point, Rhona wondered how Magnus's house, Seaview, was faring, built as it was on the shores of Scapa Flow.

'Has Magnus gone home for the Easter break?' Sean said, reading her thoughts.

'He usually does.' A professor of criminal psychology at Strathclyde University, Magnus Pirie liked to return to his native island whenever he got the chance. 'I'll maybe check on him later,' she said. 'Make sure he's not blown away.'

As Sean began to clear the table and stack the dishwasher, Rhona intervened. 'I'll do that. You'd better get ready for the jazz club – although judging by the weather, you may not have much of a crowd tonight.'

'The diehards always turn out, come hell or high water,' Sean reminded her.

'You're going to get soaked,' she warned. 'Maybe you should try for an Uber?'

'No worries. I've got dry clothes at the club.' Sean glanced at the window as another blast of wind and rain rattled the glass. 'Though if it carries on like this, I might bunk down in the back office afterwards.'

Rhona tried not to look too pleased by that, although she had been planning to suggest he go home to his own flat tonight anyway.

Sean was observing her, a small smile playing on his lips. 'You're done with me for tonight, I take it?'

Rhona smiled her answer.

'Then I'll be gone.'

She followed him into the hall and watched as he dressed for the weather. He gave her a hug and reminded her to call him.

'Of course,' Rhona promised, though not saying exactly when that might be.

He opened the door to the shriek of the wind in the stairwell.

'The garden door hasn't been shut properly,' Rhona said.

'I'll bolt it as I go out,' Sean promised.

She watched as his tall figure headed down the stairs, perturbed that she was glad to have the flat to herself again. But hadn't it always been like this? Even from that first night, when they'd met at DI Bill Wilson's fiftieth birthday party at the jazz club, and she'd taken Sean home with her.

There had been a few times since then when their on-off relationship had appeared to be at an end, but then the positives would persuade them back together again. She was pretty sure Sean didn't spend much time fretting about where he stood with her. She, on the other hand, probably analysed it too much.

As the shriek stopped, signalling that the back door had been shut and bolted, Rhona headed inside and, fetching her wine, took it and her phone through to the sitting room, where the gas fire was dancing in the draught from the chimney.

Sitting on the couch, feet up, Tom the cat on her knee, she pulled up Magnus's number.

His voice, when he answered, was rich in its Orkney

heritage. When in Glasgow he usually modified it, dropping the descriptive phrases so reminiscent of his native isles.

'Describe the wind for me,' she said after his welcome greeting.

'Well, here in Orphir we might call it a skreevar. Across on Hoy it would likely be called a katrizper. The UK weather forecasters are referring to it as Birka, which is, as you know, the name of a female Viking. So not a bad choice.'

'What's Scapa Flow like?' Rhona said.

'Pretty angry,' Magnus said. 'Throwing her wrath at the back o' the hoose as we speak. How's my favourite city faring?'

Through the sitting-room window, Rhona could just make out the thrashing trees of Kelvingrove Park via the nearby street lights. 'You know Glasgow. Nothing much daunts her.'

'So no flying roof tiles as yet?'

'Not around here anyway.'

They chatted for a few minutes more before Rhona said her goodbyes and offered her hope that Magnus might get some sleep despite the wind.

'I doubt Birka's shrieking will allow for that,' Magnus said with a laugh, 'although a whisky nightcap might help.'

Sleep proved elusive in Glasgow too as the howling wind, peppered by the distant shriek of sirens, no doubt answering emergency calls, kept Rhona on red alert.

Eventually she did doze off with Tom stretched out alongside, the cat having no issue with the Viking maiden's assault on Glasgow, or indeed on Scotland for that matter.

3

Inspector Erling Flett picked up the drilling mobile and, rising, headed for the kitchen before answering, not wanting his partner, Rory, to be disturbed. They'd had little enough sleep, what with the wind howling round the cottage all night.

Erling, being Orcadian, was used to the constant winds of the islands, but last night the storm that had battered his low-lying croft house had surprised even him in its ferocity. High on the Scorradale Road, his home faced any onslaught coming across Scapa Flow from the south and the east.

'What's up, Constable?' he said, recognizing PC Ivan Tulloch's voice.

'Looks like we have a stray ship on the rocks up by Yesnaby. I've sent over the photo Geordie Findlater took at first light this morning. The coastguard's been alerted, sir.'

Erling brought up the image, which had obviously been taken amidst the storm. Through the early light and the falling rain, he could just make out what looked like a battered cargo ship tossing about just a short distance from the famous cliff face.

'Any crew on board?'

'Coastguard says there was no Mayday call. They suspect it might be a ghost ship brought here from the Atlantic by the storm.'

Abandoned vessels, known as ghost ships, were plentiful

at sea and often ended up on Atlantic-facing coastlines, the most recent having been washed up on the west coast of Ireland. They were also a devil to deal with, especially if there was fuel still in their tanks.

PC Tulloch continued, 'They haven't managed to get near it as yet, sir, although the wind's forecast to drop by the afternoon.'

'Okay, I'll head over there.'

'What's up?' Rory had entered as the call ended, encircling Erling in his arms.

'The storm's brought a ship ashore up by Yesnaby.'

'God,' Rory said, studying the photograph. 'Who was brave enough to take that?'

'Farmer Geordie Findlater went out to check that his sheep hadn't blown away and spotted it.'

'It looks abandoned. No lights on anyway. I take it the coastguard knows?'

Erling nodded. 'No Mayday signal, so they think it's likely to have been abandoned somewhere mid-Atlantic and driven here by the storm.'

'What about the fuel tanks?' Rory said worriedly.

'My first thought too.'

If the ship was holed below the waterline and there was still diesel in the tanks, they could have an ecological disaster on their hands.

'I was due back on Flotta,' Rory said, 'but I could stay here in case I'm needed.'

They would definitely have to check out the ship's hull for any damage, and that would require a professional diver, which was Rory's job at the oil terminal. Erling was pleased he'd offered to stay, without being asked. He kissed him as a thank you.

'You want food before you head out?' Rory offered.

'Coffee and a bannock to take away would be great,' Erling said as he went to get dressed.

'Did you get the name of the ship?' Rory called after him.

'MV *Orlova*.'

'Sounds Russian,' Rory said as he set up the coffee machine and extracted cheese from the fridge to load up the bannock.

Minutes later, Erling was heading up the steps to the road and his car. Outwith the shelter of the cottage, the wind was still strong enough to nearly take his car door off as he attempted to get inside.

Pulling away from the cottage, he was presented by a fine view of Scapa Flow, still raging after the battering it had had overnight.

Erling could only imagine what the sea off Yesnaby would be like.

4

The wind had lifted a few tiles, but they were easily replaced. As for the hen house? Where it had ended up, Ava Clouston had no idea. Although she'd taken the precaution of shutting the hens in the big barn along with the wintering kye, so they wouldn't be blown away too.

Nevertheless, she'd spent most of the night awake and peering out of the window, just to check that the barn was still intact. Having lived in London for years now, she'd forgotten just how much damage the wind up here could do, and Storm Birka had apparently been the worst to hit Orkney for a while.

Heading for the byre, she said a silent thank you to her farming neighbour, Tommy Flett, who'd advised her not to let the cattle out to graze before the first of May, despite the recent bout of good spring weather and the lush green grass that awaited them.

Her heart was heavy as she trudged through the mud, not because of the storm, but because the storm had only served to amplify the decision she must take, and soon. The funeral had been nearly two months ago and she still hadn't worked out what to do with the family farm. Pain gripped her again as she recalled the terrible call that had brought her rushing home to Orkney. Her much-loved parents, both dead in a freak car accident.

Orkney rarely faced ice and snow. Wind was its main winter enemy and yet on that particular night her parents' car had hit black ice coming home from Kirkwall, which had taken them into the path of a lorry.

According to the police, their deaths had been instant, so no chance for either Ava or her teenage brother, Dougie, to say goodbye. Dougie had called her in London, his voice breaking, and of course she'd caught the first plane north to Inverness, then across to Kirkwall.

Escaping the busy city to alight in Kirkwall had always been such a pleasurable experience until that day. In fact, Ava doubted whether it would ever be pleasurable again.

Much as she loved Orkney, she had chosen not to live and work there after graduation. She'd pursued her dream of becoming an investigative journalist and succeeded. Although based in London, her work took her all over the world, sometimes into scary and threatening situations. It didn't stop her loving it.

Coming back here to run the family farm seemed much more daunting and, frankly, much less enjoyable. That thought alone was torturing her. Then there was Dougie to consider. Only seventeen, he was in no position to run the farm on his own, no matter how much he wanted to.

For Dougie, grief at the death of his beloved parents had now been replaced by anger that his sister should even contemplate selling the farm, his birthright, instead of staying here to run it with him.

Her troubled thoughts beat at her, much like the buffeting wind, as she made her way to the byre. Straight ahead she could see the boathouse, where no doubt Dougie had gone to nurse his wrath after their latest confrontation, brought on by the storm. She had lost her cool, pointing out to him how unprepared they were to deal with both the finances of the farm and the physical work it required. Plus how was she going to earn a living here, doing what she did?

Thinking about the words she'd uttered in the midst of the storm, panicked as she had been, she knew they were still inexcusable. Dougie had had every right to take refuge with his beloved dog, Finn, and his boat, the *Fear Not.*

Dougie was fearless in a way that only the young can be. Hence the name of the boat he'd learned to sail on Scapa Flow as soon as their parents had permitted it. John Rae, the intrepid Victorian Orcadian adventurer, had always been his idol and it had been sailing Scapa Flow where the explorer had tested himself as a young man, before he'd set sail for Canada as a ship's surgeon.

Entering the byre, Ava felt the warmth envelop her. The moos that greeted her showed no fear of what had happened overnight. A series of big eyes turned her way and their breath blossomed in the air. Ava suddenly remembered her childhood and how much she'd loved being in here with the cows.

The hens she'd secured in the stall next to the door came hurrying towards her, squawking their excitement at the food Ava now scattered. She would have to rebuild the hen house, of course, but in the meantime they could stay here, since the kye would shortly be released to graze on the new grass.

At that moment her mobile rang.

'Ava Clouston?'

'Yes?'

'*The Orcadian* newspaper here. We wondered if you would be interested in covering a story for us? A Russian cargo ship has foundered off Yesnaby. It's believed to be a ghost ship, probably abandoned mid-Atlantic. The coast-guard and police are on site already. Is that something you'd be interested in?'

'Of course,' Ava said, her heart lifting. 'Do we know the ship's name?'

'The MV *Orlova*.'

5

Rhona rose with the dawn, having had little to no sleep.

After setting up the coffee machine, she headed for the kitchen window to view the damage. In the neighbouring convent garden, she was pleased to see the statue of the Virgin Mary still upright, although the well-kept lawn that normally surrounded her had now been replaced by a moat. As for her own back garden, it looked as though a giant had decided to trample all over it, while scattering branches from the surrounding trees.

Taking her coffee through to the sitting-room window, she found much the same level of destruction below in Kelvingrove Park. Broken branches littered the grass and pathways, while those that hadn't come down had been stripped of their spring leaves.

Only the Gothic towers of Glasgow University on the neighbouring hill and the red sandstone Kelvingrove Art Gallery below looked unmarked by the storm.

Glasgow was battered but unbroken, just as she'd suggested it would be to Magnus. She only hoped that Orkney had managed the same.

Showered and dressed, Rhona made her way downstairs. Despite both front and back doors to the stairwell being shut, the wind had still managed to infiltrate enough to deposit a layer of wet leaves and dirt from the street outside.

Opening the heavy front door was a job in itself, as the invading wind tried to wrestle it from her hands. Once outside, Rhona swiftly made her way down the wide staircase that led into the park.

Here the shelter of the surrounding trees provided some cover, although folk heading for work against the wind were still struggling.

Her last lap was the steep path that led up the hill to the university. As Rhona emerged from the trees, the wind caught her again, propelling her into the famous cloisters, where it now proceeded to batter her from various directions until she escaped into a quiet, sheltered, grassy quadrant where all was still.

Reaching her lab, she found Chrissy already there.

'My God. What. A. Night,' Chrissy said, waving a welcome breakfast bag at Rhona. 'Let's get the coffee on and we can share experiences.'

Minutes later, they were tucking into black pudding rolls and coffee, with Chrissy weaving her tale of lying alongside her young son, wee Michael, to protect him, in case the wind blew their roof off.

'Mum had me up to high doh, telling me all about the great storm of sixty-eight when chimney pots crashed through the tenement roofs killing folk in their beds.' She made an 'oooh' face. 'I pointed out that I didn't live in a tenement, but she reminded me that you do.'

'The same thought did cross my mind, especially after the weather forecaster reminded us about that storm,' Rhona said. 'Was wee Michael frightened?'

'He slept right through it, unlike his mother.' Chrissy pulled a face. 'I never used to be frightened of, well, anything. See what becoming a mum does to you?'

At that point Rhona's mobile rang. Noting DI Wilson's name on the screen, she set it to loudspeaker.

'Morning, Bill. You survived the storm, I take it?'

'Spent most of the night waiting for the roof to take off. It didn't, although some of the guttering came down. Hope I haven't disturbed your breakfast?'

'We're almost done,' Rhona said, although Chrissy was just about to take a big bite out of her second black pudding roll.

'Good, because I need you both down at—' He gave them an address in Govan. 'A possible self-immolation in the early hours, helped on by the wind. D'you need a lift?'

'We'll bring the forensic van,' Rhona said. 'See you shortly.'

'Self-immolation,' repeated Chrissy, looking thoughtfully at her roll.

Perhaps with the news of their impending task, a well-fired black pudding roll no longer seemed so appetizing, Rhona thought.

She was wrong, of course.

'Let's get going,' Chrissy said as she popped the roll back in its paper bag. 'I'll finish this on the way.'

The locus was sheltered in part by the surrounding tenements. Despite this, the wind, though lessened, still swirled in gusts. Rhona stood for a moment taking in the location. The ground was dry. She recalled that the rain had ceased to beat at her bedroom window around midnight and the major sound after that had been the howling of the wind.

Checking the forecast this morning, she'd seen the rain would return probably by lunchtime, when hopefully the SOCOs would have combed the locus.

A tent, protecting the victim, had already been secured in a corner, a few metres from the back entrance.

There was no garden here, just gravel and a line of bins against a fence. As soon as they'd emerged from the close, where metal treads had already been set out, the smell had hit them.

'Why,' Chrissy said, 'does it always smell like fried chicken?'

Rhona didn't agree entirely, although everyone picked up the scent slightly differently. It was certainly easier to recognize the smell than to describe it, because charred flesh simply smelt like nothing else. In fact, it could be so thick and powerful that it was almost a taste.

Those on the front line of fighting fires said you never really got the smell of burning flesh out of your nose entirely. No matter how long you lived.

Rhona was inclined to agree.

Aware that however strong the smell was out here, it would hit them like a wall when they entered the tent, Rhona checked with Chrissy that she was ready.

Chrissy secured her mask and indicated that she was.

Once inside, Rhona closed the flap. They would be pretty well undisturbed now, unless they chose otherwise. She could sense Chrissy's concentration, knowing that first impressions of a scene were vital. Context was everything. Before them was the evidence of when and how the victim had died. It was up to them to find and secure that evidence.

The body was covered in part by a singed blanket, which had been thrown over the victim to try to douse the flames. According to Bill, the good Samaritan was an elderly man in the nearby ground-floor flat, who'd been watching the storm play out via his living-room window. He said he'd spied a woman on fire and went out with the blanket. He managed to put out the flames, but couldn't save her.

The victim was lying on her right-hand side. Protruding

from under the blanket was some singed hair and a portion of her legs and feet. She was barefoot and there was no sign of her shoes.

As Rhona became more accustomed to the smell of burnt flesh, she'd already picked up another scent.

Petrol.

Using an accelerant was a common aspect of self-immolation. Petrol was best, although surgical spirit might also be used. Folk sometimes poured the liquid over their head, which wasn't pleasant because it burned the eyes. If this had been the case, the face and the front of the hair would be badly scorched.

Alternatively, they might pour it into their lap instead. In that case, the fire would be concentrated on the chest and stomach. Once lit, however, victims often changed their minds and tried to put it out. In such a scenario, the palms of the hands and underarms would be affected, but not the backs, which might mean they couldn't retrieve fingerprints to help identify the victim.

Rhona began taking her own series of photographs. Once a crime scene was disturbed they could never recreate it. So everything they captured now was important.

'Ready?' she said, when finished.

On Chrissy's nod, Rhona caught the corner of the blanket and slowly peeled it back, hearing Chrissy's intake of breath as the victim was revealed.

It was a youngish woman. What was left of her hair indicated it was light-coloured and of shoulder length. She was petite and slim, her shoe size, Rhona thought, a four or five.

From the pattern of burning, it looked like the petrol had been poured over her head.

Fire burned upwards and, in this case, it had had time to destroy much of her face. But the blanket had saved other parts of her body from deep burns, including the main torso and the thighs. Rhona checked out the hands, to find no burns to the palms.

'So she didn't try to put the fire out,' Chrissy said.

'Or she didn't start it.'

People often held the mistaken belief that fire would destroy everything. Including how someone had died. It didn't. Just because it looked like a self-immolation didn't mean it was one.

Her clothing appeared to contain natural fibres, which had added another layer of protection to the skin. Natural fibres didn't shrink or burn easily, whereas synthetics shrank and bits dropped off, damaging the skin beneath.

'What's that?' Chrissy pointed at something protruding from below the body.

Moving to hunker down there, Rhona carefully extracted the item, which turned out to be a handbag. It appeared unmarked, suggesting it was leather and not a plastic equivalent.

Rhona opened it. 'There's a mobile.' She took it out and switched it off, to protect it from online interference, and placed it in a Faraday bag.

Next out was a wallet. It, too, was leather and, flipping it open, the plastic cards inside appeared undamaged.

'Do we have a possible name?' Chrissy said.

'Olivia Newton Richardson.' Rhona dropped the wallet into another bag.

'So no shoes, yet she brought her handbag?' Chrissy said.

'No jewellery, either,' Rhona remarked.

'What about tattoos?' Chrissy said.

'Nothing visible as yet, and I don't plan to remove the clothing here. We'll wait until the PM.'

'She liked nail varnish,' Chrissy said. 'Both hands and feet are painted. So why no jewellery? There's a mark on the wrist, though. Both wrists, in fact.'

Rhona checked for herself, then, without commenting, crouched for a closer look at the ankles.

'What is it?' Chrissy said.

'I think these might be plastic cable tie marks,' Rhona said. Which if true meant the victim had been bound hand and foot prior to being set on fire.

6

McNab had risen before his alarm went off. Not because he'd wanted to, but because his mobile had refused to be ignored. The boss had made no apologies regarding the early morning call. DI Wilson had just told him where to go and that his partner, DS Clark, would be outside his building in fifteen minutes.

Sniffing his oxters, he'd decided a shower would be required, despite the scarcity of time afforded him. Sadly, breakfast wasn't on the cards (mainly because the fridge was empty), although strong coffee was a possibility.

Hurrying down the stairs, he'd emerged onto a street that looked like a football horde had stampeded down it, along with a wind that he could only describe as penetrating.

Hence he was waiting, freshly bathed with coffee consumed, when Janice drew up alongside him.

'You survived the storm, I see?' Janice said as he climbed into the car.

McNab adopted a blank look.

'You slept through it!'

'I'm a sound sleeper. Was it bad then?' he said, feigning innocence.

Janice gave a grunt that signified she wasn't interested in pandering to McNab's attempts at humour, then said, 'You know where we're headed?'

'Govan. Somebody set themselves on fire in the back court.'

Janice had shot him a look at that point. 'I take it you're okay with the smell of burnt flesh in the morning?'

'I would be if I'd eaten,' McNab tried. 'On an empty stomach, maybe not so much.'

'Tough luck, then,' she retorted. 'We're not stopping.'

McNab was almost glad of that when they eventually exited the vehicle outside the required address to be greeted by that exact smell.

'It's a lot worse, I hear, where Dr MacLeod's working,' Janice informed him.

'Rhona's here too?' McNab said. 'Do they suspect it wasn't a suicide?'

'Maybe they're hoping she'll decide that,' Janice said in her inimitable fashion, chapping on a ground-floor door. 'We're to speak with the guy who called it in. A Mr Jimmy Donaldson.'

The knock was followed by an extended silence. McNab was about to knock again when they heard shuffling footsteps, before a voice called out, 'Who is it?'

McNab held his warrant card in front of the spyhole. 'Detective Sergeant McNab and Detective Sergeant Clark. We'd like to talk to you about the fire, Mr Donaldson.' After which they heard numerous locks and bolts being released.

The door was slowly opened to finally allow them a view of Jimmy Donaldson. He was short, thin and elderly, although still sporting a full head of grey hair, tinged with ginger.

'Aye, come away in then, detectives.'

They followed him through a long narrow hall and into a room that looked out on the back court. Sitting on the window ledge was a big black cat, which immediately arched its back and hissed at them.

'Shoo, Lucifer!'

The old man flung his arms about, and eventually Lucifer decided to vacate his prize spot and exit, long tail standing rigidly upright.

'Lucifer's my protection. Woe betide anyone who manages to break in here. Lucifer would spring right at his face and claw his eyes out.'

McNab believed him.

'Sorry about the smell. I've got the windows shut tight. Oh, that poor lassie.'

He looked so distressed at the memory of why they were here that Janice urged him to sit down.

'Thanks,' he said as she helped him into a seat.

Not for the first time, McNab thought it was handy having Janice around. Her glance now told him to say nothing until the old man gathered himself. McNab kept his mouth shut as requested.

'Would you like me to make you a mug of tea, Mr Donaldson?' Janice offered.

'Call me Jimmy, hen. That's kind, but I'm fine.'

'D'you feel up to telling us what happened, Jimmy?' McNab came in.

Jimmy nodded. 'Aye, son. If you think it'll help.'

They waited as he took another look out of the window. McNab wondered if his thoughts had wandered off, but then he turned back to face them.

'I sat up because of the wind. I remember the storm of sixty-eight. Folk killed in their beds when the tenement roofs fell in. So I stayed in here at that window.' He shook his head, remembering. 'It was pitch black and blowing a hoolie. The noise of the wind swirling round the back court, screeching through the close. I pulled a blanket round me.

The one I keep on the back of the sofa, for when I cannae afford to keep the electric fire on.' He stopped to brush a tear away.

'It's okay, Jimmy, just take your time. DS McNab and I can wait.'

Jimmy gave her a wan smile in thanks, then took a deep breath. 'That's when I saw her standing there, hair whipping her face. A second later, there was a whoosh and she was on fire. Jesus, the lassie was on fire. All those locks and bolts, then the bloody wind wouldn't let me open the door to the back court. I eventually got to her, but by then she was on the ground with her head a mass of flames. I doused the fire, but it was too bloody late.' He shook his head. 'My dad used to talk about the Clydebank bombings during the war, the terrible smell of folk burning. He said it never went away. I didn't believe him.'

McNab rose. 'I'm going to make you a cup of tea, Jimmy. Sugar and milk?'

'Aye, son. Do that. Two sugars. And have one yourselves.'

McNab left the door open so he could hear anything that was said, filled the kettle and switched it on. The wee kitchen was tidy. Fresh milk in the fridge. A packet of Scottish Blend teabags. Even a jar of instant coffee. Better than his place, he noted.

He swithered whether he should make tea or coffee for Janice, then decided tea would be more chummy. He settled for a double spoonful of instant black coffee for himself. In the kitchen the smell was weaker, but until they removed the body, it wouldn't go away, and even then . . .

He couldn't see a tray anywhere, so he carried through the teas, then went back for his coffee. By the time he returned, Jimmy had a little more colour in his cheeks.

'So, Jimmy, had you seen the lassie before last night?' McNab said.

'Naw, son. But then I don't see the folk going up and down the stairs. I sit in here most of the time when I'm not in the kitchen. My bedroom's at the front, but I keep the curtains shut in there.'

'You don't know any of your neighbours?' Janice tried.

'The flats up this close change hands a lot. Landlords ship folk in and out again, if they don't pay. There aren't any families. Kids used to play out the back all the time. Not any more.'

'Did you see anyone else out there last night?' McNab said. 'Or hear anybody in the close?'

'You couldn't hear a damn thing, son, except for that screeching gale. Did you no hear it yersel?'

'My colleague's a sound sleeper,' Janice said.

Jimmy shook his head, apparently finding the idea that anyone could have slept through that racket unbelievable.

At that point Lucifer strode back in and gave them both a menacing look before jumping up onto Jimmy's knee. As the old man clapped him, the cat arched his back and purred, although he still held them in his evil gaze.

'We'd better be going.' Janice nodded at McNab.

They rose together.

Janice took McNab's mug. 'I'll rinse these through, Jimmy. We'll maybe come back and see you again if that's okay?'

'Aye, that'll be fine,' Jimmy said. 'I'll have to get a new blanket,' he added, as though he'd just thought of it. 'This room doesn't get much sunshine being at the back.'

'I'll bring you one,' McNab found himself saying.

'Thank you, son. That's mighty good of you.'

Janice gave him a big-eyed look as the door closed behind them.

'What?' McNab said. 'We can't bring the old boy a blanket? Plus we'll need to speak to him again anyway. We haven't got everything yet.'

'True enough,' Janice conceded.

McNab indicated he planned to suit up and look in on Rhona. 'Are you going to interview anyone else upstairs?'

'A couple of uniforms are on it. I'm going to check. See if they've got anything.'

Minutes later, suited and masked, McNab headed out. A couple of SOCOs were combing the rough ground that served as the back court. He checked with them first, but they had little to report, apart from a fair number of discarded cigarette ends. It looked like a no-smoking policy had been implemented in one or more of the rented flats.

McNab's announcement that he wished to come into the tent was initially met by silence, then a quiet acknowledgement from Chrissy.

Outside the tent, the smell had been strong despite the still blustery nature of the wind. Once inside, the suffocating nature of the stench was almost overwhelming. McNab had seen and smelt the dead more often than he cared to think about, but this was special and, he could foresee, long-lasting.

Chrissy nodded at him but said nothing, intent as she was on whatever Rhona was doing. McNab waited, aware that disturbing their concentration wouldn't be welcomed.

Eventually Rhona leaned back on her haunches and observed him.

'I've been talking to Jimmy on the ground floor,' McNab said. 'He flung the blanket over her.'

'He was brave,' Chrissy said. 'Getting close enough to do that.'

'Any idea who she is?' McNab tried.

Rhona handed him the Faraday bag. 'The mobile from the handbag that was under her body. I switched it off. Plus Chrissy has the bag with the wallet and cards in it.'

'The credit card's platinum,' Chrissy said. 'And we may have a partial from it.'

McNab read the name out. 'Olivia Newton Richardson.' He looked at them. 'The name and the platinum card don't scream local at me. So how did she set herself alight?'

'Petrol, probably over her head, judging by the burn pattern.'

'So we're looking for a petrol can and a lighter?' McNab said. 'Both of which should be in the vicinity if she did it to herself?'

'Exactly,' Chrissy said.

'The SOCOs outside haven't found them yet. Anything else?'

Rhona nodded. 'Her clothing is of good quality and mostly natural fibres. She was barefoot, yet had her handbag with her.'

'She paints her nails, but didn't have any jewellery,' Chrissy said.

'Also, if you come closer, you'll see marks on her wrists and ankles,' Rhona added.

McNab crouched beside her for a closer look, trying to stifle his rising nausea.

'She's been bound,' he said, recognizing the distinctive marks.

'The fire didn't destroy them, thanks your good Samaritan and his blanket,' Rhona said.

McNab rose. If the victim had been bound before the fire, how did she get free? And where was she before she came out here?

7

Watching as the farm buildings disappeared from her rear-view mirror, Ava gave an audible sigh of relief. For the next few hours, at least, she could think of herself as a reporter again, and not as a big sister and pseudo-farmer.

The wind had dropped in strength, but the sky, via her windscreen, was still a swift-moving collage of cloud, with intermittent flashes of blue and rays of sunshine.

When she'd left to go to university in Aberdeen, it was the big skies of Orkney she'd missed most. That and the closeness of the ever-shifting sea.

Eventually choosing London as her base, she'd sought a high-rise apartment so that she might be nearer to the sky. The constantly moving sea, however, could never be replaced. Even the Thames didn't do that.

Dougie hadn't returned from the boathouse before she was ready to leave, so she'd left him a note taped to the fridge. Had she left it on the kitchen table, the likelihood was he would never have noticed. The fridge, however, was always a go-to location for her teenage brother.

What if I wasn't here to fill the fridge?

Ava chastised herself for that thought. Dougie was pretty self-sufficient. Probably more so than she had been at his age. He wouldn't starve without her, that was for sure.

Being early in the tourist season, the road past the Loch

of Stenness was currently devoid of the buses that ferried folk from the giant cruise liners that docked just outside Kirkwall to the key tourist sights of Orkney mainland. The loch itself was still choppy and white-tipped, despite its sheltered location.

Turning onto the Yesnaby road, she spotted the police and rescue vehicles parked up ahead. The neighbouring farm she knew belonged to Geordie Findlater, a friend of her father's, who'd apparently reported the foundering ship to the coastguard.

According to the phone call from *The Orcadian*, Geordie had crawled to the edge of the cliffs in high winds to take a photograph. Knowing Geordie, that didn't surprise her.

As she drew up alongside the other vehicles, Ava spotted another face she recognized. Of course Erling would be in charge of this, she thought. Surprisingly, he was now an inspector, when back in their teenage days in school together, he'd stated that he had no intention of remaining on Orkney. As for joining the police? His teenage self would have laughed at such a suggestion.

We don't always end up where we thought we would, she mused as she approached him.

Spotting her, Erling finished his mobile conversation. 'You're here. Great. That was the coastguard. They're going to try and bring a couple of divers round to take a look below the waterline and check the hull.'

'You're worried about the fuel tanks?'

'Exactly. It's not going to be easy, but the sooner we know whether we're facing an oil spill or not, the better. We're also hoping to get a couple of guys on board to take a look inside.'

'So approaching on both fronts?'

Erling nodded.

The onshore wind was brisk as they got near to the cliff edge, but nothing like what Geordie must have faced the previous night. They were close enough now for Ava to get her first clear view of the stranded ship. She could just make out the name: MV *Orlova*, which sounded Russian.

As the search and rescue boat came into view, rising and falling in the swell, they also heard the unmistakable beat of the approaching coastguard helicopter. Despite being only an observer and not a participant, Ava's heartbeat rose in both excitement and fear.

This was what being on the job again felt like, and she was grateful for it.

Erling stood a little away from her, his back to the wind, listening on the radio, she presumed to the rescue teams, above and below.

Ava watched as two divers positioned themselves on the edge of the boat before dropping backwards into the swell. A keen swimmer, but with very little diving experience, and only in warm Mediterranean waters, Ava could only imagine what falling into that dark choppiness felt like.

As they'd walked to the cliff face, Erling had revealed that one of the divers was his partner, Rory. 'He's an experienced oil rig diver, so this is no more difficult than that, or so he assures me.'

Despite his upbeat words, there was no doubt in Ava's mind that Erling was concerned for him.

The hovering helicopter hung above the *Orlova* now, and they watched as the first man began his swaying descent. To Ava, it seemed most of those on the clifftop were collectively holding their breath as he drew closer to the pitching deck. Then he was down and giving those on the shore the thumbs up, and the detached cable was rising again.

'One down, one more to go,' Erling said, grim concentration on his face.

The second guy was close behind. He had the added advantage of someone on the deck to steady his arrival. Once he too was down, Erling's radio crackled into life. He listened carefully before giving the go-ahead to whatever plan they'd decided on, and within seconds the two men had disappeared down into the bowels of the ship.

Now came the waiting.

Ava decided to go back to her car and dictate what she had so far into her mobile. A food van had arrived in the car park and was serving coffee. She joined the queue, exchanging a few words with folk, then carried her coffee back to the car. Once inside, she called Dougie. His mobile rang out for a while and she expected it to go to voicemail, but before it did, he answered.

'Did you get my note?' Ava said.

'Yeah.'

'Not sure when I'll be back.'

'Okay.'

'Will you see to the kye? We could maybe let them out into the fields when I get back.'

He muttered what Ava thought was an affirmative. Realizing she wasn't going to get any more from him than that, she said her goodbyes.

Her heaviness of heart came back as she cut the call. What the hell was she going to do about Dougie and the farm? Sit around in Orkney waiting for the next ship to go aground for something interesting to report on? Or was it the Dounby Show next? She felt guilty at such a thought, which belittled her fellow reporters who chose not to traipse round the world looking for trouble spots.

'Fuck it!' she said, and not under her breath, as she began to record what had happened up to now.

Once she had the key points noted, she decided to try to find out what she could about the origins of the MV *Orlova*, which turned out to be more interesting than she'd first thought. So much so that she didn't notice that the helicopter was landing on the clifftop.

Eventually the noise of its descent made her abandon her internet research, and she headed across to find Erling apparently about to be transferred to the ship.

'What's happened?' Ava said, noting his serious expression. 'Is it the hull?'

'The hull looks sound, according to the divers.'

'Are there folk aboard?' Ava tried.

'As far as we know there are no survivors.' Erling looked decidedly grim.

As he headed for the helicopter, Ava caught sight of Geordie Findlater and went to see if he knew any more.

He did. 'Word is there are bodies aboard, lass. How many, I don't know.'

8

Rhona could hear the SOCOs moving about outside, but here in the tent all was still.

She continued to write up her notes, determined to miss nothing. Soon they would take the victim to the mortuary for further examination and this exact scene could never be reconstructed in its entirety again.

The smell was still there, of course. It would linger in her nostrils for who knew how long. But here and now, the body's smell wasn't important. She thought only of the victim hidden within it. The how and the why of her being here in such circumstances, and what evidence they might capture which would help them tell the victim's story.

What had been retrieved so far suggested that Olivia, if that was indeed her name, had not chosen this end willingly, rather that someone or something had driven her to it.

The incessant tugging at the tent by the wind had ended. Now it was only the softly insistent patter of rain on the roof. Rhona quietly thanked whatever deity had allowed the back court to be properly searched before the rain had taken over from the wind.

At that point she heard Chrissy's voice and the tent flap being pulled back.

'You'd better come and see this.'

Rhona followed her assistant into the close and up the

stairwell. All the doors they passed on the way remained closed, although she suspected that whatever was happening out here was being closely followed by the occupants of the other flats.

The left-most door on the top landing stood open, and by its state it was obvious it had been forced. Rhona could hear McNab's voice coming from inside. She followed Chrissy in, moving carefully from tread to metal tread, the presence of which already declared it to be a possible crime scene.

Rhona mentally prepared herself for what might come next. At the far end of the narrow hallway stood a still-suited and masked McNab guarding an open doorway. At her approach he stepped to one side to allow her entrance.

It was a bedroom and the smell of petrol came, she suspected, predominantly from the stained and rumpled bedding. The mattress sat in a metal frame, the top and bottom of which gave ample opportunity for attaching a captive's wrists and ankles via cable ties.

Chrissy confirmed this by holding up a clear evidence bag with the apparent remains of the ties inside.

'Any sign of the petrol can?' Rhona said.

'Not in here, or anywhere else in or outside the building.'

'So how did she get free?' Rhona said.

'Some ties have ragged edges, and look' – Chrissy pointed to one of the metal uprights where traces of the plastic had lodged – 'it looks as though she may have managed to rub herself free and made her way outside?'

Rhona ran her eyes over the room again. To one side of the bed lay a pair of high heels which looked like the victim's shoe size. 'Did you find any underwear?' She had decided not to remove the outer clothes before the autopsy, for fear of disturbing evidence on the charred body.

'A black lacy thong,' McNab said. 'It's been bagged.'

The picture being painted by everything they'd already discovered in the room wasn't lost on anyone, least of all Rhona.

'I'll get a team in here and see what else we can find,' Chrissy said, 'while you finish up in the tent.'

'I'll leave you to it, then,' McNab said, indicating he was heading back to the station with DS Clark to report their findings to DI Wilson. 'I'll maybe catch up with you both later.'

The usual routine was for the team to meet up after work at the jazz club near the university where Sean played. The wind-down club as Sean occasionally called it.

Rhona gave a non-committal nod, her brain still full of what she was looking at.

Not so Chrissy. 'I'll definitely be heading there after all this,' she declared. 'With or without Dr MacLeod.' She gave one of her grins which declared that fun might be had, even in the midst of adversity.

When McNab had departed, Chrissy said, 'What are you thinking?'

'Likely the same as you,' Rhona said. 'She was held in here, probably against her will . . .'

'But not necessarily,' Chrissy added. 'Not initially anyway. We've seen the result of rough but consensual sex before.'

Rhona nodded. 'But being doused in petrol hasn't been a feature.'

'Candle wax, yes. Petrol, no.'

'Will you deal with this while I finish with the body? I'll check back once the mortuary van's been.'

'Sure thing, boss.'

*

Back now in the tent, Rhona resumed her place beside the body and continued to make her notes, this time regarding what had been discovered in the top-floor flat and how it might relate to what had happened here.

It did appear, as Chrissy had suggested, that the victim had managed to break free, or else her captor had freed her. Whichever way it'd happened, she'd come down here, already doused in petrol, barefoot, and in the midst of the storm.

Perhaps she'd believed she'd escaped and that was why she had her handbag with her? Alternatively, her attacker had wished it to appear that way.

When the mortuary van finally arrived, Rhona said a silent goodbye. Emerging from the tent, she stood to one side as the body bag was carried out on its stretcher. At that point she noticed the figure of an elderly man at a ground-level window, a large black cat in his arms. Both were avidly watching the proceedings.

That, she realized, must be the good Samaritan who had tried to save the girl's life.

If only the wind hadn't been so strong that night. If only he had got out here sooner with the blanket.

Rhona could only imagine what was going through his mind as he watched them carry the girl away, although, she thought, it might be both of those things. What she did know was that none of his thoughts were of any comfort to him.

Heading into the close, she met Chrissy on her way down the stairs.

'The SOCOs are going over the rest of the flat. The evidence from the bedroom is already in the van. Shall we head for the lab?'

The sky on the way back was an ominous grey, the wind

now noticeable by its absence. Glasgow had been busily cleaning up the effects of Storm Birka, the flying litter and broken glass swept up and the waste bins returned to their rightful places.

Chrissy, always the talker, was noticeably quiet, which suited Rhona for the moment. Having departed the locus, it was obvious they had brought the smell with them as a reminder. It permeated the van and she could taste it on her lips.

By the studied look on her face, Chrissy was suffering from it too.

Watching the rain stream down the windscreen, Rhona was already imagining herself standing under the shower, the spray beating her head, her mouth turned upwards to be rinsed. That alone wouldn't be enough to kill the smell that had invaded every part of her body, but it would help.

9

*The ship, the MV Orlova, was boarded today by Inspector
Erling Flett, along with two of the coastguard search and
rescue team. As this was happening, two experienced
divers, familiar with North Sea conditions, examined the
hull of the stranded ship.*

*Thankfully, it was found to be intact, with the fuel
tanks undamaged by the storm and its aftermath.*

*As we understand it, the interior suggests it had been
internally upgraded to allow its use for adventure cruises,
possibly in colder latitudes.*

*Adventure cruising has become internationally popular
of late. It often includes travel to more hostile locations
with the possibility to take part in extreme sports.*

*Our sources tell us that there was a great deal of
computer equipment on board the ship which allowed
for sophisticated virtual gaming to take place.*

*Sadly, three bodies have also been located aboard, of
two men and one woman who apparently died in suspicious circumstances.*

*Initial results on the history of MV Orlova suggest it
may be a Russian ship abandoned off the Florida coast
two years ago, when the registered owners were declared
bankrupt. It appears to have been upgraded since then,
but by whom?*

What we do know is that the Orlova *made its way east across the Atlantic Ocean, perhaps still manned or already abandoned, to be driven ashore on the cliffs at Yesnaby in Orkney.*

The abandoned ships that litter our oceans are often referred to as ghost ships. A relatively common phenomenon, the most recent was the MV Alta*, the derelict 77-metre freighter which was driven onto rocks at Ballyandreen in east Cork, Ireland, during Storm Dennis. It had been derelict since the US Coast Guard rescued the ten-man crew from the vessel in October 2018.*

Intriguingly, the story of the MV Orlova *is shrouded in more mist than the MV* Alta*. No one it seems lays claim to the ship either currently or in the recent past.*

An initial search throws up a mixture of international companies which no longer exist, together with a number of shell companies around the world, although word is circulating online that the gaming ship has been advertised on the dark web. If that is true, then it suggests what was happening on board needs further investigation.

So, who currently owns the ghost ship MV Orlova*? What was she being used for? Who are the three dead people aboard and how or why did they die?*

As an investigative reporter who has pursued illegal activities around the world over the last ten years, I fully intend to try to answer these questions.

Once made secure, the MV Orlova *will be towed into Scapa Flow, anchoring off Houton Pier, which will allow access for the major crime investigation team expected from Glasgow, assisted by Inspector Erling Flett from Kirkwall police station.*

*Maybe then we can discover who the victims are, and
in what circumstances they lost their lives.*
Ava Clouston, Investigative Reporter

Ava read over her article. She had been careful by simply
stating that two men and one woman had been found dead
in suspicious circumstances. She'd not given away any aspect
of their deaths, which, as in any small close-knit community,
had quickly become common knowledge. She had made no
mention that one guy had been found in the computer
room. Nor that the couple found in a mock arena may have
been duelling with one another.

What the hell had been going on aboard that ship?

Ava pressed the send button with the same surge of
excitement that always surfaced when she began another
investigation.

The MV *Orlova* and its reincarnation from a cargo ship to
a pleasure craft, apparently with high-class guest accommodation for up to eight, plus service personnel and crew,
suggested a stay on board would not have come cheap.

So what had really been on offer via the *Orlova* and who
was interested in sampling its pleasures? And how did that
apparently lead to their deaths?

The story would appear in *The Orcadian*, of course, but by
also sending it to her London editor, David Morris, it would
reach numerous international news outlets and channels. David,
a keen advocate of her investigative reports over the years,
especially those from Afghanistan, would recognize the international interest this one from her home island would generate.
A report no doubt would also go out on tonight's BBC News.
The world would soon know of the MV *Orlova* and be asking
what had really happened on board the abandoned ship.

Ava rose from the kitchen table and went to refill her coffee cup. The trip to Yesnaby and the resultant article had taken up most of her day. Also, they hadn't eaten as yet. Although she'd told Dougie they would set the kye free tonight, she decided that would have to wait now until the morning.

Dougie hadn't emerged from his music-filled bedroom since she'd arrived home, but she'd been delighted to find that he'd put a casserole in the Aga for their evening meal. Something that smelt delicious.

Maybe it was a peace offering, Ava thought. Or maybe he planned to have the discussion they'd been avoiding since their fallout.

Ava baulked at the thought, mainly because today's events had convinced her even more that she couldn't give up her day job and stay on Orkney to run the farm. Not and keep her sanity. Such a thought made her feel even worse, as though she was not only letting Dougie down, she was betraying her much-loved parents too.

Grabbing her jacket, she headed for the barn.

Entering the warmth of the place, and hearing the lowing of the cattle, she found herself swaying again towards staying.

She had always thought that if anything went drastically wrong with her life and work, she could always come back here and be renewed, either temporarily or permanently. She'd imagined the farm, her real home, would be available to her forever. And it would have been, had her parents lived into old age, and Dougie had taken over as planned, married and had children of his own. Dougie would always have welcomed her home, whenever she might want to return.

And she was planning to take all that away from him, and from herself.

The weight of her grief at the loss of her parents bore down on her in that moment. They had been, she now realized, the rock on which she stood. That rock had gone, and if she let herself go, she would flounder, making Dougie even more of an orphan.

Exiting the barn, she found a bright moonlit sky. The wind having dropped, the air was filled with the smell of new grass and all things growing. She breathed it in, saying a silent thank you for a moment of peace.

Looking out over the moonlit waters of Hoy Sound, she spotted the lights of the two newly commissioned tugs, named *Thor* and *Odin*, that had towed the ghost ship from Yesnaby. Behind them was the dark shadowy shape that was undoubtedly the MV *Orlova*, making its way to Houton Bay, where its secrets would hopefully be revealed.

10

The sound of Sean's saxophone met them at the top of the stairs leading to the cellar bar. He was being accompanied by a pianist, which prompted Rhona to ask if Chrissy was still seeing Danny, the young jazz guitarist who'd recently played with Sean at the club.

Chrissy shrugged. 'I can't be doing with a roving musician for a boyfriend. Who knows what they get up to when they're on the road?'

Rhona tried not to laugh, since there was no one more casual than Chrissy regarding boyfriends. Not since wee Michael's dad, Sam, had returned to Nigeria had a relationship lasted more than a couple of weeks.

'Have you heard from Sam recently?' Rhona ventured.

'He FaceTimes wee Michael once a week. And we chat for a bit. Just as friends. In fact, he's getting married soon. Apparently she's a doctor too. They're having a big African wedding.'

Chrissy's tone suggested she was okay about that. After all, Sam had asked her to go back with him to Nigeria and be his bride, but she'd refused. Rhona knew how difficult that decision had been for Chrissy.

They headed for the bar and Chrissy ordered up their usual. Sean, spotting them, raised his saxophone mid-tune to acknowledge their arrival.

'Does he play for you at home?' Chrissy said.

'Only the jazz pieces I like,' said Rhona. 'Those that have a recognizable tune,' she added.

Their conversation shifted to McNab.

'Rumour has it,' Chrissy said conspiratorially, 'that he's back in touch with Mary Stevenson.'

McNab had gone to school with Mary, when she was the teenage Mary Grant, a girl from the Highlands who'd moved to Glasgow. Sadly, despite McNab's adoration, Mary had chosen to marry McNab's pal, the owner of multiple betting shops in Glasgow, who was now serving a prison sentence for some pretty unsavoury crimes.

'So he and Ellie aren't a thing any more?' Rhona said, a little saddened by that.

Ellie, a biker, had stayed around longer than most of the others. Rhona liked her. She was certainly fit for McNab.

'She wants an open relationship. McNab doesn't, apparently. So he broke it off,' Chrissy said.

The last case they'd all been on together had caused a few personal difficulties, both between herself and Sean, and Ellie and McNab. Sean had made himself scarce shortly after that, heading for gigs in Paris. At the time it looked as though it might be over between them. However, their time spent apart, as always, seemed to do the trick, and they'd fallen back into the same old routine.

'Maybe she's fed up being stood up when he heads out on a job?' Rhona said. 'Though in the past, McNab wasn't that keen on exclusivity. On his part, anyway.'

'Aye, there's always one rule for the goose and another for the gander,' Chrissy said. 'Talking of which, here comes the gander now.'

Rhona followed Chrissy's gaze to the door, where McNab and Janice were heading towards them.

'Okay, what's going on here?' He looked swiftly from Chrissy to Rhona and back again. 'My ears were definitely burning on the way down the stairs,' he said accusingly.

Chrissy guffawed. 'Who says we were talking about you?'

'Hope it wasn't me then?' Janice said, eyebrows raised.

'You're definitely the more interesting half of the crime duo,' Chrissy said. 'How's Paula?'

'Complaining that I work too much. So I'm taking her out to dinner nearby tonight. Hence my presence here.' She smiled.

'What about you?' Chrissy looked to McNab. 'You have plans?'

'Sadly, no. A pint here and a carry-out at home for me. Something that definitely doesn't smell like fried chicken,' he said with vigour.

His remark was followed by a short silence, before Chrissy eventually said, 'There's no avoiding it, so why not talk about it? Any leads on the victim?'

'Olivia Newton Mearns—' McNab halted as a chorus of moans went up. 'Okay, sorry, but if she *was* from Glasgow, she would definitely have come from Newton Mearns. However, the owner of the credit cards, Olivia Newton Richardson, who might not actually be our victim,' he reminded them, 'apparently lives in North London. Her bank account, according to the Tech guys, is very, very healthy. She's involved with a business called Go Wild and is a party planner.'

He toasted that with his pint.

'Some party that turned out to be,' Chrissy said. 'Why the hell was she tied up in a tenement flat in the East End of Glasgow?'

'Exactly,' Janice said.

'And the mobile?' Rhona asked.

'It looks like the data was deleted remotely,' Janice told her, 'before you discovered it and switched it off. So more work to do on that.'

'Someone is covering their tracks?' Rhona offered.

'It looks like it,' Janice said. 'First thing is to identify our victim. Find out if she really is Olivia Newton Mearns—' She halted, a pained look on her face, and pointed an accusing finger at McNab. 'That's your fault.'

'He likes his nicknames, does McNab,' Chrissy said. 'He has one for all of us.'

McNab tried to look horrified at such a suggestion, but the three women just laughed.

'And we have one for you,' Chrissy said.

McNab looked worried. 'What is it?'

'You show us yours and we'll show you ours,' Chrissy declared.

'Okay,' Janice said, 'I'm off before this turns into the sort of game we used to play behind the bicycle shed.'

Rhona and Chrissy announced that they were planning to do the same, whereupon McNab made an attempt to persuade them to stay for another drink.

'I'm off home to see wee Michael, your namesake,' Chrissy announced.

'And I'm just off home,' Rhona said.

'You're not staying to talk to Sean?' McNab asked.

'I saw him last night,' Rhona said. 'You ready to go then?' she asked Chrissy.

'You bet.'

They both glanced back when they reached the door to find McNab's woebegone expression following them out.

'What did I tell you?' Chrissy said as they exited. 'He's

McNab all alone at the moment, which makes a meet-up with Mary all the more likely.'

Rhona didn't know what to say to that, so said nothing.

Leaving Chrissy at her bus stop, Rhona set off home through the park, which had almost returned to its normal self, the broken branches either gone or else stacked neatly awaiting removal.

When she opened her front door, Tom seemed inordinately pleased to see her, suggesting she'd forgotten to refill his pet feeder. When she discovered she had, Rhona apologized and set things to rights, at which point Tom lost interest in her again.

As for her own evening meal, she ordered in a vegetable curry, hoping the spicy smell and taste would supplant the ones she still carried with her.

Despite her earlier shower at the lab, she had another, sticking every item of clothing into the washing machine and donning a fresh set, convinced the smell was emanating from her pores. Her timing was spot on as the buzzer went shortly after, heralding the arrival of her curry.

At that point Tom decided she was interesting again, but, for the sake of peace in which to eat, Rhona opened the kitchen window and let him out onto the roof. Something that didn't happen often since the Sin Eater case. And definitely didn't happen when Sean was about.

Standing at the window, Rhona took solace from the fact that the Virgin Mary was no longer surrounded by water, and order had been restored.

Not so, though, in real life.

After her meal, with Tom back inside and the window shut, Rhona settled by the fire, her laptop on her knee, to read over her report from the locus. Deep in thought, she didn't register the drill of her mobile at first, then, seeing the name on the screen, answered with a smile.

'Magnus. You've survived Birka's visit?'

'I have. What about you?'

'Still have a roof, although the park was in a state this morning when I headed for work.' Rhona waited, aware that Magnus had called her for something other than a chat about the weather.

'I wondered if you'd caught the news about the ship that was washed up at Yesnaby during the storm?'

Rhona listened to Magnus's tale of the MV *Orlova*.

'So it's a crime scene?' she said, her interest now truly sparked.

'Yes. It's been towed into Scapa Flow. In fact, it's sitting within view of my dining-room window as we speak. Erling's expecting an MIT to be sent up, plus of course forensics. He's planning to ask for you, since you've been to Orkney in that capacity before.'

'Excellent,' Rhona said. 'Chrissy will be well chuffed about that.'

'And you must both stay here, of course. It'll be handier than being in a hotel in Kirkwall.'

Magnus was barely off the phone before the official call came through. They would be taken by police helicopter to Kirkwall airport first thing, where a police officer would pick them up and take them to Houton Bay and the MV *Orlova*.

11

On his way home, McNab found himself taking a detour via the tattoo parlour, where it had all begun. Standing in the door of the pub opposite, he let his mind replay the moment he had first encountered Ellie.

When he'd told Mannie, who owned the shop, that he wanted a skull inked over the bullet wound in his back, Mannie had called Ellie in, because apparently inking skulls was a speciality of hers.

McNab recalled the way the dark-haired girl had looked at him, her exposed flesh a painted tribute to her art. Not skulls, but a fairy tale of colour and imagery. Up to that point he'd only really thought of multiple tattoos as a male thing, but had definitely changed his mind at that moment.

She'd taken him into her cubicle and shown him a selection of possible tattoos. His shirt off by then, she'd studied the scar he wanted to cover. He could feel her wish to know the circumstances in which he'd been shot. So he'd jokingly told her it had been inflicted by an angry woman he'd cheated on, and he was lucky she hadn't shot a hole through his prick.

Laughing at his fictional story, she assured him that they inked penises too. She'd showed him some samples, and then told him a tale of tattooed testicles, which he'd been horrified by.

The chemistry between them . . . Fuck, he could feel it yet.

It was in her cubicle that they'd first made love, but not on that night. In that moment, McNab had thought that life couldn't get any better.

So why had he messed it all up?

All the fault of the job, of course. Except that was just a cop-out. He'd let Ellie down far too often. And she wasn't a girl to be messed with. Something he'd loved about her.

I did warn her what it would be like getting in tow with a detective. I was straight with her about that.

And she was straight with you from the beginning. She said if you were going to get together, that you both had to be honest if you wanted to have sex with someone else.

I couldn't believe that at the time. I didn't think I would want that. I didn't think she would.

That was the arrangement. So Ellie hasn't changed. You have.

The lights were still on in the shop, which meant someone was definitely there. Plus there was a bike outside, although it wasn't Ellie's Harley. Ellie didn't always bring her bike, especially if she was planning on going for a drink after work. So the likelihood was that it belonged to a customer.

McNab contemplated going in, on the off-chance. But if Ellie was there, what would he say to her? *I've changed my mind. If you want to screw someone else, that's fine by me, as long as you continue to screw me.*

Yeah, that would work, he thought grimly.

McNab tried to recall if this was one of the days Ellie had a shift in the Harley shop during the day and worked here in the evening. Surely he should know that at least?

He was suddenly shocked to realize he couldn't recall

Ellie's regular shift pattern at all. Had he ever really committed it to memory?

At the beginning, Ellie was always at the forefront of his mind, even when he was on a job, but gradually, McNab realized, she had become merely background as the work had taken over again.

Even finding time for sex had become an issue, particularly during the last major investigation. God, no wonder she wanted to have an open relationship. She certainly wasn't getting what she needed from him.

At that moment in his deliberations, he saw the lights go out, followed by the front door opening and a figure emerging. It was Ellie. His joy at seeing her almost resulted in him calling out her name. Until he saw the bloke. Tall, head shaven, he came out right behind her, and they were chatting and laughing together as she locked up.

He's just a customer, McNab told himself.

He realized that if Ellie turned, he would be right in her line of sight, so he pretended an interest in his phone.

They were at the bike now. McNab silently urged the bastard to get on the damn thing and ride off into the sunset. Then he would shout over to Ellie, make out he'd come to meet her and ask her to come for a drink with him.

The guy had pulled out a helmet, but instead of putting it on himself, he was handing it to Ellie. From then on things just got worse because he bent over and kissed her.

Ever since Ellie had told him she wanted their relationship to be open, McNab had imagined a number of images of her with some random bloke. They were all bad, but at least they'd been a figment of his imagination. Until now.

McNab turned just enough to get the fucker in view and clicked. Now he had a picture, he could check him out.

– First port of call would be Ollie in IT. If the bastard was anywhere on the system, he would find him.

Even as he decided this, he knew he was behaving like an arse, but that didn't change his mind. What if the guy *was* bad news? Wasn't it better to know, so he could warn Ellie? After all, he wanted her to be safe, didn't he?

As the two roared off together, Ellie's arms about the guy's waist, McNab realized that not only had he been dumped, he'd also become a sad bastard stalker.

12

The trip north had been verging on pleasant. Little to no wind. Great views. Rhona had almost relaxed. Despite her frequent helicopter rides, her attitude to flying never changed. She understood the physics of flight, but she still didn't really believe it, despite being a scientist.

Chrissy, on the other hand, was in her element. Chatting to the co-pilot, exclaiming at the scenery. Whooping as they crossed the swiftly moving Pentland Firth. Pointing out the Old Man of Hoy. The list of her joys was endless.

In contrast, Rhona was keenly awaiting the first mention of Kirkwall airport, which meant they would soon be on terra firma again.

Her wish finally granted, she and Chrissy headed across the tarmac and into the terminal to find PC Ivan Tulloch waiting for them, his eyes lighting up at the sight of Chrissy. She had been a favourite of his when they'd worked on the excavation case on his home island of Sanday.

Chrissy seemed equally delighted to see the young constable again and chatted to him enthusiastically on their way to the vehicle.

'Inspector Flett is waiting for you at Houton Bay,' he told them as he put their bags in the boot. 'The police launch will take you out to the *Orlova*.'

Ivan was keen to give them the full story of the storm

and how it had brought the ghost ship ashore at Yesnaby. How Geordie Findlater had gone out to check on his stock, and had spotted the MV *Orlova* and called the coastguard.

'The weather was too coarse to get anywhere near it until later in the day. Divers took a look below the waterline, but thank God there was no leakage from the fuel tanks. The coastguard helicopter managed to drop two guys on board. That's when they found the bodies. After that, Erling . . . Inspector Flett went on board.'

Rhona didn't interrupt him, although she already knew the story after Erling had sent her through his report first thing this morning. Following that, they'd had a brief face-to-face chat, where he'd suggested that rather than have her brought to Kirkwall police station, she should come straight to the jetty at Houton and be taken out to the ship. Rhona had immediately agreed. The sooner she was at the locus, the better.

Heading south out of Kirkwall, they were soon within sight of Scapa Flow, which, as Ivan had promised, was fairly calm. Rhona noted in passing the lush green of the fields and the roadside verges bright yellow with primroses, known here as mayflowers, according to Magnus.

Despite the circumstances, Rhona was pleased to be back in Orkney.

Approaching Houton Bay, she had her first clear view of the *Orlova* anchored offshore. Approximately 80 metres in length, a rusted red, she resembled a supply vessel for an oil installation, with a flat cargo area at the rear. Although, according to Erling, the interior crew quarters had been substantially upgraded. If it was as luxurious as he'd suggested, there was no evidence of that on the outside. Word was that its origins were Russian and that it may have been abandoned in the Atlantic before being upgraded to become some sort of cruising ship.

As they pulled up in the ferry car park, Rhona spotted Magnus and Erling outside Magnus's house, next to the jetty, where the police launch was tied up.

Chrissy leaped out of the car and swiftly took off towards Magnus, Rhona and Ivan following.

'He's another of Chrissy's favourites,' Rhona told Ivan with a smile. 'She loves the Orcadian accent.'

Ivan gave a half-smile, as though thinking he was already outmatched by the tall professor Chrissy was currently embracing with gusto.

'You'll both stay with me,' Magnus said after greeting Rhona warmly.

Rhona looked to Erling.

'Makes it easier to come and go to the ship. Plus Magnus, as you know, is an excellent cook.' He paused for a moment before saying, 'Considering the strangeness of the crime scene, I suggest Magnus accompanies us. As a behavioural psychologist he might be able to interpret what's been happening out there.'

That agreed, they donned life jackets and boarded the launch. Within moments they were cutting through the waters of the Flow towards the red hulk that was the *Orlova*.

'How do we get aboard?' Chrissy said.

'By ladder,' Erling told her. 'Think you can manage the climb?'

'Nothing to me,' Chrissy said, her eye drawn upwards as the launch approached to nudge the ship's side. 'After Kilt Rock.'

Rhona enlightened Erling. 'It's a cliff face on Skye. We abseiled down.'

In fact, it did turn out to be trickier.

On Skye she'd been attached to Jamie McColl as they'd dropped down the steep cliff face. Jamie was a pal from her teenage years when she'd spent her summers with her family on the island. He was also a member of the local mountain rescue team, so the descent had demanded little effort on her behalf, except controlling her fear.

This was different. Here she would have to climb a steep ladder on her own volition, while trying not to look down at the swirling sea below.

Erling indicated he would go first, followed by Rhona then Chrissy, with Magnus bringing up the rear.

'I'll be there to catch you if you fall,' Magnus assured them.

Of the actual climb, Rhona registered nothing except the image of Erling's boots a rung or two ahead, and her delight at being helped over the railing at the top to find her feet on solid ground again.

'Okay?' Erling said.

'Fine,' Rhona assured him. 'Glad I didn't have to carry my gear though,' she added, seeing it carefully stacked on the deck, having been brought up in advance of their ascent.

Chrissy appeared next, doing her best to look unfazed, although Rhona had heard her forensic assistant give voice to a few well-known Glasgow oaths on her way up.

'Nae bother,' Chrissy announced. 'Right, let's get the kit on.'

The act of donning their forensic suits changed the mood. By all accounts so far, they had now entered a crime scene, where three people had died in suspicious circumstances.

Once they were ready, Erling led them across the cargo deck, which housed three Portakabins.

'Dorms for the crew and catering staff, we believe,' he told them. 'The original indoor accommodation had been significantly upgraded. There's a helicopter pad on the bow, too badly damaged to use at present, although that looks like the original method for bringing folk aboard.'

After circling the dorms, they came across what looked like a boxing ring tucked in behind, the base a similar size, but constructed with rough wooden planks, a single thick rope serving as a barrier.

'Some sort of fighting ring,' Erling said. 'The base is pretty badly stained with blood.'

Entering the main structure, he showed them the guest accommodation. 'Four suites but possibly only one in use. We found clothes in here belonging to a male and a female.'

The king-size bed was made up. The room was tidy, as though housekeeping had been in. An open wardrobe revealed a row of clothes hanging up, both male and female.

'The victims' clothes?' Rhona said.

'We're assuming so.'

'Anything to identify them?'

Erling indicated there wasn't. 'Only the clothes and toiletries. Which is odd. But then everything about this ship is odd.'

They moved then through the staterooms, which had the same air of sudden abandonment. The long mahogany dining table had a centrepiece of two candelabras, and it looked as though two people had eaten there.

'We found the remains of prepared food in the galley. I won't open the door because it doesn't smell too good.'

From there they headed down another set of stairs. This time Rhona had a sense that she was entering the bowels of the *Orlova*, perhaps already below the waterline.

Ever since they'd come aboard, she'd been aware of the

constant shifting of the ship at anchor as the tide continued to turn. Down here, the movement was accompanied by creaking and groaning sounds, and the scraping of metal on metal.

It was as though the dead bones of the ship were rattling.

'We're coming to the first locus,' Erling warned them.

They turned a corner in the metal staircase to see a door that led into a box-type room just above the lower deck. And it was there the smell they'd been living with recently hit Rhona again. Chrissy caught it too because she muttered as much from behind her mask.

Erling pushed the door wider, so that they might view the interior.

The man was seated on a swivel chair facing a wall of screens. The fire had damaged both him and the computer equipment he'd been operating. The scent of an accelerant hung in the air, mingling with that of burnt flesh. There was the mild buzz of flies disturbed at their sudden appearance. Rhona could see that the fire had consumed his left arm and hand, and the left side of his head. His left leg and lower body weren't visible from where they stood. The equipment nearest that side appeared to be the most damaged.

At first glance, you could have imagined that an electrical fault had caused the fire, but the presence of an accelerant suggested otherwise.

'Someone trying to cover their tracks?' Chrissy said.

'That's what we thought. He hasn't been disturbed. This is exactly how we found him,' Erling told Rhona. 'We'll head for the second locus now.'

They continued down the staircase. The vast open space they were about to enter was obviously the gaming area. From where they stood on the stairs, they could see what looked like a maze, built of fake walls, the central portion opening out to become an arena.

'It's like the Night of the Undead at the Arches,' Chrissy said.

Rhona gave Erling a quick explanation. 'It's an underground space beneath Central Station in Glasgow.'

'Where they held an overnight combat game killing zombies,' Chrissy finished for her. 'It was ace.'

'So you'll be able to find your way through this maze?' Erling joked.

'Of course. Since it looks as though you've already laid down the treads.'

As they stepped via the metal treads towards the entrance, they were suddenly blinded by light, while above, a virtual audience began to scream down encouragement at them from an animated balcony.

'Sorry,' Erling tried to shout above the noise. 'I should have warned you. This happens intermittently and we're not sure how it's controlled. We didn't want to remove any of the equipment from the computer room until you'd had the opportunity to process the body. It'll cut out again shortly,' he promised.

'The second locus,' Erling said as they reached the main arena in sudden and blessed silence. 'A warning, though. Someone's vomited just inside.'

Under the arc lights, already set up, the image presented was garish and disturbing. The victim nearest them was female, dressed in a leather, Viking-like tunic, her long blonde hair, which was threaded with braids, partially covering her face. She lay on her back, exposing a long open gash that ran from her neck to her stomach. The tunic was short and pleated, exposing her legs, which were pitted with smaller surface wounds.

Rhona registered all of this, then switched her attention to the male.

He was similarly dressed, his head shaved at the sides and spiked on top, so that his face was in full view. He too had a gaping neck and chest wound. Plus his left leg had been severed below the knee.

Between them was a metre of bloodied floor and two discarded swords.

'Jeez,' Chrissy said. 'This was no virtual game. This was definitely for real.'

Their arrival had caused a small cloud of spring flies to rise in frustration at being disturbed.

'I have my net and some fly-papers,' Chrissy said. 'Plus these little beauties may help us determine the time of death.'

Magnus had remained silent throughout their path through the ship, although Rhona had been conscious of his benign and thoughtful presence. She was here to analyse death. Magnus, as a professor of psychology and a criminal profiler, was focused on what the locus might tell them about any perpetrator.

'Could they have killed one another?' Chrissy ventured what was an obvious question.

'Or it's been staged to look like it,' Rhona said. 'Okay, we'll begin here and tackle the computer room victim after that.'

13

Janice was already at her desk when McNab strode into the office. She looked him up and down.

'So you're back on the Harley then?'

McNab didn't respond, since it was perfectly obvious by his outfit that was how he'd come into work today.

He hadn't been on the Harley since he and Ellie had parted company. Janice was quietly aware of that, of course, so she would interpret this move as a sign he was either over Ellie or, alternatively, that he wasn't.

McNab had the fleeting idea that he should ask her which it was, because he didn't have a clue himself.

'Strategy meeting on the fire victim in ten minutes,' she informed him. 'You look like you need a coffee.'

She was right. He'd managed to sleep through Storm Birka, but hadn't been able to sleep after seeing Ellie climb on the back of that bike and ride off with Baldy.

His solution in the early hours had been to send the photograph he'd taken to Ollie in IT and ask him to check if they had the guy on file. That small mean gesture had resulted in a couple of hours of tortured sleep before he'd had to rise again and come to work.

The gang was moving into the meeting room when he got back from the coffee machine, and McNab joined Janice there.

'Have you heard the news?' she said as he came along-side her.

'What news?'

'Rhona and Chrissy headed off to Orkney early this morning. An abandoned ship was driven onto the cliffs at Yesnaby and three bodies were discovered aboard.'

'They get all the fun jobs,' McNab said, although he didn't mean it. The emptier parts of Scotland held no appeal for him, and his memories of being blown about on the island of Sanday were only now thankfully beginning to fade.

The place fell silent as their boss, DI Bill Wilson, appeared. Having drawn their attention to the photos of the scene on the board, together with the names of key witnesses who'd been interviewed, he now addressed the team.

'We've spoken to everyone who was in the surrounding buildings that night. Most folk reported that they were in bed asleep, or lying worrying whether their roofs were coming off.

'No one,' he continued, 'except Jimmy Donaldson, an elderly man in the ground-floor flat, claims to have seen the girl alone out there immediately before the fire. The first thing mentioned was the sudden roar of the flames that had drawn folk to the window.'

DI Wilson confirmed that a handbag containing identifi-cation had been found at the locus, and that they now had an address for an Olivia Newton Richardson in North London.

Despite the boss's correct rendering of the victim's possible name, McNab was still hearing Newton Mearns in his head. A sideways glance at Janice indicated she did not want him to voice it.

The boss continued. 'We have passed the information to the Met and asked them to make enquiries regarding this person. They have designated an officer to be our liaison on the enquiry.' He looked into the audience. 'DS McNab.'

McNab didn't register that he was the one being called until Janice nudged him.

'Yes, sir?' He stood to attention.

'You will be our contact here for that, so confirm with IT what they have on Ms Richardson, then give DI Cleverly a call and get him up to date on where we are.'

'Yes . . . sir,' McNab managed to say in return.

Janice gave him one of her piercing looks as the boss began doling out other tasks.

'What?' McNab said, obviously failing to temper the emotion he'd experienced at the name of his contact in the Met.

'What's wrong with DI Cleverly?' she said.

McNab considered how much of the story he should give her. Eventually he said, 'One, he's a wee shite. Two, he's not clever.'

'You know him, then?'

McNab sucked air between his teeth. 'He almost got me killed when I was in a supposed safe house in London, after I was shot.'

'You've never mentioned him before?'

'If I listed every arsehole that's pissed me off, you would have demanded not to be my partner.'

'I've thought about it for less,' Janice conceded. 'Does the boss know you're sworn enemies?'

McNab didn't know, since he'd never reported on Cleverly's actions. He'd just abandoned the safe house and gone into hiding on his own volition, until it was time to give evidence in court.

'It wouldn't stop him giving me the job, even if he did,' McNab said. 'The boss doesn't do vendettas.'

Janice didn't say 'unlike you'. What she did say was, 'So time to let bygones be bygones?'

McNab smiled in reply. 'I'm off to speak to Ollie. See what else we've learned about Ms Newton Richardson, in preparation for my phone call to DI Cleverly.'

That wouldn't be the only question he planned to pose, McNab thought, as he headed in the direction of the IT department.

He was in the cafeteria stocking up on goodies for Ollie when his mobile rang. The screen gave him nothing but a London number, but McNab guessed who it would be.

He left the goodies on the counter, motioned he had to answer this call before he could pay for them, then took himself off into a corner.

'DS McNab here,' he said.

The pause that followed was long enough for him to wonder whether Cleverly had actually been given his name as the contact in Glasgow. And if so, had he recognized it?

Eventually the response came. 'DI Cleverly here from the Met.'

The tone suggested he either didn't recall McNab's name or he was being studiously neutral on the subject. McNab remained silent.

'It's about the possible self-immolation case . . .'

McNab continued to wait. If information was to be given out, it would not be by him. Besides, he hadn't yet seen Ollie to be brought up to date.

'And the possibility that the victim might be one Olivia Newton Richardson of—' Cleverly quoted an address.

'So what have you got?' McNab said.

'Nothing as yet. We've just begun enquiries.'

This time the intervening silence lasted even longer, before Cleverly finally said, 'We'll be in touch, Detective Sergeant.'

And that was it.

Grasping a can of sugar-free Irn-Bru and a packet of mixed nuts, McNab found himself pining for the days of sugared ring doughnuts, now apparently banned by Ollie's recently acquired girlfriend, Maria.

Still, you were the one that introduced them, he reminded himself. *So you only have yourself to blame.*

Now outside the IT suite, McNab took a deep breath before entering. He was as averse to rooms full of tech as he was to the countryside. Fortunately for him, he wasn't often required to spend time outside his home city of Glasgow. Avoiding this place was less easy.

He stood for a moment to locate Ollie, then headed over there.

Plonking his offerings on the desk, he gave Ollie a grin, while also noting that the new diet imposed by Maria seemed to be working. Either that or Ollie had increased his physical activity levels since he'd met her. Or maybe both, McNab thought.

Ollie caught the grin, and looked mildly embarrassed, which he often did.

'Nuts and sugar-free Irn-Bru,' McNab pointed out. 'Just what Maria ordered. Things still good between you two?'

Ollie's eyes behind the glasses took on a shine. Something McNab had only seen previously when Ollie had located some excellent and enlightening piece of information online.

'Of course,' he said. 'Maria says to say hi.'

So I continue to be in the good books, McNab thought. *That bodes well for getting info on Baldy.*

'You're here about the credit cards from the fire?' Ollie said.

'I am sent from the boss on precisely that mission.'

'Well,' Ollie began, 'Ms Richardson, owner of the cards, lives at—'

McNab repeated the address given him by Cleverly.

Ollie shot him a look of surprise. 'Yes . . . how did you know?'

'Go on,' McNab urged him.

'The address is in a very desirable area. She leases the flat. Her bank accounts are healthy. She earns a lot and spends a lot. She also works for, or has a company called, Go Wild, which as far as I can gather, provides extreme adventure holidays.'

'How extreme?' McNab said, ears pricking up.

'Still checking this out, but it definitely involves travelling to difficult locations. Taking part in extreme sports. That sort of thing.'

'Not cheap, I take it?'

'Definitely not cheap.' Ollie's head bobbed in his enthusiasm.

'So a short stay in a tenement flat in Govan is unlikely to be included in the itinerary?'

Ollie gave a little laugh. 'Exactly.'

'So why was our girl there? Have you found any links to Glasgow?'

'Not so far,' Ollie said, sounding apologetic. 'But I've only just started.'

'Any word on her mobile?' McNab tried.

'Trickier . . .'

When Ollie started out on the reasons why this was so, McNab cut him off. 'Just let me know when you do.' He sat back in the chair. 'Now, the photo I sent?'

'Is he a suspect in the fire case?' Ollie said.

McNab considered a lie, albeit briefly, then shook his head. 'I just want to know if he's been anywhere on our radar.'

'Okay, but I take it the Go Wild thing has higher priority for now?'

Ollie had done favours for him in the past, and McNab didn't want to jeopardize their arrangement. 'No hurry,' he said, 'just when you can fit it in.' He tried to look easy about it, even as he thought the opposite. If the guy was a felon, he wanted evidence to present to Ellie, and fast.

Then another outcome presented itself. Ellie might not care. Might think he was the creepy one in this scenario.

'Okay, send me everything you find on this Go Wild thing, and any evidence to suggest that Ms Richardson is still alive.'

'You think the cards didn't belong to the victim?'

'There's always that chance.' McNab hesitated. 'We're liaising with the Met on this one, in case the victim is one of theirs, and I'm the contact on that. If a DI Cleverly gets in touch directly, can you refer him back to me, please?'

'Sure thing,' Ollie said.

McNab left then to head to his next port of call, which was Jimmy. The old man hadn't given them much. Maybe he was just too upset. Then again, if he had seen a perpetrator, he might not have been keen to make that known.

If some guy was up for setting a woman on fire, an old man who was witness to that might be his next victim.

14

The flies hadn't been the only visitors to the crime scene. That became obvious as Rhona and Chrissy quietly went about their work.

'You hearing them too?' Chrissy said, her whisper muffled further by the mask. 'They're getting braver.'

'We stole their future dinner once they'd finished with the kitchen,' Rhona said. 'Do you have your mobile with you?'

'Never without it,' Chrissy assured her.

'Then let's have some music. That might keep them away.'

'Good idea. Any requests?'

'Something rats won't like,' Rhona said, well aware that she might not like Chrissy's choice of music either. Whatever it was, it would be better than listening to the squeaking.

Rhona wasn't against rats per se. In fact, there was much to be admired about them. Still, she didn't want them scuttling around her when she was on a job.

They'd erected a tent over their workspace, and brought the arc lights inside. The strange virtual world that surrounded them had exploded into life roughly every forty-five minutes. Shielded in part by the brightness of the spotlights, they'd gradually come to ignore the sudden screaming of their virtual audience, knowing they were stuck with it anyway until the body in the computer room had been processed.

She had chosen to leave the arena victims clothed, but

had gone through the usual meticulous routine of photo-
graphing, examining and taping them.

Their position and that of the swords seemed to Rhona's
judgement to suggest neither sword had been used to inflict
the major blows. Added to that, the angle and depth of the
chest wounds implied that both blows had been struck by
someone taller, and possibly left-handed.

The swords themselves had been bagged for further examination, but in her minimal handling of them, neither blade
had appeared sharp enough to result in such penetrating
wounds. Added to that, the male's lower leg had been sliced
cleanly off, and she couldn't see the slightly built female
being able to do that.

If she was right, then a third person had been present,
and that person had been taller, more muscular and had
had a weapon capable of bringing about this carnage.

When this had happened depended on multiple factors.
A body exposed to the air decomposed more quickly than
a buried body. The virtual game might be still playing, but
any heating that had been on was no longer in operation.
In fact, the area was cool, verging on cold. That, and the
fact it wasn't yet summer, had meant the flies weren't
numerous.

The bodies had gone through rigor mortis, which broadly
happened between twenty-four and thirty-six hours after
death. Post-mortem decomposition usually began immediately after death, often not visible at first until greening of
the skin began in the right flank of the abdomen at around
two to three days, gradually extending to cover the whole
abdominal area.

In this instance, decomposition had progressed further,
showing swelling in the face, genitals and abdomen, but

hadn't yet progressed to marbling of the skin, where the vein patterns are visible. At a broad estimate, the two fighters had died three to five days ago.

Chrissy had been concentrating on the small wounds on the legs. Their initial interpretation, that they might have been caused by the points of the swords, had been tempered by the presence of the rats, which was also feeding into their interpretation of the overall state of the bodies.

It was a slow and laborious process, but just as in the Glasgow fire, they had to retrieve as much as possible before the bodies were removed.

Kneeling back, Rhona signalled that the music should be turned off. Chrissy did so. The sudden silence, from both the rats and their virtual audience, seemed deafening, until they gradually registered again the metallic creaks and clangs as the ship circled its mooring with the shifting tide.

'I used to fancy going on a cruise,' Chrissy said. 'The Norwegian fjords, or maybe the Mediterranean for the sunshine. Don't fancy it so much now.'

'Did you get the vomit?' Rhona said.

'I can confirm I have taken possession of the pavement pizza,' Chrissy said, using a favourite Glasgow expression.

Not for the first time did Rhona say a silent thank you for Chrissy's take on the world in general.

'How's your own stomach?' she said, returning Chrissy's smile.

'The rats have retreated because it was growling so loudly.'

Rhona checked the time only to discover just how late it was.

'Can you finish up here while I photograph the first locus? After that, we'll head back. Eat and get some sleep, then come back at first light,' she said.

'Which, as it's Orkney, will be very early,' Chrissy warned her.

Erling had left them a radio to keep in touch. Rhona called him now, saying they were ready to transport the evidence and the two bodies ashore from the arena, and that they would return at first light tomorrow.

'I'll send Ivan out with the launch. The guys will see you safely down the ladder and back to shore, where Magnus is ready with the food.'

At the promise of food, Chrissy's eyes lit up, the bannocks and cheese which Magnus had packed for their lunch having been consumed long since.

Rhona glanced back at the rusty ship as the launch powered its way to shore. The decision had been made to land the coastguard helicopter on the cargo deck, now possible after the Portakabins had been moved. The bodies of the two Vikings would be transported to the Glasgow mortuary in the morning. After that it would be the forensic pathologist's job to discover their secrets.

'When we were shown the fancy quarters,' Chrissy said suddenly, 'I noticed something.'

'What?' Rhona said.

'The bedding all had an embroidered symbol on it. I took a photo out of curiosity. Then I noticed the same symbol was on the handles of the swords. So I presume it was a company mark. You'll no doubt have captured it in your photographs.'

She handed Rhona her phone. It was an insignia. The swirling adjoining letters looked like a G and a W intertwined.

'I wonder if Erling's picked up on that,' Rhona said.

Chrissy grew ever more excited as the image of Magnus's house got closer.

'I've always wanted to stay there,' she announced to Ivan, who looked a little put out by that.

'The sea comes up and round the foundations, you know,' he warned. 'Two fishermen built it below the high-water mark because that land was free.'

'How romantic,' Chrissy said, much to Ivan's chagrin.

Rhona now suspected her assistant was definitely having the poor man on, and kicked her to register that. Chrissy, however, when rapturous about something, wasn't likely to be dissuaded.

Chrissy was out of the launch first, and heading straight for Magnus's front door. Rhona thanked Ivan and reiterated that they'd like to go back out at dawn the next day.

'Sun's up just after five tomorrow,' he checked. 'Shall we say six o'clock for our trip out?' He looked worried that she might suggest even earlier, so Rhona complied.

'We'll be ready,' she promised.

Opening the front door, Rhona caught the scent of something delicious. The relief at having her feet back on dry land was now further enhanced by the anticipation of a hot shower and a meal.

Magnus appeared from the kitchen to greet her. 'I've put you in the room you had last time. Towels are on the bed. Take as much time and hot water as you need.'

Entering the room, Rhona went straight to the window, remembering how much she'd loved this view the first time she'd stayed with Magnus.

Luckily, the hulk of the MV *Orlova* had shifted out of sight, and she still had a clear line to the hills of Hoy. Magnus had joked on her first visit that if you could see Hoy then the rain was on its way. If you couldn't see Hoy, then the rain was already here.

Rhona undressed and moved swiftly to the shower. As the water beat down on her head, the image and smell of the locus began to fade and she could focus on the forthcoming dinner.

According to Magnus, they would be joined tonight by investigative journalist Ava Clouston. It seemed Ava was reporting on the ghost ship for *The Orcadian*, plus various national and international outlets, since she was back home for a while, after the death of her parents. Rhona was intrigued to meet her and perhaps get her take on the mysterious MV *Orlova*, although, of course, there couldn't be a discussion of what had happened on board today.

Heading downstairs, she found Chrissy and Magnus outside on the stone jetty admiring the view. Sunset had now turned the sky blood red against the dark hills of Hoy. It was stunningly beautiful and also devoid of wind, as though a Norse god was holding his breath at the splendour.

Chrissy was staring transfixed at the wonder before her. She might be a city girl but, unlike McNab, she could appreciate a world outside its boundaries. She had definitely taken a liking to the remote cottage they'd occupied during the Sanday case, once she was sure that the larder and fridge were well stocked.

'A dram?' Magnus offered, indicating the bottle of Highland Park and glasses set out on the outer wall of his own little harbour.

As Rhona smiled a yes, they heard a woman's voice call his name.

'That'll be Ava,' Magnus said, going to answer.

'D'you know this Ava woman?' Chrissy asked. 'Apparently she's an investigative journalist.'

'I've read some of her reports, but never met her,' Rhona admitted.

Chrissy lowered her voice. 'Her parents died in a car accident, and she has to decide what to do with the farm. It's over there.' She pointed westwards. 'Apparently there's a teenage brother who wants to keep it on.'

As Chrissy finished, the woman they'd been discussing appeared. Tall and dark-haired, she observed them with a cool, clear, interested gaze.

'It's good to meet you, Dr MacLeod, and you must be Chrissy. I've heard all about you both from Magnus.'

She accepted her dram and they all toasted their meeting and the stunning sunset.

'I forget when I'm in London just how long the spring and summer days are in Orkney,' she said. 'It's always a revelation when I return. As is the wind,' she added, laughing.

'What wind?' Magnus indicated the flat calm of the water gently lapping against the stone jetty.

They spoke mainly of Ava's work during the meal and Rhona discovered a mutual connection between them. Ava had been working on the disappearance of immigrant children in London, which had links with the torso of a young Nigerian boy found in Glasgow's River Kelvin. Rhona had been involved in the case, and the subsequent search for another little Nigerian boy snatched from a garden in Glasgow.

'Michael's father, Sam, helped us with that,' Chrissy told Ava. 'Rhona and DS McNab eventually travelled to Nigeria to help find and rescue little Stephen.'

After that, they'd moved on to Ava's reporting on the MV *Orlova*.

'Of course, I'm aware of the restrictions on talking about the crime scene,' she said. 'What I am intrigued by are the ship's secrets. Who owns it, what was happening on board in general? I've spent all my time since its arrival trying to discover its backstory.'

'And have you?'

As Chrissy asked the question, Rhona was conscious of water lapping against the thick stone walls of the house. It was like being aboard the *Orlova*, yet not like it at all. In here was warmth and light and a knowledge of permanence. Out there – she glanced through the glass at the moonlit darkness beyond – the ghost ship would be juddering and creaking in its perpetual circle round its anchorage.

'Did you hear that, Rhona?' Chrissy said, breaking into her thoughts. 'Ava says the *Orlova* was offering trips aboard via a company called Go Wild. So that's what the GW insignia stood for,' she added triumphantly.

'I understand from Erling that a couple of detectives are arriving tomorrow to take a look at the ship?' Ava said.

Chrissy looked to Rhona. 'It wouldn't be McNab, would it?'

'I'm sure if it was we would have heard by now,' Rhona said.

'This is the McNab from the Nigerian story?' Ava said, sensing Chrissy's excitement at such a prospect.

'My wee boy's named after him,' Chrissy said proudly. 'Michael McNab saved my life when I was pregnant.'

'Wow,' Ava said. 'A friend indeed, then.'

Ava left after that and Rhona, mindful of the prospect of their early rise, and the fact she wanted to update her notes, indicated she was bound for bed. Chrissy, already yawning, joined her.

'I'll leave a packed lunch out for you and set the timer

on the coffee machine, although I may not see you before you leave,' Magnus said. 'Good luck tomorrow.'

Now in her room, Rhona settled in bed with her laptop. The meeting with Ava had been fruitful, she thought. If anyone could discover the hidden world of the MV *Orlova*, she suspected it might be her.

15

The close seemed back to normal. Tape was down, litter was appearing on the stairs instead of metal treads. Only the door on the top landing remained sealed.

Having taken a look, McNab proceeded down again and approached Jimmy's door. This time, his knock was swiftly answered and he was greeted with a big smile.

'Come away in, Sergeant. Just in time for a cuppa.'

McNab was shown into the sitting room where Lucifer eyed him with evil intent from the windowsill.

'He likes you. I can tell,' Jimmy assured him, before heading, McNab assumed, to fetch his tea.

Minutes later he came back with two mugs. One supporting Glasgow Rangers, the other Celtic. He handed McNab the Celtic one.

'Am I right?'

'I don't follow football much, but if I did . . .' McNab toasted him.

Jimmy smiled at that. 'I'm glad it's just you, son, this time. It's not that I didn't like the lassie, but I'm not sure it's safe to have women on the front line. The world can be a terrible place for them. Like that poor lassie.' He glanced towards the window, following Lucifer's fierce gaze into the back court.

They supped for another minute or two, before McNab said, 'I just wondered if there was anything else you remembered that you wanted to tell me. Or maybe something you didn't want to say in front of DS Clark?'

Jimmy threw him a shrewd look. 'If you guessed that, then no wonder you're a detective, son.'

'So what was it?' McNab prompted.

'There was shenanigans going on up in that flat.'

'Shenanigans?' McNab said.

'Sexy shenanigans,' Jimmy explained. 'I followed Lucifer up there. He pees on the stairs sometimes, and folk complain.' He hesitated.

'And?'

'They were going at it in there. Hell for leather,' he added, his eyes wide. 'Screaming even.'

'A woman was screaming?'

'Screaming and moaning. The man too.'

'Was someone being hurt?' McNab tried.

'It's difficult to say nowadays. What with this rough sex stuff you read about in the papers. Women asking men to choke and hit them. I cannae believe it.'

'You think that was what was going on?' McNab said.

'I'm just telling you what I heard, son.'

'Was that the night of the fire?'

He shook his head. 'Naw. I didnae go up there that night. Too frightened to move for the wind. And Lucifer was in here with me.'

'When was the last time you heard the . . . shenanigans?' McNab found himself saying.

'A couple of days before the fire.'

'Do you know who owns or rents the flat?'

'Naw. But folk come and go regularly. I thought at first it was a druggie place – you know, where they buy the stuff – but there's been no syringes or nothing about the close, and no weird smells, except for the flat across the landing from it. Ah think they're on the wacky baccy.'

'Did you tell this to any of the officers taking statements?'

'Och, naw. Ah saved it up for you, son.' He smiled. 'Maybe get you a promotion, eh?'

I've already been there and done that, McNab thought. His time as a detective inspector hadn't lasted very long. He rose to go.

'Oh, you're off, are you?' Jimmy looked disappointed. 'Will you come back if I remember anything else?'

McNab handed him a card. 'Call me if you do.'

He was well aware that the old boy was lonely, and talking to the police about that night might have been his only contact with the outside world for God knows how long.

Heading up the stairs, he wondered if he was destined to end his days like Jimmy Donaldson. Sitting in his flat alone – he definitely wouldn't be having a cat – not knowing any neighbours. Hey, he didn't know any of his neighbours now, he realized. What would happen to him if he didn't have the job to hang on to, the company of his workmates to rely on?

Reaching the door of the so-called wacky baccy brigade, he pushed such thoughts away and rang the bell. After a minute or two he heard footsteps approach the door, followed by silence, when no doubt his ID was being examined through the peephole. Eventually the door swung open and he was confronted by a bearded bloke wearing a T-shirt and shorts.

Since the storm, the weather had brightened, they'd even been blessed with some sunshine, but weather for shorts? McNab didn't think so.

Jimmy had said the place stank of weed. McNab made a

point of taking a deep and obvious breath in. As he did so, the guy's face took on a worried look.

'Can I help you, officer?'

McNab took a couple more sniffs, and wrinkled his nose, causing more consternation. Finally he said, 'The neighbouring flat.' He gestured towards the crime scene tape.

The relief on the guy's face at what he saw as a change of direction was obvious. 'Yes?' he said eagerly.

'There've been reports of noises from the flat of a sexual nature.'

The guy stared at him. 'You're really asking me if I've heard folk fucking next door? Well, the answer's yes, as I'm sure they've heard me at it too.'

'The reports suggest it was of a violent nature. Screaming and moaning?' Even as he heard himself say the words, he knew what would happen.

'Sex can sound that way at times,' the man said with a knowing grin. He'd relaxed now over his fear of getting busted, and was enjoying himself.

'Do you know who owns or rents the flat?'

'The uniforms who interviewed us already asked us that and the answer is no one knows. But there's definitely a big footfall. Maybe an Airbnb? Then again, who would want to stay here for a weekend break?'

Heading down the stairs, McNab wondered if Jimmy had set him up. Anything to keep his company for a bit longer. He met the cat on the way, heading upwards, intent on what? Peeing on the top landing? Glancing up, he saw Lucifer staring down at him through the bars, a malevolent glint in his eye.

McNab got quickly out of the way, just in case Lucifer's latest spray of urine was directed at him.

Back on the bike, his stomach reminded him how late it was. His day, he accepted, had evaporated and he was no further forward on anything. He contemplated returning to the office to report just that, or alternatively head for the chippy and satisfy one hunger at least.

Did he decide to go by the tattoo parlour or did the bike take him there of its own free will? Whichever it was, that's where he found himself. This time the place was in darkness. So no one was in there getting inked, or laid, by Ellie.

He pulled up alongside to answer his phone, hoping against hope that it might be Ellie, while knowing full well that it wouldn't be. There was a female name on the screen, however. It just wasn't the one he wanted. Still smarting from his previous thought, he answered.

'Michael? It's Mary. How are you doing?'

'Good,' he said, even though it wasn't true.

'How's the Harley going?'

The Harley you gifted me, you mean, McNab thought, but didn't say.

'Great, thanks. On it now.'

'Glad to hear it.' She sounded pleased. 'I wondered if you fancied an Italian and a catch-up soon?'

It was something he'd promised her, but reneged on. Because of Ellie, a wee voice reminded.

'Sure thing. When?'

'Later tonight?'

McNab contemplated the evening stretching ahead with only thoughts of Ellie and Baldy and sexual shenanigans to fill it, and made a decision.

'Okay. Text me where and when. I'll be there.'

16

Erling knew the two men were the visiting detectives as soon as he spotted them walking across the concourse. It wasn't because he'd met them before, rather that they stuck out from the troop of returning Orcadians, who knew how the whole thing worked, including the gusts of wind that tried to lift their feet from the tarmac.

He waited until the men had composed themselves before he moved forward to greet them.

'DS Campbell and DS Neville? Welcome to Orkney. How was your flight?'

It was DS Neville who answered. 'Bumpy, especially over the Pentland Firth. So no hot drinks allowed, but I enjoyed my caramel log.'

'Do you want to pick up a coffee here before we head for Houton Bay?' Erling offered.

'No need,' Neville said. 'We'll survive.'

They kept the discussion until they were inside the vehicle and on their way out of Kirkwall. Erling did his best to give a quick overview of the events up to now, including Dr MacLeod's examination of the bodies from the previous day.

'Have the remains been taken south yet?' Neville, the apparent spokesman, asked.

'Should have gone first thing, but we delayed because of

the wind this morning, which means you'll get a chance to see them in situ.'

'What was Dr MacLeod's opinion?'

'That there was likely an assailant,' Erling said. 'She and Chrissy are working on the computer guy this morning.'

'Chrissy McInsh's here too?' DS Neville asked.

'She is,' Erling said. 'No show without Punch.' He laughed. 'I take it you know Chrissy?'

DS Campbell, who was seated in the front, motioned to his colleague in the back. '*He* does. Or I should say he wishes he did.'

They talked a bit after that about the SOCO team that had been working the ship.

'We know you've done a good job here,' DS Neville said. 'The powers that be just thought it would be a good idea for us to see the locus in person. The ghost ship, as they're calling it, has grabbed the news, with much of the press stating it has Russian backers.'

'I suspect it may be even more international than that,' Erling said. 'We have Ava Clouston, the investigative journalist, home on Orkney at the moment. She's covering the story.'

DS Campbell shot him a look. 'She's a friend?'

'Everyone knows everyone else on Orkney,' Erling said. 'That doesn't mean we reveal police business.'

They were approaching Houton Bay and the men's eyes were drawn to the image of the ghost ship anchored offshore.

'An old cargo ship?' DS Neville said.

'From the outside,' Erling said. 'Once aboard, it's a whole different world.'

'How do we get out there?' DS Campbell said.

'Police launch and a climb up a long ladder.'

*

Their trip out earlier that morning had proved choppy, and the ladder climb a little more hair-raising, although Chrissy for one hadn't flinched. In fact, Rhona had got the impression that her assistant had begun to relish the experience.

Despite plans to transport the first two bodies south, they were still here, with a revised time of departure later today. Which meant the two Glasgow detectives from the serious crime squad who'd landed earlier at Kirkwall would get a chance to view them.

Rhona had just announced a loo and coffee break, which had provided Chrissy with the opportunity to watch for the arrival of the police launch and the said detectives. Her assistant, of course, really wanted to view their ascent of the ladder.

While Chrissy was on watch, Rhona was enjoying a cup of Magnus's coffee, and one of his bannocks, while she considered what they'd discovered so far about the body in the computer room.

Electrocution occurred when a victim became the fastest pathway to earth for an electrical supply. To achieve this they had to touch an exposed live electrical cable or a metal surface connected to such, and to be standing on the ground or on something that conducted electricity.

Barefoot was best because the rubber soles of shoes prevented conduction to earth, or at least slowed it down – so the victim might get zapped, but not be killed.

Electrocution didn't severely burn a body, except at the point of contact, where you would likely see very deep burns, blackening of the tissues and sometimes a loss of fingers.

The myth that if you were in contact with water and an energized electrical cable was placed in the water then you would be immediately electrocuted was just that, a myth.

Such a thing didn't happen unless the water was able to conduct the electricity in the first place. That only happened if it was contaminated, for example with salt.

In this case, no water was present, either with or without salt.

Something else had happened here. The figure in the chair had been on fire, but that hadn't been the cause of his death. The bloodshot eyes, the fibres and oil deposits she'd retrieved from around the mouth and nose suggesting a cloth of some kind, the pressure bruising, all of these pointed to suffocation.

The fire, she'd concluded, had been set to primarily destroy the computer equipment, the partially charred body being an appending causality.

Rhona was writing her notes alongside the victim when Chrissy reappeared.

'They're on their way,' she said. 'You should have seen them on the ladder. DS Neville looked positively green. Mind you, it's rougher than yesterday,' she conceded.

'Did they see you spying on them?' Rhona said, already feeling sorry for the visiting detectives.

'No way,' Chrissy said. 'I'll save that up for later.'

Seeing Chrissy's mischievous grin, Rhona suddenly realized, 'You know DS Neville?'

'I do, but not in the biblical sense,' Chrissy assured her with a smile.

At that moment the two detectives arrived, suitably kitted up. While Erling did the introductions, Rhona observed a swift look pass between DS Neville and Chrissy. So there was a tale to tell there, and no doubt she would hear it in due course.

Rhona gave them a brief résumé of what she'd read from her examination of the computer room victim. After which they headed downstairs to the arena.

All murder scenes were unique and frequently bizarre, but she suspected neither man had viewed anything quite like this one before. Silence prevailed as they all stepped their way across the treads and into the centre of the maze.

As luck would have it, the ear-splitting sound and lights of the bloodthirsty crowd came into action as they entered the locus. Even having been forewarned of this, the two men were visibly disconcerted, though trying not to show it.

Erling and Chrissy stayed outside the tent while Rhona led the detectives in to view the bodies. After a silent and close examination, Campbell asked about the weapons found on site and Rhona produced the bagged short swords.

'So you don't think either of these swords inflicted the fatal wounds?' Campbell said.

'The major cuts to the neck and chest caused them to bleed out. I don't think the swords are capable of inflicting those wounds. They aren't sharp or heavy enough. Neither would they be able to chop off a leg,' Rhona said. 'Some of the smaller cuts on the arms and legs may have been inflicted when they were actually fighting one another. There is also a resident rat population, although they wouldn't have liked the intermittent bright lights and screaming from the virtual audience.'

They'd emerged now from the tent.

'So they were actually trying to hurt each other?' Neville said.

'I think that was the idea.'

'They booked a holiday on the *Orlova* with a company called Go Wild. One assumes they knew what they were coming to do,' Erling said.

'But a fight to the death wasn't on the cards?' Neville asked.

'Men will go to all sorts of lengths to kill their partner,' Erling said.

'But I don't think the male victim was the perpetrator,' Rhona reminded him. 'I believe we have evidence to suggest the presence of a third party. And hopefully at post-mortem, forensic proof that neither sword inflicted the fatal wounds.'

'I assume you've not located another weapon in the vicinity?' Campbell said.

Erling indicated they hadn't. 'And it would be easy enough to dispose of it overboard.'

'We also collected vomit from the crime scene,' Rhona said. 'Which we can compare with the stomach contents of the victims.'

'Do we have a passenger list or captain's log?' Neville tried.

'No. We have no idea who was on the ship when this happened or what happened to them, other than the three bodies left behind.'

'The *Orlova*'s a ghost ship,' Chrissy said. 'It doesn't really exist.'

17

'Cleverly's flying up for the PM, and you've to pick him up at the airport,' Janice informed him on entry.

'What?' McNab struggled to deal with a sentence that contained the words Cleverly and PM in it, since he disliked both.

'The boss's orders,' Janice added, examining him more closely.

It was, McNab thought, like being sniffed all over by a Rottweiler.

'Are you hung over?' she eventually demanded.

McNab considered the question. There had been drink taken last night. Red wine with the meal, and whisky afterwards with the coffee, and later back at his place.

God. He'd taken Mary back to his flat, he recalled again with horror. What was he thinking?

But she hadn't stayed, he reminded himself. She'd called a taxi and gone home to her big house overlooking the park. Her husband might be banged up, but Mary still maintained the lifestyle he'd provided for her.

'I am not hung over,' he said, in part to convince himself. 'Anything else you need to tell me?'

'The boss wants a word.' His partner gave him one of her sweetest smiles. 'As soon as you arrive.'

McNab composed himself before knocking on the glass

door, recalling the single terse exchange he'd had with Cleverly and how he might report it. Which was undoubtedly what the boss wanted to discuss. When the call to enter came, McNab already had a plan.

DI Wilson looked up at him from behind the desk. 'You've heard DI Cleverly is coming for the post-mortem?'

'DS Clark told me, sir. And that I should pick him up at the airport.'

'Good.' DI Wilson studied him. 'You've already spoken to him, I assume?'

'Yes, sir.'

Noting McNab's expression, DI Wilson sat back in his chair. 'He gave nothing away?'

'Nothing, sir. He led me to believe they hadn't yet established whether Ms Richardson lived at the given address, nor whether they might have evidence to suggest she might be alive. He also didn't mention Go Wild, the company Ollie in IT says she worked for.'

Silence followed, while the boss considered this, and McNab took his chance.

'Sir. Might the Met be viewing this as their case, even though the death happened here in Glasgow?'

'Why do you say that, Sergeant?'

How did he explain that the entitlement in Cleverly's voice told him? Along with his avoidance of any information-giving. And now his attendance at the PM.

'Might the fire victim be more important than we realize, sir?' he tried.

DI Wilson nodded. 'I was thinking that myself, Sergeant. See what you can glean from our visitor at the PM.'

'He's not coming in, sir, to speak to you?'

'He is not. A flying visit, I was told. Hence my decision

that you should pick him up at the airport. I'm relying on you, Sergeant. To find out what you can.'

McNab was in a better state of mind exiting the boss's domain than when he'd entered it. He headed back to his desk and gave Janice a satisfied smile.

'So it went okay then?'

'Of course. I'm to suss out what Cleverly is really up to as I chauffeur him round Glasgow.'

As he took his seat, he spied the coffee Janice had no doubt fetched for him in his absence. McNab toasted her with it.

'I spoke to Jimmy Donaldson again.'

'And?'

'He thought you were a really nice lassie, but there were things he didn't think he should say in front of you.'

Janice pulled a face. 'You're joking. What exactly?'

'The sexy shenanigans he claims were going on in the flat where the victim was being held.'

'Sexy shenanigans,' Janice repeated with a smile.

'Once it's in your head you can't get rid of it,' McNab promised her. 'However, he did say there was screaming and moaning, which may have been consensual. He's been reading stuff in the papers about rough sex.'

'I'm beginning to be grateful I wasn't there,' Janice admitted.

'I checked with the bloke in the flat opposite, who confirmed it. It may have been operating as a brothel of some sort.'

'With a link to Go Wild?' Janice suggested.

'Ollie maintains Go Wild was for high-paying customers only. Why come to a tenement in Glasgow for sex?'

'Maybe more than just rough sex was part of the package?'

'You mean you get to set fire to the girl afterwards?' McNab said, his face displaying his horror at such a thought.

'It doesn't get rougher than that,' Janice said.

18

Ava had spotted the police launch heading for the *Orlova* mid-morning and assumed it was ferrying out the two Glasgow detectives. She'd asked Erling if she might have a quick interview with them at Houton, but he'd been categorical in his refusal.

'I'm your go-to person for information. Let's keep it that way,' he'd told her.

Ava had conceded to that, of course. Erling kept her in the loop with Police Scotland, but he had no jurisdiction over her own investigations. Although she wasn't allowed on board herself, she still knew what had been found there. The information had arrived via an anonymous email which included details of the virtual games set-up, a description of the arena and the deaths of the two fighters.

Ava had no reason to disbelieve this. There was enough local info circulating from those who had boarded the ship while making it secure to suggest the information was correct. Plus she'd already discovered enough about the ship to pair it with the company known as Go Wild.

Her initial leads, however, had now begun to dry up, suggesting Go Wild was likely removing material from online sources and generally battening down the hatches.

She did, of course, have another line of enquiry open to

her, should she choose to use it. Ava poured herself a coffee and considered this.

She and Mark went back a long way. They'd spent time together in Afghanistan and worked on exposing a number of high-profile international organizations, companies and politicians. If anyone could help her it would be Mark Sylvester, scourge of anyone high-ranking and influential who had something to hide.

The problem was, would he want to work with her again?

She'd kidded herself that their break-up had been mutually decided upon, when it definitely hadn't been. She'd been the one to end it, abruptly and without explanation. If Mark chose not to answer her call, she had no one to blame but herself.

She pondered this by the kitchen window, taking heart from the vision of the kye freed from their winter lockdown. When she and Dougie had released them, their delight had been wonderful to watch. They'd literally pranced their way into the fields. Their mooing at the discovery of acres of luscious spring grass and the ability to roam wherever they wanted had lifted her spirits. Dougie had been the same, the joy on his face confirming what she already knew. Dougie was born to be a farmer.

And she was about to take that away from him.

Dragging her thoughts back to the problem she could resolve, Ava picked up her mobile and brought up Mark's number, her thumb hesitating over the call button before pressing, almost hoping he wouldn't answer.

It only took three rings before he did.

'Ava, how great to hear from you. Are you still in Orkney?'

Momentarily shaken by the sound of his voice again, and the obvious delight in it, Ava hesitated. When she did so, Mark came back in.

'I was so sorry to hear about your mum and dad. How are things? How's Dougie doing?'

In those few moments, Ava realized how much she missed Mark, as a friend, a colleague and a lover. Back when they were together, she would have confided in him about the farm and Dougie, but she had no right to offload her troubles on him now.

'We're okay, thanks. You'll have heard about our ghost ship?'

'I've been following your reports. Fascinating stuff. In fact, I've been meaning to get in touch with you about it. See if I might be of help with your investigation into the *Orlova*.'

It was, she realized, an answer to her prayers. How could she ever have imagined that Mark would have reacted any differently? To her, or to the type of work he relished.

She brought him up to date, giving him the background to what she'd discovered so far regarding the set-up aboard the ship, and the obvious involvement of the company called Go Wild.

'It's not the first time I've heard that name,' he said. 'In fact, I've already been trying to find out more on their operations.'

Her heart lifted even further at that.

'I'll send you everything I have, which is more than I feel able to put in the public domain as yet,' she said.

'Right, I'll get back to you when I've taken a look,' Mark promised. 'I don't suppose there's any chance you'll be back down in London soon?'

'Maybe for a visit,' Ava conceded. 'I need to check in with David, about this and other things.'

'Great. I'll see you then.'

Ringing off, Ava was struck by the feeling that Mark believed, as she did, that what had happened on the *Orlova* was merely the opening to a much larger story. What if revealing that story brought repercussions for them both?

It wouldn't be the first time an investigation had put them in the firing line.

Mark relished a fight. She did too in normal times. Now, when she was Dougie's only remaining family, could she take the same chances as before?

Deep in thought, she was unaware of Dougie shouting for her until he threw open the kitchen door, his face reddened by running.

'What is it? What's wrong?' Ava said, seeing his distress.

'You'd better come and look.'

The calf was two days old. She and Dougie had birthed it together, after the mother had got into difficulty. Her young brother had taken the lead, demonstrating all he'd learned since she'd taken off to roam the world, leaving the farm and Orkney behind.

None of this had been lost on Ava and the experience had brought them together, however fleetingly.

Now the calf lay inert beside its distraught mother, whose lowing was painful to hear.

Ava dropped onto the grass beside it, searching for any signs of life.

'It's dead,' Dougie informed her. 'I checked. That was round its neck.' He pointed to a piece of wire lying in the grass.

'How?' Ava said. 'We inspected the fences before we let them out.'

'We must have missed a break somewhere.'

Ava took a closer look at the twisted length of wire, still bloodied from biting into the calf's neck. It was new, no rusting, and the ends were cleanly cut. It certainly didn't look as though it had been broken from a fence.

Dougie was regarding her, wondering what she might say.

'Okay, fetch the digger. We'll bury the body away from the mother.'

They were dirty, sweaty and distressed when they eventually headed back to the house. They'd buried the carcass in the field closest to the shoreline. Dougie had manned the digger, scooped up the calf, dumped it in the hole and shovelled the earth in to close the grave.

When he was a child, he'd always asked for the graves of dead calves he'd seen born to be marked. Not any more. Dougie, she accepted, was a child no longer.

As they made their way back to the house, they could see the *Orlova* floating like a dark stain on the horizon.

'What do you think really happened out there?' Dougie said, his face grim.

Ava wanted to say 'something bad', but knew it was more than that.

'I'm not sure, but I aim to find out,' she said.

Dougie was silent for a moment, his eyes focused on the track that wound up to the house, his mouth set, a nerve twitching his cheek. His jaw, Ava realized, was squarer, the softer contours of his teenage face being moulded into a man's.

'I heard what you told Mark,' he said sharply. 'D'you want me to help you check out this Go Wild lot?'

'You'd want to do that?'

'I'm part of an online gaming community. If Go Wild's in the business of selling virtual gaming, I'll find them.'

After they'd eaten, Dougie headed for his room, to check out his virtual pals and what they might know of Go Wild.

Ava had mixed feelings on this, but couldn't stop him, and wasn't sure if she wanted to.

Pouring herself a glass of wine, she sat down in front of her own laptop to transfer the photos she'd taken of the dead calf from her phone. It was weird, she thought. They always lost some calves and lambs, but not normally like this.

They'd walked the nearest fences and nowhere had there been a breakage that might have caused a length of wire to wrap round the calf's neck the way it had.

Of course, animals were sometimes attacked on purpose. Knives being the usual weapon of choice. Most farming communities had experienced that at one time or another, with no real explanation as to why.

She had good neighbours here. She couldn't imagine any of them would want to harm her cattle. But what if someone on the island wanted her to give up the farm? Would that have been reason enough?

As she studied the blown-up images, she realized she'd caught Dougie in one of them, behind the dead calf. The way he was standing, the look on his face. What did it tell her? That he was distressed, angry? Or something else?

Might her wee brother know more about this than he was saying?

Her mobile vibrated loudly against the table, pulling at the connecting wire. Seeing Mark's name on the screen, Ava disconnected it and answered.

'I've found something you have to see. ASAP. Can you come down tomorrow?' he said, his voice sharp.

Ava didn't hesitate. 'I'll catch the first flight,' she told him, her own exhilaration quelling any misgivings she might have about explaining her sudden departure to Dougie.

19

McNab was trying to recall what Cleverly looked like, and couldn't. His voice on the phone had rung a bell, mainly by its supercilious tone, but it hadn't conjured up an image of the man.

Of course, Cleverly might well recognize him, although he had definitely given the impression on the phone that he'd never heard of a DS McNab.

The road out to the airport was quiet, which resulted in him being there well in advance of the Met officer's expected arrival. That suited McNab, who, having parked, now made for the nearest coffee shop.

His mobile had pinged twice en route, one message from Ollie to say he had some news for him. The other was from Chrissy to say they were heading back to Glasgow from Orkney and that Rhona would be at the post-mortem for the fire victim.

Checking the arrivals board, he noted the Gatwick flight was on approach and would land five minutes late, so he had plenty of time to check in with Ollie before he had to meet Cleverly.

The mobile rang as he was about to do so. He observed the name on the screen with something approaching horror, before pressing the dismiss button.

Agreeing to meet with Mary last night had been a mistake.

One he feared he would pay for. It wasn't that he didn't like her. He did. And they'd had a good time.

'That was a fun night,' she'd declared as she'd headed downstairs to the taxi. 'We must do it again sometime. No strings attached.'

Her proposal had sounded much like Ellie's, and last night he'd thought it possible, even pleasurable. Then just before he'd left the station this morning, Janice had asked if he and Ellie would like to come to dinner with her and Paula. He had found himself strangely pleased by the invitation, before realizing that Janice had no idea he and Ellie had split up. Of course he could have made that plain, but he hadn't, because the thought had immediately entered his head that he might ask Ellie.

After all, she'd only said they should be free agents again. She hadn't actually ended their relationship. That had been down to him.

'No hurry,' Janice had said, when he'd fallen silent. 'Just let me know when you get a chance to ask her.' Her smile then had stopped the truth in his throat.

Strange how not voicing a truth outright resulted in an unspoken lie.

Ollie answered his call almost immediately. 'I'm texting you an old address I dug up for Go Wild in Glasgow. By the location, it doesn't look as though it was aiming for the high end of the market.'

'I'll have a look,' McNab said, thinking he could take Cleverly along with him. Maybe get him to talk a little more. 'Anything else?'

'I found your guy on the system.'

'Oh?' McNab tried to sound only mildly interested.

'He has form. I can send you details?'

'Do that. And thanks.'

So what was he planning to do with them? Flash them in Ellie's face? Like that would be a good idea. He toyed with the idea that he would say he was just protecting her. Would she buy that? Unlikely. Would it stop her seeing the bald guy? Doubtful. Would she be pissed off at him? Definitely.

McNab shifted himself as a trickle of passengers started to appear at the arrival gate. Downing the last of his coffee, he exited the cafe and watched for any bloke that might be Cleverly.

It wasn't hard to spot him. Or maybe it wasn't hard to spot the only man who looked like a police officer.

Face on now, it wasn't difficult for his shadowy memory of the detective to take form. The dark, close-cropped hair, the high colour, the thick neck, the look of a bouncer. Back then, McNab now recalled, Cleverly hadn't been so beefy. More lean and mean. The lean had definitely gone. What about the mean, he wondered?

'DI Cleverly?' McNab held out his hand.

Cleverly eyed him as he might a suspect. 'My God, it is you. The guy from the safe house.' His face grew puzzled. 'But I heard you'd been promoted to DI? I assumed when they said DS, it was another McNab. Let's face it, there's a lot of Mics and Macs up here,' he said with a laugh.

McNab gritted his teeth, and remote-opened the car.

As Cleverly slid in alongside him, he reminded himself that orders were to wring as much information out of Cleverly as he could, rather than wring his neck.

'So what's with the Met's interest in a lassie burned to death in Glasgow? Not enough to be going on with in the capital?' he said as they headed into the city centre.

Cleverly kept his eyes firmly ahead. 'If there's a London connection, we want to know.'

'So the visit's nothing to do with the fact that the victim might work for a company called Go Wild?' McNab said.

The twitch to the right of Cleverly's mouth suggested Go Wild were two words he was definitely familiar with, but didn't want to acknowledge.

'I'm here solely for the PM,' he said, confirming this.

McNab nodded. 'Fair enough. However, we now have an address for a Go Wild premises in Glasgow. So I'll be heading there on our way to the mortuary. Of course, you're free to stay in the car while I take a look.'

Five minutes later, McNab drew up on a yellow line and, hopping out of the vehicle, went to check the semi-boarded-up shopfront. A quick glance through the letterbox found the usual pile of junk mail.

He immediately headed round the back, if only to get out of Cleverly's view and express his irritation with a string of Glasgow expletives. There he found a small paved area with a shed for refuse bins and a party space as evidenced by the assortment of empties.

A quick examination of the back entrance suggested it could be easily forced if he wanted a look inside. Through a dirty window he caught a glimpse of an open inner door to what was an office, with a poster on the wall featuring the words 'Go Wild'.

The place was definitely worth a closer look.

Trouble was, if he took the time to do that, Cleverly would no doubt come to see what he was up to. And McNab didn't want that. Maybe later tonight when he'd rid himself of Cleverly, he decided, before heading back to the car.

Just in time, it seemed.

As he turned onto the main street, Cleverly was in the act of getting out of the car.

'Something interesting?' he said as McNab approached.

McNab shook his head. 'Just a hang-out for kids. If Go Wild ever operated from there, they're long gone.' He checked his watch. 'Time to head for the post-mortem. Your sole reason for visiting Glasgow.'

20

'Self-immolation in the open air has access to huge amounts of oxygen,' Dr Sissons was saying. 'Which means you die from ferocious heat and burns, and not carbon monoxide. To put it bluntly, you incinerate.'

The scent of burnt flesh hung in the air. Rhona had grown used to it again, her memories of the fresh air of Orkney sadly dissipated.

Sissons turned to Rhona. 'Am I to understand someone tried to put her out?'

'An elderly neighbour saw her and ran out with a blanket,' Rhona told him.

He nodded. 'Without that, two-thirds of the body would have been cremated, with perhaps only the feet and lower legs spared. In that case, we would have expected to see a more pugilistic attitude as the muscles contracted with perhaps the skull splitting. As it is, both the blanket and the natural fibres of the clothing have helped protect the body.'

Evidence of Sissons's words were obvious, now that the clothes had been removed. Rhona met McNab's eyes across the table. He was never at ease at a PM, and they were nearing the point in the proceedings he was least comfortable with . . . the dissection.

The Met detective Rhona had never encountered before. She assumed he was here to hopefully identify the victim as the owner of the credit cards, Londoner Olivia Newton Richardson.

In no way was that going to be possible visually because of the fire damage to her face. When a disappointed Cleverly had mentioned the possibility of digital reconstruction, Sissons had immediately declared that that was for others to discuss and not here in his mortuary.

'One assumes the Met can use her dental report to help establish her identity,' he'd finished, his voice slick with sarcasm.

Rhona had noted a twinkle in McNab's eyes at that point, plus she was certain he wore a smile behind his mask. So whatever the reason for the Met officer being there didn't sit well with McNab.

Undaunted by Sissons's sharp response, Cleverly had then tried to establish whether she'd been set alight or had committed suicide, whereupon the pathologist had told him to speak to Dr MacLeod about that as she had collected the scene-of-crime evidence.

As the pathologist declared them ready to open up the body, Cleverly indicated he would like to speak to Dr MacLeod and DS McNab outside.

So here they were.

His suit now discarded, Rhona could get a proper look at the man who was likely McNab's current nemesis. A native Londoner by his voice, he wore the air of someone here on sufferance. He also asked a great many questions, while not obviously keen to answer any that were directed at him.

Rhona explained that for the moment the crime-scene evidence suggested a third party was involved. Plus the victim had been kept in the top flat prior to her death.

'She had been bound to the bed and the bed had been

doused in petrol. So when she escaped or was taken down-stairs, she was already covered in accelerant.'

McNab shot Rhona a look that suggested she curtail the details. So it wasn't all about sharing. At least not at this point.

'Why were the cards undamaged?'

'A leather handbag was found under the body. The wallet and cards were inside. As you're probably aware, leather doesn't burn.'

'And the mobile?' Cleverly said as though he knew of one's existence already.

'There was a mobile, which I switched off and put in a Faraday bag as protocol dictates,' Rhona said, growing increasingly wary of Cleverly's tone.

McNab came in at that point as though intent on taking the heat off her. 'We're examining the mobile, along with the connection between Ms Richardson and the company we think she's linked to, Go Wild.'

Rhona's ears pricked up at this. 'You think the victim definitely had something to do with Go Wild?'

McNab nodded. 'Why?'

'I'm just back from a crime scene on board an abandoned cruise ship that ran aground off Orkney in the storm. The MV *Orlova* is apparently owned by a company with that name.'

McNab looked surprised by this development, Cleverly not so much – or else, Rhona thought, he was pretending not to be. His next request suggested that might be the case.

'I'd like to take a look at the fire scene now. Speak to the old man.'

'Okay,' McNab said. 'We're not far from there.'

He threw Rhona a wide-eyed look as Cleverly quickly stuffed his forensic suit in the bin provided and prepared to leave.

When it was obvious that Cleverly was ready, McNab said, 'Thank you, Dr MacLeod. I'll maybe see you later?'

Cleverly, jolted into action by this, reiterated his own curt thanks.

'No problem,' Rhona said, thinking, as the two men left, that there was definitely a problem, she just wasn't quite sure what it was yet. She stepped back into the post-mortem room.

Noting her re-entry, Sissons stopped what he was doing to remark, 'The Met seem very interested in our fire case, do they not, Dr MacLeod?'

Aware, from long experience, that this was not a question to which she was required to give an answer, Rhona waited.

'So much so that they sent DI Cleverly on a flying visit to Glasgow.'

The pathologist started up the drill and shouted above the whine.

'Next thing we know, there will be a request, or perhaps even a demand, that the victim's remains, plus the scene-of-crime evidence, be transported south.'

The scream of the drill almost buried his final remark, but not quite.

'You mark my words, Dr MacLeod. You mark my words.'

21

'How far?' Cleverly said as they exited the hospital grounds.

'Ten minutes from the Death Star to the locus,' McNab said.

'The Death Star.' Cleverly pretended a smile. 'Is that what's known as Glasgow humour?'

'We were told to call it the Queen Elizabeth,' McNab said. 'That was the joke. So Glasgow folk took it into their own hands.'

Cleverly looked as though he might come back on that, then changed his mind. 'Tell me about the eye witness.'

'In his seventies. Lives . . . alone.' McNab had been about to mention the cat, then realized that Lucifer might prove a nice surprise. He could only hope so.

He expected a few more barbed comments about Glasgow as they made their way across Govan, and found himself slightly disappointed when they didn't materialize. Maybe he was reading Cleverly wrong, he thought. Holding his past misdemeanours against him. After all, he'd screwed up plenty himself over the years.

Drawing up outside the flats, McNab imagined he could still smell the residue of the fire, maybe even the female victim, before he reminded himself he'd just left her company fifteen or so minutes ago.

Leading Cleverly to Jimmy's door, he gave a couple of knocks.

Jimmy was either there in a flash or he'd spied their arrival via the street-facing window of the flat. As the door opened, there he was, a big smile on his face. 'Sergeant McNab,' he said, the smile widening at a double helping of police officers.

'This is DI Cleverly from the Metropolitan Police,' McNab told him.

Jimmy looked suitably impressed. 'You're very welcome here, sir. Come away in, both of you.'

McNab followed Jimmy through to the rear room expecting to find the big black cat in his usual spot at the window.

'Where's Lucifer?' he said when he saw the place was empty.

'Out on the prowl,' Jimmy said. 'He'll be back soon, I expect. Tea or coffee, gents?'

McNab returned Cleverly's questioning look with a little nod. 'Coffee for me, Jimmy. Strong.'

'And you, sir?'

'Same as DS McNab, thanks.'

When Jimmy headed for the kitchen, Cleverly said, under his breath, 'You two are very pally. Sure he's not got you coming back just for company?'

'It was you who asked to speak to him,' McNab reminded him.

'So I'll ask the questions,' Cleverly said.

'Here we go.' Jimmy set a tray down with the three mugs. 'Celtic for Sergeant McNab, Rangers for me. No idea who you support, Inspector, so I've given you my Scotland mug,' he announced with a twinkle in his eye.

Cleverly was still wearing his serious look, which didn't budge at Jimmy's wee joke.

'Okay, Jimmy. Give me your story.'

Jimmy set off. 'Well, it was the night of the big storm. Me and Lucifer were in here at the window waiting for the roof to take off. That's when I saw the flames and—'

'Nothing before?' Cleverly interrupted. 'She must have arrived out there before the fire started,' he insisted in a voice that suggested he didn't believe Jimmy. 'And you have a clear view of the back exit from here if you were, as you say, seated at that window.'

'I wasn't actually at the window,' Jimmy said. 'I was sitting on the couch.'

'So you weren't at the window?'

'I went to the window when I saw the flames.' Jimmy looked confused. 'It all happened so fast.'

'How did you know it was a person on fire?'

Jimmy's face crumpled. 'The screaming. It was terrible. That's when I took out the blanket.'

'So you saw no one out there along with the victim?'

McNab watched as Jimmy struggled with the question.

'I might have seen someone in the light from the close.'

'You never mentioned that before, Jimmy,' McNab said.

'I'm sorry. The police lassie was here. I didn't want to frighten her. I didn't mention the sex games thing either.'

'Mention it now,' Cleverly said.

McNab listened while Jimmy retold the tale of the top flat in which the words 'sexual shenanigans' weren't uttered. After that Cleverly seemed to have had enough and so, too, did Jimmy.

At that moment Lucifer arrived to claw at the window, his eyes staring malevolently in at them.

'I told you he'd be back soon,' Jimmy said, sounding relieved to get backup.

On entry, Lucifer took a moment to study both detectives before focusing all his spitting hate and arched back at Cleverly.

'I'm very sorry, Inspector. Lucifer's my guard dog. He knows when I'm upset about something.' He scooped up the cat and tried to placate him. It worked with the spitting, but didn't put an end to the malicious look.

'Thank you for your help, Mr Donaldson,' Cleverly said, making for the door. 'We can let ourselves out.'

McNab lingered to say goodbye, now that he knew Lucifer's wrath was not directed at him.

'Thanks, Jimmy.'

'I'm sorry I never mentioned the figure at the door, Sergeant. I wasn't even sure I saw it. What with the wind and rain that night and my eyes on the lassie and the ball of fire. If I remember anything else . . .'

'Just give me a call,' McNab said, patting him on the shoulder.

'An unreliable witness,' Cleverly said as McNab unlocked the car. 'There's no way from his statement we get to know that it wasn't a suicide.'

'A young woman is bound to a bed, someone had sex with her, according to the swab taken at post-mortem, the bed is doused with petrol, then she gets free and runs outside to set herself alight? Does that sound the right finale to you?'

Cleverly's mobile rang as they departed Govan. He listened to some instructions, gave monosyllabic replies and rang off.

'Change of plan. I'm staying here overnight and flying down first thing tomorrow.'

'Why?' McNab said.

Cleverly threw him a look. 'So that we can get to chat

more, Sergeant. And to that end I suggest we ditch the car and go get a drink. It's knock-off time anyway.'

'So you're all nine-to-five in the metropolis?'

'Or five at night to nine in the morning,' Cleverly said.

McNab was about to say he had other plans, then thought what the hell, maybe he could get a better take on why the Met were so interested in Glasgow's burn victim.

'So where are you taking me?' Cleverly said.

McNab had already dismissed the jazz club, even though he'd planned to go there to meet with Rhona and hear more about Go Wild and her ghost ship crime scene. Instead, he proposed a place in the centre of town, where he and Ellie had been a few times.

'We can eat there too,' he said. 'If you're hungry, that is?'

'Copy that. I'm booked into an airport hotel. I'll catch a taxi there later.'

McNab wondered when all this had been decided, seeing as he'd been with Cleverly since he'd picked him up at the airport. Maybe he'd never intended flying back tonight?

The last person he wanted to spend time with this evening was Cleverly, but maybe, just maybe, if they had a drink together he might glean a little more information from him. Or vice versa, a wee voice reminded him.

The area around George Square was busy with folk coming back from work or heading out on the town.

'The place hasn't changed much,' Cleverly said as they walked through the square, having ditched the car.

'You've been to Glasgow before?' McNab said, surprised.

'Had a Scottish girlfriend for a while. She had a flat in the West End, near the university. I liked coming here. Then she decided she didn't like me any more.'

'It happens,' McNab offered in solidarity.

As McNab led him up the stairs and into the chosen bar, Cleverly took an appreciative look around. 'Very nice. Hope it's not just fancy cocktails they serve?'

'Also good beer and fine whisky,' McNab assured him.

'So, we start with a beer, eat, then move on to your whisky recommendation?' Cleverly suggested.

'Okay by me,' McNab said.

After a pizza each with the beer, they did move on to whisky. They hadn't talked shop during the meal, Cleverly just reminiscing about his trips to Glasgow.

'Sadly,' McNab said, 'I don't have fond memories of my last time in London.'

They eyed one another.

It had to be said, McNab thought.

'How's the bullet wound?' Cleverly said.

'I got it tattooed,' McNab told him.

'Really?'

'Covered it with a skull.'

Cleverly raised an eyebrow. 'Impressive. Plus you made the Kalinin trial alive.'

The Russian, Kalinin, who'd ordered him shot in front of a pregnant Chrissy, had believed him dead. As had Chrissy and Rhona. Jesus, they'd even buried what they thought was him. McNab wasn't proud of that part of the story, although he hadn't had any choice in the matter. Eventually he'd risen from his fake death to become the prime witness in the Russian's trial.

As for Cleverly's poorly played role as his minder . . .

'Only because I bailed out of the not-so-safe house and came home,' he reminded him.

Cleverly nodded. 'Fair comment.'

The semi-admission of guilt, although he'd been looking for it, still surprised McNab.

'All in the past,' he heard himself say. 'So what's the real story about your visit?'

Cleverly thought for a moment, then shrugged. 'Just trying to establish if the victim's a Londoner or not.'

McNab didn't believe him, and said so. 'You and the Met are fucking us around. What's this really about?'

Female laughter from a nearby booth halted McNab's attack. Was that Ellie? He rose and, slipping into the aisle, took a look.

She was seated two booths down, Baldy opposite. The bastard looked very comfortable and keen. Ignoring the warning voice in his head, McNab decided to go with the hot-blooded approach.

'Hi, Ellie. Thought I heard your voice.'

She looked up at him in surprise. 'Michael.'

McNab almost flipped when he read her face. A mixture of embarrassment, discomfort and defiance.

Baldy, on the other hand, was observing him with extreme annoyance, like he'd been stopped in the sex act just prior to climax. It was an image McNab didn't relish.

'Your new friend here,' he heard himself saying. 'Did he tell you about himself? Like, the fact he's been charged with stalking?'

When Ellie's face fell, McNab knew he'd fucked up, but he still couldn't stop himself. 'Dating a detective is crap, but dating the folk a detective is looking for is the bigger shite by far.'

Turning on his heel, McNab returned to his table, but did not resume his seat. The truth was he'd had enough of DI Cleverly's face too.

'We're over, Cleverly. Go suck blood somewhere else.'

McNab made for the door. Was it the whisky or jealousy or just plain being a detective who'd read too many situations and people and found them wanting?

At that moment he didn't give a damn.

22

'So what's going on?' Chrissy wore her intense look. 'Between you and Sean?'

'Nothing,' Rhona said, because it was true. She hadn't seen him since he'd left for work in the eye of the storm.

Chrissy eyed Rhona in her inimitable fashion. 'I suggest you seek the Irishman out and make contact.'

Rhona was about to say no, but since they'd established Sean was on the premises, and it only involved a short walk to his office . . .

'Anything to get you off my case,' she said with a smile.

How many times had she walked this corridor since she'd met the Irishman with the blue eyes and the ability to play her the way he teased sweet music from his saxophone?

She recalled one instance, back when Sean had had a brush with the law because of a girl Chrissy was convinced was dealing drugs on the jazz club premises. Her suspicions had proved false in the end, but Rhona remembered how she'd initially been more freaked by the thought that Sean and the girl had been having sex than by the drugs angle.

All in the past, she reminded herself.

As she approached the door, she heard Sean's raised voice. Was someone in the office with him?

She hesitated before easing the door open, only to discover

Sean alone, phone anchored to his ear, his normally easy-going look transplanted by one of fierce annoyance.

'Fuck off, then,' were his last words before he slammed the receiver down.

'Rhona,' he said, coming towards her, his expression suddenly transformed into one of pleasure. 'You're back.'

'I am.'

Sean enveloped her in his arms. 'How was Orkney?'

'How did you know where I'd gone?' she said.

'It was on the news and in the papers. Forensic team visit the ghost ship *Orlova*, wrecked off the west coast of Orkney. Something about a bloodbath aboard?' Sean was reading her expression. 'Apparently I have the tabloid version. Are you planning on telling me the real story?'

'I attended a crime scene on board the *Orlova*. That's all I'm willing to say,' she told him with a smile.

He kissed her. 'Good. I'd rather talk of other things.'

'Like what your Mr Angry phone call was about?' Rhona tried.

Sean pulled a face. 'Club matters. Like you, that's all I'm willing to say. Are you sticking around for a while?' he added hopefully.

'I have to work tonight,' Rhona said. 'Catch up on my report from Orkney.'

'Okay,' he said, slowly releasing her. 'I'll await your command. Until then, I too have work to do.'

Rhona retreated, although she was unconvinced by Sean's brush-off regarding the phone call since he rarely, if ever, lost his cool regarding anything, including being turned down by her.

'What's up?' Chrissy said on her return.

'Nothing,' Rhona assured her with a smile.

Accepting this, Chrissy changed the subject. 'I hear a detective from the Met was at the autopsy on the fire victim?'

'Your army of spies were right. McNab brought along a DI Cleverly. Although they did not look the best of pals,' Rhona added.

'Know why?' Chrissy said.

'No, but I guess you're going to tell me?' Rhona said, catching the glint in Chrissy's eye.

'Cleverly was part of the safe-house team, when McNab did a runner. He told Janice that Cleverly was an arse.'

Now the scene in the mortuary began to make sense.

'I'd assumed he didn't like the Met getting involved with our fire case, but then again, we work with their officers all the time.'

'Janice says it's all take and no give on this one.' Chrissy sipped her drink. 'The boss doesn't like it either. He sent McNab to the airport to pick up Cleverly, to try and get the real story out of him.'

Rhona contemplated this. 'Cleverly wants digital reconstruction so the face is recognizable, but if they already have a possible identity via the credit cards and dental records, surely they would be pursuing that first?'

Chrissy assumed a thoughtful expression. 'Something smells in all of this and it isn't fried chicken,' she said. 'And look who's here to tell us all about it.'

Chrissy's face broke into a grin as McNab approached, although his expression did not match her own. In fact, he didn't acknowledge them until he'd ordered and received his drink.

'Whisky,' Chrissy said as he sampled it. 'Tough day?'

The icy look McNab threw her made her step back for effect. 'Wow, that bad?'

'That bad,' McNab agreed, pushing his glass over for a refill.

'Easy, partner,' Chrissy said. 'We need the story before you start slurring your words.'

'Has he gone?' Rhona said, drawing the conversation back to its obvious target.

'No. He's staying over. Back in the morning, apparently.'

Chrissy glanced swiftly at the door. 'You didn't bring him here, did you?'

McNab shook his head. 'No chance, although I did have to eat with him.'

'So tell all,' Chrissy demanded.

'He used to have a girlfriend who lived near you.' He motioned to Rhona. 'She dumped him and he's not been back to Glasgow since.'

'That's it?' Chrissy said accusingly. 'That's all you got out of him?'

'Pretty much.'

'Now we know why you're so pissed off.'

McNab ignored that and turned to Rhona. 'How does Go Wild feature in your ghost ship story?'

'It was me who discovered that,' Chrissy broke in. 'Or at least it was Ava who gave me the idea.'

'Ava who?' McNab demanded.

'Ava Clouston, an investigative journalist, home for the moment in Orkney.' Rhona brought him up to date on what Ava had discovered about the ownership of the MV *Orlova*.

'So Go Wild is a lead on both stories.' He looked at them. 'In which case, why was Cleverly not interested in it?'

23

'Are you sure about this, mate?' The Uber driver gave him a warning look. 'Gets pretty rough in there, or so I've heard.'

'How long has this place been up and running?' McNab said.

'Word is, it was shut for a while. Maybe they went bust or the cops found out. Been back up a couple of weeks. You a punter or a fighter?'

'Neither. Just fancied a look,' McNab told him as he exited the vehicle.

'Your funeral.'

Chrissy's earlier question as to why Cleverly had seemed so disinterested in the Go Wild connection had fired up his own interest again. Why was the bastard set on ignoring it? So he'd returned to his original plan and made a swift departure from the jazz club before he drank too much whisky, heading back to the boarded-up offices.

This time the back entrance was occupied by a wee gang of teenagers in the thirteen-to-fifteen age group sharing a couple of bottles of vodka.

Their initial reaction when he'd appeared had been one of bravado. Things changed when he'd flashed his badge and asked for their names and ages. He could have confiscated the bottles but, deciding that was too much hassle, he'd just ordered them to scram, which they did.

Left to his own devices, he'd re-entered the premises and had a good look round.

That's when he'd found the out-of-date ticket to the Go Wild fight club, which he'd pocketed, promising himself to check out the location at least.

The place looked all shut up when he got there apart from the red light above the door. McNab stood for a moment listening, convinced he could hear voices raised somewhere in the building. He banged on the door three times and waited.

When nothing happened, he tried again. Having got there, it would be unfortunate if he never crossed the threshold. He fished in his pocket and brought out the invitation he'd found in a desk drawer of the boarded-up Go Wild office. Out of date, of course, but they might accept it, especially if the place had been closed down for a while.

A slot in the door opened and a pair of mean eyes stared out at him. McNab displayed his invite.

'Out of date,' came a voice. 'You'll have to pay again to enter.'

'Sure thing,' McNab said. 'How much?'

The door opened and he was faced with a guy as broad as he was tall. 'Fifty to watch. Bets extra.'

He was waved towards a booth where a young woman was only too willing to swipe his card.

'You placing a bet?' she said with an interested look.

McNab wasn't sure if the smile was for him or the contents of his wallet.

'I'm just here to watch,' he said.

'Shame, I was going to recommend you bet on the blond.'

McNab tucked his card back in place. 'Maybe the next bout.'

'This is the last tonight. You should have come earlier.'

She pointed him in the direction of another door. 'It starts shortly. Bar's inside. No photos,' she warned him, indicating the bouncers. 'Or you'll lose your phone.'

If entry was fifty pounds, McNab wondered what a drink would cost. As he approached the inner door, it was opened by the first bouncer's twin brother, who examined his receipt, then stood out of his way.

The smell that hit him like a wall was a mixture of male sweat and fresh blood with a splash of piss, coming from somewhere near the back. McNab made for the bar, skirting round the crowd of about sixty men of varying ages. He had a quick scan of the faces, but none were recognizable from this distance. As well as the bouncers at the entry point, he spotted two other guys who looked like handlers. They had certainly marked his late entry.

There was no ring as such, just a concrete floor, turned a slippery red, and a single rope to keep the punters back. In opposite corners, the blond, who the lassie in the booth had referred to, was the taller, with a gym-built physique and a tan that definitely wasn't out of a bottle. His opponent was smaller and wirier with a shaved head and a red beard. It only took a moment to work out who wasn't from round these parts.

The bare-knuckle fight invite had promised high stakes and high winnings; only one of the two men he surmised may have paid for the privilege of taking part, and it wasn't the Glasgow bloke.

McNab placed himself next to an old guy who, by his intense interest, had definitely placed a bet. McNab introduced himself as Micky and asked what the odds were.

The old guy shot him a look. 'You're too late, son, they're about to start.'

'Who are you rooting for then?'

'Kenny Boy. The wee bloke with the beard. He's about to smash that posh fucker's face in.'

'I take it Kenny's local?'

'Aye. The posh fucker's from out of town. Been here before, I hear. Pays money to have his pretty face punched.'

McNab wasn't as sure as his new friend about the outcome. To his eye, the posh fucker looked like a player.

'Has he got a name?'

'If he has, I don't know it. Arrived in a limo with blacked-out windows and two minders.'

McNab was keen to ask who was running the show, but that, he realized, might be a step too far. The last thing he wanted was to be slung out on his ear before he found out what he wanted to know.

A bell was rung and the two men, stripped to the waist, moved towards one another. The only thing McNab knew about scrapping he'd learned as a teenager. After which he'd realized it was better to carry a knife as a first level of self-defence, even if he never actually used it.

He'd got good with a knife, trick-wise. Even shown off his prowess when he was a young recruit at the Police College. Until he was taken aside by the brass and given a severe warning about being in possession of an illegal weapon.

There were no weapons on display here apart from bloody knuckles. The posh fucker's tan was already spotted, but he was giving as good as he got.

The noise in the room was deafening, the jeers and shouts of encouragement bouncing off the walls. By the expressions around him, there was a lot of money riding on the outcome.

What struck him most was the difference between the two players. Kenny wanted to win, no doubt about that. He was skilful. An artful dodger, whose every punch counted. As for the posh fucker, he had the look of a killer. He wasn't here simply to win. He wanted to beat the wee guy into the ground. For him, this looked like a fight to the death. For a terrible moment, McNab wondered if it might be. There was enough blood spraying about the place to resemble a Friday night in A&E after a gang fight.

'When is it over?' he asked his new pal.

'When one of them doesn't get up again.'

The crack that put Kenny on the concrete sounded like a bone snapping. If Kenny had even considered trying to drag himself up, the posh fucker put an end to that when he made a move to stamp on his head.

McNab heard his own shout before he realized he'd uttered it.

'Fuck's sake. You'll kill him.'

The voices dropped to nothing as McNab entered the ring to stand in front of a prostrate Kenny.

The steel-blue eyes were now fastened on McNab. 'You have a problem with me finishing the fight?'

'The fight's finished,' McNab said. 'He went down. It's over.'

'Not until I say it is.'

McNab thought his reactions were fast, but they weren't quick enough. As the fist came towards him, he dodged, but not quite in time. A roar went up from the crowd and he heard bets being thrown around, all of them on him to lose.

His brain suggested he declare himself a police officer, but he knew if he did it might make things worse. And who would find his dead body here in this warehouse?

So he swung back, getting a jab in at those blue eyes, before the man's two minders grabbed his arms and let their boss finish him.

Another face swam in front of him, suggesting it was over and they had better leave.

The last thing McNab remembered was the lights going out as a mad scramble of male bodies stepped over and on him to get to the door.

24

They'd taken a break from dealing with the evidence from the Glasgow fire scene to compare notes, Chrissy being particularly keen to tell Rhona about the handbag.

'It's a Mayfair bag from Aspinal of London,' she quoted, 'and is hand-crafted from the finest deep shine black croc print Italian calf leather. It features two inner compartments separated by a central zipped pocket, secured with our enduring shield lock closure.'

Rhona studied the set of images, both outer and inner views of the aforementioned bag.

'It does look the same,' she admitted.

'And it costs six hundred and fifty pounds,' Chrissy finished triumphantly. 'At that price they probably have records of the purchasers.'

'Or the sale will be on one of Ms Richardson's credit cards,' Rhona said.

'But that still doesn't prove the body is hers, does it?' Chrissy said, reading Rhona's expression. 'For that we need the DNA of the owner of the credit card.' Something that surely the Met could have provided by now. 'Why did Cleverly come up here to try and identify the body, and never mention whether they'd collected sample DNA of the supposed victim? After all, they would have access to her apartment and her place of work.'

Chrissy was voicing Rhona's own train of thought.

'Do you think this death could be a link to something bigger, something they're already investigating, and they don't want to divulge anything?'

That did make sense, and Rhona said so. 'Especially since Cleverly seemed to pointedly ignore any mention McNab made of Go Wild.'

Chrissy hadn't finished her handbag story. 'If we can prove that the handbag is not the victim's, then someone carried it down to the back court and placed it with her, and that same someone may have set her alight.' She paused. 'I did manage to get some DNA off the bag handle. Which we could try and match with the victim.'

'Dr Sissons collected semen from the vagina,' Rhona said. 'If we get a DNA match between that and the handbag . . .'

'We have a possible perpetrator.' Chrissy's mobile buzzed an incoming text. 'That's weird,' she said, checking the screen. 'It's from Sandra.'

'Your nurse pal?'

'It's about McNab,' Chrissy said, wide-eyed. 'Sandra says he turned up at A&E last night, pretty beaten up. Told them he got run down by a cyclist in a twenty-mile-per-hour zone.'

'That's got to be a lie,' Rhona said.

'Sandra thought so too.'

'Is he okay?'

'They wanted to keep him in overnight in case of concussion. He insisted on calling a taxi and went home.'

McNab answered on the third ring. 'What's up, Dr MacLeod?'

Rhona switched to loudspeaker. 'Where are you?' she demanded.

'At work, of course,' he said.

'What happened last night that meant you ended up in
A&E?'

'Ah.' There was an exasperated sigh. 'I see your forensic
assistant has eyes everywhere.'

'Well?' Chrissy got in on the act.

'I had a run-in with a cyclist,' McNab said in an irritated
fashion, 'as I explained to the nurse.'

The groan that followed sounded real. But the rest? Rhona
suddenly thought of Ellie. Had McNab got into a fight over
her? She didn't get a chance to ask because McNab swiftly
changed the subject.

'On a more important topic, Cleverly's gone back to
London, having given us zilch on our fire victim and without
speaking to the boss.'

'What does Bill think about that?' Chrissy said.

'I plan to run the whole Go Wild thing past him. If the
incidents in Orkney and here in Glasgow are connected, the
boss will want to know.'

As he rung off, Rhona exchanged looks with Chrissy.

'He's lying,' Chrissy said. 'Sandra says his injuries suggested
he was in a fight.'

'Over Ellie maybe?' Rhona voiced her thoughts out loud.

'Exactly what I was thinking.'

25

She'd left before Dougie got up. His reaction the previous evening to being told she was off to London had been one of anger. So there had been little point in saying goodbye.

Ava realized then that by offering to help with the investigation, he'd been trying to prove that she didn't need to leave the farm to do her work.

'Mark has something to show me,' she'd insisted.

'He can show you online.'

At that point she'd stopped arguing because she didn't want to tell Dougie that Mark had been reluctant to do that.

During the brief stopover in Glasgow, she'd rung Mark's number but it had gone to voicemail. She'd tried again on landing, but still had had no luck. Mark had told her not to email. *Just in case.*

Looking around the packed Underground carriage, the myriad voices and the sheer number of people reminded her how long she'd been away from London. From Kirkwall airport to Glasgow to Central London it had just kept on multiplying exponentially.

When she'd first departed Orkney for London, she'd revelled in the city's hordes, not missing the wide sky and empty landscape of the islands. Coming back now felt different, as though she were an insignificant ant among an army flowing around her.

Mark had arranged to meet her in a coffee shop in St Martin's Lane, after she'd spoken to David Morris, her editor. If Mark didn't turn up, what would she do?

Emerging from the Underground, Ava made her way to the cafe, and wasn't surprised to find she was there first because she'd factored in time for a longer meeting with her editor than the one that had taken place.

At the onset, David had appeared keen on the emerging *Orlova* story, until she'd brought up Mark's imminent involvement. That's when things had changed.

'You didn't mention Mark when we spoke on the phone,' he'd said.

'I hadn't talked to him at that point,' she'd begun.

'Mark can be a wild card,' David said. 'Treads on a lot of important toes.'

He didn't give an example because he didn't have to. The British government preferred to be seen as the good guy in the Middle East in particular. Mark's various investigations there had tarnished that image.

'He gets results.' Ava had found herself rising immediately to Mark's defence, even though what David said was true.

David had sat back in his chair at that moment and his expression should have been a warning. 'The word is Mark's under investigation by the Met,' he said firmly, as though that was the end of the matter.

Was this investigation linked to Mark's current interest in Go Wild? He'd told her he already knew about the company. Which was probably why he'd agreed so readily to help her when she'd called him, and why he'd asked her to come to London so soon after that call.

As for the Met, he'd rubbed them up before now. By what David had said, he must have done it again. Which could explain why Mark hadn't wanted to reveal anything he'd found out over the phone.

Whatever the truth of David's statement, their meeting had ended at that point, and not in a positive manner. In fact, David's parting comment of 'Let me know when you're back down permanently and we'll talk again' had left her in no doubt that the *Orlova* investigation would only be of interest should Mark *not* be a contributor.

Ava checked her watch again. How long should she wait before abandoning her post? When she'd raised that question with Mark last night, he'd just laughed. 'You know me. Always late to the party. I'll find you at home if need be.'

Deciding the party was over, Ava abandoned her spot in the now busy cafe and headed for her flat, just managing to hit the rush hour. A phenomenon she'd almost forgotten about.

Rush hour on Orkney could be construed as passing a couple of cars on the road home to Orphir, but only if she didn't know either of the drivers.

Out of the Underground now and moving swiftly into the residential streets, Ava breathed a sigh of relief as humans became scarcer and an occasional tree or hedgerow appeared. She'd been away from her Chelsea flat for work on numerous occasions, but the Orkney stay had had a degree of permanence that had made her feel like a stranger here. Slipping her key in the lock, she was suddenly relieved to open the door on her previous life again.

She stood briefly in the hall, revelling in its familiarity, before heading to the sitting room. It was as she glanced into her office that it struck her that something was wrong.

She came to an abrupt halt as the hairs rose on the back of her neck. It was the smell of the place, she realized. It had been empty for over two months, yet didn't smell like it. Walking into her office, she ran her eyes over her untidy desk. The piles of articles, the books. Her back-up laptop. An abandoned coffee mug. Was everything as it had been when she'd left, after the devastating phone call from Dougie?

She realized that she had no idea. All she knew was that someone had been in here. Walking through the rest of the flat just confirmed the feeling. Looking for a logical explanation, she decided to check with Mrs Rosen across the landing, who held her spare key.

'Ava, you're home.' Mrs Rosen looked delighted to find her on her doorstep.

Ava stopped her neighbour from beginning her commiserations on what had taken her to Orkney and asked if anyone had come looking for her in her absence.

Mrs Rosen looked surprised, then nodded. 'A man did knock to ask me when you would be back and I told him I didn't know.'

After being given a description of her visitor, which she didn't recognize, Ava asked, 'Did this man give a name or say why he wanted to see me?'

'No, dear, he didn't. Should I have asked?'

Ava tried to look unconcerned. 'No matter, Mrs Rosen. It couldn't have been important.'

Re-entering the flat, she contemplated the latest development. The man hadn't left a name, but whoever he was, he'd learned from Mrs Rosen that the flat was empty.

Which gave him the opportunity to break in and do what? There was no mess, so he hadn't been searching for anything. Plus her back-up laptop was still here and when she'd switched it on to check, it was working okay.

That didn't mean it hadn't been interfered with. Ava shut it down again, then began looking for bugs in all the usual places.

She was on her knees under the desk when she heard the front door open and footsteps enter the hallway.

She froze, unsure what to do next. She could stay hidden and hope whoever it was didn't come in here. Or she could call out and challenge them. Chances were, they might leave if she did.

She shouted, 'Who's there?' in as commanding a tone as she could manage.

'Ava?' Mark's voice answered in return.

Relief sweeping over her like a warm wave, she ran into the hall and threw her arms about her former lover as though they'd never split up in the first place. 'I forgot you still had a key.'

It was then she registered the cut mouth, the swollen right eye already turning fifteen shades of purple.

'What the hell—' she began.

Mark raised a hand to stop her. 'First things first. Is there any whisky in the house?'

He followed her into the kitchen where she poured him a shot of Highland Park. Taking a gulp, he swirled it round his mouth before swallowing it and offering up the glass for a refill.

'So,' he finally said, 'is David going to cover the *Orlova* story?'

When Ava shook her head, Mark showed no surprise. 'Did he give you a reason?'

'He says the Met are after you.'

Mark gave a strangled laugh. 'I wonder who told him that.'

'Then it's true?'

'Well, it wasn't the boys in blue who did this to me,' he assured her.

He'd taken a seat at the kitchen table as though his legs would no longer hold him up. Ava set the whisky bottle before him. With an attempt at a smile, he refilled his glass. After which he bent over, removed his left shoe and extracted something.

'This is what I wouldn't send you by email.' He handed Ava a memory stick. 'Everything I have gathered so far on Go Wild is on there.'

She gestured at his face. 'Is this why you were attacked?'

'Maybe. But I have my fingers in many pies, as you know. On the current subject, I heard that the Met sent someone up about a fire victim in Glasgow, who apparently had a link with Go Wild.'

Ava had no knowledge of that and said so.

'Is there someone you can approach in Police Scotland to ask if that's the case? Because, if so, that would make four deaths so far linked to the company.'

She doubted if she approached Erling that he would be familiar with the Glasgow case. So it would have to be someone close to that.

'I met a Dr Rhona MacLeod in Orkney,' she said. 'She was the forensic scientist on the *Orlova* and I believe on the Glasgow fire too, although we obviously didn't discuss either case.' She paused, remembering. 'Except when I mentioned looking into Go Wild and Rhona's assistant realized an insignia she'd spotted on board might stand for the company.'

'She's your way in, then,' Mark said, his eyes lighting up.

'To do what?'

'The guy the Met sent up, a DI Cleverly – there's evidence on the memory stick to suggest he's involved with Go Wild in some way.'

Ava's head was spinning. 'You're talking about a Met police officer,' she said in a shocked voice.

'I know.' He held her gaze. 'Which is why someone in Police Scotland should be made aware of that.' He gave a half-smile. 'And that information should come from someone with an unblemished investigation record. And that's clearly not me.'

'I'm flying home tonight via Glasgow.' Ava hesitated. 'I could make a stopover. Talk to Dr MacLeod.'

'Great.' He took hold of her hand. 'After that, promise me you'll return to Orkney and stay there?'

'I got you into this,' she said.

'And I'm glad you did.' He forced a smile past his bruised lips. 'We've always been good together at getting the bastards.'

Before he left he gently kissed her and held her tightly to him.

'Be safe,' he said, and Ava murmured back, 'You too.'

Those words had always served as their goodbyes while in the middle of an investigation. Ava couldn't prevent the feeling of foreboding they had begun to generate.

What if this was their last farewell?

That question had become the reason for their break-up, or – more honestly – her reason for ending their relationship.

Hearing Mark head downstairs, followed by the bang as the front door shut behind him, she felt again that familiar feeling of loss. He wanted her to be safe, yet discussing his safety was never permitted. She stood in the hall, wondering why she hadn't told Mark of her possible intruder.

What would have been the point, she argued.

She was about to leave shortly for the airport. As to whether she would ever return to London, that was a decision she had yet to make.

26

'Who was that on the phone?' Chrissy said, removing her forensic suit.

'Ava Clouston. She's in Glasgow tonight and wants to meet up. I suggested she come to the jazz club.'

Chrissy's face fell like a ton of bricks. 'Bugger it. I'm heading straight home tonight. Mum's got a date.' Before Rhona could ask, Chrissy carried on. 'His name is Euan and he works for the Scottish Fire Service. I've met him. He's very nice. Although his appearance is about to curb my social life.'

'I'll tell you what happens first thing tomorrow,' Rhona promised.

'Okay,' Chrissy said. 'Or you could call me later?' She made a begging face.

'If it's not too late,' Rhona said, laughing.

Stuffing her own suit in the bin, she headed for the shower, wondering what the proposed meeting was really about. Ava had intimated that she'd been in London briefly and had been booked to fly back to Kirkwall via Glasgow tonight.

She'd hesitated then, before saying, 'It's a tight connection, and it looks as though I might miss it. So I thought it better to book in somewhere in Glasgow and head north in the morning.'

'Sounds sensible,' Rhona had said, already suspecting that

wasn't the real reason for the overnight stay. 'It'll be nice to see you again.'

Ava had sounded so relieved at this point, Rhona almost asked if everything was okay, but bailed out and gave her directions for the jazz club instead. 'That's our hang-out place after work,' she'd explained.

As she walked towards Ashton Lane, Rhona pondered the real reason for Ava wanting to meet up. Was this to be a fact-finding mission regarding the *Orlova* case? Ava had shown no desire to interrogate them in Orkney. In fact, she'd been the one giving out the information, leading to Chrissy mentioning the GW insignia aboard the *Orlova*.

The autopsies on the three victims from the ship were scheduled for tomorrow morning and McNab had called her late in the afternoon, informing her that he planned to attend.

'Campbell and Neville are the investigating officers,' Rhona had reminded him.

'If I'm right and the cases are connected, I need to be there.'

Something she couldn't argue with.

McNab was propping up the bar when she arrived, Sean alongside. They appeared deep in conversation as she approached, and a little put out when she suddenly appeared.

McNab and Sean were not best pals; in fact, at times they'd been adversaries, even rivals for her affections. Although on more than one occasion they'd also been each other's supporter.

Which was it this time, Rhona wondered?

It was Sean who spoke first. 'I've been keeping McNab company while he waited for Chrissy's arrival,' he said.

'So you weren't talking about his battered face?'

'He was run over by a mad cyclist,' Sean said with a smile.

'So he spun you that line too?' Rhona was taking in the injuries in all their glory, in particular the bruised and skinned knuckles. 'Did you beat up this mad cyclist?' she said.

'Bloody back-lane cobbles did that,' McNab said, taking a mouthful of his beer.

Sean, obviously keen to get out of what appeared to be a tricky situation, slapped McNab on the back. 'Next one's on me, mate.'

'Great,' McNab said.

Rhona's white wine was delivered at that point, which gave McNab an excuse to change the subject.

'Why's Chrissy not coming?'

Rhona gave him the mum's boyfriend story.

He winced as he tried a smile. 'That makes a change from hearing about Chrissy's latest conquest.'

Rhona, not one to give up when in dogged pursuit of the truth, said, 'About girlfriends and boyfriends. How's the situation with Ellie?'

'Okay,' he said breezily. 'We've been invited to Janice and Paula's for dinner.'

'And Ellie's accepted?'

'We're waiting on a date to confirm. What?' McNab said, catching her look.

Realizing she was unlikely to get anything more on the Ellie front, Rhona decided to spring her surprise.

'Chrissy's not coming, but Ava Clouston is. She's having a stopover in Glasgow on her way back to Kirkwall.' When McNab looked blank, Rhona reminded him of who she was talking about.

'You invited a journalist here to interrogate us?'

'I was thinking it might be the other way round,' Rhona

said. 'She knew about Go Wild and the *Orlova* connection before we did.'

McNab began to show some interest. 'So what's the plan?'

'We take her somewhere to eat and see what we can find out,' Rhona said.

'Without giving anything in return?'

'Exactly.'

Rhona was on her second packet of crisps to stave off her hunger when the text pinged in, announcing Ava had arrived in Ashton Lane. McNab followed her outside, keeping back a little as agreed.

Rhona recognized the tall figure immediately and went towards her.

'Ava, you found us.'

'I found the lane,' she said. 'I hadn't found the jazz club yet.'

'It's right at the end and down the stairs, but it doesn't serve food and I'm starving. Have you eaten?'

'Not yet,' Ava said.

'Do you like curry? It's a big Glasgow favourite.'

'Great. Lead me there.'

At that point McNab appeared.

'McNab is going to join us,' Rhona said.

Ava checked him out, then held out her hand. 'I've heard a lot about you from Chrissy,' she said. 'All of it good.'

'And I've heard all about you from Rhona. So we're even.' McNab even managed a smile.

Introductions over, they walked the few yards past the evening crowds to Ashoka.

'You're not familiar with Glasgow?' McNab asked on the way.

'I did my degree in Aberdeen, then headed to London.

And from there to anywhere there was a story worth investigating.'

'So none in Glasgow?' McNab said.

'None until now.'

The first flurry over, they settled down to their meal with little more than chit-chat involved. McNab became the friendly, funny version of himself. The one women in general enjoyed. Telling Ava the story of his time on Sanday, and how an irate group of locals had tossed him over the wall at the Kettletoft Hotel and into the North Sea.

'That's terrible,' Ava said laughingly. 'I apologize for my fellow islanders.' She indicated McNab's injuries. 'You didn't get these in Orkney too, I hope?'

'No. These were inflicted locally,' McNab said, his voice more serious now.

Rhona waited, knowing this was the moment when the real reason for the stopover was likely to be revealed.

Eventually Ava said, 'My colleague, Mark Sylvester, who's working the Go Wild story along with me, turned up at my London flat today looking very much like you do. He didn't explain what had happened either. Although I'm pretty sure it was linked to the Go Wild investigation.' She paused, her face serious.

'That's why you wanted to meet with me?' Rhona said.

Ava nodded. 'Mark asked me to locate a contact at Police Scotland in order to pass on a message.'

'What message?' McNab demanded.

'The Met sent up a detective for the post-mortem on the fire victim—'

'How d'you know about that?' McNab interrupted her.

Ava ignored the question. 'Mark's message was that DI Cleverly can't be trusted.'

A moment's silence followed, before McNab laughed out loud. 'Jesus. Tell me something I don't know.'

At the arrival of the waiter with the coffee, they fell silent, although Rhona could almost hear McNab's brain working. Until now, his distrust of Cleverly could have been construed as personal. If suspicion was being levelled at the police officer from another quarter, albeit an investigative journalist, maybe it improved his argument.

'What does this Mark have on Cleverly?' McNab demanded.

'He didn't say. Just asked me to warn you.'

'Not enough,' McNab said.

Rhona didn't think so either. 'If you have information related to this case, you must inform the police.'

'Mark's being investigated by the Met, according to my editor. Seems he's upsetting some important people who don't want Go Wild exposed for what it is . . . supplying the wealthy with ways to commit murder and get away with it.'

'Or he's the one that's not to be trusted,' McNab challenged her.

'There are four people dead who were connected to Go Wild. You look as though you could have been number five.'

Rhona turned to McNab. 'Are your injuries connected to the investigation?'

She watched as he tried to figure out his response.

'You can't accuse Ava of withholding information if you're doing the same thing.'

'It's not the same,' McNab finally said.

The drill of Ava's mobile broke the silence that followed. She'd laid it alongside her on the table as though concerned that she might miss a call.

Her face was fraught as she listened. 'Call Erling. Tell him what's happened. Then stay inside. D'you hear me, Dougie? I'll be back first thing tomorrow.'

'What is it?' Rhona said as soon as the call ended.

'One of our cows has been knifed to death in the field.' She looked stricken. 'That's the second in days and I left Dougie there on his own.'

'Why would anyone do such a thing?' Rhona said.

Ava shook her head. 'All I know is that it began when I started investigating what was going on aboard the *Orlova*.'

27

There was a light on in the second-floor window and a motorbike parked up next to the front door. McNab lifted the cover and recognized the markings.

It looked like Ellie was home and hopefully alone, although he couldn't be certain of that.

He stood for a while, his eyes fastened on that window, and saw no movement inside. Of course, she could be in the kitchen or the bedroom, both of which were at the back of the building.

He wrestled with his decision, knowing that walking on was the easier thing to do, but maybe not the wisest. That's the way Rhona had put it. They'd sat for a bit after Ava had left, discussing what had been said.

Rhona had eventually extracted a potted version of what had happened to him at the fight club, but only because he'd planned to come clean to the boss tomorrow anyway. She'd also prised out of him what he and Sean had been talking about when she'd arrived at the club.

'It's not another woman,' he'd told her.

'So what the hell's going on?'

He'd contemplated a lie, but there was something in the way she'd looked at him. Their past was fraught enough, with him mostly the cause. So he'd decided to tell her the truth.

'The club's in debt.'

'It's not anything to do with drugs again?' she'd immediately asked.

Sean had been closed down once before because of drugs found on the premises. It had been a rough time for all of them.

'It's not that,' he'd told her.

She hadn't looked totally convinced, so he'd added, 'I would tell you if it was.'

And she'd believed him. He could see that in her eyes. Not for the first time, he thought that she was with the wrong man. That it should be him.

Until that wee voice of truth reminded him that he'd screwed up once with her and wouldn't be allowed a retry.

Taking another glance upwards, he made up his mind. He would do as Rhona had suggested. He would try to talk to Ellie. 'She just might give you the sympathy vote for that face,' she'd said.

McNab had smiled then, knowing he needed all the help he could get.

When they'd left the Indian restaurant, he'd made for the main road, whereas Rhona had gone back to the jazz club. He'd turned at the corner to watch her re-enter, knowing what she was planning. He'd found himself wishing her luck, at the same time as wishing it were him she was going back to.

The main door to the tenement was unlatched, which meant someone had either lost or forgotten their key again. Ellie was always unfazed by the front door being left open. It was something McNab had often lectured her on, much to her irritation.

Remembering that caused him to recall other warnings

he'd dished out, usually citing being a police officer as a valid reason.

No wonder she wanted time off from me, he thought.

Despite being able to enter, he rang the buzzer anyway. A few seconds later, he heard her pick up.

'Ellie. It's Michael.'

'I know. I saw you from the window.'

Silence.

'Can I come up? I need to speak to you.'

She must have known that the main door was already open. Was it an advantage that he hadn't appeared unannounced? Or might Ellie think he was just making a point again?

When he hit the landing, she was waiting for him. As soon as he was in full view, her hand jumped to her mouth in shock at his battered face. McNab had had a quick survey of it in the Gents prior to leaving the restaurant, and even he'd been taken aback by the swelling mosaic of colours.

'Sorry,' he said. 'It's not as bad as it looks.'

'My God. What happened?' She was about to reach out to him, then didn't.

'I tried to stop a fight.' He shrugged. 'Which didn't go down well with the bloke who was winning.'

And with that he was in.

McNab hoped the invite might take him as far as the sitting room, but every door off the hall was firmly shut. On a positive note, he saw no sign of a strange jacket where his had once hung.

He shifted his gaze back to Ellie, who was silently awaiting whatever he'd come there to say. He tried to read her expression but couldn't.

'I wanted to tell you . . . I'm okay about sharing you with someone else.'

In the silence that followed, the stupid words echoed in his brain.

'Fuck it,' he said. 'That came out all wrong. What I meant to say was, I really want to see you again – on your own terms, that is.' He tried his cheeky grin as a finale and was miraculously awarded with the ghost of a smile from Ellie.

'I'll think about that,' she said.

'Oh and Janice asked if we would like to come to dinner with her and Paula. Seems Paula's a great cook . . .' He slowed to a halt.

Ellie's eyes were fixed on him. He had this notion she was reading his soul and finding it dark and tortured. So no surprise there then.

'When?' she said.

'The date's still to be decided,' he rushed on. 'I've to let them know when you're free.'

'Will your face be back to normal by then?'

Was that a yes? McNab wasn't altogether sure. 'It might get worse before it gets better,' he offered.

'Hope you gave as good as you got,' Ellie said. 'I'll text you when I'm free.'

And that was it. McNab found himself swiftly back on the landing with the door shut.

Rhona had warned him not to mention Baldy and the altercation when he was out with Cleverly. He was glad he'd taken her advice.

He found himself whistling as he descended the stairs. He was in again. Maybe just a little, but it was a start.

Emerging onto the street, he found the rain had come on. He didn't care. A wee drop of rain never hurt anyone, his mother used to say. He paused for a moment to look up at Ellie's window, hoping she might be there again, waiting for him to appear. She might even look down, see him and wave.

His hopes in that direction didn't last long.

There was a figure at the window, but it wasn't Ellie. It was Baldy and he was giving him the finger.

28

They'd begun with the computer room victim.

Sissons had recorded the state of the body into the overhead mike, establishing the burn patterns on the left arm and hand. He'd quickly dismissed the possibility of electrocution, and determined that the victim had likely been dead before the fire had started.

The lingering scent of an accelerant on his clothing had been obvious as they'd taped and undressed him, and the tracking of the burns showed where most of it had been poured.

'If this was an attempt at disguising the method of his death, it wasn't successful,' Sissons had remarked in a laconic voice.

At this point Campbell and McNab had walked in. Luckily for McNab, the suit hood and mask covered the worst of his injuries, so the pathologist didn't get to view the increasingly colourful damage.

Dr Sissons acknowledged their entrance, then carried on relating his thoughts to the overhead microphone, as though in conversation with God on the demise of one of his creations.

'It is now obvious that the fire did not kill the subject, who, by the state of his bloodshot eyes and bruising round the nose and mouth, was most likely suffocated before the fire was set. High levels of carbon dioxide in his blood and no evidence of soot in his lungs will confirm this.'

He turned to Rhona. 'Was any evidence found of a pad or a plastic bag at the scene?'

Rhona explained about collecting fibres from the nose and mouth. 'The cloth used wasn't in the room, or it was destroyed in the fire.'

'Do we know anything more about the victim apart from the fact he's male and likely in his twenties?' Sissons said.

It was Campbell who responded. 'There was no record of the crew or passengers. Neither did the search find any personal belongings that might help identify them.'

'What happened to the other people on board?'

'We suspect some will have been lifted off. Alternatively, some may have gone overboard.'

It was a scenario Rhona had imagined herself. What had happened after the killings? Where had the crew gone? The kitchen and waiting personnel? Those who'd been sleeping in the units set up on deck.

The *Orlova* had been a ghost ship before, and it was a ghost ship again.

Having finished noting all aspects of the body, Sissons now indicated he was ready to open it up. This was the cue for McNab to withdraw. Campbell didn't look that keen to stay either.

'There are two more bodies after this,' Sissons reminded them as they left.

Rhona assured him she would be back, before following in the wake of the two detectives.

Once in the changing room, Campbell said, 'You'll keep us informed about the results on the other two autopsies, Dr MacLeod? DS McNab and I are better occupied with investigating how the fire death is linked to the *Orlova*, via this Go Wild company.'

So McNab and Campbell were allies on this, which boded well, Rhona thought.

'Has there been any more news from DI Flett?' she said.

'He wanted to know when we've finished with the ship, then they'll arrange for it to be taken south for scrap.'

'When would that happen normally?' Rhona said.

'Not immediately,' Campbell assured her. 'You think you'll need to get back on board?'

There was always the chance a forensic team might want to go back for another look. She said so.

'Then I'll tell DI Flett to wait to hear from you, before any arrangements are made.'

McNab had been hanging on, obviously wanting to speak to her. Once Campbell had closed the door, he said, 'Can we get a coffee before you go back in?'

'Sissons won't be starting on the other two for a while yet.'

They walked through the hospital to the nearest cafe, attracting curious glances on the way. Even in a place full of sick or injured folk, it seemed McNab's face was still a draw.

'So what happened with Ellie?' Rhona said as they settled at a table.

'I followed your instructions,' he said. 'She let me in. We talked. She'll think about it.'

Rhona knew by the guarded look that wasn't all that had happened. 'And?'

He shook his head. 'The skinhead was in there. He gave me the finger from the window.'

'Before or after you were inside?'

'What does it matter, she's still seeing him?' He shrugged. 'How about you?'

'Sean and I talked.'

They'd done more than just talk in the back office, but she wasn't going to tell McNab that.

His blue eyes fastened on her and he smiled. 'Good for you, Dr MacLeod. At least one of us had fun last night.' He finished his coffee. 'Another?'

'I'm fine, thanks.'

She watched as his tall figure headed to the counter. Whatever he said to the barista made the girl laugh. Rhona wondered how many tales he'd told to explain his battered face and if even she'd been told the truth.

The pretty barista didn't want him to leave, delaying him with responses to his banter. The queue that had built up behind had also joined in. Eventually McNab sauntered back, a smile on his face.

'So some people *don't* want to punch your lights out?' Rhona said.

'Just the ones who *don't* know me,' he quipped in return. 'Let's talk Ava Clouston.'

McNab's reaction to Ava and her involvement had changed when the name Einar Petersson had been dropped late in the conversation the previous night. There was a good reason for that. Petersson, apparently a colleague of Ava's, had played a vital role in McNab's survival during the Kalinin case. 'No thanks to DI Cleverly,' he'd told her.

After that, McNab had become more inclined to listen to the reporter. It had struck Rhona, as they'd discussed Mark's run-in with the Met, that there were definite similarities between the way he and McNab went about their jobs.

'So you're determined to go to London?' she said to McNab.

'If the boss okays it. And I think he will after I talk to him this afternoon.'

'When you explain how you got that face?' A sudden thought occurred. 'You have told Janice?'

'So you tell Chrissy everything?' he came back at her.

She didn't. Hadn't. In fact, McNab had been her confidant more often than Chrissy. And he knew that, even though it remained unspoken.

Rhona changed the subject. 'When you speak to Bill, can you stress we need a DNA sample from Olivia Newton . . .'

'Richardson,' he completed for her.

It was ridiculous that the Met hadn't supplied that as yet. Either the real Ms Richardson was alive or the fire victim had died accompanied by her handbag and wallet.

'I'm also planning a visit to IT,' McNab said. 'Seems like we have a digital reconstruction of the fire victim and a photograph of the elusive Ms Richardson to compare.' He rose.

Rhona glanced at her watch. 'And I'm heading for a double autopsy on the two Viking warriors.'

'I'd rather get beaten up in a fight club,' McNab said.

Stripped now of what little they'd worn and laid out side by side, the difference in height and weight between the two victims was obvious. Dr Sissons registered the male as five foot ten inches, the female as five foot five. They would have made an unequal match whatever game they'd been playing.

Medically, injuries were divided into blunt force trauma and those due to sharp cutting instruments. Stabbing injuries usually killed by penetrating a vital organ or major blood vessels, massive haemorrhage or bleeding out being the most common cause of death.

In both victims, there was some evidence of gnawing from the resident rats, which could be distinguished from the puncture wounds, which were located mostly on the legs and arms, more on the male than the female, and probably inflicted by the points of the short swords found next to the bodies.

'Pinpricks of pain,' Sissons had recorded. 'Perhaps inflicted for sexual gratification. As Dr MacLeod has recorded, both blades were relatively dull, only the points sharpened.' He paused there. 'The major incised wounds, however, were made by a different instrument. Sharp, clean-cut wound margins demonstrate a keen blade. Deeper at the entry point, with tail abrasions. Such wounds can be less dangerous than stab wounds, but in both cases I believe the wielder knew where to inflict the most damage. I suspect what was used was a long sword, heavy and very sharp, and whoever was wielding it was intent on death.'

The couple had been there to fight one another, Rhona thought, even to inflict real damage. Hence the small stabbings on the legs and elsewhere. Probably for sexual satisfaction. If so, the female had inflicted, or been encouraged to inflict, the most damage.

If they were on the *Orlova* to play such games, why had they died by another's hand?

Someone offered more money to kill them, was her immediate thought. Or were they killed as a warning to someone?

All of which got them no nearer to finding out who the dead were, or their killer. Only unravelling Go Wild would do that.

Before leaving, she confirmed with Dr Sissons that they would need to do a comparison between the pool of vomit found at the scene and the stomach contents of the deceased.

Once washed and changed, she called Chrissy and told her how it had gone.

'You sound knackered,' Chrissy said sympathetically. 'Still, you were right about both scenes.'

'But no closer to discovering the identity of the victims or the killer.'

'Not strictly our job,' Chrissy reminded her. 'You coming for a drink?'

'Not tonight. I'm off out on a date.' Rhona told her the unexpected news.

'With Dr Walker?' Chrissy tried.

Rhona laughed. 'No, he's still cutting up bodies, and I'm pretty sure he's lost all interest in me. I think I've been replaced by one of the mortuary assistants, Rachel.'

Chrissy sounded disappointed, since discussing complicated love lives was one of her favourite pastimes. They'd spent most of breakfast discussing the McNab/Ellie/Baldy story from last night.

'Who then?' she demanded.

'Sean. He's booked us a table at the Ubiquitous Chip for dinner.'

'Mmmm. Lucky you.'

'I'll see you tomorrow, when I won't be telling you what happened.'

29

The boss was scrutinizing him as only he could.

'What are you suggesting?' DI Wilson finally said.

'That the two cases are connected via the Go Wild company, so they should be followed up together, sir,' McNab said.

'Has this got anything to do with your face, Sergeant?'

McNab had his answer ready.

'We located a Glasgow address for Go Wild. DI Cleverly and I took a look. It was abandoned, but I found something there that led me to believe that an illegal bare-knuckle fight had been arranged by the company.'

DI Wilson sat back in his chair. 'And you went to this fight?'

'Just me, sir. DI Cleverly didn't know about it.' He halted, seeing the boss's expression.

'You withheld this information from Cleverly?'

McNab cleared his throat. The next bit of the explanation was tricky since it might involve mentioning breaking and entering.

'I revisited the former Go Wild office address after we parted company, sir. That's when I found the invitation.'

McNab held his breath as DI Wilson interpreted this partial information, then quickly broke in before the boss could pose a further question.

'The fight was held at an abandoned warehouse. It was a bout between a local called Kenny and a Londoner – they called him the posh fucker – who'd paid for the privilege of putting the guy down, sir, but then he proceeded to stamp on his head.'

'And you intervened at that point?'

'I think he'd paid to kill him, sir.'

'Did they learn you were a police officer?'

McNab indicated no. 'It seemed wiser not to mention that, sir.' He paused. 'The fight club is a direct link with Go Wild. We could put an undercover officer in there and maybe learn more. I've discussed that possibility with DS Campbell, plus what I'm about to say next, sir.'

He waited for the boss to indicate he could continue.

'So far, the company has been linked to four deaths. Three on the *Orlova* plus the fire victim, all under our jurisdiction. I got the impression from Cleverly that the Met is not happy about that, which is why he won't share anything with us regarding identifying Ms Richardson as the deceased. Plus Dr MacLeod and I had a meeting with Ava Clouston last night.' McNab began to outline to the boss exactly what had been discussed, before ending with, 'I think I should take a trip to London, sir. A reciprocal visit, so to speak.'

'How'd it go?' Janice said when he finally reappeared.

'As we hoped. At the next strategy meeting we'll consider the Go Wild connections to the four deaths under our jurisdiction.'

'With no help from the Met?'

'I'm off to London,' McNab said with a smile. 'Two can play at Cleverly's game.'

'Good stuff.' Janice looked impressed. 'Want to see what Ollie just sent through?' She turned her screen towards him.

The facial reconstruction of the fire victim sat alongside an image they had of Olivia Newton Richardson.

'Well?' Janice said.

'Could be, then again, maybe not. I'd like to see what the super recognizer thinks.'

McNab made his usual visit to the cafeteria en route to IT, this time choosing two iced doughnuts as an offering since Ollie's girlfriend wasn't around to see.

When McNab produced the doughnut bag with a flourish, Ollie took a look inside, then horror suffused his face.

'I can't eat those.'

'Maria isn't working today,' McNab reminded him, before extracting a sugary concoction and taking a bite.

Ollie fought off his fear of Maria's wrath and helped himself to the other one.

They munched together for a moment as Ollie brought up the images McNab had just viewed.

'Okay,' McNab said. 'You're the super recognizer. Is that her or not?'

'I can't be sure,' Ollie admitted.

McNab nodded. That was good enough for him. 'So how or why did she have Ms Richardson's handbag, wallet and cards?' It was a question he didn't expect an answer to and Ollie didn't give him one. 'How's the mobile doing?'

'Remotely wiped and set to factory settings before it was found.' Ollie looked a little guilty, as though that was his fault – or perhaps his guilt was the result of having eaten the doughnut.

'Okay, let's move on to Go Wild,' McNab suggested.

'I've been following up shell companies that may be linked

to Go Wild. Remember the Scottish Limited Partnership registered here in Glasgow that was used to transfer £160 million out of Russia last year?'

'You think Go Wild involves Russian money?' McNab said.

'Not just Russian. American, European and British too.'

'So how does it work?' McNab said.

'You outline your Go Wild fantasy and they supply it at a cost. The important thing is they promise no comeback for whatever you choose to do.'

'That could account for what happened at the fire death and the ghost ship,' McNab said. 'Which reminds me. Who's dealing with the computer equipment from the *Orlova*?'

Ollie wasn't sure.

'Find out what's on that equipment. We're all in this together now.'

'Will do,' Ollie said.

'Now, the bloke who tried to destroy my good looks,' McNab said. 'Known as the posh fucker. Arrived in a limo with darkened windows. Had a couple of minders.' His mind flashed back to their arms pinning him as the fucker got stuck in. Then the different face swimming above him, urging that they leave.

'He's a felon?'

If he was they might find him in a database.

'I think more like a member of the county set,' McNab said, realizing how impossible that made it. Little wonder no one had been allowed to take photos.

As he rose to leave, Ollie said, 'There's one other thing you should know. We're not the only ones digging into Go Wild on the dark web.'

McNab immediately expected Ollie to mention the Met. He didn't.

'An investigative journalist . . .'

'Ava Clouston,' McNab finished for him.

'She's covering her tracks well, but maybe not well enough,' Ollie said.

30

It was already approaching dusk as Ava watched the cow being loaded onto the truck and driven away. Mother and child butchered in the space of a couple of days. What the hell was going on?

A squally wind tugged at her hair, covering her face again. She'd forgotten how irritating the combination of long hair and an Orkney wind was and vowed to have it cut soon, and as short as possible.

A grey Scapa Flow seethed with the moving tide and gusting wind, the MV *Orlova* rising and falling in its wake. *Like a curse on the landscape*, Ava thought.

Or was she the curse for having written about it, for trying to discover its secrets? Maybe she should give up? Maybe then the killing on the farm would cease?

Her mobile buzzed and she checked it anxiously to find it wasn't Dougie. He hadn't been here when she'd got back mid-morning and she'd heard nothing from him all day. Erling had said he'd taken off with Finn, too upset to wait for the dead cow to be removed.

It was what Dougie did when things got too much for him. Head off on foot with the dog or take out his beloved boat. Seeing the seething waters of the Flow, Ava hoped it was the former, but she would have to check to be sure.

Her heart jumping a little, she made her way to the

boathouse, all the while repeating the mantra that the *Fear Not* would still be inside. Even before she reached there, she knew it had gone . . . but where?

Her first thought was Hoy, because it was one of Dougie's favourite islands. If he was over there, chances were he wouldn't have got her text messages. Ava clung to that thought for comfort.

Checking the contents of the boathouse, she thought some of his camping gear might be missing. Surely if he planned to stay away, he would get in touch to tell her? Ava wasn't so sure he would. Anger at her London trip, followed by a cow being killed in her absence, might just mean he'd keep her waiting and in the dark as to where he was.

He was seventeen, he'd reminded her constantly. A man. He didn't need to answer to her any more. Just the way she chose not to answer to him.

A feeling of defeat accompanied her back to the house. That and the terrifying thought that Dougie might have had something to do with the animal deaths in order to persuade her to stay.

It was a ludicrous thought, but once it lodged in her brain, it demanded to be considered. On the other hand, if the cow deaths were connected to the *Orlova* investigation, that meant there was someone on Orkney with a vested interest in shutting her up.

How realistic was that? Not very, she thought. A local was unlikely, which meant it had to be an incomer with links to Go Wild. And, if they wanted to shut her up, why not just shut her up permanently?

Mark had sent her home to Orkney because he believed it to be the safest place in the present situation. *Although I didn't tell him about the dead calf*, she thought.

That brought her thoughts back to where they'd begun. With Dougie. Was her wee brother capable of killing the cows in an attempt to make her stay here with him?

Remembering his face when he showed her the calf strangled by the wire made her want to weep. Dougie was a farmer, a natural one. He could no more stab a cow than she could.

Reaching home, she pulled the big kettle onto the hot ring of the Aga, then tried to call Mark, intent on running the latest developments by him. What she didn't expect was to be told the number was no longer operational.

Why would that be the case? Her sensible side moved in to quash the fear. Mark had a number of mobiles. Stopping the use of one was par for the course, especially during an investigation. Her mind conjured up a vision of his face, which had resembled the detective's last night. Who had jumped him and why?

Ava admonished herself. Mark was more than capable of looking after himself and had done so in far more dangerous places than London.

As is Dougie and as am I. It was a comforting thought but stayed only fleetingly.

She headed upstairs to check out Dougie's room. Surely if he'd decided to stay away for a few days, there would be evidence there to prove that.

Walking into his room after so long (he'd never allowed her to enter when resident) brought back memories of the little boy she'd left behind. He had worshipped his big sister because she'd indulged him constantly. Twelve years' age difference had made her into a second and more accommodating mum. And she had relished it.

The bedroom now was not the one she'd left behind.

This wasn't a boy's room any longer, but a young man's. Dougie had become a grown-up, and the death of both his parents had hastened that.

Shaking herself, Ava checked for possible missing clothes, for his rucksack. Then she spotted the most significant missing item of all.

Wherever he had gone, Dougie had taken his laptop with him.

31

Anchored in the waters of the small, sheltered inlet, he had a clear view of Houton Bay and the rusting hulk of the ghost ship.

Here, all was calm, but out there was a different matter. The *Fear Not* had braved the waves on the way over, Finn at the bow, but Scapa Flow was now made rougher by the changing tide and a rising wind.

Dougie laid his hand on the collie's head, whispering words of endearment while the intelligent eyes watched him intently, ears on high alert.

The sun was sinking into the west, the sky a fiery red line below a threatening cloud mass. He felt the first sting of raindrops on his face as he started up the engine.

He had been sailing these waters since he could first handle a boat, encouraged by his father. Before that he had sat in the bow like Finn, confident that his dad could take them safely to wherever he chose.

Now it's my turn, he told the dog.

The engine purring, the small boat began to trace a line across the calm waters of the bay. Two seals, who'd been his curious companions while at anchor, followed until the bow of the boat hit open and choppy water. Halting there, they regarded his departure from safety with large questioning eyes.

A wave broke over the bow, soaking Finn, who still stood as resolute as a figurehead. Dougie tasted salt on his lips, washed off intermittently by the raindrops that fell from an increasingly leaden sky.

There was a moment's hesitation as he grew closer to the *Orlova*. A shift to port or starboard would decide. Finn, sensing his hesitancy, offered a little whine of encouragement.

Dougie had no need of it. He knew where he was going, and it wasn't home.

32

McNab swirled the whisky round the glass, then paused to admire the colour before tasting.

He'd made the right choice with the Caledonian Sleeper, although it had been a rush. He wasn't a keen flyer and by the time he'd agreed things with the boss, it was too late to get himself on a late flight anyway.

This way he would wake up in the centre of London, and avoid having to find a place to stay.

The boss had called him in again after his trip to IT, and it was obvious there had been a development. McNab had rarely seen the boss so angry. Whatever attempts he'd made to secure more cooperation from the Met had seemingly fallen on deaf ears.

The most likely next step, from what he could gather, was that the *Orlova* investigation would shift to London. The excuse being that the ship had been in international waters until the storm had blown it ashore on Orkney.

'What about the fire death?' McNab had immediately asked.

'That's where you come in, Sergeant.'

So here he was, sitting comfortably, having enjoyed a satisfactory meal, drinking his dram, all of which made up for the fact he would wake up in London.

There were three others in the bar with him. A couple of

businessmen who were deep in a combative conversation about work, and a single female. Late twenties and classy, she was currently reading a book and enjoying a cocktail the barman had mixed for her.

She'd noted his bruised face on entry, and had quickly tried to cover her reaction. Meeting this with a grin had resulted in a warm return smile from her. In fact, at this moment, McNab was considering trying to draw her attention to him again, rather than the book.

As he took possession of a second whisky, his mobile vibrated in his pocket. Hoping it might be Ellie phoning to discuss when she would be free to come to the dinner party, he was initially disappointed to find Ava Clouston's name on the screen.

'What's up?' McNab said.

'I can't reach Mark. His mobile's out of action and his landline just rings out.'

McNab could hear the mounting fear in her voice, and Ava Clouston hadn't struck him as a woman who scared easily.

'Text me his address. I'll go round there.'

There was a short silence. 'You're in London?' she said.

'I'm on my way there now.'

'Is this to do with Go Wild?'

'It's police business, that's all I can say.'

The tense silence that followed made McNab ask, 'What's happened?'

'My brother's disappeared. He took off after the cow was found stabbed to death.'

'Does DI Flett know?' McNab said.

'I've spoken to Erling. He knows Dougie does this when he's upset. He did it when our parents were killed in the car accident.' She sounded as though she was trying to persuade herself. 'Erling believes he'll be back when he's thought things through.' She halted there and a pregnant silence followed.

McNab knew avoidance when he heard it, having played that tune many times himself. Ava was hiding something. And he thought it might, just might, have a link to her brother's disappearance.

'If there's anything you're not telling me?'

A pause, then . . .

'Mark suspects people high up were using Go Wild's services. Hence the reticence by the Met and the probability of a cover-up.'

'Okay, I'll find him and talk to him,' he promised.

He felt her sense of relief, even over the phone.

When she rang off, he found the woman at the next table watching him. How much had she heard and did it matter?

The two businessmen had gone. They were alone now, apart from the hovering barman.

McNab thought of the made-up bunk, the chance for a sleep. But would he sleep?

She was smiling over at him, and the next thing he knew he'd ordered up another cocktail for her and a whisky for him.

Any doubts he'd had about such an encounter he blotted out with the image of the new boyfriend giving him the finger from Ellie's front window.

33

He'd told Erling that the ship was haunting his life. That he wanted it to go.

'It will soon,' Erling had promised. 'They'll tow it down to the Central Belt where it'll be scrapped.'

In Erling's keenness to reassure Dougie, it had slipped out that there was no one aboard now that the bodies and evidence had been removed.

'The coastguard are keeping an eye on it,' had been his parting shot.

Dougie reached out now and grabbed the rusty ladder, tying the *Fear Not* to the bottom rung. Daylight almost gone, he'd already donned his head torch and fastened the climbing harness on Finn so that he could pull him up once he reached the deck himself.

If he reached the deck.

Ignoring the small voice of doubt, Dougie told Finn to wait, then grabbed for the ladder, hitching himself up and onto it.

He'd sent his drone out a few times, assuring himself that what Erling had said was true. The coastguard visited the surrounding waters or flew over intermittently. To all intents and purposes the *Orlova* had become a graveyard, without the resident dead.

Halfway up, he lost his nerve. What the hell was he doing,

leaving Finn alone down there? And would he manage to pull him up even if he did get to the deck himself?

Concentrate on how you're going to get Finn up and put one hand after the other. That's all you have to do.

He'd been sheltered from the wind during the climb, but as he finally pitched himself over the railing and onto the deck, he realized the wind had dropped and a haar was rolling in.

Which was even better, he told himself, as the thick fog closed around him.

Dougie secured the rope and began to pull Finn up. Orkney wasn't known for its mountains, but there were plenty of cliffs and stacks he'd climbed with the dog. Many caves they'd lowered themselves into.

Finn, he knew, would likely be less fazed than him by this latest adventure.

Safely now on deck, Dougie freed the collie, who immediately sniffed the air.

'So where to, Finn?'

As though in answer to his question, Finn set off, Dougie following, his head torch focused on the waving white tail.

Dougie still wasn't sure what he was looking for, except perhaps that he wanted to see if what he'd learned from the online gamers about the ghost ship was true.

Inside now, he stood for a moment, trying to get his bearings. According to the material he'd collected about the ship, the virtual games area was on a lower deck, so he needed to find the nearest stairs.

The emergency lights might be working, but the heating definitely wasn't. He could see his breath condensing, the further he descended into the bowels of the ship.

Glancing into the staterooms and sleeping quarters, his

headlamp picked out the black dusted surfaces where SOCOs had taken prints, the crime scene tape still strung across entrances or broken and trailing over the floor.

The lower he went, the more the cold smell of the upper decks began to change, subtly at first, then more swiftly and strongly as he descended. There had been talk about a fire death, as well as two deaths during a game.

Was that what he could smell?

Finn had caught the scent too and had taken off down the next set of steps, to halt on a landing outside an open door, his hair standing straight up.

Dougie joined him there.

This was the control room for the game, he thought, viewing the empty shelves where the equipment had been. The smell of burnt plastic and something else, which he realized might be burnt flesh, assaulted his senses, and he covered his face with his hand and retreated.

A turn in the metal stairs finally brought the games arena into view.

This time he stopped in awe at the maze laid out below, at the centre of which was an arena. Even from here he could make out a large dark mark, which might be blood.

Finn knew exactly what it was, and howled to indicate that.

Noting the complexity of the maze, Dougie shouted at the dog to wait for him, aware that without Finn he might take a while to reach the centre.

Finn did as bid, waiting at each turn until Dougie appeared behind him.

Reaching the arena, Dougie halted in shock at the now obvious bloodstains, imagining the bodies that had lain inside the markings. A male and a female, according to reports.

Above was the gallery, which, during the duel, would have been populated by a computer-generated screaming crowd, all baying for blood.

Despite his horror at the evidence of death, his skin prickled with excitement as he envisaged the real-life game being played out here. No wonder people were willing to pay large sums of money to take part. So much better than duelling with an imaginary enemy via a computer screen.

Finn's bloodlust was waning, another scent taking its place. The collie was keen to leave the arena, and whining at Dougie to follow.

They were heading down another level, Finn definitely following a trail. Dougie wondered if the dog was simply after a rat. Any ship this size would have a resident rat population, and Dougie wasn't keen to meet one, but his calls to heel were being ignored.

Eventually the dog, way ahead now, fell silent. This seemed scarier than when he had been whining with excitement. Dougie upped his speed, skirting round some containers, until he almost fell over the collie scratching furiously at what looked like a low metal door.

'What is it, boy? What's in there?'

Finn answered with a bark, indicating that he had no intention of moving until his master opened the door.

Dougie imagined what might be in there. Another body, missed in the search of the ship? Or a family of rats that hadn't eaten for some time?

Finn was staring up at his master, intelligent eyes willing him on.

'Stay,' Dougie ordered the dog before reaching for the handle.

The screech as the metal freed itself a little set his heart racing.

The smell escaping through the narrow opening was like his bedroom when he hadn't opened the window in a while.

He waited, listening. Nothing.

Intrigued now to know what lay beyond, he dipped his head and the bouncing beam from his torch alighted on what looked like tins and bundled bedding.

So someone had been in here.

Behind him, Finn whined, keen to enter.

'Wait, boy,' he ordered. The last thing he wanted was the collie wrecking the place before he examined it properly.

Moving towards the far wall, he noted a partially drunk bottle of vodka and some eating utensils. Then a pile of what looked like clothes.

As he crouched to pick up an item to see if he might identify it as male or female, the door suddenly clanged shut behind him.

In that moment he knew someone was in there with him. Someone intent on keeping the dog out.

He tried to rise, but it was already too late, as something hard and heavy met the back of his head.

Dougie registered Finn barking his distress as he slumped to the floor.

34

Rhona sniffed the air. The aroma of shower gel it was not. Sean was cooking and it smelt like a fry-up. She found her mouth watering at the prospect.

He was at the cooker in his boxer shorts, humming a tune she recognized, which meant it wasn't jazz. When he heard her enter, he turned.

'Slice sausage and eggs all right?' he offered.

'You trying to do Chrissy out of a job?' Rhona said, eyebrows raised. 'My assistant always brings in our breakfast in the shape of filled rolls. Usually with three offerings on each.'

He checked out the contents of the frying pan. 'I can probably manage all of this myself – after the busy night I had,' he added with a smile. 'Coffee's on the table.'

Rhona poured herself a cup and sat for a moment to drink it, or maybe to admire Sean from afar.

The evening had gone well, although she wasn't sure she had been given the entire story of the club's debt level and what Sean planned to do about it. Her mind went back to seeing Sean and McNab huddled together at the bar. Sean wasn't keeping McNab company until Chrissy arrived. That hadn't rung true then, and it didn't now.

She suspected Sean was asking for advice, which suggested the trouble the club was in might involve the law.

None of which had been discussed last night.

Sean's easy Irish attitude to life's complexities and troubles had been one of the reasons she'd been drawn to him in the first place. It was enticing to be with someone as laid-back as he was. Especially considering the nature of her own work.

'Okay, I'm off,' she said.

Sean followed her into the hall. 'I'll see you later?'

She smiled a yes.

'I hope for your sake Chrissy isn't back on the porridge,' he shouted as the door shut behind her.

The sausage aroma followed her down the stairs. Rhona tried not to picture the scenario Sean had just pitched her. *No*, she thought. *We're over the porridge phase. Please God*.

Crossing the park in spring sunshine, she noted that the devastation of Storm Birka had almost totally disappeared, council teams busy loading the remains of the debris onto pickups.

She found herself looking for the ancient yew tree, a player in an earlier case, wondering if it too had survived the storm. She almost veered off the walkway to check, but stopped herself in time.

There were some memories better not stirred.

'Yay, you're here,' Chrissy called when Rhona arrived. 'How did it go with Sean last night?' she said with a big smile. When Rhona didn't answer, Chrissy added, 'Look, I'm not getting any at the moment and I can't ask Mum about her love life, so I'm left with you.' She assumed a crestfallen expression.

Rhona succumbed. 'He wanted to serve me breakfast, but I declined because I didn't want to do you out of a job.' She looked around, realizing to her dismay that there was no sign of the paper bag, nor the smell of breakfast.

Chrissy gave her a studied look. 'That's a shame.'

'Chrissy,' Rhona said threateningly.

Her assistant's adopted innocence should have warned her.

'Sean called me. Said you were keen to get back on the porridge.'

'I'll kill him.'

Chrissy sighed. 'That voice of his would persuade me to do anything.'

'Find your own Irishman, then,' Rhona said.

'He's offered to introduce me to his cousin when he's next over from Dublin.'

Rhona wondered what else they'd been plotting behind her back, but the only thing she was worried about at the moment . . .

'The rolls are in the microwave,' Chrissy informed her. 'For a forensic scientist, you're very easily fooled, Dr MacLeod.'

Over breakfast, Rhona gave a brief update on the previous day's autopsies and Dr Sissons's conclusions on the deaths.

'I like it when we're right,' Chrissy said. 'Oh, I almost forgot, a preliminary report's back on the vomit we sampled at the second locus. It doesn't look like a match to the stomach contents of any of the victims.'

Might it have come from the perpetrator? Rhona mused on that briefly.

It wasn't unknown for someone to kill on the spur of the moment, only to be so shocked at what they'd done that they were sick. The killings in the arena had been pre-meditated, so that seemed unlikely.

Chrissy was thinking, her brows knitted. 'We've judged the deaths to be around three to five days before the ship was boarded and we know that you can't officially judge the age of vomit, only what it contains.' She halted there to look at Rhona. 'Might it be more recent than that?'

If it was, then someone may still have been alive before the *Orlova* hit the rocks.

35

The shunting of the train woke him. It shuddered then began to move again, clicking and clacking, gaining speed, eventually streamlining its sounds. A chink of light crept round the blind.

McNab, coming to properly, realized he was alone again. A waft of memories from the previous night's encounter swept over him, all of them pleasant. He tested himself for guilt, and found none.

Ellie had wanted to be free to choose her sexual partners. He hadn't wanted her to. Yet here he was among the bedclothes that smelt of another woman. A woman he would never see again. A woman he had no desire to see again.

But he did want to be with Ellie. That much he did know.

Up and dressed, he was ready when breakfast was delivered to his door. He'd roughly formulated a plan the previous evening before Ava's phone call, then shelved it for an hour or two as he focused on other more pleasurable activities.

He revisited it now, deciding he would check out Olivia's flat first, then see if he could locate Mark Sylvester. According to Ava, the Met were currently displeased with Mark and his investigation into Go Wild, which made him a man McNab wanted to meet.

*

Crossing the railway concourse, McNab recalled that the last time he'd been in this particular railway station, he'd still had a dressing over the bullet hole in his back.

Having escaped the safe house, he'd gone looking for lodgings, thinking he might stay in London for a while, and had eventually found a place run by a Mrs Morrison. She'd been the one to help him re-dress the open wound and she'd never asked how he had come by the injury in the first place. Older than him, with a son in the army whom she doted on and whose father was never mentioned, McNab remembered her now with affection. In fact, staying there had reminded him of his own home life, where his mum had also never spoken of his father.

He briefly thought that if he needed to stay in London longer, he could always check up on Jean Morrison, then dismissed the idea. He would definitely get the job done here as quickly as possible and be on the night train back to Glasgow.

Seated upstairs at a terrace cafe, he had another coffee and reworked his plan. After thinking over Ava's phone call, he decided it might be better to check out Mark's flat first, to put her mind at ease. Mark being out of touch didn't strike McNab as that unusual. He often went off the radar himself when on a job.

Ava's increased anxiety probably came from the antics of her brother and the worry about the farm. McNab couldn't see why the dead animals should have anything to do with her investigation into Go Wild. More likely someone wanted her to sell the farm and was exerting a bit of pressure to make that happen.

Or maybe the brother was trying to keep his sister there, and the attack on the animals was part of that? McNab had never met the boy, so couldn't say. What he did know was that he'd been a prize arse at seventeen, with a desire to have his own way whatever it took.

Of course, he hadn't suggested that possibility during the call, keen as he was to keep Ava onside.

Rising, he made his way down the escalator and threaded through the crowds on the concourse, heading for the Underground sign.

Emerging at Victoria to follow Ava's directions, he found Mark's place easily enough. The red-brick mansion flats she'd described were only a short walk from the station, tucked down a side street.

With no answer from the buzzer, he awaited the next entrant and slipped in behind them. Ava had indicated that the flat was on the third floor, number 309.

Ignoring the lift, McNab took the stairs two at a time and made his way along the corridor, still nursing the hope that Mark might be home and just unwilling to advertise that fact.

After three attempts at knocking, with no sound or response from inside, he decided it was time for his lock pick.

Closing the door quietly behind him, McNab stood for a moment, breathing in the smell of the place and the silence. Instinct told him the flat was empty, plus the scent wasn't of death but of spilt blood and sweat.

He followed it into the kitchen where it was clear that a fight had taken place. The blood was mostly splattered lightly across the walls and surfaces, with no pools present. He hoped that meant serious damage hadn't been done, to Mark at least. Ava had told him Mark's face had been much like his own, so had the altercation happened here? If Mark had been attacked on his home turf, it didn't look as though he'd come back to clear up the mess.

Returning to the hall, he retrieved the couple of letters he'd spotted lying behind the door. Both were dated after Ava had said Mark had visited her, which suggested he may not have returned home at all in the interim.

Moving into the bedroom, he found the wardrobe and drawers lying open, discarded clothes scattered about. Either Mark had been packing in a hurry or someone had been searching the place, and perhaps been disturbed by Mark's arrival.

With the bathroom remarkably empty of everyday toiletries, and the study minus a laptop or any evidence of work currently going on in there, McNab came to the studied conclusion that Mark Sylvester had taken up residence elsewhere.

He then spent some time checking for bugs, but found none in the usual places, although Mark had ordered Ava not to email or text him, so he'd obviously believed someone was interested in his various social media and mobile accounts.

Including the Met, McNab suspected.

After trying Mark's mobile number one more time, to no avail, he then called Ava.

She answered almost immediately. McNab explained where he was and what he'd found.

'If he returned here, after speaking to you, it was only to collect what he needed,' McNab said. 'So can you think of anywhere he might have gone, where he would feel safe enough to continue with his investigation?'

'God, yes,' she said as though just remembering. 'There's an Afghan cafe he visits, run by the family of Abu-Zar, who we met when we were working out of Kabul. Mark helped save the life of Firash, Abu-Zar's young son, during our time there. He has a room there where he works sometimes. It's not far from the flat. It's called—' She struggled to remember, then came up with a name, which she had to spell out for him. 'You can't phone there and ask for him. They'll deny he exists. You'll have to visit in person. Even then, they may not let you in.'

36

McNab had taken note of the cafe's address, then ended the call without further comment, leaving Ava wondering if he intended to check whether Mark was actually at the Afghan cafe.

She knew she couldn't force the issue. After all, he was a police officer, apparently in London to do something in that capacity. Exactly what, she had no idea. Although she had a strong suspicion it was connected with the investigation into the *Orlova*.

She contemplated whether she shouldn't go back down to London herself. See if she could make contact with Mark again.

Mark told you to come back to Orkney and stay here, she reminded herself. He was adamant about that.

Plus she couldn't leave the farm until Dougie came home.

Ava tried calling her brother's mobile one more time, even though she'd left a dozen messages already. Maybe Dougie was ignoring her calls and texts in order to punish her? She realized she would be more than delighted if that were the reason. As long as he was okay.

Pocketing her phone, she went outside. The thick haar of last night had cleared, revealing a sky full of scudding clouds, both dark and light.

She'd gone out first thing to check on the cattle, and seeing them grazing the fresh grass had lifted her spirits a little.

The *Orlova*, sadly, was in view again, floating like a dark blot on the landscape. The ghost ship had switched from being an important investigation to a threat to herself, her family and her friends.

When her work had proved life-threatening in the past, she'd given no thought to her Orcadian family and what they might feel if anything bad happened to her. She'd blithely ignored the danger and did whatever she thought necessary for success.

But back then Mark was with you, a small voice said. His courage and conviction made her stronger.

Plus I never stopped hoping.

Ava now made for the boathouse, picturing herself opening the door to find the *Fear Not* inside and Dougie, having returned during the night, still asleep aboard, something he'd done on numerous occasions before. Why not this time? She began to run, hoping that what she wished for might yet come true.

The closer she got, the more the hope began to dissolve, and she knew before she reached for the door that there would be only emptiness within.

Staring into the darkness, Ava now pictured another future. One in which she'd also lost her brother. The thought almost overwhelmed her and she had to grip the door post to prevent herself from falling.

It was the sound of a vehicle coming down the farm track that roused her from her frightened trance.

From this distance she couldn't tell who it was, although it definitely wasn't a police car. So it probably wasn't news of Dougie. Good or bad.

Steadying herself, Ava set out for the house.

'Ava.' Tommy Flett came striding to meet her. 'I'm sorry

I didn't come over earlier. I've been off the island this past week. Erling's just brought me up to date on what's been happening.'

Erling's father looked a lot like his son, she thought. Their voices too had a similar ring. Quietly spoken, Tommy's Orkney accent was the richer. Ava had loved to listen to him and her father talking together in the kitchen, struggling sometimes to work out exactly what was being said, they'd used so many of the old words and expressions.

'Come away in,' Ava said. 'I'll make us tea – or coffee if you prefer?'

'A mug of tea will do fine,' Tommy said.

Once they were both seated with their tea, Tommy said, 'Any news of Dougie?'

Ava shook her head.

'Well, I wouldn't worry. The boy's had a lot to face recently and, frankly, he's dealt with it remarkably well. Your mum and dad would be proud of you both.' He met her eye. 'Dougie will be back when he's ready. He needs time alone. He'll not come to any harm. The boy can handle his boat in all weathers. Plus he knows these waters like the back of his hand.'

Ava felt a wash of comfort at his words. After all, she reasoned, Tommy had been here more than she had as Dougie had grown into a man.

'Now, I have a proposal to make and I hope you'll think on it, for your sake and the boy's.'

As his words flowed over Ava, it was as though a light had come on at the end of a long dark tunnel. Tommy was proposing that she keep the farm, with his help. He and Dougie would work it together. They could share labour to cut costs. He could rent some of the land if that helped.

'Dougie loves the farming life. He's a born farmer. I've seen it. He just needs a peedie hand to get over this patch. Then it can stay in your family, as your mum and dad would want.'

Tommy was looking at her, trying to judge her response.

'You wouldn't need to stay on here. You could come and go as before. I would keep in touch, speak to you about any decision that needed to be made.'

Ava found herself at a loss for words.

Realizing this, Tommy put his hand on hers. 'Think on it, Ava. That's all I ask. We can talk again when the boy gets back. See what he thinks.'

Ava watched his pickup climb the track to the main road. Was this a way to solve her problem? Dougie wanted her to stay, he'd made that plain enough, but maybe he would go for Tommy's suggestion.

But then Dougie wasn't here . . . and what if he never came home again?

37

When he'd eventually surfaced, he'd found Finn anxiously licking his face. Assuring the dog he was okay, Dougie had dragged himself into a sitting position and gingerly examined his head. It was then he'd seen her. She was sitting with her back against the wall, shining his head torch on him. At that point Finn had gone over and nuzzled her hand, indicating he at least liked her.

For some time following, the girl hadn't spoken except to apologize for hitting him and to say that she had not killed those people in the arena.

Dougie believed her.

Eventually he'd opened his backpack and offered up some food. Passing the kitchens on the way down, he'd noted the smell of rotting food. No doubt she'd kept going on anything tinned she could find.

The bannocks loaded with Orkney cheese proved a hit, even to the point of her fetching the bottle of Polish vodka and two shot glasses.

After that, things had got a little easier, as she decided he wasn't to be feared. Finn helped with that, of course, staying close and allowing himself to be petted.

They'd talked far into the night about how she'd come to be on board the *Orlova*.

Her English was excellent, just like the Polish people who

worked in the fish processing in Stromness, and the frightened way she told her story had convinced Dougie of its truth.

She'd answered an advertisement for a job in Ibiza. As a language student, she was much in demand, they'd explained, since their clientele came from the UK, Russia and beyond.

'It was good at first. A bit wild, you understand? Special parties where women were brought in. I remember hearing gun shots, but I never found out what happened because when I started asking questions they moved me to a cruise ship.'

'The *Orlova*?'

'Not yet. It was on the Med. Smaller, very expensive. Guests arriving by helicopter. I was there to clean, make up beds, that sort of thing. There was gambling, partying, frightened women brought aboard who never left again. I wanted to give up the job, then discovered I couldn't. If I tried to leave they would kill me.'

She'd filled their glasses again at that point, her hands trembling.

'Then one day I was brought here to the *Orlova*. I had the feeling that the ones who were expendable ended up here. If we objected to what was happening here, then we would die.'

Fear had radiated from her body. Dougie had wanted to put his arms about her, tell her she was safe now, but knew he shouldn't.

'They came here to play games. All involved violence. Some death. We knew that, but never saw it happen. Our job was to clear up the mess they left behind. Just before the storm hit, something bad happened. I hid in here and didn't come out until we got to this place.'

'You've been on deck. You've seen the coastline?'

'Only after I couldn't hear anyone else on board.'

'Why didn't you talk to the police?'

'I couldn't take a chance. They would come looking for me.'

The terror on her face had brought fear to his own heart.

'All my friends are dead,' she'd said, as though admitting it for the first time. 'They killed them and threw them overboard. They never thought the ship would be blown ashore. They never thought it would be found.'

Dougie's head was reeling a little from the vodka, but he knew he wouldn't be able to persuade her to give herself up, even to Erling.

But there could be something else she might consider.

He'd told Nadia about his sister. What she did for a living. About her investigation into Go Wild. That Nadia could trust her. She could stay hidden on the farm. No one would know she was there. She could tell her story to Ava. Ava would tell the world. The company would never know where the story had come from.

She'd agreed then to his plan and he'd come up on deck, keen to use his mobile before the charge ran out.

Late afternoon now, they would need to wait until it was dark enough to go ashore.

He sent a text to Ava saying simply that he was fine and would be home soon.

38

It was clear from the number of people gathered, and the display of evidence, that the fire death and the *Orlova* killings had become a joint investigation.

Rhona spotted DS Clark and the two detectives who'd examined the *Orlova* crime scene in the throng of attendees, plus the bespectacled Ollie from IT who McNab favoured. The one person she'd expected to see wasn't there and conspicuous by his absence. Of course, McNab might yet turn up, good timekeeping not being his strong point.

News was that McNab had taken a late booking on the Caledonian Sleeper after a prolonged meeting with the boss the previous evening. Since Chrissy's intelligence was rarely wrong, Rhona suspected he'd gone south with Bill's blessing.

When DI Wilson appeared stage front, the din quickly diminished, leaving an expectant silence. He began with an acknowledgement that it was now believed that the Glasgow and Orkney cases were linked via a company called Go Wild. Something DS McNab and DS Clark had established. DS McNab was currently following up this link, hence his absence, and DS Clark would give them an update.

Janice appeared beside him.

'We have not yet verified our fire victim as Londoner Olivia Newton Richardson, although credit cards in that name were discovered with the body,' she said. 'However, it has been established that Ms Richardson ran a holiday company, which has links with Go Wild. Go Wild has also been involved with the staging of illegal bare-knuckle fights in Glasgow and elsewhere. Something DS McNab encountered first-hand,' she told them.

There was a ripple of laughter from those who'd obviously viewed McNab's face.

She continued, 'Since then, it has also been established that the MV *Orlova*, which was washed ashore on the west of Orkney during the recent Storm Birka, was operating as a cruise ship under the ownership of Go Wild. So we currently have four suspicious deaths associated with this company. We have not, as yet, identified any of the victims.'

When Bill gave her a nod, Rhona knew she was up soon.

'Most of you will be familiar with the facts surrounding the fire death,' Bill said, taking over from Janice. 'Dr MacLeod and her team also examined the *Orlova* crime scenes and recently attended the autopsies on the three recovered bodies. DI Flett from Kirkwall, who took charge of the *Orlova*, joins us online while we look at the images from the ship and hear what was found there.'

Most of those in the room were new to the scenes now appearing on the screen. The arena and maze were shown from above in a short video, which also featured the sudden explosion of sound from the virtual audience, while Erling gave a brief résumé of the initial boarding of the ship to discover what looked like a mutual death by combat.

'It became clear,' Erling said, 'that the arena games were being played out using a mix of the real and the virtual. The equipment controlling this is now with you in Glasgow.'

Rhona took over then to begin with the first locus, explaining what she and her assistant, Chrissy McInsh, had concluded from the computer room, now confirmed at post-mortem.

'Although appearing initially to be a possible electrocution, the deceased was dead by suffocation before the fire, which was probably started in an attempt to destroy the equipment.

'The other two deaths were from exsanguination following major injuries caused not by the small swords you can see at the scene, but by a longer, sharper blade, not yet located, and wielded by a third party. Evidence of cuts to the arms and legs by the smaller weapons suggest the couple did in fact initially fight to draw blood.

'Near the bodies we found a pool of vomit. We cannot age vomit other than to say it's fresh or that it's dried out a bit, meaning it's probably older. What we can do is compare the contents of the vomit with the stomach contents of the deceased.

'The vomit contained evidence of a recent meal of beans and hot dog sausages. The last meal consumed by the victims consisted of steak with mushrooms and cut chips, eaten probably less than four hours before death, potentially less than two hours.' Rhona paused before making her next comment, aware of the reaction it would bring. 'We estimate the deaths to have happened approximately three to five days before we examined the bodies. However, we think the vomit may have happened after that, which could suggest someone was still alive on board after the deaths of the three victims.'

There was an outbreak of discussion about this as Erling came in. 'You think someone might have been present on the ship during the storm?'

'It's possible, yes. As you saw, the fresh food was already rotting and the power was turned off on the freezers. Tinned food and alcohol were, however, still available.'

'We searched the ship thoroughly after we boarded her,' Erling said, 'but if there was someone on board who was familiar with the layout, they could have escaped the search.'

'Might they have come ashore once it was anchored in Houton Bay?' Bill asked.

'The sea stayed rough in the aftermath of Storm Birka, even in Scapa Flow. Plus the water's currently around eight degrees,' Erling said. 'A seasoned swimmer might cope with rough seas and a low water temperature, but they'd have to find shelter quickly if they were to make it to shore.'

Bill came back in. 'Let's take another look at the *Orlova* and question the locals in case we've missed something.'

Next up was Ollie with a map of all the countries he believed Go Wild might be working in and how they publicized their games.

'There are an estimated 2.7 billion gamers across the globe. And embedding subliminal links to advertise real death games provided by companies such as Go Wild is a huge money-making exercise.'

He brought up a sample advert for such a gaming holiday, emphasizing the way in which participants might physically engage via virtual software to fight, maim or kill an opponent, supplied by Go Wild at a cost.

'Their guarantee is that there will be no comeback, whatever the level you participate at. DS McNab got his injuries by stepping in to stop a fight he believed might result in death.'

There was a murmur from the crowd. Now McNab's injuries didn't seem so amusing.

'Have we ID'd either of the fighters?' a voice asked from the floor.

'We're working on it,' DS Wilson told him.

As the crowd dispersed, Bill waved Rhona over.

'We need to talk,' he said, ushering her into his office and closing the door. 'McNab told me about your meeting with Ava Clouston.'

'He mentioned what she said about DI Cleverly?' Rhona immediately asked.

She could tell by Bill's expression that the name hadn't come up in their conversation.

'What about Cleverly?' Bill asked.

Rhona couldn't lie, not to Bill. 'Ava said that Mark Sylvester, her colleague, wanted us warned that the detective the Met sent up wasn't to be trusted.'

Bill gave a half-smile at that. 'McNab managed to convey his concerns about some of the Met's non-cooperation on this without pointing the finger at anyone in particular.'

'He's gone to London?'

'Ah, I see the McInsh telegraph's been at work,' Bill said. 'We're keen to know what the hold-up on the fire victim's ID is all about. The Met seem to be hampering that. I suspect it's because there are a number of high-profile names on Go Wild's books, so we need to tread carefully on this one. We have no intention of allowing this investigation to be taken out of our hands. Let me know if you receive any requests to share forensic evidence outwith Police Scotland.' He added, 'I'm assuming you're in touch with Ava Clouston?'

Rhona nodded.

'If she reveals anything else or asks any questions, let me know. McNab's due back tomorrow morning. Things might be clearer by then.'

39

The white, two-storey terraced houses, with pillared entrances, appeared even more upmarket than Mark's impressive red-brick mansion, McNab decided. Ollie had indicated that Ms Richardson's flat was on the first floor.

Pressing the doorbell, and not expecting an answer, McNab was surprised when he got one.

'Yes?' a male voice said.

'Detective Sergeant McNab, Police Scotland, here to see Ms Richardson.'

There was a studied silence, while whoever had answered absorbed this information, then the voice said brusquely, 'I'm afraid Ms Richardson is away on business.'

'I'd still like to come in, sir.' McNab's tone didn't brook a refusal.

'Do you have ID?'

'Of course.'

A moment later, the door buzzed open.

The mosaic-tiled entrance hall led to a set of stairs, at the bottom of which stood a man, who looked to be in his fifties. He wore a slightly haughty expression.

'As I said, Ms Richardson is away on business,' he repeated as though McNab was slightly deaf.

'May I ask who you are, sir?' McNab said.

'Henry Wollstone. I live on the ground floor. Ms Richardson is the upstairs tenant.'

McNab proffered his ID. 'Can you tell me when you last saw Ms Richardson?'

Mr Wollstone thought about that for a moment, then, shrugging his shoulders, said, 'She's away a lot. Maybe a week ago.'

'Then I'd like to check Ms Richardson's flat.'

McNab had fully expected the man to mention the Met somewhere in their conversation, but it didn't look as though he planned to.

'Has something happened to Olivia?' he said instead, looking worried.

'That's what we're trying to establish, sir.'

'But why Police Scotland?'

'Because Ms Richardson's handbag and wallet were found in Glasgow.'

'Glasgow! Why on earth would Olivia be in Glasgow?' He sounded genuinely surprised.

'That's what I'm here to hopefully find out, sir. If you could let me check her flat now?'

McNab followed the man up the stairs, his mind already working on the fact that it appeared no one from the Met had been here. Which probably meant they already knew the fire victim wasn't Olivia Newton Richardson and possibly had done all along.

So why had Cleverly come to Glasgow, attended the PM and demanded facial recognition software be used to identify the victim?

'There you are.' Mr Wollstone threw open the door, allowing McNab to enter, then attempted to follow him inside.

'You can wait on the landing, Mr Wollstone, or I can call you when I'm ready to leave,' McNab said firmly.

He expected a possible argument and was relieved when the man's only reaction was a disgruntled look.

As soon as he heard footsteps descending the stairs, McNab closed the door. Despite the classical nature of the building's exterior, in here was open-plan and modern, a sitting area with a study at one end, a kitchen at the other.

The place felt and smelt as though no one had been in here recently. There were a few dishes in the sink and a half-empty bottle of Polish vodka sitting on a coffee table, two shot glasses beside it, both used, one with a lipstick imprint.

There was no laptop in the study area and no paper evidence of any work done there.

The bedroom was a mess. Not that different from Mark's. Clothes and shoes scattered about. Wardrobe open. A space above that may have held a suitcase.

The bed was rumpled, the duvet thrown back, the bottom sheet stained by what might be semen. It was then he saw the photograph. The frame had been turned over next to the bed. On purpose or by accident, he couldn't tell.

Olivia and a man, cheek to cheek, smiling at the camera. With a start, McNab realized where he'd seen the man before. Only then, he'd been bare-chested, his fists up.

It appeared the man who'd put his lights out in Glasgow and Olivia Newton Richardson knew one another very well.

McNab bagged the shot glasses, then went in search of alternative sources of DNA, the bathroom providing a couple of toothbrushes, a hairbrush and a discarded earring.

Hearing the front door being opened, he concealed his booty and went to greet Mr Wollstone.

'All finished here, thank you.'

'Did you find anything that might help locate Olivia?'

McNab ignored the question and asked one of his own. 'I take it the Met haven't been here as yet?'

Mr Wollstone's face fell. 'The Met are involved too?'

'I'd expect them to visit soon,' McNab said, although he believed otherwise.

Out on the street now, he pulled out his mobile and rang Cleverly's number.

The voice that answered was gruff and distinctly unwelcoming. McNab decided to make things even worse.

'I'm in London. We need to talk.'

40

As the moon escaped the clouds again, Dougie urged Nadia to lie down at his feet rather than sit in the bow. They were coming within sight of the shore, and there was always a chance of being spotted by someone out late in the fields.

The girl was shivering, either from fear or cold. He couldn't blame her. His own heart had been racing ever since he'd urged her from her hiding place to cross the slippery decks. She'd frozen at the sight of the ladder and it had struck him that she was as fearful of ending up in the sea as she was of being discovered.

He'd spoken encouragingly to her as he'd put an unprotesting Finn in his harness and begun lowering the collie onto the boat.

'Now us,' he'd told her as he'd roped her to him. 'I'll go first and then you follow. Don't look down, but even if you do, you'll only see my face smiling up at you.'

She'd relaxed a little at that, the fear in her eyes diminishing.

The descent had taken longer than he'd wanted, conscious as he was that the gradual turning of the *Orlova* at anchor would soon expose them to anyone who might be watching from the shore. The periodic unveiling of a bright, almost full moon only increased his concern, but he couldn't let Nadia see that. So every time she stopped, seemingly frozen to the ladder, he'd spoken calmly, telling her they would soon be on dry land and in the warmth of the farm kitchen. That she could have hot buttered bannocks with bacon and fresh eggs from the hens.

He had no idea if she'd heard or understood his wittering, anxiety strengthening his Orkney accent, but eventually she got close enough for him to grab her by the waist and ease her aboard the *Fear Not*.

Feeling Nadia shiver now against his legs as a squally shower added to the sea spray hitting the boat, he ordered Finn to get down beside her, which the collie did, pushing his warm body into her arms.

In sight of the slipway now, Dougie watched as the moon slid behind a cloud, plunging them into shadow once more.

'It's okay,' he told a silent Nadia, 'I know my way in the dark.'

Seconds later, he felt the bow scrape against the slipway. The tide, he knew, was well in, so they were very close to the boathouse. Finn, familiar with the routine, jumped out, Dougie following, before holding out a hand to help Nadia.

He was shocked at how cold her hand was and realized he had to get her into the warmth, and soon. She scrambled onto the slipway and waited while he drew the boat up and secured it.

Dougie's plan was to stop at the barn, get Nadia settled in the warmth of the hay, then approach the house alone to talk to Ava.

He explained this to Nadia as he opened the barn door. 'You'll be safe here,' he told her. 'I won't be long.' Worried about her low temperature, he told Finn to stay with her to keep her warm.

Once he saw them settled, he apologized for leaving her there. 'Don't go outside. Finn will stay with you until I whistle for him. Okay?'

She nodded, the whites of her eyes barely visible in the gloom.

As Dougie walked swiftly towards the house, he saw a pair of lights turn off the main road to make their way down to the farm. He held his breath as he realized that it looked like a police car.

Had Ava got his message and called Erling?

Dougie mustered himself. He would return home as promised. *But what of Finn?* he thought. *Won't Ava think it odd that he's not with me?*

He contemplated whistling for the dog, then decided against it. Nadia might get freaked or follow Finn out, assuming it was safe and he was summoning her. Better to have an excuse for the missing Finn, he decided.

By the time he reached the house, the police car was parked and the driver already inside. Dougie took a deep breath and, before he could change his mind, opened the door and walked into the kitchen.

41

McNab was still seething when he walked into the Afghan coffee shop. Having just wasted an hour waiting for Cleverly to show up at an agreed location, he was in no mood to be thwarted a second time.

The guy behind the counter listened to his demand with an openly hostile look, which McNab duly returned. He wasn't the only one in the cafe throwing him dirty looks. In fact, it was a little like walking into a Rangers' pub wearing a Celtic top on the day of an Old Firm match.

'Tell Mark McNab's here to see him. And I'm in a hurry.'

The dark look only got darker. McNab could see where all this was heading and the result would be a refashioning of his face again.

'Tell him Ava sent me,' he added as a last resort.

At Ava's name, something changed. The guy looked less likely to punch him or throw him out. McNab decided to take that line a little further.

'Tell Mark Ava's in danger.'

'Sit down,' the voice said, gesturing to a nearby table.

Thinking he might be getting somewhere at last, McNab chanced his arm and asked for a coffee, the scent of which had been assailing him since he'd walked in the door.

He duly took a seat, aware that whatever interest the

circle of other male customers had had in him had lost its edge. His face, it seemed, wasn't about to meet another fist.

Five minutes later, the coffee arrived, delivered by counter guy, but with no invitation to come and see Mark. McNab threw another glance at the curtained doorway, which he presumed led to more private accommodation and through which counter guy had gone earlier.

Drinking the remainder of his coffee, he ordered another, which didn't arrive. In fact, everyone was now doing a fine job of pretending he didn't exist. Either the journalist was here or he wasn't, McNab decided, and there was only one way to find out which.

Ava had said he had a room here where he worked and sometimes slept, and to McNab's eye it had to be beyond that curtain. He rose and made for the Gents just long enough for counter guy to clock him and turn away. Then he made his break.

A warning shout followed him beyond the drapes, down a corridor towards a door. McNab reached it before his pursuer caught up. He flung it open, stepped inside and shut it behind him, just as a shoulder slammed it.

A tall figure rose from behind a desk. 'DS McNab? I wondered when you'd decide to come through.'

Counter guy, in now, fired something unintelligible at the man, and was duly ordered out in English together with a request for more coffee. 'My visitor looks like he needs one.'

He waved McNab to a seat and introduced himself.

'Apologies for the wait. My Afghan friends take my security very seriously. They didn't like the look of you.' He paused. 'You said Ava was in danger. Is that true?'

'You weren't answering her messages. She told me you

might be here. She asked if I would check up on you,' McNab told him.

'So here I am. Alive and well. What about you?' He gestured to McNab's facial bruising, which matched his own.

'A little argument at a bare-knuckle fight.'

Mark looked interested. 'So they're on offer in Glasgow too. Any names?'

McNab didn't answer. If an exchange of information was expected, he wasn't going to be the one to go first.

'You told Ava to warn me about Cleverly. Why?' he said instead.

Mark sat back in his chair. 'The Met don't want me investigating Go Wild. In fact, they're trying to stop me. I suspect they're doing the same with Police Scotland.' He eyed McNab. 'Am I right?'

McNab didn't answer.

'You're planning to meet with the Met while you're down here?' he said.

When McNab still didn't respond, Mark gave a little laugh. 'The girl in Glasgow is not Olivia Newton Richardson. But hey, you knew that already.'

'Who was she?' McNab demanded.

'My guess? A trafficked female supplied by Go Wild for one of their games.'

'And the handbag?'

Mark shrugged. 'You're the detective, not me.' Reading McNab's expression, he added, 'You've checked out Olivia's flat? Any sign of the Met having been there?' When McNab said nothing, he looked thoughtful again. 'What did you remove for DNA sampling?'

McNab thought about the glasses and the Polish vodka display.

'If someone wants you to believe the dead girl is Olivia, then you'll get a match from the flat with your fire girl. If not . . .'

He gave a half-smile, before adding, 'Even you, as a police officer, cannot imagine the kind of cover stories those in authority can cook up, even when you yourself know the real truth.'

McNab thought of Mr Wollstone. The ease with which he'd allowed McNab to enter. The likelihood that the Met had never been there. The whole scenario had screamed 'wrong' at him. Then that photo of Olivia with the posh fucker who'd been in Glasgow around the time of the storm. Maybe the missing Olivia had been there with him?

He tried to bring up an image of the fight room. The audience had been mostly men, but there had been females too. He cursed himself for not registering them properly.

If he hadn't been knocked out cold, he would have likely seen the posh fucker leave with one of them on his arm, and that one might have been the real Olivia.

Coming back to the present, he found the journalist studying him.

'My interpretation? Cleverly was sent north to check out your moves on the fire death because they believe a high-profile bastard was involved in the torture and death of the victim,' he said. 'As for the *Orlova* coming ashore on Orkney, thus involving Police Scotland even further in what the Met see as their case . . .' He made a face. 'My bet is you'll shortly be getting requests, which are really demands, to send south all evidence relating to the investigation into Go Wild. In the interests of national security, of course, which supersedes everything.'

42

Dusk had settled over the park, with a clear sky and the prospect of a full moon. The call from Bill had come as she'd headed down the path from the university, having decided to go home rather than to the jazz club.

Which was just as well, since what he'd had to say meant that she was headed back to Orkney next morning and would have to pack again.

'Give Erling a call,' Bill had told her. 'He'll give you the full story.'

Opening her front door, Rhona was greeted with some enthusiasm by Tom, which only lasted until she'd checked his dish and replenished the contents. After which food became much more interesting than she ever could be.

Rhona extracted a ready meal from the freezer and put it in the microwave, then poured herself a glass of wine and set about calling Erling.

'I take it DI Wilson told you what's happened?' he said after the usual greetings.

'Only what was required to get me to agree on a return trip tomorrow.'

'The body was discovered this evening. A male, probably in his twenties. We had to move him further up the shore because of the tide. We've covered him but the wind's up, so no tent. D'you want us to move him to the mortuary?'

'It's better if I see him in situ first,' Rhona said.

'He's dressed like a waiter, so we think he may be off the *Orlova*.' Erling answered the next question before she could ask it. 'I don't think by the state of the body that he's been long in the water.'

Erling would have pulled enough folk from the sea over the years to be a reasonable judge of that.

'Any obvious wounds?'

'Not on his back and I haven't turned him over as yet.'

She heard a hesitancy in his voice. 'But?' she encouraged him.

'I think there's a neck wound, but I can only see a little of it.'

'I'll be up at first light,' Rhona promised. 'Where is the body exactly?'

'I'll send you a location reference and you can take a look. It's on a beach near the Broch o' Borwick, just north of Yesnaby. The helicopter should be able to land you nearby. I'll meet you there,' he promised. 'Oh, and we plan to check out the *Orlova* again tomorrow at first light. See if we can find anything that might fit your theory of a possible stowaway.'

Rhona rang off and, fetching her laptop, waited for the incoming arrival of the map reference. Her previous caseload in Orkney had seen her called to the Ring of Brodgar and, of course, Sanday, but she'd only boarded the *Orlova* once it had been towed into Scapa Flow. The cliffs at Yesnaby, where it had come aground, she hadn't yet seen.

Opening the map, she noted that the area lay about a half-mile from the Yesnaby car park. It wasn't far north of Stromness, although the main road that ran along the Loch of Stenness gave way to smaller farm routes leading in the direction Erling had indicated.

Online, photos of the bay showed it as slated stone and gravel with a layer of sand closest to the fields. Which definitely looked flat enough to land a helicopter.

Fetching her food from the microwave, she refilled her glass and settled down to eat. A series of incoming emails from Erling offered a set of initial flashlight photographs taken at the scene, to give her context. The body in the first set was in its original position lying below the high-water mark.

He was on his front, head turned to the right. Dark skinned, with close-cropped black hair, he was wearing a light-coloured shirt, black trousers and shoes. The images were of a high resolution, but lighting had obviously been a factor in the quality of the resulting photographs.

The second set had been taken in his new position above the waterline. They'd managed to maintain the pose and it was obvious they'd moved him just enough to not be encroached on by the incoming tide.

Studying the images at closer quarters, Rhona was inclined to agree with Erling's conclusion that the body hadn't been long in the sea. Cold water slowed decomposition and the water round Orkney was cold enough to do that.

Daylight would begin early tomorrow, so the sooner she could arrive to view the scene in reality, the better.

Setting her phone alarm for the morning, she realized she had a missed call from McNab's number. She contemplated calling back, then decided against it. Bill would explain where she was and why, and if McNab had managed to collect evidence for DNA analysis, Chrissy was there to start processing it.

Still, it seemed ironic that McNab would arrive back in Glasgow just as she left again for Orkney.

Packed and ready, Rhona climbed into bed and, glancing at the time, realized there was little sleep to be had between now and take-off.

43

Glasgow was well known for rain in all its forms . . . from a penetrating drizzle to the full 'stoating down' version. What he hadn't realized was that it could stoat down in London too.

McNab had attempted to stay dry by standing just inside the allotted Underground exit, but the crowds of people trying to get past him were pissing him off even further. Why would Cleverly choose a busy place like Leicester Square to meet if it wasn't designed to punish him for coming to London in the first place?

When the Met officer had eventually called him back, he'd apologized about the earlier misunderstanding, saying he'd been held up at work. 'You know how it is, Sergeant?'

McNab had known it was a lie, but he'd kept his temper in check and asked for an alternative meeting place and time.

He checked his watch again, knowing it was barely past the time he'd last looked at it. It was also fast approaching the hour when he would need to start thinking about making his way back across London to Euston and the overnight train home.

Scanning the crowds again, he finally spotted Cleverly approaching – or thought he did. McNab stepped out into the pouring rain. At that moment the bustling crowd surrounded him and he almost lost sight of the detective. He halted, checked again and spied him. He imagined Cleverly had spotted him too because he raised his hand in recognition.

Just as McNab acknowledged his presence, Cleverly appeared to change his mind, turning to duck into a nearby doorway.

Almost simultaneously, McNab felt the sharp point of a blade in his lower back angled towards his kidney. 'Get in,' a voice said, forcing the point in deeper. 'Or you're dead where you stand.'

He had seen the result of enough knife attacks to know that the threat was real enough. Better alive in the back of the van than bleeding out on the pavement.

The dark interior got even darker as a black bag was thrust over his head. He couldn't see his attackers, but he could still scream abuse at them. Until the needle was plunged into his neck.

'Shut the fuck up, Jock pig' was the last thing he heard before his world collapsed and all the angry words died in his throat.

44

'Why was Erling really here?' Dougie said when the car drove away. 'Was it about me? I told you I was coming home, didn't I?'

Dougie's sudden arrival with Erling there had been awkward, although she'd been overjoyed to see him home again. Erling, perhaps sensing this, had simply welcomed Dougie with a smile, and made a swift departure.

'His dad came round earlier to offer you help with running the farm. Erling was talking to me about that.'

Dougie's expression changed from anger to one of surprise. 'Is that possible?'

'We're definitely going to talk it over with him,' Ava said, glad she had some good news at least. She stopped there, struck by something. 'Where's Finn?'

'Outside,' Dougie said.

His face clouded over again and she thought maybe the collie was hurt in some way. 'Is something wrong with Finn?'

'No,' he said sharply. 'I have something to show you.'

Ava's immediate thought was he'd found another dead cow, but when she asked, he shook his head impatiently and beckoned her outside.

'Where are we going?'

'The byre.'

Dougie led the way, moving so quickly that Ava had to almost run to keep up with him. He'd put on his head torch and the beam bounced along the muddy track before them like a runaway ball. Ava's brain was racing with thoughts of what it might be that was so mysterious. None of her imaginings were good.

Now at the barn, he threw open the door. 'It's me, Finn,' he called.

The dog gave a little welcome bark and jumped up from the hay where he'd been lying.

It was then Ava saw the girl, her eyes blinking in the sudden light. Ava was aware she was staring, open-mouthed, but couldn't help it. Had Dougie found the girl here? If so, how long had she been in the barn and who was she?

She turned to Dougie, hoping her startled expression asked all those questions.

'Her name's Nadia,' he said. 'She's from the *Orlova*.'

Before she could comment, or even absorb this, he continued, 'She's a witness to what happened there. If the men from Go Wild find out she's alive, they'll come looking for her and kill her like the others.'

The girl had said nothing, her teeth chattering from cold and, Ava suspected, fear.

Dougie rushed on. 'I told her you're trying to expose Go Wild. I told her you would help. She'll give you her story. Once you publish it, she'll be safe,' he said, his expression determined and pleading at the same time.

The girl was staring up at her, like a rabbit frozen by oncoming headlights.

If she was the only witness to what had happened on that ship, then what Dougie had just said was true. Whatever she thought of the danger to Mark or herself from investigating Go Wild, it was nothing in comparison to the girl's possible fate.

She reached out to draw the shivering girl to her feet. 'Let's get you up to the house. Don't be frightened. You'll be safe here with us.'

Once they were inside, Ava locked the door. 'Although,' she said, to assure the girl, 'Finn always lets us know of approaching visitors. Plus we can see the headlights of any car that turns onto our road.' She urged Nadia to the seat next to the stove. 'Come on, let's get you warmed up, then we'll get some food into you.'

'I promised her warm bannocks with bacon,' Dougie said, his face flushed with relief.

'Then bannocks and bacon it is,' Ava said, welcoming the chance to do something practical.

The girl hadn't yet uttered a word. With a name like that, might she be foreign? Ava wondered what age she was, where she'd come from and why she'd been on the ship in the first place. But she knew those questions would have to wait for now.

'Tea, coffee or something stronger?' Ava said. 'I have beer or Orkney gin?'

Seeing the girl's reaction to the word gin, Ava immediately fetched the bottle and, pouring two shots, handed her one. They downed them together, almost like a toast. Ava topped up their glasses again, pleased to see some colour coming into the girl's cheeks.

'Now we eat,' she said.

Devouring the spread Ava set out before them prevented conversation for a while. Ava noted it was the most enthused she'd seen Dougie about food since she'd returned home. Up to now, his habit had been to take any meal she'd prepared to consume alone in his room.

As the plates were cleared, Ava suggested Nadia should

head for bed. 'I'll take you up and show you where everything is. We can talk properly in the morning.'

The girl glanced at Dougie, who nodded his encouragement. 'Finn will come with you. Keep you company.'

The girl smiled her thanks, then turned to Ava. 'You won't tell anyone I'm here? Please.' They were the first words she'd uttered, and the fear in them was obvious.

'I won't. I promise,' Ava said.

Dougie looked up as Ava arrived back in the kitchen. 'You can't tell Erling she's here. No one must know. No one,' he stressed, his face determined.

Ava fetched her mobile and set it to record. 'Tell me about the *Orlova*. Tell me everything.'

The story poured out of him, like a tide rushing to shore. His trip first to the bay on Hoy, then out to the ship. His fear on the ladder, then finding the bloodstains where the bodies had lain. The terrible smell of burnt flesh that lingered in the computer room. He'd halted briefly at that point, his eyes haunted.

He told her how Finn had led him down to the bowels of the ship where they'd discovered the cell-like room she'd been living in. Her initial attack as he'd broken into her hideout, then Finn showing her that they weren't going to hurt her.

'We drank Polish vodka and ate the remainder of the food I'd taken from home,' Dougie said. 'That's how I persuaded her down the ladder and into the boat. I promised her warm bannocks and bacon.'

His face broke into a tentative smile. Something Ava hadn't seen in a long time.

'You'll record what Nadia tells you tomorrow? I'm certain there's more to her story.'

215

Ava realized he believed in the girl . . . totally. She wanted to do that too, but in her job you couldn't just accept everything someone told you. There was no questioning Nadia's fear of being found, but why be so afraid of being found by the police? Why was Erling a threat?

The girl had told Dougie she was a virtual prisoner on the *Orlova*, yet she'd been working for Go Wild for a while. Had she entered their employment willingly? What had they asked her to do for them during that time?

'What?' Dougie said, catching her expression.

Ava forced a reassuring smile. 'Nothing really. Let's talk in the morning. Nadia's safe. You're safe. That all that matters for tonight.'

When Dougie went upstairs, Ava poured herself another gin. Having held her emotions in check since Dougie's safe return, she now allowed herself to face them head on.

She'd promised not to reveal Nadia's existence. *Promised.* How could she keep her word without being on the wrong side of the law? The girl was a possible witness to murder and the workings of the company she was currently investigating.

If only I could talk this over with Mark.

The huge hole she'd made in both her personal and professional life by walking out on their relationship gaped open in front of her. She recalled his beaten face, his determination to pursue Go Wild, even if he was being watched by the Met.

He told me to come home, while he stayed in the firing line.

The dilemma she was in stared back at her. She desperately wanted to tell the girl's story. What a scoop that would be. Her editor would never turn it down, despite his reservations about Mark. But if she did that, Erling, Magnus, Rhona, everyone who'd been involved in the Orkney part of the story, would know she'd broken the law or, at the very least, defied it.

Taking a deep breath, she picked up her mobile and, saying a silent prayer, dialled Mark's number again, only to hear the same grating message signifying an unknown number. The short and pleading email she then sent, asking Mark to get in touch as it was an emergency, bounced back almost immediately. Mark had disappeared off her radar and there was no way of reaching him.

Despair swamped her. She gave it time to ebb and flow, then re-emerged to try an alternative. She would have to be careful what she said to the Glasgow detective, but she could at least check if he'd succeeded in making contact with Mark.

Bringing up McNab's name, Ava pressed the call button.

45

They were over the cliffs at Yesnaby now. Rhona had spent most of the flight across the Highlands studying the photographs from last night, keeping her mind off the fact she was up in the sky with only a rotary blade keeping her there.

Interspersed had been the co-pilot's enquiry as to why Chrissy wasn't with her this time.

'Too much work to do in Glasgow,' she'd told him.

'She's an enthusiastic flyer,' he'd said, somewhat wistfully.

'Chrissy's enthusiastic about most things,' she'd assured him.

'A busy love life too?'

'Usually.'

'So I'd have to stand in line?'

'Chrissy likes being pursued,' Rhona had offered as way of encouragement.

There were a few moments of thoughtful silence before he drew her attention to where they now were.

'There's where the *Orlova* came ashore.' He indicated a series of jagged cliff faces, frothed by crashing waves. 'It was some job getting personnel on board and then towing the ghost ship into Scapa Flow.'

Rhona could see what he meant.

'Your bay is just ahead. After that's the bigger Skaill Bay and the Neolithic Skara Brae settlement. Magic place.'

They were dropping towards green fields and grazing

cattle. Rhona spotted a row of police vehicles parked along a farm track and someone waving up at them. It appeared Erling was there as promised.

Minutes later she thanked the crew and, dipping her head, walked towards his tall figure.

'You're back,' he said with a smile. 'Although I wish it was under better circumstances.'

'All in a day's work,' Rhona said. 'But the scenery always helps.'

He pointed the way ahead. 'It'll take ten minutes or so to walk there.'

'I'm glad to have my feet on solid ground again,' Rhona assured him.

Erling brought her up to date as she got kitted up. How a local farmer had spotted what looked like a body on the beach late yesterday afternoon and called it in.

'I'd been expecting a body to turn up from the *Orlova*,' he admitted. 'And I don't think it'll be the last, although the tide might deposit them elsewhere on the islands.' He went on, 'The beach we're heading for is easily accessible. If the body had been spotted at the bottom of the cliffs it would have been another matter.'

'So nothing like Kilt Rock,' she said. 'That's good.'

'The weather's set to stay breezy and dry, but the light will start to go by nine o'clock,' Erling said as they reached the beach. 'Just give us a shout should you need anything.'

The seashore was small and curved, tucked between two headlands. The great slabs of rock that Orkney was famed for framed it with shingle and sand layers between. Here the air was ripe with the smell of seaweed, fresh and rotting, while clouds of small flies rose to follow her as she walked towards the cordoned-off area.

Stepping across the tape, Rhona approached the tarpaulin and carefully drew it back.

The young black male lay on his front, his head to one side, partially exposing his right cheek. The images taken last night in fading light had been, she acknowledged, a poor substitute for seeing the real thing.

Her first thought was that the sea had been kind to him, the low water temperature delaying bacterial action on his body until he'd reached the shore at least. His back hadn't been feasted on by fish. Nor had the rocks of Orkney battered and broken his skin. In fact, in this position he looked virtually intact, apart from the wound just visible on the right side of his neck.

Rhona tilted his head a little for a better view. Even at this angle you could see his neck had been sliced with a sharp implement, the wound most likely stretching from ear to ear.

Often it wasn't possible to distinguish injuries inflicted before a body entered the water from those inflicted afterwards, by rocks, sea creatures or even boat propellers. Not in this case, though.

Turning the head a little had also exposed the GW insignia on the shirt collar. If there had been any doubt that the body had come from the *Orlova*, there was no longer.

By the time she'd requested help with turning him over, the wind had strengthened, indicating that any tent they might have erected wouldn't have stayed upright for long. The light, however, had remained as promised, allowing her the opportunity to study the victim face on.

The frontal evidence of feeding had been more obvious, his eyes partially consumed, the soft fleshy lips nibbled on, as well as general feasting at the knife wound.

When she'd completed her examination, four officers had helped lift the waterlogged remains onto a stretcher and carried it up to the waiting van, just as the sky was welcoming the advancing dusk.

'Well timed,' Erling said as they walked to his vehicle. 'Even in Orkney, the day ends eventually. Now if it had been midsummer . . .'

'I remember it well,' Rhona said with a smile.

'How long do you want at the mortuary?'

'Just enough time to bag his clothing and photograph and tape the unclothed body. He'll get a full forensic examination at the PM.'

'I've had a report back from the second search of the *Orlova*,' Erling told her. 'They found a hidden room in the hold, possibly created for drug smuggling, where someone had obviously been living. Looks like you were right, someone might have been there when we searched before. I assume you'll want a look in the morning?'

She would, Rhona told him.

Her mobile rang just short of Kirkwall. Answering it, she found Bill keen to know how the day had gone. Rhona gave him a brief résumé of the recovery of the beach body, plus Erling's latest find on the *Orlova*.

'So you'll check out the ship tomorrow?'

Rhona assured him she would, before asking, 'How did McNab get on in London?'

There was a short but pregnant silence, before Bill said, 'McNab wasn't on this morning's sleeper and we can't reach him. DCI Sutherland has been in touch with the Met. It appears McNab arranged to meet DI Cleverly in central London, but never turned up.'

46

The smell of frying bacon met her on the way downstairs. Ava hesitated before entering the kitchen, knowing Dougie would be keen to engage her in a further conversation about Nadia.

After they'd both gone to bed, she'd sat up well into the night, trying to find if the name Nadia Kowalski occurred in any of the Go Wild literature she'd assembled, or anywhere in the material given to her by Mark. Both searches had drawn a blank.

Despite all her brother's assurances, his pleadings not to inform the authorities of Nadia's existence, Ava still had misgivings. Something she would have to face up to today.

'Hope you're hungry,' Dougie greeted her. 'I've cooked loads.'

Ava made a point of fetching a plate and pouring herself coffee, waiting for Dougie to start the expected conversation. Eventually he did.

'You want to tell Erling about Nadia?' he said, apparently reading her thoughts.

Ava didn't answer right away, mentally choosing the words. Aware no matter what she said, it would be wrong.

'Someone's been attacking our cattle. I think it may be because of my investigation of Go Wild. It might not be safe for Nadia to stay here.'

Dougie shook his head vehemently. 'The cows have nothing to do with the *Orlova*.'

'How can you know that?' Ava said.

'I just do.' His mouth formed a stubborn line.

'That's not enough, Dougie. Not nearly enough. You bring a girl here that the police will undoubtedly be looking for—'

He cut her off. 'They have no idea she was on the ship. They searched it and didn't find her.' His voice rose to a higher pitch.

'What do you know about our cattle?' Ava demanded, the terrible thought replaying that Dougie might have killed them to keep her there.

He was avoiding her eyes, hesitating, as though he couldn't say the words. Eventually they emerged quietly through gritted teeth.

'I pissed a bloke off. Didn't pay him for dope. He did it to threaten me.'

Ava stared at him in disbelief. 'If that's true, you have to tell Erling.'

'Fucking Erling. He's your answer to everything.'

At that point they heard Nadia's footsteps on the stairs.

'Do what you promised,' Dougie hissed at her. 'And if you breathe a word about her to Erling, I'm out of here for good.'

If Nadia had heard any of their exchange, she didn't show it on entry. Dougie immediately jumped up and offered her some breakfast, asking if she'd slept well.

Ava attempted a smile too. There was no point freaking the girl out any further than she obviously was already.

'After breakfast, I want to tell you my story,' Nadia said, her voice determined. 'Before anything happens to me.'

Ava felt a surge of guilt in case she'd heard them arguing.

'You're safe here, Nadia. We won't let anything happen to you,' she tried.

'You don't know these people. They're everywhere, even in the police, and they're very powerful. I've seen what they are capable of.'

They all jumped as Ava's phone suddenly buzzed loudly on the tabletop.

'It's Erling,' she said, reading the screen. She hesitated, wondering whether she should let it go to voicemail.

'Answer it,' Dougie ordered.

Ava drew the phone towards her. 'Erling, hi. How are things?' She listened in studied silence, trying to form suitable replies to what he was telling her without alerting her audience to the horror of it. 'Okay. I'll see you then.'

'What?' Dougie demanded as soon as she ended the call.

'Dr MacLeod is back on Orkney. Magnus has invited me to have dinner with her and Erling at Houton tonight.'

Dougie's alarmed reaction matched her own. 'Why is *she* back?'

'A body came ashore, they think from the *Orlova*. An unidentified black male.'

Nadia's face drained of all colour as she sank to a chair. 'It's Guido,' she said. 'They threw him overboard.'

47

He was drowning in his own vomit.

The realization that the nightmare was, in fact, true forced McNab to turn over, crawl to his knees and disgorge the bile that had stopped the breath in his throat.

The noise of his retching echoed back at him in what, it dawned on him, must be a cavernous space. It was still pitch black, but he was definitely no longer in the back of the van.

His head swimming, he turned to sit, knees drawn up, head between them, and tried to remember.

He'd spotted Cleverly. Been walking towards him, then bam! He was in the back of a van, a needle in his neck. A sudden thought forced its way through his muddled brain.

Cleverly. Was Cleverly here too?

He shouted out the name once, then panicked at how loud it sounded. The last thing he wanted was to alert his captors to the fact he was awake.

He tried a little softer this time. 'Cleverly?'

The eerie whisper came back at him, once, twice, three times, until he was suddenly surrounded by it. *Cle . . . ver . . . ly Cle . . . ver . . . ly Cle . . . ver . . . ly . . .* like a circular fairground ride.

His stomach began to spin in unison and suddenly he was seventeen again and on the Waltzers with a girl he wanted to impress. He'd certainly managed that, spraying horrified onlookers with the half-dozen beers he'd downed before climbing on board.

He covered his ears and concentrated on slow, deep breathing. The smells of vomit, piss and shit that occasionally wafted towards him were bad enough. He had no desire to supplement them any further.

That sudden thought sent his hand to his crotch.

Thank Christ. He hadn't pissed himself . . . yet.

As the drug continued its retreat, he registered that he no longer had his jacket on. In fact, his upper half was bare. He was still wearing his trousers, thank God.

He checked his pockets, both front and back.

No wallet and no phone, of course.

None of which meant that he couldn't walk out of here, providing he could find the exit in the dark.

As he rose gingerly to his feet, he heard the clang of a door opening and with it the entrance of a shaft of electric light. He froze in its beam as three figures entered and began to walk swiftly towards him.

Even as he tried to sidestep on unresponsive legs, two of them had him by the arms, dragging him backwards against a wall to rope and hook him up there, his feet trailing the ground.

McNab cried out as his shoulders were drawn from their sockets.

'Not too high,' the third guy ordered. 'We want him conscious.'

The ropes loosened a little, and the balls of his feet met the ground. The third figure moved towards him in the shaft of light.

'Back for another round?' McNab spat between his teeth.

The mouth curled into a smile. 'You won't be up for that when we're finished with you.'

McNab gathered a blob of spit and launched it in his direction. It missed.

'Smell that shit and piss, Jock pig? Well, by the time we're finished with you, it'll be your own that you're smelling.'

48

'That'll be Ava,' Magnus said. 'Can you let her in?'

Rhona went to do his bidding.

'I thought everyone just walked into friends' houses in Orkney,' she said as she opened the door.

'I've been too long away from Orkney. I forget the rules sometimes.'

Magnus called from the kitchen. 'Help yourselves to a dram in the sitting room. I'll be through shortly.'

The fire had been lit and banked up with the warm glow of peat, the scent of which met them on entry.

Ava smiled. 'God, I used to love that smell in winter, especially if I managed home for Christmas. Nowadays Orkney is inclined to a more renewable form of energy.'

'The wind can be a blessing, although it doesn't feel like it at times.' Rhona indicated the drinks tray. 'What can I get you?'

'I'm driving, so I won't, but you go ahead.'

As they settled on either side of the fire, Rhona said, 'I hear your brother's back home safely. You'll be relieved about that.'

Ava looked annoyed rather than relieved by her remark. 'He was never really away. Dougie often takes his boat out and camps on one of the islands for a bit. It's his way of coping with the world *and* the fact he lost both parents not long ago.'

Rhona, feeling she had overstepped, apologized.

Ava shrugged. 'Don't worry. Everyone knows everybody's business round here. Why should you be any different? Even if you are a visitor,' she added.

Rhona took refuge in sipping her whisky. Apparently her presence here offended Ava for some reason, which was puzzling after all they'd shared at their Glasgow meeting.

Magnus's entry brought relief to both of them. Rhona watched as he read the atmosphere and, pouring himself a whisky, took a seat between them, before turning to her. 'Any news of McNab?'

Before she could answer, Ava came in. 'What's happened to McNab?'

'He was due off the London train this morning, but didn't appear,' Rhona said. 'And he's not been reachable since—'

Ava interrupted her. 'I spoke to him on his way to London. I asked him to check in on Mark.'

Now Rhona was even more concerned.

Magnus glanced at her. 'What did DI Wilson say exactly?'

'That the Met said he arranged to meet DI Cleverly in Central London and didn't turn up.'

Magnus looked thoughtful. 'It's not the first time he's gone off the radar.'

'But this time he wasn't doing his own thing,' Rhona said. 'The boss agreed his visit south because of—' She halted there, aware she was straying into police business.

Thankfully, a shout from the hall announced Erling's arrival.

'Come away in,' Magnus called back. 'We're in the sitting room.'

Rory appeared first. 'Great,' he said, acknowledging the whisky glasses, 'we haven't missed the aperitif.' He grinned all round. 'And this must be Ava who went to school with Erling.' He offered his hand.

Ava looked a bit taken aback but, rallying, said, 'And you must be Rory.'

Instructing Erling and Rory to help themselves, Magnus requested Rhona give him a hand in the kitchen. 'Serving up in five minutes,' he announced.

Once inside, Magnus closed the door. 'Why did McNab go south or can you not say?'

Magnus had been involved since the beginning, so Rhona didn't hesitate to tell him.

He listened attentively before commenting. 'So the Met's a problem?'

She nodded. 'Bill thinks they're likely to request that all evidence in both cases be sent south.'

'They're pursuing Go Wild themselves?' He caught her expression. 'Or it's a national security issue?'

'Could be either – or both,' Rhona said.

'Okay, let's eat.' Magnus indicated which dishes she should carry through, then led the way to the dining room, where the others were already seated.

Rhona barely registered the food, despite how good it was, all her thoughts centring on Ava. Something had definitely spooked her since they'd last met. But what?

As for McNab's part in all of this, if Ava had requested he check on Mark's well-being, Rhona didn't doubt that he would have done so. Was his non-reappearance this morning in Glasgow due to that? Or had he just reverted to type and gone off on his own tangent?

Ava seemed a different person from the one who'd met with them both in Glasgow. Then she'd been totally committed to discussing and investigating Go Wild in tandem with herself and McNab. Tonight, Ava had chosen to sit as far away from her as possible, although occasionally when Rhona turned her way, she would find Ava studying her.

The conversation hadn't featured the *Orlova* until they reached the coffee stage, even though, from where Rhona sat, she could just make out its shadowy presence via the window.

Finally, it seemed, Rory could wait no longer.

'So they think there was a stowaway on the *Orlova* when we pulled her into Houton.' When Erling threw him a discouraging look, he said, 'What? It's all over the island and maybe even bigger news than the black guy found on the beach last night, which brought Dr MacLeod back.'

'What's being said about this possible stowaway?' Ava immediately asked.

Erling's pointed looks weren't working on Rory, who carried on with his story.

'That it's likely a female and she might have seen what happened on board.'

'So where is she now?' Ava said.

Rory shrugged. 'Lots of wild theories. Maybe they found her and threw her overboard like the black guy, or she was still alive when the ship was brought into Scapa Flow and she managed to get to shore.'

There was a sudden silence and Rhona wondered if Erling had been kicking his partner below the table.

'If this stowaway is alive,' Ava said, 'she's in terrible danger.'

'This is Orkney,' Rory said. 'If a girl came off that ship, she would have been spotted by now.'

Magnus shook his head. 'Orkney's already full of tourists. There's a cruise liner docked in Kirkwall, with a thousand folk aboard.'

Picking up on the tense atmosphere, Magnus suggested they all retire to the sitting room for a dram. At this point Ava indicated she wouldn't as she was the only one to have brought the car.

'Plus I'd like to be back for Dougie's sake,' she said, rising.

With a swift look to Magnus, Rhona indicated she would see Ava to the door, making a joke of the fact she was leaving her alone here, with only the men to talk to.

As Ava donned her jacket, her worried expression prompted Rhona to finally ask her what was wrong. Ava looked as though she might answer, then shook her head. 'I just have to get back.'

'Ava okay?' Erling asked quietly when Rhona rejoined the chatting men.

'She just wanted to get home for Dougie,' Rhona said, aware that simply wasn't true.

49

'How well do you and Erling know Ava?' Rhona said as Magnus poured her morning coffee.

'As a teenager or now?' he asked with a smile.

'Both.'

'Well, I was in love with her aged fourteen. Erling had other crushes. Then we all left the island for university. Erling came back and settled here, whereas I became a regular visitor from Glasgow. Ava, on the other hand, rarely returned. Christmas occasionally. She was always away working on some international story. I take it this is about last night?'

Rhona indicated it was.

'She and Mark were together both professionally and personally for a long time. That, I think, had ended by the time she came back here in the aftermath of her parents' death. It looks as though the *Orlova* investigation has triggered a revival of their partnership, on the work front at least.' He continued, looking thoughtful. 'She's obviously worried about Mark, and now there's McNab,' he said. 'You met with her in Glasgow. Was she different then?'

'Definitely. Strong, determined to carry on with the investigation. Fearless even.'

'Dougie gives her a hard time. Heading off without telling her. Then the cattle being attacked.'

'You think that might have been because of her investigation?'

'It happens sporadically in farming communities. No one knows why exactly. The police will find out who it was, in time,' he assured her. 'There's also the matter of what Ava does with the farm, although it seems Erling's father, Tommy, has stepped in and offered a partnership on running it with Dougie.'

That was good news, which suggested that neither Dougie nor the farm had been Ava's main concern the previous night.

'Do you want to take a packed lunch with you?' Magnus said.

Judging from the view of white horses from the window, the ride out to the *Orlova* wasn't going to be pleasurable. Plus the ship itself would likely be pitching a bit. Rhona decided to forgo lunch on board.

'If Chrissy was with me, her answer would be yes, but I'm happy to wait until I get back,' Rhona said with a grim smile.

Erling was waiting for her on the jetty, the launch rising and falling alongside. 'You ready for this?' he said.

'Just don't let me fall in,' Rhona told him, already wondering how she would get from the launch to the ladder.

The trip over didn't allay her fears, especially when the pilot told her that Orkney fishermen in the past didn't learn to swim. 'Better to die quickly if you fall in, rather than fighting to stay afloat and freeze.'

On that cheery note, they drew alongside the *Orlova*.

As luck would have it, getting up the ladder seemed less of a trauma than on the previous occasion, although Rhona missed Chrissy's humorous take on the proceedings.

Safely aboard, Erling led the way past the previous loci and down another level into the hold. Rhona followed him as the *Orlova* rose and fell, the metal clanging and sighing, the thick smell of unmoving air encompassing her.

'The hold, we've now discovered, has a number of small hidden compartments, possibly for drug running at one time, although now all empty. Of course, when we boarded the *Orlova*, we weren't actively looking for drugs, and once we discovered the crime scene, that became our primary focus. Once you alerted us to the possibility of a stowaway . . . Here's the place.' He came to a halt in front of a low metal door. Undoing the padlock, he pulled the heavy door open for her.

Rhona peered into the well-lit space.

'We set up an arc light for you,' Erling said. 'Otherwise you would have only had a head torch to work by.'

'Whoever was here was in the dark?'

'Some lighting was still functioning when we brought you on board earlier. Remember the mad chorus from the audience in the arena? We switched it off when you'd completed your examination of the computer room victim.' He handed her a radio. 'How long will you need?'

'A couple of hours minimum.' She began getting kitted up.

'Give us a call when you're finished. Good luck,' he offered.

Rhona listened to Erling's retreating steps. Eventually silence fell except for the continuing creaks and groans of metal on metal, plus the constant drip of water from somewhere close at hand.

The cell, she estimated, was roughly six foot by six, the height a little more than that. She took a series of photographs from the low doorway, then, stepping inside, took a full 360-degree video.

There was a bed of sorts along the back wall, a little pile of clothing on the right-hand side. On the left was the food and rubbish area. A stack of unopened tins of beans, tuna, corned beef; a plastic bag with the empties. A cutlery set was there, but no plate or bowl. It looked as though whoever had hidden here had been eating straight out of the tin. There was also a stack of water bottles, one partially drunk.

Before lifting DNA samples, she checked the clothing. Jeans, tops, jumpers and some underwear which all suggested the stowaway had been female.

Erling had exhibited some unease at Rory's announcement of that the previous evening. Most likely because she hadn't yet examined the hideout and its contents.

However, if a girl had made it to shore from the *Orlova*, the best way to find her would be to alert the local population to her existence. And the sooner the better.

As she worked, Rhona was conscious that the *Orlova* was never still or silent, but constantly ringing with sound as it strained against its anchor. The noises, of course, were never of human life. It was as though the ghost ship had swallowed everyone, including whoever had taken refuge here in this hidden room.

Two hours later, she had collected her evidence. Long strands of human hair, dark blonde in colour, DNA saliva and blood samples and, interestingly, some short animal hairs, both white and black.

The thought had crossed her mind that the room may have been used in one of the many games played on board, so the animal hairs might relate to costumes similar to the Viking outfits, the blood spots to minor injuries sustained. Then again, from experience, when viewed via her magnifying glass, she thought the hairs had possibly come from a dog, although she would have to confirm this under the microscope back in the lab.

Shortly after she'd bagged everything, Erling reappeared.

'It's getting a bit wild out there, so we'd like to get you off and safely back to Houton.'

'What about Glasgow?'

'The helicopter won't go now. You're here for another night, I'm afraid.'

Making their way up on deck, Rhona was surprised at the increased pitching of the *Orlova*, something she'd missed during her time in the cell. The wind having risen, its gusts now threatened to take the feet from under her, until Erling grabbed a hold.

At the ladder, he lowered the evidence bags first before roping her to him. 'I'll go first,' he said. 'Just look straight ahead, not down.'

Their descent passed in a blur, much like when she'd abseiled down Kilt Rock on Skye, the difference being she didn't land on solid ground this time, but on the rocking police launch. There was a brief welcome from the pilot, then they were slicing through the waves towards the Houton slipway.

'I'll take the evidence through to the station,' Erling told her as they parted on the jetty. 'It'll go down with you tomorrow.'

Stepping into the solid stone of Magnus's house, Rhona said a silent thank you to whatever Norse god had seen her safely back.

Magnus, working in his study, came out to greet her. 'You've had a couple of phone calls,' he said. 'They tried me when they couldn't reach you.'

'Who?' Rhona said, hoping one caller might have been McNab.

'Check your mobile.'

Reaching her room, Rhona did exactly that. There were, in fact, three messages. One from Chrissy demanding Rhona call her, one from Bill asking the same.

The third wasn't from McNab, but from Ava Clouston.

I need to speak to you alone. Can you come to the farm. Now.

50

The rain was on in earnest. Driven by the wind, it splattered the windshield so insistently that Rhona had to slow to a crawl to spot the track down to the Clouston farm. Untarred, the route was already puddled and muddy.

She could see the house lights in the distance, the Flow beyond, the distant hills of Hoy looming through the rain. Although still daylight, the scudding dark rain clouds made it seem more like dusk.

She'd stopped registering the presence of the *Orlova*. Perhaps because its ghostly shape felt more threatening than the dark sky, the wind or the rain.

Approaching the farmhouse, she found a long stone building, two-storey, with three attic windows facing the sea. Between the house and Scapa Flow stood a cluster of farm buildings, the largest, probably the byre, the furthest away. Nearest the shore was what looked like a small boathouse.

As she pulled up in front of the house, Ava appeared at the front door to welcome her in.

The kitchen was bright and warm, a laptop open on the kitchen table. Alongside the range was a dog basket lined with a tartan blanket.

'You have a dog?' Rhona said.

'Finn. He's down at the boathouse with Dougie.'

'They're not going out in a boat in this weather?' Rhona said.

Ava shook her head. 'Dougie likes to spend time on the *Fear Not*, whatever the weather. Can I get you a tea or a coffee?' she offered, waving Rhona to a seat at the table.

'Coffee, please,' Rhona said.

Ava prepared the coffee in a silence which didn't end when she joined her at the table. Whatever she'd wanted to say to Rhona in person, she was finding it difficult to do so, now she was here.

Eventually she blurted it out. 'You were on the *Orlova* today looking for evidence of the girl Rory was talking about.' It was less of a question than a statement.

Rhona gave a brief nod.

'Did you find it?'

Rhona saw no reason to lie. After all, Erling would no doubt be relaying the news to the island, asking for folk to look out for a possible survivor from the *Orlova*.

'I can't discuss what I found, but yes, I believe someone has been hiding there. Probably female.'

There was a long pause, while it appeared Ava was fighting herself as to how she might respond. Eventually it arrived.

'She's here,' Ava said. 'Dougie brought her from the ship.' The words finally out, she was waiting on Rhona's response.

Rhona hadn't wanted to examine the dog's blanket, but sitting so close to it, she'd already registered the white hairs against the blue of the tartan, which had made her suspect that the dog and Dougie may have been on the *Orlova*. To hear he'd brought the girl ashore was both surprising and wonderful news.

Before she could say this, Ava rushed on. 'Dougie told Nadia she would be safe here with me. That I was investigating

Go Wild, and I would tell her story, but no one could know she was here.'

Rhona now understood what last night's behaviour had been all about. Ava's reaction to their discussion at the dinner table and her wariness of Rhona being on Orkney again.

She knew I would examine that room in the ship. She knew a forensic search might reveal that Dougie and the dog had been there.

'You need to tell Erling about this,' Rhona said. 'She's a witness in a murder investigation and has knowledge of Go Wild.' She avoided the words 'possible suspect' although conscious of that possibility too.

'She begged me not to, not until I release her story. She says the company has connections everywhere. They'll find her and kill her. She's convinced they're already on Orkney. It was never imagined the *Orlova* would come ashore anywhere. It was just another ghost ship floating about in the Atlantic. What happened aboard would never have been discovered, and if it was, it would be years from now, when the bodies were nothing but skeletons.'

What Ava said was more than likely true. The *Orlova*, like many of the ghost ships littering the world's oceans, was a curiosity, nothing more. Until it had come ashore at Yesnaby.

'Nadia would be placed in protective custody,' Rhona said.

Ava dismissed that. 'You don't know who you're dealing with here, you can't imagine their reach and influence.' She fell silent and Rhona realized there was something more she wanted to say. The real reason for her request that Rhona come here.

'Why are you telling me all this?'

'If the story of a possible survivor is leaked from Glasgow, anyone sent to kill her will look there. That takes the focus away from Orkney.'

'Can I talk to Nadia?' Rhona said.

'That can't happen. If Dougie finds out I've betrayed them, they'll run. He's threatened as much.' Glancing at her watch, she rose. 'They'll be back soon. You have to go.'

'What do you want me to do?' Rhona said.

'I was planning to ask you to speak to DS McNab but—' She came to a halt.

'I can speak to his boss, DI Wilson,' Rhona said.

'Can he be trusted?' Ava asked.

Rhona didn't hesitate. 'I've trusted him with my life before this.'

Ava nodded, relief showing in her face. 'Now you have to go.'

'What about Magnus?' Rhona said as she donned her jacket. 'I had to borrow his car so he knows I'm here.'

'Tell him I wanted to write a piece about a forensic scientist who experienced PTSD after she was targeted by a stalker.'

'I wouldn't agree to that,' Rhona said.

'Exactly – despite all my efforts to persuade you, you said no,' Ava said with a hint of a smile.

51

I am he and he is me.

In his drug-addled state, he thought himself back in Kelvingrove Art Gallery, standing in front of Dalí's painting of Christ, hanging forward on the cross, his hands and feet free of nails.

Just like I hang here, half naked above . . . what?

His eyes snapped open and he saw that he was looking down not on a stretch of water, as in the painting, but on a pool of his own piss.

And I am no saviour, of myself or anyone else.

What had he told them during the beatings? His mind flitted with individual images of the people he might have betrayed, Mark and Ava in particular.

Did he talk about the coffee house, where Mark was holed up? What about Ava? Had he said where she was? What she was doing?

And what about Go Wild? Did he spill everything he knew about them?

No, he thought. *I haven't told them everything . . . not yet. Because if I had, I wouldn't be hanging here and still breathing.*

As whatever drug they'd injected began another retreat, the cold advanced its attack. The shivering would start again soon, knocking his teeth together, burning his extremities, clawing at his chest with long, sharp fingernails.

A ripple began, then a long shuddering icy wave washed up from the soles of his feet, scrabbling up his thighs to focus on his crotch. He would have urinated again, had he had any liquid left in his body.

At this point he heard them approach, the clang of the door and then the advance of the long shaft of light which ended at him.

It seemed it was time to rock and roll again.

The three figures came forward together, the outer two almost as broad as they were high, replicas of one another. Only their tattoos differentiated between them. He'd named them Mutt and Jeff, after the Second World War double agents who had spied for the Allies. They were playing out their good cop, bad cop roles. Having time to study their torsos through drug-addled eyes, McNab knew that Mutt preferred being adorned with naked women. Jeff was more inclined to Nazi symbols. McNab had observed this at close quarters.

At first he hadn't clocked where he might have seen them before, because back then they'd been fully suited, and the truth was most minders looked much the same. But the more he saw them, the more he believed that they'd been at the bare-knuckle fight with the posh fucker. Which was probably why they were enjoying themselves so much.

Their boss had never stripped or taken part himself. He was the Kommandant, the one, McNab suspected, who dictated when, where and how. Had he seen him before? McNab couldn't be sure.

By the look of their pupils, Mutt and Jeff were always high on something, probably cocaine. How many times had McNab wished they'd give him that drug instead of the cocktail that was supposed to free his tongue to answer their questions?

He tried to prepare himself for the next bout, but at that moment all he wanted was for them to put his lights out, like they'd done in Glasgow.

Then something happened. The boss proceeded to take off his shirt and, with a smile, said, 'It's my turn.'

With a nod from him, Mutt and Jeff freed McNab's wrists from the rings and he slumped forward onto his knees. The excruciating pain stopped the breath in his throat, just as his heart raced off into a bloody sunset.

Through all of this, he heard the two henchmen being dismissed and, struggling to lift his head, realized the Kommandant and he were alone.

In seconds, his head was dragged back and a knife placed at his throat.

'Well done, Jock,' he hissed. 'You haven't told us a fucking thing. Heard you were good with a chib. You're going to grab this off me and take yourself out of here.'

52

As Rhona took the turn-off to Houton Bay, she spotted a police car parked outside Magnus's place, which had to mean Erling was there.

God, now she would have to face not only a forensic psychologist, but a detective as well.

Two thoughts had accompanied her on the drive back from the Clouston farm. The first and most important was that the girl from the ship had to be protected at all costs. The second was that Ava's suggestion of involving Glasgow might have merit. The decision on both of those she would now pass to Bill.

A final thought assailed her as she drew up behind the police car. *I have to decide what to tell Chrissy.* And Chrissy of all people knew her well enough, both by her expression and her voice, to recognize when she was avoiding the truth.

No one appeared to have noted her return as yet, so Rhona took her chance. If she could tell Bill the truth, it might be easier to face those indoors with a lie. Praying for a quick response, Rhona rang Bill's number.

'Rhona.' He sounded relieved to hear from her. 'How'd it go today?'

'There was a stowaway,' she confirmed. 'A female. Her name is Nadia Kowalski.'

Rhona told him word for word what she and Ava had

discussed. When she'd finished, there followed a moment's silence, before Bill said, 'Don't repeat this to anyone, including Erling and Magnus. The fewer folk know about the girl's whereabouts, the better.' He paused. 'When are you back?'

'I'll come with the body in the morning. Any more news on McNab?' Rhona said.

'No. I'm beginning to hope he's gone rogue after all.'

The admission, Rhona knew, showed just how worried Bill was.

'Let's talk when you're back,' he said, before ending the call.

Rhona breathed a sigh of relief. The call to Chrissy, she would delay until she was inside.

She found Erling and Magnus drinking coffee in the kitchen. Both men turned expectantly on her entrance.

Rhona immediately focused on the reason for Erling's presence. Sounding concerned, she said, 'Is everything okay for tomorrow morning?'

'It is,' Erling assured her. 'I just came in to say that I'll pick you up at eight.'

'Good. I've just spoken to DI Wilson and brought him up to date.'

In the short silence that followed, and before she could make her getaway upstairs, Magnus asked how it had gone with Ava.

'Okay. Better than last night anyway,' Rhona offered.

The two faces suggested that wasn't enough, so Rhona added, 'She wanted to talk to me in private about a piece she was writing on front-line workers and PTSD. She'd read up about the sin-eater case and wanted to feature my experience.'

Magnus looked slightly taken aback by this. 'Did she mention this last night?'

'She broached the subject, yes,' Rhona lied. 'That was the reason for the awkward atmosphere when you walked in on us.'

Stop talking, she silently reproached herself. Magnus and Erling knew enough about interviewing techniques to recognize that giving too much information was usually done to cover a lie.

The moment ended and with it some of the tension, but not all.

'If you'll excuse me, I need to write up my notes from today.' And with that Rhona escaped to her room.

She had survived the first encounter, but dinner later with Magnus might not prove so easy. Plus she still had Chrissy to deal with. For that she would have to rely on Chrissy's need to talk, more than her own obligation to reply.

Chrissy must have been holding her mobile, so quick was her response. 'I was just about to try you again,' she said accusingly. 'I thought you were supposed to fly down with the body tonight?'

'If you could see and hear the weather at this moment, you'd know why I'm here until the morning,' Rhona told her.

There was a *harrumph* as Chrissy digested this, then, 'What happened on the ship?'

Rhona was happy to describe what she'd found.

'So there was someone,' Chrissy said thoughtfully. 'And the beached body?'

'A young black male, wearing a shirt with the Go Wild crest. Looks like his throat was cut before he went overboard. I'll send you the images shortly of both the body and the room on the *Orlova*. Body will come down with me tomorrow.'

When Chrissy next spoke, there was a catch in her throat. 'You've spoken to the boss? They can't find McNab and I know something's wrong. I just know it.'

Rhona repeated Bill's words. 'If Bill holds out hope for that,' she said, 'then so will we.'

53

'Here, snort this.'

McNab watched in disbelief as a double line of coke was shaken across his hand. When he just stared at it, the voice said urgently, 'It'll take the edge off the pain. Hurry.'

'Who the fuck are you?' McNab said.

'You don't need to know.'

To McNab's astonishment, his erstwhile tormentor angled the knife to score a bloody line across his own neck, followed by a couple more across his bare chest and arm, then handed him the knife and his jacket.

'Through that door and turn left. There's an emergency exit. Once outside, head for the gates. They're padlocked, but there's a loose bit of fence to the right of them. After that, it's up to you. Now hit me and fuck off, Jock, back to Glasgow.'

His head singing with joy via the coke he'd just snorted, McNab happily obliged with the fist. Harder maybe than required. Certainly enough to see the guy fall with a painful grunt.

Pocketing the knife, McNab made for the door and quietly opened it. The concrete passage was empty and he could see the fire exit ahead. He made for there, his legs screaming out from lack of use, and pushed it open to darkness and a blast of fresh air.

A quick look round and he spotted the gates as promised, lit by a street light. He forced his battered body in that direction, running like someone drunk or demented.

Scrabbling for the fence opening, he squeezed through, tearing another gash along his cheek. Then he was outside the perimeter fence.

The cocaine racing through his veins, he took a swift look left, then right, choosing the route leading to a busy road junction, knowing the sooner he hid among people, the better. At this time of night most of the shops he passed were shut, but the pubs were still open, with groups of smokers outside. McNab chose what looked like a crowded bar and, registering BrewDog Clerkenwell as the pub name, slipped inside and made straight for the Gents, getting a few odd looks on his way.

The mirror over the sink told the truth. He looked terrible and no doubt smelt worse. He splashed his battered face with cold water and headed into a cubicle. His trousers, he decided, were second in line after his face. Taking them off, he flushed the crotch in the hope it would lessen the scent of urine, while thanking God he hadn't shat himself.

His head suddenly swimming, he sank onto the toilet seat and put his head between his knees. The cocaine rush was on the way out, he realized, and the real state of both his mind and his body was not superhuman after all.

He struggled to process what had just happened.

The Kommandant had let him go, but why? Was he really free or was he supposed to lead them somewhere or to someone? Or had they got everything they'd needed from him?

The Jock that told all.

McNab tried revisiting the scene at Leicester Square.

Cleverly had definitely been nearby. He must have seen it happen. Had he told the boss? Had he even reported it to his own superiors? Or had the whole thing been prearranged?

Another thought wove its way into the puzzle. He'd arranged to meet Cleverly in the morning, but the Met detective hadn't turned up – or had he? If he had, yet didn't show himself, Cleverly could have followed him to the Afghan coffee shop, thus revealing where Mark Sylvester was hiding.

Christ. McNab didn't like that particular train of thought, nor where it might lead.

Retrieving his trousers from the floor, he did his best to wring the excess water from the crotch before putting them back on. Meanwhile, he thought of all the drunks he'd picked up over the years, smelling of piss, their faces a mess, just like his. He hadn't been strong on sympathy then.

So now the shoe was on the other foot.

Exiting the toilets, he passed a female who looked at him in horror, her nose wrinkling in disgust. Figuring he had about sixty seconds to get what he could before being thrown out, McNab took ownership of an unwatched pint and a packet of crisps. The crisps went swiftly in his pocket, the pint he downed in a oner.

The owner, arriving just as the last mouthful disappeared, saw fit to throw a punch at him, which McNab miraculously managed to sidestep.

Then, together with his accompanying smell, he made swiftly for the door.

Outside again, he had a quick look round for his captors, who surely by now would be out looking for him. And let's face it, he wasn't difficult to spot among the clean, well-dressed male throng.

So where to now?

Having staggered sufficiently far away from the bar, he ducked into a doorway both to hide and to try to think. His brain, he realized, was attempting to formulate a plan, but the dregs of hallucinatory drugs, combined with the snorted cocaine, kept fleetingly reasserting themselves.

Truth was, he was a fucking mess. Plus his legs no longer worked.

He contemplated sitting down where he was, but if anyone came looking for him around here, he was in full view. He needed somewhere off the main street and preferably in the dark.

Dragging himself to his feet, he staggered off towards what looked like the opening of an alleyway. He made it in and stumbled as far as a wheelie bin, then slid in slow motion down the wall, only to meet with the current incumbent of that particular piece of London real estate.

McNab decided the face that stared out at him from under the blanket looked in better shape than he did.

'You okay, mate?' a gruff voice said.

'Where am I exactly?' McNab answered in a slur.

'In shit alley, mate. You're down and out in shit alley.'

54

As luck would have it, Ava was outside with Finn when she spotted the police car turning onto the farm track. Running back inside, she shouted up to Dougie that Erling was on his way, and neither he nor Nadia should make a sound.

Once she'd heard a grunt in return, Ava tried to regain her composure by pulling the kettle onto the hotplate and instructing Finn to go to his basket and stay there.

Erling surprised her by knocking, which wasn't his usual method of entry. This alone should have alerted her to the possibility that he might be the harbinger of bad news.

When she opened the door, she knew that had to be the case. Had Dougie still been missing, she would have imagined the worst by the look currently on Erling's face.

'Can I come in?' he said, his voice both serious and formal.

'What is it?' Ava immediately said.

'Let's go into the kitchen,' he suggested, leading the way. Inside now, he took off his hat and suggested she sit down.

Ava wasn't one for swearing. Brought up by parents who simply never cursed, it was a habit she had never acquired. Yet, at this moment, in her head was running a stream of invective that would have made both her parents blush.

'Tell me,' she demanded.

'I'm so sorry, Ava. Mark's dead.'

The words 'Mark' and 'dead' chimed together in her brain,

ringing as loudly and incessantly as a church bell. Her legs no longer willing to hold her up, Ava slid onto the seat she'd scorned only moments before.

'That can't be true,' she heard herself say. 'DS McNab was going to check on him when he was in London. Who told you this?' She stared accusingly at Erling.

'It came via the Met. I checked it out first thing. His body was pulled out of the Thames last night. Your editor, David Morris, identified him.'

If David identified him, it must be true.

Now this vocalized thought became her internal mantra, replacing the string of curses. 'It must be true,' she uttered out loud. Then, 'How did he . . . Mark die?'

'Still to be confirmed by post-mortem.'

'They killed him. The bastards killed Mark to stop him telling their story,' she muttered under her breath.

'That's part of the reason I'm here, Ava. As someone working with Mark on Go Wild, you could be in danger.'

'But this is Orkney,' she said stupidly.

'Nevertheless, I think I should put an officer here with you, for the next few days anyway.'

God, she couldn't let that happen. Not with Nadia here.

'No,' she said firmly. 'That's not necessary.'

'What's going on?' Dougie appeared in the doorway. 'Why is *he* here?' He threw Erling a look of distaste.

Ava pasted a smile on her face. 'Remember I mentioned Erling's dad was keen to help us with the farm? Well, Erling's suggesting we all get together sometime soon to discuss it.'

By the look on Dougie's face, he wasn't buying her explanation. Thankfully, however, he didn't pursue it.

Erling said, 'You'll think about it, then?' to Ava, and she nodded, then indicated she would show him out.

'You need to be careful, Ava,' Erling said at the front door. 'Orkney's not as far off the beaten track as some folk think. We have over a thousand visitors currently on mainland Orkney. Many have been down to Houton Bay just to view the *Orlova*.'

'Then the quicker you arrange to have it towed south, the better,' Ava snapped at him. 'Has Dr MacLeod left yet?'

'I'm about to take her to Kirkwall to meet the police helicopter.'

Ava tried not to show her disappointment. It seemed that talking to Rhona about the recent developments would have to wait.

Re-entering the kitchen, she found Dougie had been joined by Nadia. Both threw her an accusatory look.

'You told him about Nadia,' Dougie said. 'That's what brought him here.'

'I didn't,' Ava said. 'And it wasn't.'

'Well, it was nothing to do with the farm. That much I do know.'

Unable to say the words 'Mark is dead', Ava went over to her laptop and fired it up.

Her hands shook as she entered Mark's name, and immediately watched a long string of news clips rolling up the screen. She chose one, clicked on it and turned the screen towards Dougie. 'That's why Erling was here.'

Dougie approached the table, Nadia standing hesitantly behind him.

Ava watched his eyes run over the headline, then drop to read the text below, something she was dreading doing herself.

'Oh no.' His eyes met hers. 'I'm sorry, Ava. So sorry.'

Nadia had no idea what was going on, but it was obvious

it was bad. She pulled up a chair next to Dougie and turned the laptop screen towards her.

'This journalist, you know him?' she said, her voice strangely staccato, revealing her Polish accent clearly for the first time.

Ava nodded. 'We worked together for years.' Her voice stumbled a little. 'Mark and I were both investigating the Go Wild story.'

'They killed him,' Nadia said, raising her chin in defiance. 'I told you what they would do, didn't I? They'll kill anyone who might expose them.'

Dougie glanced from Nadia to Ava. 'That means you're in danger too now,' he said, his voice hushed with fear. 'That's what Erling was here to tell you, wasn't it?'

Ava gave a weary nod.

'What does he want you to do?' he demanded.

'He wants to put a guard on the house, an officer from Kirkwall.'

'But we can't have a policeman hanging about . . . not with Nadia here.'

'I told him no,' Ava said.

Dougie was pacing now. 'I can take Nadia away. We'll camp on one of the islands.'

'No,' Ava said. 'Someone will spot you. Locals make a point of finding out who's on an island. Anyway, no one knows that Nadia exists. That she came ashore. That she's here.'

It wasn't true, of course, but she hoped she sounded convincing. 'No,' she said again, thinking. 'You don't go anywhere. I do.'

Dougie looked perplexed. 'I don't understand. Where would you go?'

'Glasgow,' Ava said. 'I'll announce that I'm going there to help Police Scotland with their enquiries into Go Wild.' She thought about the memory stick Mark had given her. Maybe it was time to hand it over to McNab . . . She cut that thought, remembering that McNab was missing too. Might he also be dead? Had she, by sending him to Mark, sealed his fate as well?

'What?' Dougie said, seeing her troubled expression.

'You and Nadia will stay here. Nadia out of sight at all times. I'll announce my intention to go to Glasgow. That way, the focus moves there. I'll speak to Rhona about—' She came to an abrupt halt, realizing too late that this was too much information.

'Rhona?' Dougie latched onto the name. 'The forensic woman who came back to check on the ship for a stowaway? Why would you speak to her?'

Nadia was regarding her with those big dark eyes. 'You told her about me. Didn't you?'

55

Time had been short. She'd had to leave with Erling almost immediately to get to Kirkwall and her flight south. Rhona had said her swift goodbyes to Magnus, knowing the likelihood would be that he would visit Ava to talk the situation over with her.

My God, she could hardly believe what Erling had told them about Mark. Yet another death associated with Go Wild. An assumption at this point, she knew, and yet . . .

Erling had been adamant about his desire to have a constable stationed at the Clouston farm, despite the fact Ava had refused his offer.

And Rhona knew exactly why she had.

Heading east out of Orphir, they met a bank of haar that blanketed the vehicle and blotted out the surrounding landscape. Glancing seawards, she could no longer make out the red hump of the cargo ship, something she'd been keen to happen, yet strangely felt no pleasure in now.

'The haar's due to clear by nine at the latest, or so the Met Office promised,' Erling told her. 'Although there may be a slight delay with your chopper coming in.'

At least she would be on her own in the airport, Rhona thought, and could call Ava from there.

Ava wasn't the only one she should call to talk about the latest and terrible event, but Bill would know what to do.

Of that she was sure. Anyway, the plan to keep Ava and the girl Nadia hidden in Orkney no longer seemed safe nor feasible.

Her biggest fear when Erling had told her about Mark was that McNab might have suffered a similar fate. Ava had told them she'd asked McNab to check on Mark and he'd agreed.

Might they have been together when Mark was killed?

Erling's information was that Mark had been found in the river, and it was being trailed as a possible suicide. Something he hadn't told Ava. Whether he'd been dead before he'd gone in or drowned would no doubt be established at post-mortem.

Erling broke into her thoughts to tell her that the evidence bags and the body from the beach were already at the airport. 'With any luck, you'll be back in your lab before lunchtime.'

'That would be good,' Rhona said.

They'd navigated Kirkwall by now and were heading out on the airport road. True enough, the mist was thinner here, as Erling had said it would be. Glimpses of sky suggested an elusive sun would hopefully burn it off.

'I'll have to get back to the station, so I'll drop you at the door, if that's okay?' Erling said. 'I've instructed Officer Tulloch to make sure you and the body get away all right.'

As they drew up outside the terminal building, Rhona thanked Erling for his help.

'No bother,' he said. 'You'll hear from me direct if your missing stowaway turns up. And we'll look after Ava, I promise.'

Now, she had to find somewhere private to try to contact Ava. The airport was a size that befitted the islands' population. Glasgow it was not. Open-plan, with a small cafe, a few tables, the rest of the area taken up by seating for the waiting passengers.

Rhona had a quick glance around and spotted Ivan Tulloch right away, even as he noted her own entrance. There would be no hope of talking privately to Ava with Ivan by her side.

She gave the police officer a little wave of acknowledgement, then indicated she was heading for the Ladies. Once inside, she chose a cubicle, went in and locked the door.

Ava's mobile rang out, but went unanswered. Rhona stopped the call, waited a few moments then tried again. If Ava wouldn't answer her, what could she do?

Her frustration was eventually curtailed when the call was picked up.

'Yes?' an Orcadian male voice said, who she presumed must be Dougie.

'It's Rhona MacLeod here,' she said. 'May I speak to Ava, please?'

'Ava's not here,' came the terse reply.

That seemed odd, Rhona thought. Where would she have gone without her mobile?

'When will she be back?' she tried.

'No idea,' he said rudely, and hung up.

Emerging from the toilets, Rhona saw PC Tulloch waving her over.

'The helicopter's here and loaded. Would you like me to walk you out, Dr MacLeod?'

Rhona gave him a smile. 'That won't be necessary, Officer Tulloch. Walking across the tarmac's the easy part. It's the flying bit that's the problem.'

Glasgow was overcast as they came in to land, much like Rhona's mood. Even the co-pilot hadn't been as chatty as usual, Chrissy's name not mentioned once on the flight back.

A thick drizzle accompanied her through the city centre, so that she might have been back in Kirkwall in the haar. Entering Kelvingrove Park via Kelvin Way, the cloud cover broke for an instant, the light catching the spires of the university and lifting her spirits.

Her hope now was that Chrissy would have food available, since she hadn't been able to eat any of Magnus's carefully prepared breakfast. Arriving at the lab, she wondered why she had ever doubted that to be the case.

'Great, you're back.' Chrissy gave her a hug. 'Food first. I'll log the evidence while you eat, then we'll talk. Oh, and Bill's called a strategy meeting for two o'clock and wants you there.'

As soon as Rhona indicated she was suitably replete, Chrissy said, with a serious air, 'The print you managed to lift from the burn victim doesn't match the one I retrieved from the credit card.'

Rhona nodded. 'Well done.' Yet another indicator that the victim was unlikely to be Olivia Newton Richardson, and a reminder of why the now-missing McNab had gone to London.

She had known without asking Chrissy that there had been no further news of him, and that her forensic assistant was aware of the death of Ava's journalistic partner.

'How is Ava taking the news about Mark?' Chrissy said.

'Badly, according to Erling, although I haven't spoken to her in person yet,' Rhona said.

Chrissy, obviously judging it was probably better to stick with talking about work, said, 'So tell me about this possible stowaway. And the beach body.'

They spent the next hour poring over her photographs of both loci, Rhona constantly reminding herself to talk about the hideaway minus Nadia's name, in the full knowledge that Chrissy had an almost uncanny ability to spot both a lie in practice and one by omission.

Eventually Chrissy said, 'You believe whoever was in that room is still alive, don't you?'

'I'm *hoping* that's true,' Rhona countered.

Chrissy gave her a look, but didn't comment on her response. Instead, she focused on one of the images of the hideaway. 'See here,' she said, pointing to the blanket covering the makeshift bed. 'Those look like white animal hairs. I take it you brought some back for analysis?'

Rhona nodded.

'I suppose they might have come from one of the Viking outfits, although I think any fur on those was fake. These look real. Never mind, I'll know what they belong to when I take a look under the microscope.'

And she would, Rhona thought. After which would come the enquiry about why a dog was on board the *Orlova*. Rhona could only hope that, by then, she would be free to tell Chrissy the truth.

Chrissy was now pointing to the contents of the refuse bag. 'These tins the stowaway's been eating. Peas, beans, hot dog sausages.' She paused. 'Well, a full report's now back on the make-up of the vomit. Whoever puked up near the crime scene had been eating hot dogs and beans, which suggests the vomit may well have come from your stowaway.'

Rhona was in the act of constructing a suitable response, when Chrissy suddenly declared, 'You'd better watch your time.'

When Rhona looked blank, she added, 'The strategy meeting?'

Lying or omitting to tell the whole truth was an exhausting business, Rhona acknowledged on the way to the police station. She could only hope that after talking to Bill she might be freed from keeping any more secrets, from Chrissy at least.

They had moved the strategy meeting to a larger venue, the number of combined officers now exceeding the original. On stage was DCI Sutherland, backed by Bill. The chief inspector called the meeting to order, then immediately spoke of DS McNab who, he said, had not yet been located.

'I have been in discussion with my opposite number in the Met, who assures me that we have their full cooperation on this and other matters associated with both the fire death here in Glasgow and the deaths on the *Orlova*.'

At this point Rhona felt compelled to ask a question.

DCI Sutherland noted her raised hand, but there was a brief moment when he looked as though he might not acknowledge it. A murmur from the surrounding officers changed his mind.

'Dr MacLeod?' he offered.

'Are you aware that the Met has yet to provide us with DNA samples that would allow us to establish if, in fact, the fire victim is Olivia Newton Richardson?'

The silence that followed begged a response from the commanding officer, although he didn't look keen to supply it.

Eventually, looking a little put out, he assured Rhona that that was being dealt with and added, with a sombre look, that the investigation was now associated with matters of 'national security'.

After which DCI Sutherland beat a hasty retreat.

Beside her, Janice muttered a word beginning with 'p' to perfectly describe him, which Rhona found herself agreeing with. She threw Janice a look of support as Bill called her up to brief them on the latest forensic evidence findings.

Having voiced her concerns about matching the body to the actual Go Wild employee Ms Richardson, Rhona revealed Chrissy's discovery of the discrepancy between the fingerprint retrieved from the fire victim and the one on her supposed credit card.

To those working on the fire case, this wasn't a revelation, just one more small step in proving the victim wasn't who they were being led to believe she was.

Rhona moved now to the *Orlova* case. Despite a number of officers in the room not primarily working on that area, the interest was intense and the questions numerous, all of which Rhona answered in evidence terms as best she could.

The Met might believe the Go Wild case was exclusively theirs, but the men and women in this room did not.

Her delivery complete, Rhona followed Bill into his office, where he shut the door behind them.

'Essentially the word from on high is that the bigger story mustn't get out. We've been told to focus on the fire and the bodies associated with the ghost ship. Nothing about the wider implications of what had been happening on board.'

'What about Nadia?' Rhona said. 'Does the chief know about her?'

When Bill didn't immediately answer, she added, 'You think she'll be taken south of the border if the Met learn about her?'

Bill nodded. 'Which takes her out of Police Scotland's jurisdiction.'

'And protection,' Rhona said, thinking about McNab. 'She may, of course, have played a part in some or all of this. After all, she was an employee of Go Wild.'

'You have DNA from the hideout?' Bill asked.

'I do, and I can compare it with that collected at the crime scenes,' she tells him. 'Also, analysis of the vomit suggests the person hiding in that room was probably the person who was sick in the arena. However, that doesn't mean she's not implicated in their deaths.'

They moved on to discuss what was in Ava's investigative report. The question was, could it be published as Ava wanted, now that they had been told not to publicize the case?

One thing Rhona had learned over the years was that DI Bill Wilson didn't make decisions without careful consideration. Plus he always put his front-line officers first. And, Rhona thought, Bill was definitely unhappy about the way McNab's disappearance was being handled, which was bound to affect any decision he made.

'Have you spoken to Ava since the announcement of Mark's death?' he said.

'I tried her mobile, but her brother answered and told me she wasn't there.'

'Is she avoiding us?'

Rhona didn't think so. She was more concerned that Ava wasn't being permitted to talk to them.

'The boy's worried about Nadia. If he thinks his sister broke her promise and told anyone about her . . .' Rhona ground to a halt.

'Ask Ava to send the piece to her London editor. Tell her to make sure he mentions that the reporting came from Glasgow, where the first Go Wild body was found. Hopefully any interested parties will think she's here.'

'And Nadia?'

'We keep the girl in Orkney for the moment.'

56

As his eyes flickered open, he was assailed by the same sounds and smells as before . . . dripping water, piss and shit. A face stared down at him. Or was it just his own reflection?

Am I dead, he wondered? If he was, then he definitely hadn't gone to heaven.

'You're in bad shape, mate,' a voice said. 'You need a doctor.'

McNab realized with sudden clarity that it was his street companion from the previous evening talking.

'The Simon folk'll be round here soon. They'll sort you out. Can you sit up?'

McNab tried. He'd been dreaming about his mobile, wishing he had it, but more than that, something he should remember about it. *Your brain's fucked,* he told himself.

As his good Samaritan helped him sit against the wall, McNab noticed that he'd gained a blanket round his shoulders. He tried to say thank you, but his mouth just flapped open and shut like a stranded fish.

At that moment two dark-clothed men appeared at the entrance to the alley and looked in, checking for – what? Him?

'Who's there?' a voice called.

McNab cowered back against the wall. 'Don't answer,' he hissed.

'It's okay. They're the Simon guys I told you about.' His companion stood up and called out. 'You need to help this guy.'

After that, things passed by in a blur. The voices that seemed to surround him murmured their concerns. Questions were asked of his erstwhile mate. He heard him say, 'he sounds Scottish' and 'he's beaten pretty bad'.

Another blanket was laid over him. Then he found himself rising in the air and realized he'd been loaded onto a stretcher. The alley passed him by and he emerged onto the street, and from there into the back of an ambulance.

All of which he could do nothing about, although his mind screamed at him that it wasn't a good idea.

The alley had smelt bad, but in here the stink seemed even worse.

'Jesus,' he heard himself say, 'what's that fucking smell?'

A male voice laughed. 'That's you, mate. All you.'

McNab, shocked, attempted to apologize.

'Forget it,' the voice said. 'I'm more concerned about your injuries.' He turned to whoever else was in the back with them. McNab's swollen eyes denied him the ability to view the other paramedic, but he heard her voice, a soft series of notes, which became a song in his head.

His jacket lay open, he knew that, and someone was mouthing concern at the exposed battered version of himself. He said he was sorry, again. Why, he had no idea.

His eyelids were eased open and a light shone in.

'You taken anything, mate?'

'Not by choice,' he tried to tell them, although that wasn't strictly true, if you counted the cocaine.

The female voice asked, 'Who did this to you?'

When McNab remained silent, she said to her partner, 'We should inform the police about this.'

'No,' McNab managed to say. 'I just need patching up.'

He realized the moment to declare himself a police officer had come and gone and he'd chosen not to. Despite the pain and the scrambled brain, McNab knew why.

57

'Why is she calling you?' Dougie demanded.

'Because of Mark's death,' Ava tried again. 'Mark told me to tell Dr MacLeod and DS McNab that a Met officer who wasn't to be trusted was being sent north. This was all before you brought Nadia here.' She paused to emphasize that fact. 'It'll raise suspicions if I stop talking to them now. Plus,' she added, 'DS McNab went to London to check on Mark, and Mark's been found dead. They can't locate McNab now, which means . . .'

She stopped there. It wasn't the whole story, but it was enough to get them thinking.

'So it's not all about you, or me,' she said directly to Nadia. 'Don't you want the people who killed Guido and your other friends to be caught?'

'That's why I gave you my story,' Nadia said, her voice suddenly tired. 'You said you would publish it.'

'And I will,' Ava said. 'But I need to do it in a way that doesn't lead them here to you.'

Finn padded over at that point, but instead of nuzzling Dougie, he put his nose in Ava's hand. It made her want to cry, all the sorrow at Mark's death welling up inside, threatening to swamp her.

'Sorry,' Dougie suddenly said. 'I'm sorry for all of it.'

Ava's heart ached for him. 'None of this is your fault.

None of it,' she repeated. 'But what happens now *will* be down to us.' That much she did know. 'Which is why I have to talk to Dr MacLeod, and in private.'

Dougie eventually nodded. 'Can we go down to the boat-house with Finn?'

The tension in the room had eased. She may even have made some headway, but there were decisions to be made and a route to publication decided. One thing was certain, Mark would not thank her for taking time to mourn him now. His first desire would be for her to finish what they'd begun together.

'Do that,' Ava said, relieved at the thought of no longer being under constant scrutiny.

She told them to go straight to the boathouse and stay there until dark. 'Nadia shouldn't really be outside in daylight. Orphir folk have long-range vision. Here,' she said, grabbing her own jacket from the rack. 'Put this on and pull the hood up. If anyone spots you from a distance, they'll likely think it's me. Now go. Scram. And let me make my phone call.'

She watched them from the window until they reached the byre, then extracted Mark's memory stick from the place she'd hidden it and sat down at her laptop. Mark's death had changed things. His material, together with what she had discovered, was further topped by the existence of a witness.

Who could she trust with the story now?

David had always backed her and Mark up before, even in difficult circumstances. But Go Wild had identifiable links with central government and the upper echelons of British society. And not only the UK government. Mark had evidence linking Go Wild with both Russia and the USA, and a number of European countries too.

Rich and powerful people who believed they were above and beyond the law. Who owned and managed the system. Who both ran and controlled the press.

Could . . . should she send it to David or would he believe it to be too hot to handle, especially in view of Mark's death?

Mark's voice came back to her at that point, urging her to do what was right. What was necessary.

In the past, she would have agreed with him, relished the challenge, maybe even the danger. She also knew that in the last year alone, at least twenty-five journalists around the world had been murdered for exposing stories like this one. Mark had just been added to that list.

Her mind made up, Ava brought up David's number – or thought she did. Too quick. The last few numbers she'd contacted were on the screen and she'd pressed too quickly before realizing the highlighted number was actually McNab's.

She expected it to ring out unanswered, as before, but waited just in case. Then a man's voice answered.

'Yes?'

'DS McNab?' she said, surprised and delighted. 'It's Ava Clouston here.'

'Yes?' the voice said, again.

Fear came crashing in to swamp the joy, because the voice, she realized, wasn't McNab's at all. Ava cut the call and threw the mobile on the table.

She'd given her name to whoever had McNab's phone. If they were searching for her whereabouts, it would be easy enough to locate her now.

58

Dr Sissons had been reserved, even reticent; Dr Walker even more subdued than usual. Rhona knew why. No DS McNab to walk through those doors, usually late, to be harangued in Sissons's inimitable fashion.

McNab wasn't there. Couldn't be there. Because he was missing in the line of duty. At times like these, the team was a squadron with a missing member.

Even Sissons, with all his faults, was aware of that.

The autopsy on the beach body went as planned. The young male had entered the water still alive, but probably barely so, his throat having been cut. He had nevertheless tried to breathe and got some seawater into his lungs rather than air.

His other injuries were slight. He hadn't crashed against rocks or the cliff face, but merely washed up on a partly sandy beach on the west of Orkney mainland, after the Atlantic had tossed him about for a while.

'How many more bodies can we expect from MV *Orlova*?' Sissons enquired, as though Rhona was responsible for the body count coming their way from the northern isles.

As Dr Walker cringed for her, Rhona said, 'Only the Atlantic currents can tell you that.'

Entering the changing room, Rhona immediately sat down. The PM had felt more about McNab's probable death than the poor victim on the table.

273

Although she'd toyed with the idea that McNab was in fact dead and would soon be dragged out of the Thames, not far from where Mark's body had been retrieved . . . still she couldn't, or wouldn't, believe that to be true.

I would know if he were dead. Chrissy would know if he were dead.

'You okay?' Dr Walker said, appearing suddenly beside her.

'Of course.' Rhona rose and removed her mask. 'Been here, there and everywhere the last couple of days. Travelling by helicopter will do that to you. Or at least to me.'

She stepped out of her suit and tossed it in the nearby basket.

A shout from the mortuary sent Dr Walker back inside, but not before he told her how sorry he was.

For what? That McNab is dead? Or that he hasn't been found yet? she said silently to his retreating figure.

Rhona called Chrissy, keen to hear her voice. 'Any word?' she said.

'Nothing . . . as yet,' Chrissy added. 'I'm clearing up here. Planning to head for the jazz club. Want to meet me there?'

A fleeting glimpse of home, empty of company and food, played with her briefly, before Rhona said, 'I'll get cleaned up and meet you there.'

The shower worked, up to a point. The beat of water took away the scent of death, but it didn't remove the fear of it. Not hers, not this time, but of someone she cared about.

What might life be like without McNab?

Easier, certainly. Less annoying, less colourful, less real . . . definitely.

Sean crossed her mind. Any problems they may have had seemed superfluous and unimportant at this moment. Sean,

Chrissy, McNab, Magnus, even Erling . . . All of them played a role in her life. All were the linchpins of her existence.

She stepped out of the shower. She would go to the jazz club. She would talk to Chrissy and she would re-engage with Sean.

That was life. That was reality. That was what McNab, wherever he was, would tell her to do . . . Dr MacLeod.

The mist still lingered, softening the hum of traffic on Byres Road. Stepping into Ashton Lane was like stepping into a ghost story. Free of vehicles, the only sound was of footsteps on the cobbles, their owners looming out of the mist to do a quick sidestep when they saw her.

No one sat at the outside tables because the mist was really a smirr, a Scottish rain that could not make up its mind to fall but hung on every droplet of air, just waiting.

The light and sound of the jazz club beckoned her down the stairs. She recalled the last time she'd been here, going to meet Ava, with McNab following on behind. A short time ago, in which too much had happened.

On the way here, she had made up her mind about one thing, at least. Depriving her forensic assistant of information regarding her recent examination of the stowaway's room had to stop. It wasn't professional, nor was it fair.

Chrissy could keep a secret, probably better than she could. Plus Chrissy's advice at times such as these had in the past proved invaluable. Bill hadn't ordered her not to tell Chrissy about Nadia, just stressed that they should keep it between themselves. And Chrissy was, without doubt, one of them.

Relieved at her decision, Rhona entered the room with a lighter heart, which was quickly noted by Chrissy.

'Here to spill the beans?' she said, a twinkle in her eye. 'Good.' She indicated the large glass of chilled white wine awaiting Rhona. 'I thought I was going to have to ply you with drink first.'

She laughed when Rhona got to the bit about the dog hairs. 'I knew they were dog hairs, even from the photos. So how'd a dog come to be aboard?'

The rest of the story came out then, to include Ava's new house guest, which brought a low whistle from Chrissy.

'And you've read Ava's interview with the girl?'

Rhona nodded. 'So has Bill.'

'None of which was mentioned at the strategy meeting?'

Rhona shook her head.

Chrissy fell silent, her face clouding over again. She was, Rhona thought, considering what part McNab had played in all of this.

'Think I'll head home now,' Chrissy said. 'Give McNab's namesake a hug.'

She gave Rhona one too before she left. 'You'll be all right here on your own?'

'Sean's here. We're off out to eat shortly,' Rhona told her.

'Good.' Chrissy approved of that.

Sean had obviously been watching for Chrissy's departure, because he arrived on cue.

'You ready now?' he asked.

Rhona nodded. 'Ready and hungry.'

They walked down Byres Road and into Partick, still accompanied by the mist. As Sean slipped his arm around her shoulders, in that easy way of his, Rhona sensed something might have changed since their last meal together, when he'd revealed the situation at the club. Either the worries regarding the club's finances had been fixed or Sean, in his inimitable way of looking at the world, had decided not to let them weigh on him any more.

Rhona silently wished she might be capable of doing the same.

Waiting for their order to arrive, he asked her about Orkney.

'A washed-up body from the MV *Orlova*,' she said.

'God, are there likely to be more?'

'Erling Flett suspects so, yes. When and where they might appear is anyone's guess.'

They were avoiding talking about McNab, but could only do that for so long. Sean suddenly reminded her that when McNab was last in trouble, he'd hidden out at the jazz club.

'If he asks to do that again,' Rhona said with a half-smile, 'I want you to tell me, right away. Promise?'

Her mobile rang before Sean could respond. Checking the screen, hoping as ever that it might be McNab, she saw Ellie's name.

With a quick glance at Sean, she answered.

'Rhona?'

'Hi, Ellie.' Rhona waited.

'I've been trying to get hold of Michael,' Ellie said. 'We'd arranged to go to dinner with Janice and Paula, and I can't reach him to confirm . . .' Her voice faltered. 'His mobile seems to be dead?'

'He's maybe out of power,' Rhona said. 'He's had to go to London on a case.'

Sean caught her eye, urging her to be truthful with Ellie.

'He's been out of touch for a while,' Rhona admitted. 'That sometimes happens when he's on a job. I'll make sure he gets in touch with you the moment we hear from him.'

'If you would, please,' Ellie said, her voice breaking a little.

Ringing off, Rhona looked to Sean, saying nothing. She didn't have to. Her worried silence said it all.

59

Looking up at a pristine white ceiling, he registered that he no longer smelt of anything but mild antiseptic. McNab breathed it in and allowed himself the ghost of a smile before reality hit.

Dragging himself upright, he checked his visible wounds, to find all were stitched or bandaged. He loosened the ties on the hospital gown and eased it off his shoulders to get a better view.

His body was colourful and definitely not pretty. But hey, he was semi-upright and warm, which meant he was alive. It also meant he had to get out of there.

A beating such as this would have to be reported to the police. And while he was out of the box, he was pretty certain that would have happened. He glanced at the clock above the door, noting the late hour, plus the fact he'd been here since early morning. A uniform would no doubt appear tonight or early tomorrow.

How soon would it be before Cleverly was made aware of his whereabouts?

He'd replayed the scene of his capture endless times in his head since he was hanging up in that warehouse. The one and only thing he knew for certain was that he still did not trust Cleverly. And what of the Kommandant? How did he play out in all of this?

The door opened and a nurse looked in. Seeing him

sitting up, she gave him a big smile. She was, he registered, small and dark, and very easy on the eye. Especially to someone who'd been viewing nothing but big male bastards for too long.

'You're awake. Good.' She came up close to take a swift look at his dressings.

'Was it you who cleaned me up?' McNab said.

She nodded.

'Then I'm sorry for the mess and the smell.'

She dismissed his apology with a small shake of her head. 'How are you feeling?'

'Great,' McNab said, throwing back the cover and swinging his legs out of the bed. 'Good to go, in fact.'

She looked a little taken aback by this. 'You haven't been discharged yet.'

McNab gave her a big smile. 'I'm discharging myself. So if you could give me my clothes?'

'I don't advise it,' she said pointedly.

McNab observed her determined expression. This wasn't going to be as easy as he'd thought.

'The guys who beat me up are likely to come looking for me,' he said. 'Even in here.'

Her face clouded over at that.

'Which is why I need to go.'

She was mulling it over. McNab couldn't imagine she hadn't faced a similar scenario before now, working as she did in the Accident and Emergency department of an inner-city hospital. She certainly would have in Glasgow.

'My clothes?' he tried again.

With a shrug, she pointed to the bedside cabinet. 'They're in there.' A pause, then, 'Is there someone you could call to pick you up?'

'Sadly, the bastards stole my mobile and wallet,' McNab said.

'You could use my mobile,' she offered.

McNab considered this, but only briefly, since he already knew where he was going and only required the means to get there. He said as much.

'If you could just lend me enough money for a taxi to my safe place?' He checked her name badge. 'I'll pay you back, Nurse Jenny, I promise.' He gave her what he hoped was a winning smile.

He watched as she sized him up, wondering if she would ever see the money again.

Eventually she nodded. 'I'll call you an Uber. You'll need to tell me where you're headed.' She checked his expression. 'Which I won't repeat to anyone.'

McNab smiled a thank you.

He'd had a small hope that Mark might have returned to his flat since they'd last met, but that didn't turn out to be true. It didn't stop him getting in, of course, and when he did, McNab found the place exactly as he'd left it.

His main reason for going there was to get a change of clothing. And hopefully to get some cash or a card he might use in the interim. The clothes were easy. Mark was taller than him, but not a lot, and in build they were similar.

McNab selected an outfit, then disposed of his own stained clothing. After which he headed for the drinks cabinet and poured himself a glass of whisky before entering the kitchen to look for something to eat.

He was rewarded in his search with a large pepperoni pizza he found in the freezer, which he popped in the microwave as per the instructions. After that, he took a seat in the living room to sip his whisky and await the ping telling him his first meal – *for how long?* – was ready.

The pizza, he decided, almost tasted better than the whisky, but not by much. In fact, the combination was pretty perfect. Having assuaged both types of hunger, he now noted that whatever pain relief he'd been dosed up with in the hospital was wearing off.

A search in the bathroom cabinet produced some paracetamol, two of which he swallowed along with another whisky. A quick glance at his face in the mirror was a stark reminder of what had happened to him since last he'd been here.

Sinking on to the couch, he accepted he now felt sufficiently human to make a decision about staying in London to find out more or trying to get back to Glasgow. Neither would be easy without access to cash.

But if he could make contact with Mark . . .

Rising again, he went in search of the house phone and located it in Mark's study. A call to Directory Enquiries got him a helpful operator who was happy to give him the number for the Afghan cafe or, alternatively, to put him straight through without the need to dial.

McNab chose the latter, listening to it ring out unanswered before registering just how late it must be. Of course, the cafe would be shut by now, with Mark no doubt asleep in his own little room.

Resigning himself to waiting until tomorrow, he decided he would turn up at the cafe in person.

He tried to work out exactly how long he'd been out of action for, but the time-lapse between the moment of his kidnapping and now was too hazy. More than likely long enough for concern to be raised back home in Glasgow.

Then another thought struck him, even more forcefully. His captors had his mobile and wallet. They therefore knew who and what he was. They'd demanded to know why he was here in London. What he knew about Go Wild. They would have examined his mobile. Discovered everyone he'd messaged or spoken to in the run-up to his abduction.

And Ava Clouston, investigative reporter and one-time co-worker with Mark Sylvester, was on that list.

McNab had a sudden flashback to having his head yanked back by his hair and various names shouted at him.

Had Ava's been among them?

Fear that it might have been roused him still further. How the hell could he warn Ava that they might in fact be looking for her? Even as far away as Orkney.

He had no memory of her mobile number. He didn't even know her address up there.

But he knew someone who did.

60

Ava came to and was shocked to discover she was lying on the couch in the semi-darkness. When had she fallen asleep?

She remembered working at her laptop, redrafting her material to fully include Nadia's description of how Go Wild recruited people for locations in Ibiza, for the luxury yacht *Hibiscus* off the coast of North Africa and, of course, for the recently discovered ghost ship, the MV *Orlova*.

Everything was there in as much detail as possible. To that she'd added what had been found on the *Orlova* by the police and what her source believed had happened on board the virtual gaming ship.

The biggest revelation, and one she hadn't yet shared with Rhona, was Mark's belief that the male victim was Damian Charles Lloyd, son of Lord Alfred Lloyd, a serving cabinet minister. The girl, Mark had said, was likely Damian's current girlfriend, Penny Addington.

It appeared Damian Lloyd had a chequered history and had skirted police involvement in his activities on numerous occasions, mainly through the intervention of his family. Penny was one of the county set, with little on record, except for the fact she was a keen fencer, something Damian had also taken part in.

If Mark was right, then a cover-up was already in action, and in his opinion the Met were involved.

Ava dragged herself to her feet and went to shout upstairs. She'd told Dougie to stay at the boathouse until dark and, judging by the silence, they'd followed her instructions. Just to be sure, she went up to check their rooms, to find them both empty.

Aware that they certainly should have appeared home by now, Ava opened the kitchen door to discover a blood-red sun setting the horizon aflame, the image of which suddenly filled her with foreboding.

She'd ordered Dougie not to take the boat out. He'd agreed to that easily enough, but had he stuck to it? He'd been pretty strong in his argument that he should take Nadia across to Hoy and he always kept his camping gear on board the *Fear Not*.

To see the boathouse clearly, she would have to walk as far as the barn. Ava reached for her coat, then remembered that she'd given it to Nadia, so headed out without one.

The May evening was chilly, the sky clear with the promise of stars and a moon. She would forgo a torch and trust to luck she could get down there and back without one. After all, she knew the route well enough, even in poor light.

Upping her speed, she decided to check the byre first. There was always a chance they'd gone in there. Ava had come to realize there was a strong bond between her brother and the rescued girl. Whether sexual or not, she had no idea, but the barn would be a warmer place to hang out than the boathouse.

Throwing open the door, Ava called into the shadows, hoping Dougie's voice would answer and dismiss her fears. With only the hens still in residence, there was none of the soft breathing and movement of the kye . . . and no answering human shout.

As she emerged, she picked up the scent of something burning. What? And from where?

Her first thought was for the cattle. Might whoever had killed the calf and his mother have lit a fire in their field? Horrified at the thought, she scanned nearby and saw that her fears were unfounded, the herd apparently grazing unperturbed.

So where was the smoke coming from? She stood for a moment. It wasn't close, but it wasn't far away either.

Then she saw the first flames to the west. With horror, Ava registered it had to be in the area of the boathouse. Or even the boathouse itself.

Terrified she might be right, she ran in that direction, screaming Dougie's name, running down the rough track.

Well caught now, the flames were leaping sky high, their colours dancing against the orange and red sunset.

Within yards of the building, her screams were swallowed by the cracking and spitting as the fire took control of the wooden structure.

Hearing someone crunch over the foreshore behind her, Ava turned, praying it might be Dougie. The figure emerging from the smoke was tall and male, which gave her hope, but only briefly, as Magnus took form and came towards her, his face horrified.

'Is Dougie in there?' he shouted over the mounting roar.

Ava shook her head, tears running down her blackened face. 'I don't know. I don't know.'

'Stay here,' Magnus ordered.

She watched as he steadfastly approached the blaze.

'No, Magnus,' she called. 'Don't.'

Whether he heard her plea or not, he didn't stop, even though he must have known that if there was anyone in the boathouse, they didn't stand a chance.

Eventually he retreated, although obviously loath to do so.

'Might he have taken the boat out?' he asked her.

'I don't know. Maybe,' she said, in hope now.

'I need to get closer,' he said. 'If someone is still in there . . .'

Ava knew what Magnus was trying to say. She remembered the trouble he'd had at school because of his hyperosmia. They'd all tormented him mercilessly about his ability to smell things so powerfully. Made him the butt of so many stupid teenage jokes. She felt sorry for that now, as she saw him try again, his expression determined.

He was concentrating, allowing his sense of smell to take over. She watched as the power of it seemed to almost overwhelm him, as she'd seen happen in the past. She imagined what it must be like . . . the smell of scorched wood, tar, a mishmash of hot metal and seared stones and, worst of all . . .

He turned to face her, and in that instant she knew. Nowhere among it all had he caught the smell of burning flesh or the scent of singed animal hair.

'Dougie isn't in there,' he told her. 'And neither is Finn.'

'You're sure?' she said, her relief obvious.

Magnus nodded. 'I'm sure.'

'Then where are they?'

'They?' Magnus said, his voice wary.

Ava thought of saying Dougie and Finn, but she could tell by Magnus's expression that that wouldn't wash. Only the truth would work here.

'Dougie has the girl from the *Orlova* with him, Nadia,' she said.

He nodded, as though he had suspected that all along.

A thought suddenly struck Ava. 'Why did you come over? Was it because you saw the flames?'

'I had a call from DS McNab in London. Go Wild thugs

have been holding him. He escaped but they still have his mobile. He wanted to warn you that they could have traced your number and there's every reason to believe they have someone already on Orkney.'

Fear crept back to swamp Ava's relief. She stared at Magnus. 'Then they could have taken Dougie and the girl and lit the fire to make us think they were in there.'

Magnus considered this. 'What about Finn? He wouldn't have gone with them without a fight. Did you hear him barking?'

Ava admitted to having fallen asleep. 'I'd told Dougie not to come back from the boathouse until it was dark. I didn't want anyone to spot the girl and wonder who she was.' She paused, thinking. 'Could we tell if the boat's gone? If it's not in the wreckage, then maybe the three of them took off in the *Fear Not*, despite me telling Dougie not to.'

Please God, they did, she thought.

'We can't check that out until the debris cools,' Magnus said. 'In the meantime, we should take a look around for Finn.'

He didn't say 'a hurt or dead Finn', but that was what Magnus was implying, because if the faithful collie was alive, and in the vicinity, he would surely have made his presence known by now.

For Ava, a picture of a dead Finn had now supplanted the one of a burning Dougie in her mind.

61

The vibration of her mobile broke through her dreams as it rattled across the bedside cabinet. Rhona's first thought was that it must be her alarm, then reaching out, she realized it was barely light outside.

Grabbing the phone, Rhona rose, taking it through to the kitchen to answer. If Magnus was calling her at this hour, then it had to be important.

She barely got to greet him before he said, 'McNab's okay. He called late last night. He'd been lifted off the street when he went to meet Cleverly and held captive, but got away.'

The relief was instantaneous. 'Thank God,' Rhona said, her heart lifting. 'Where is he now?'

'Still in London. He called to warn me that the people who grabbed him have his mobile and he was worried they would use it to locate Ava.' He hesitated. 'I think they may already have done that.'

Rhona listened as he described the fire.

'When I got there it was well ablaze, but from the smell, there was no one inside, although Ava said that Dougie and the girl from the *Orlova* had gone to the boathouse earlier.'

'Ava told you about Nadia?'

'Yes.' Magnus didn't ask how long Rhona had known because he didn't have to.

'You think Dougie and the girl have been abducted?' Rhona said.

'The rain's just come on, so the embers will soon be cool enough to check if Dougie's boat was in there. If not, there's a chance they may have got away.'

'Then who set the fire?'

'No idea, but someone did. I could smell the diesel.' He continued, 'Erling's spoken with DI Wilson and there's a search party out for Dougie and the girl.'

So Erling knew about Nadia now too, which was a relief. 'How is Ava?' Rhona said.

'I asked her to come to my place, but she won't leave the farm. PC Tulloch's stationed at the house with her. There's something else,' he said. 'McNab didn't know that Mark Sylvester was dead.'

What would McNab do with that news? Probably something rash was Rhona's immediate thought.

'Can I get in touch with him?' she said, keen now to hear his voice. And to convince him not to take any more chances.

'He called me from Mark's landline. I tried calling him back this morning, but it was engaged. When I tried again, it just rang out, so it's likely McNab's gone from there.'

'Gone where?' Rhona said.

Magnus had no idea.

'Does Bill know all of this?'

'He does now,' Magnus said.

There was no telling what McNab would do in such circumstances, except that it probably wouldn't be what they thought. Stuck in London with no money or mobile phone, and no means of getting home, unless he presented himself at a police station.

Which he didn't appear keen to do.

After Magnus rang off, promising to get back to her were there any further developments, Rhona saved the number he'd given her for Mark's flat.

McNab had gone there after his escape from his captors. Why? Because he'd hoped Mark would help him? Do what exactly?

He's not ready to come back, she thought. *And Mark's death won't have changed that. Not one little bit.*

62

McNab had thought the early call to the landline would be from Magnus, Rhona or the boss. It hadn't been. When he'd picked up, it was the Kommandant's voice he'd heard.

'I told you to fuck off back to Glasgow, Jock. They know where you are. So get the fuck out of there. Now.'

McNab had done exactly that.

Saying a silent thank you to Mark for what he'd taken from his house, he also made him a solemn promise that he wouldn't give up until he'd nailed the bastards.

The pawn shop he'd identified online was in the business of turning a wide variety of everyday items into cash. There had been a few, apparently made famous by some TV programme, that were looking for yuppie stuff like designer handbags, gold, jewellery and artwork.

In truth, Mark had a few paintings that McNab thought might be worth a bit, but he'd stuck to stuff he could easily carry. After this was over, he would try to replace them, he'd told Mark silently, while aware now that Mark was in no position to complain and most likely was cheering him on in what he was about to do.

His big fear on entering the pawn shop was that he would be required to show ID. Maybe it was because of his smart appearance in Mark's clothes, or the beat-up face, but he wasn't asked for any, just swiftly offered a sum of money for the goods, which though obviously too low, he'd accepted anyway.

Feeling much the better for having some cash in hand, he headed for a nearby Tesco and bought a burner phone and some credit. Then he sat in a cafe window seat, with a view of Mark's building, and watched for any visitors, aware that he might well have missed them in the interim.

His luck was in, however.

While he was enjoying his first coffee of the day, the black van drew up outside. What looked like the same two guys emerged along with the Kommandant, which suggested they'd swallowed his story of McNab's escape.

McNab smiled as he took photographs of all three entering the building, plus, of course, the number plate of the van.

While he waited for them to come back out, McNab called the station and asked to be put through to Ollie, who sounded verging on the ecstatic to hear his voice.

'Hey,' McNab reminded him. 'This isn't Maria you're talking to here.'

'What do you need, Detective Sergeant?' Ollie said, the smile still in his voice.

McNab fed him an image of the van's number plate first. 'It's connected with Go Wild in some way. Find out how.'

Next were the twin bruisers. 'Mutt and Jeff,' he told Ollie. 'Jeff's the one on the right. They're both heavily tattooed. Mutt likes naked women, probably the only way he gets to touch one. Jeff's more of a Nazi lover. I would expect both to be somewhere on the system.'

'The third guy, the Kommandant. He's the one that let me go. He's the one I'm interested in.'

None of the images he'd managed to take were face on, but with a super recognizer like Ollie that shouldn't be a problem.

'Call me back when you have something.' McNab cut the

call as he spotted the Kommandant and the two stooges re-emerge and climb into the van.

If they'd confirmed he'd been staying there, and it was pretty obvious by the mess, then they'd think there was a chance he would return, unless the Kommandant persuaded them otherwise.

Nevertheless, it looked like the comfy couch and Mark's whisky were now out of bounds.

McNab finished his coffee and requested another. He would stay here until Ollie came up with the goods, which, judging by his enthusiasm, wouldn't be that long, on the vehicle front at least.

By the time the call came, he was on his third espresso.

Ollie, still on a high – *How many sugar-free Irn-Brus had he drunk?* – had traced the owner of the vehicle which was, 'wait for it, a Go Wild subsidiary called Combat,' he said in obvious delight. 'I'll text you the address.'

He went on. 'As for the Kommandant, he doesn't exist on the police crime photo database. However,' he paused, 'I did find him on a trawl of social media. It's not a great image but it's him all right, although I don't have a name. It was taken in a nightclub somewhere in London and he was in the background of a group of females. It's on an Instagram account of one Lily Peony.'

McNab groaned. 'Okay, keep trying to find out who the guy is. I suspect he may be a plant in this set-up, but who put him there, I'd like to know.'

'Maybe he's Met or serious crime squad?' Ollie said. 'I have a super-recognizer pal down there. I could ask him to take a look?'

It was a good idea. 'Can he keep this under the radar for the moment?' McNab said.

'I've done the same for him in the past,' Ollie said. 'So yeah.'

It was worth a shot, so McNab okayed it. He would have to inform the boss, of course, but maybe not immediately.

'When will you be back?' Ollie said. 'You need to see what we've been retrieving from the gaming software on the ship,' he added excitedly.

McNab wasn't ready or willing to answer that question . . . yet. 'Just tell the boss I'll be in touch.'

The Afghan cafe was open. McNab caught the rich aroma of their coffee on approach.

He had no idea how he would be greeted since Mark's death, but it was unlikely to be good. Glancing down, he suddenly remembered he was also walking about in Mark's clothes, which might not go down so well either.

The guy on the counter looked him over, his expression darkening.

McNab decided to dive in anyway. 'I'm here to talk about Mark,' he said in what he hoped was a non-combative tone.

If looks could kill, McNab realized, he would now be flat on his back, taking his last breath on this earth. But looks couldn't kill, he reminded himself. Being strung up and beaten might, but luckily it hadn't.

'I think the same folk that did this to me' – he raised Mark's shirt for effect – 'may well have murdered Mark.'

'You coming here caused his death.'

McNab didn't have a response for that, apart from saying he was intent on catching the bastards who did it, and to do that he needed access to Mark's laptop.

After a moment's silence, his sparring partner pointed to a table. McNab, taking that as an instruction to wait, went and sat down.

His hope of being served coffee in the interim was destined for failure. Watching the minutes tick by, he was on the point of barging through, as before, when he was summoned to enter the world beyond the curtain.

Reaching the room, he found a man sitting at Mark's now empty desk. His dark curly hair streaked with grey, he was wearing what McNab presumed was traditional Afghan clothing. Below thick eyebrows, a pair of green eyes silently studied him before he spoke.

'Detective Sergeant McNab of Police Scotland, I believe?'

Taken aback at being so clearly identified, McNab nodded, then waited for what might come next.

'My name is Abu-Zar. My friend Mark explained about your role in all of this. I see you have had your own battles to fight in this particular war.' The man paused there, his expression solemn. '*You*, however, unlike my friend, have survived them.'

At that moment the coffee arrived and McNab was invited to sit down. Eventually the man said, 'What is it you wish to know?'

'I'd like to know what happened after I left here.'

The man nodded, then said, 'Mark received and made a number of phone calls, and worked on his laptop as normal. He then said he was going out to meet someone.' He paused for a moment. 'He did not return.' Collecting himself, he continued. 'We searched for him, of course. Then we heard that Mark's body had been pulled from the river. The newspapers have suggested it was suicide, using his time in war zones as a reason.' He gave a grim smile. 'Who would believe that a man who spent all those months in Afghanistan in the mountains travelling with the mujahidin would kill himself? I was there with him.

Mark was afraid of nothing and no one, intent only on reporting the truth of what he saw.'

McNab was inclined to agree with such a summary, although he had met the man only once. He indicated the cleared desk. 'I'd like to take a look at his laptop, phone, notes?'

The man shook his head in an apparent apology. 'That won't be possible, I'm afraid. The police came and took all of that away.'

McNab swore under his breath. Of course they had. He wondered how long the Met had been watching this place, following everything Mark did. No doubt they'd seen him visit here. Is that why he'd been picked up and interrogated?

There seemed to be no clear blue line between the Met and the people they were supposed to be investigating.

McNab, deflated and defeated, decided it was time to leave.

'However,' the man said as McNab got to his feet, 'Mark gave strict instructions that if anything did happen to him, then this envelope should be given to the Scottish detective.'

McNab accepted the small envelope and, opening it, he looked inside.

'Thank you,' he said with a smile.

63

'You're sure?' Ava said for the second time.

'No one was in the boathouse. No people and no dog. Dougie's boat wasn't there either.'

Ava felt the horror retreat. Dougie hadn't died in that fire, just as Magnus had said. She thought of how long and hard they'd searched for Finn while they'd waited for the embers to cool. They'd still been searching for the collie when Sandy and the fire team had come rolling down the track to take charge of the site.

'Thanks, Sandy,' she said, with an attempt at a smile.

'He's out somewhere in his boat, like always,' Sandy told her.

Ava nodded, as though accepting that. Sandy Balfour was, after all, an Orphir man, living on the hill not far from Erling. He'd known Dougie all his life and probably better than she had during the time she'd been away.

'Was it accidental, the fire?'

'I can't tell you how it started. Not for sure. You'd need a forensic fire investigator for that. We could request one, but since—'

'No one died,' she finished for him.

He nodded. 'The whole of Orkney's on the lookout now for Dougie, and the girl. We'll find them soon enough.'

So all their attempts to keep Nadia hidden from view had

failed. In fact, they'd only made her more visible to anyone from Go Wild who might be looking for her.

Which meant she could delay her decision no longer.

She walked Sandy out to his vehicle, said her goodbyes, then went swiftly inside to make her phone call.

David was quick to answer, perhaps because he'd been expecting to hear from her.

'Ava, how are things?'

'I've been waiting for you to get back to me,' she said pointedly.

'I know and I'm sorry.' David's tone was conciliatory. 'Your piece is currently with our lawyers. I have to be sure we're safe to print it.'

His voice, she realized, had changed. She'd rarely heard fear from him before, but it was there now.

'What's going on, David? You've never been afraid to print our material before.'

There was a moment's silence before he said, 'The police have been here about Mark's death. They're aware he was working on an exposé of Go Wild. They asked if it had been for this paper because Mark's material can't be published as it's now evidence in a suspicious death. This survivor you have . . . you have to tell the police about her.'

'Police Scotland already know,' Ava told him, not mentioning Nadia's recent disappearance.

The voice on the other end went quiet . . . Then, 'The Met are trying to kill this story. There's high-up people involved.'

'Which is exactly why it should be printed,' Ava told him. When silence fell again, she said, 'I'll publish it myself,' and cut the call.

Shaking with anger, she tried to focus. What she'd said to Dougie and the girl still held true, she reasoned. What they chose to do now would affect the outcome of all their lives.

Had Dougie decided to flee and hide or had someone else chosen his fate for him? An image of Nadia's face when they'd discussed their plan came to mind. Had the girl always intended to run? Had she been the one to persuade Dougie to do that?

Stop and focus, she told herself angrily. *Imagine you could call Mark and talk to him. What would he tell you to do?*

She thought of other times and other places, where they'd had to decide . . . to hold back or not. How many times Mark had put himself in the firing line. A soldier of the truth, without the means to protect himself.

Fuck it, Ava . . . what are you waiting for? his ghost-like presence demanded.

She smiled. 'You're right. What am I waiting for?' She sat down at her laptop. It would take a while to get it properly out there, and then for people to find it.

Dougie had told her that when she was ready, the story should be released to the online gaming community first. That way it would spread as swiftly as a virus. He had even set up an automatic link for her to do that. 'So you don't need me here when you decide,' he'd told her.

The knock at the door broke her concentration.

'Ava, I have some news for you.' PC Tulloch's voice sounded too tentative for the news to be good. Or was she just imagining that?

Ava opened the door and invited Ivan inside.

'What?' she demanded when she saw his face.

He hesitated, only making things worse.

'For God's sake, Ivan,' she said in distress.

'The coastguard have just reported finding the *Fear Not* abandoned and drifting.'

'Where?'

'Hoy Sound.'

'Close to shore?' she said, more in hope than expectation.

'It's not clear,' Ivan said, his expression a picture of misery.

Ava took pity on him. 'Thanks for letting me know, Ivan.'

Alone again, Ava tried to focus on the possible scenarios which might have led to what Ivan had just described.

Dougie was somewhere on Hoy and had released the boat to suggest they'd drowned.

They had drowned, but since Dougie knew these waters, prevailing tides and winds, that didn't seem likely.

They were dead by someone's hand and the boat released to give the impression they had drowned.

They'd been captured and were possibly still alive.

No matter which way she played it out, instinct told her it was one of the last two.

The forces ranged against them were just too strong, she acknowledged. In London, and also here on Orkney. They simply couldn't win.

That's the coward's opt-out, she heard Mark say. *Words are powerful and have reach. Use them.*

He was right. There was only one thing to do now. And that was to put the story out there.

There would, no doubt, be a price to pay, and in that moment, Ava both accepted that and almost welcomed it.

64

McNab sat back in Mark's chair and surveyed his new abode. Provided with Mark's backup laptop, which Abu-Zar had not surrendered to the police, a smartphone and a vehicle at his beck and call, he was back in business.

Plus he had a place to sleep, food when required and all the coffee he could drink.

Also, judging from the big burly guy hanging around outside his new office, they'd provided him with a bodyguard. He suspected the bodyguard was armed, but had decided not to question this. As a police officer, it was better not to know.

It appeared that taking Mark down may have been an error on the enemy's part. *Who pisses off associates of the mujahidin?* Added to all of that, he'd been assigned Firash as his driver, Abu-Zar's son, the one whose life Mark had saved, according to Ava, and now a knowledgeable man about town, who had been a confidant of Mark's.

A full and frank conversation with the boss about his present circumstances had allowed him another forty-eight hours in London, after which he was expected to get the train back to Glasgow. McNab hoped and intended that it would be enough time for his plan to unfold, especially with his new allies on board.

During his conversation with the boss, he'd stressed his

concern for Ava's safety. 'Most of her investigation was done in tandem with Mark. And he's dead.'

The boss had assured him that Ava was under police protection on Orkney. Then he'd sprung the bad news. McNab had listened with mounting concern to the story of the brother, missing again. This time with the girl he'd rescued from the *Orlova*.

'We're hoping they've gone into hiding, but we can't rule out the possibility that they've been picked up by associates of Go Wild. If so, there's a chance she may have been taken south,' the boss had said.

McNab had asked about cruise ships at that point. 'According to Ollie, the Go Wild empire has exclusive cruise ships operating worldwide, all of them with helicopter pads for the transfer of visitors. It wouldn't be that difficult to get her off the island.'

In his mind's eye, he could already see the girl being whisked away from under their noses.

'Police Orkney are checking everything within their manpower capabilities,' the boss had told him.

There had been some positive news from the call, with the identification of the Glasgow fire victim.

'We've found a match via dental records for Charlotte Weiner, a missing student at the London School of Economics,' the boss had said.

It appeared Olivia's belongings were left at the scene to suggest it was her. 'Why, we don't know,' Bill had said. 'Unless they wanted her to disappear, presumed dead. Folk still think that fire destroys everything,' he'd finished.

McNab checked the time. He had fifteen minutes before he should log on for the strategy meeting, when apparently Ollie was going to reveal what had been retrieved from the gaming equipment on board the *Orlova*. There was, however, still time to make the call he'd been putting off, despite Rhona's reminder when they'd spoken earlier.

Listening to it ring out, part of him hoped it wouldn't be answered. When it was, he said nothing for a moment, forgetting that his name wouldn't be on the screen because he wasn't using his own phone.

'Hi, Ellie, it's Michael.'

The moment's silence that followed saw his heart slowing to what felt like a stop.

Then, 'Michael. Thank goodness you're okay. I called Rhona when I couldn't reach you. She said you were away on a job.'

'Yes, sorry about that. My phone died.'

'It's about a date for the dinner party you mentioned. I expect it can't be decided until you're back from wherever you went?' she said, a smile in her voice.

Over the course of her words, McNab's heartbeat had risen first to normal, then above. Ellie actually sounded pleased to hear from him. She wanted to see him again.

'True,' McNab said.

'So you'll let me know when you're back in Glasgow?'

'I will,' he promised.

After a short silence, she said, 'Please stay safe, Michael.'

In that sweet moment McNab imagined maybe, just maybe, they might be back on firmer ground.

'You too,' he said, adding, 'I'll definitely give you a call when I get back, if that's okay?'

'Yes. It is.'

He found himself smiling, which felt strange, and also reminded him that parts of his face weren't fully healed yet.

Thank God Ellie hadn't suggested they have a video call.

65

Bill called them to order, then explained that DS McNab would be joining the strategy meeting from London.

When McNab's face appeared on the big screen, there were a few whistles of approval, even one or two wolf whistles, belying the state of his face.

Apart from that, Rhona thought, *he looks okay.*

'Stupid bastard,' Janice announced beside her. 'When he gets back, I'm going to kill him.'

Rhona understood the sentiment. 'I'll help you,' she said.

Ollie was now up on stage and, in his usual, hesitant fashion, described what they were about to see.

'There was some fire damage to the equipment, but not enough to prevent us from recovering the games software, plus the recordings taken of various bouts, including the one to the death, which you are about to see here. I should say we believe these bouts were recorded so that participants might view themselves later . . . some were also made commercially available online via various virtual gaming platforms.'

Most of the police personnel had already viewed Rhona's footage of the crime scene, the route through the maze to the arena and the virtual audience. All of which had been taken after the event. This promised to be something quite different, as the tension in the room suggested.

There was an intake of breath as the first image appeared on the screen.

A seemingly frightened female was being dragged by two men through the maze and then abandoned in the centre of the arena. Rhona recognized the victim, but here, she was alive.

A roar from the virtual crowd signalled their mounting excitement at what was to come.

It resembled a scene from a gladiator-type movie, just as Chrissy had suggested. However, the female combatant appeared not to want to be there, which threw up an alternative interpretation of the crime scene to the one she and Chrissy had imagined.

Chrissy's current task involved comparing DNA samples from the female victim with those collected from both the staff and visitor quarters, in order to hopefully establish her role aboard the ship. Had she perhaps not been a paying guest, after all, but someone brought on board to take part in the scene they were now viewing?

The virtual audience fell silent as all eyes turned to a lone male now entering the arena. He strode in, effectively giving a bow to the adoring crowd. He appeared to be the favoured one, the 'hero' of whatever game was being played out here.

The appreciative roar from the balcony emphasized that.

In contrast, the watchers in the strategy room were completely silent. Whatever happened next would result in two actual deaths, and that wouldn't be comfortable for anyone there to watch.

The female, although possessing a weapon that looked like the one found at the scene, kept it by her side. She appeared not to want to fight, which obviously angered her opponent, and the watching crowd, who proceeded to boo and shout obscenities at her.

Egged on by the male, they continued to call out for blood to be spilt. The male, obviously aroused, was eager for that too. He began prodding her, the point of his short sword nicking the skin on her arms, then her thighs, culminating in her exposed breast. This led to a roar of approval.

And still the female didn't defend herself or retaliate.

Rhona thought of her own interpretation of the manner in which the scene might have played out, and suspected something was about to change.

And change it did.

Suddenly it was the female attacking the male, and not without skill. The male, who had behaved as though he thought himself invincible, found himself being outfought. The female appeared swifter and fleeter of foot than her opponent, using her smaller stature to attack the lower half of his body. Blood was spraying from wounds inflicted on his thighs, his hips, his groin, the point of her sword getting perilously close to his most vulnerable spot.

The interest in the strategy room was sharpened by this. As for the virtual crowd, their howls of delight were now focused entirely on the female, screaming their pleasure at the fighting pair below.

The contest appeared to be evenly matched. Neither of the two participants looked as though they were there for the purpose of killing one another, although the intensity of the bloodletting was so blatantly sexual that Rhona suspected they were watching the foreplay, the culmination of which would be the sexual act itself.

At this point the scene was plunged into darkness before a single spotlight came on above them and the virtual crowd fell silent. The combatants stopped, obviously puzzled. This, it appeared, had not been in the script.

The male swore loudly, demanding that the game be continued. Consternation then apprehension registered on his face. The female became more watchful, certain, it seemed, that they must be on their guard.

Blinded by the spotlight, they did not at first see the masked swordsman emerge from the maze. Taller than the male, his upper body bare, he strode towards the surprised couple, his much longer sword raised.

The attack was over in seconds. As he swiftly sliced into necks and legs, the two fell heavily bleeding to the ground. Their assailant stood over them for a moment then, turning, walked out of sight.

The video stopped at this point, the final image being the scene Rhona and Chrissy had met on board the *Orlova*.

Bill came to the front again, allowed a few moments for the company to come to terms with what they'd just watched, then said, 'According to the murdered investigative journalist Mark Sylvester, the male victim is Damian Charles Lloyd, son of Lord Alfred Lloyd, a cabinet minister. This has not been confirmed, despite repeated requests to the Met to do so, after they insisted that both bodies be sent south.

'Mark also identified the female as Penny Addington, who apparently Damian was seeing. Both were keen fencers.'

He brought up a photograph of the two of them together, dressed in their fencing gear.

'Our resident super recognizer,' he gestured to Ollie, 'assures me they are one and the same. However, without official confirmation from London we can't be sure. Should it be Damian Lloyd, the implications are far-reaching.

'This, we believe, is the reason for London's reticence on

the matter. I must stress here that nothing stated in this room goes any further than here.' He looked around the assembled officers. 'Do I make myself clear?'

The murmurs indicated he had.

It was DS Clark up next, looking all the better for her partner being alive. She opened by saying as much, eliciting a cheer.

'The fingerprint on the credit card found with the burn victim is that of Steven Willis, who has previous convictions for people-trafficking, amongst other things. We are currently looking for him. The victim, as some of you already know, has been identified as Charlotte Weiner, a student from the London School of Economics, who disappeared three weeks ago. We believe Willis was engaged to dispose of Charlotte Weiner in a way that suggested it was Olivia Newton Richardson, who Interpol think may be currently in the south of Spain.'

Rhona could tell by the faces around her that the significance of all of this, especially the Met's failure to share information, had not been lost on the assembled company, the time wasted over the identification of the fire victim being particularly galling.

The briefing now moved to Orkney, where Erling joined them from the conference room in Kirkwall. Tense and pale, he proceeded to give them an update on the stowaway, Nadia Kowalski, a key witness to what had happened on the *Orlova*.

For many it was the first time they'd heard of the existence of a witness, then only to hear that she had now gone missing, along with Dougie Clouston, brother of Ava Clouston, who had been working with Mark Sylvester on the exposé of the Go Wild conglomerate.

'Dougie's boat has since been found abandoned in the Sound of Hoy, some distance away from his home in Orphir,' Erling said. 'There is concern that both he and the girl may have been taken to prevent her from providing evidence of what happened on the *Orlova*. Or worse, she has already been disposed of.

'We now know that Ava Clouston recorded the girl's story while she was hidden on her farm, which also puts her in considerable danger, and she is currently under police protection.'

The last person to speak was McNab. Rhona had expected him to give an account of what had happened since his arrival in London, to include his incarceration. Instead, he said, 'Run the video back to the killer's entrance.'

It was well worth a second watch, from a forensic scientist's point of view. The killer was left-handed, as suspected, the pattern of the cuts in Rhona's study of the bodies matching what was being played out on the screen.

As the killing ended, McNab shouted, 'Freeze.' In this shot the killer was caught face on, except they couldn't see his face under the mask. What they did have was a clear view of his torso. Tanned and blood-splattered, the tattoo, a swirling GW centring on the left nipple, was obvious.

McNab gave a little laugh. 'I've seen that bastard close up.'

'Where?' Bill demanded.

'At the bare-knuckle fight. That's the posh fucker who knocked me out.'

66

'You should have let Harim come with us,' Firash said. 'You forget what these people are capable of.'

McNab hadn't forgotten, and maybe wouldn't for a long time. He just didn't want his resident bodyguard, offspring of the mujahidin, going in all guns blazing.

'The plan is to take a quiet look at the Combat office, nothing more,' he said, hoping that would turn out to be true.

Firash didn't argue but adopted instead a grave countenance, as though considering how he was going to keep the Scottish detective alive when McNab didn't appear committed to the idea.

In the short time since McNab had met Mark's minder, he'd been impressed with his knowledge of Mark's work. There was also no doubt he blamed himself for his death. Apparently Mark had refused to take Firash with him when he'd left for the final meeting, and Firash had had no idea who Mark had gone to see. Something that obviously haunted him.

As Firash deftly wound his way through the central London traffic, McNab checked his mobile to realize he'd missed a call from Ollie. Listening to his voicemail, he found a frantic message asking him to call back.

The phone had barely begun to ring before it was snatched up and answered.

'The shit's hit the fan. Ava's released her material online, initially to the worldwide gaming community. It's everywhere now,' Ollie's stunned voice declared, 'with millions of hits. All the details are there. Mark's death because he was investigating the Go Wild connection with the *Orlova*, where rich people went to play torture and killing games. She gives pretty full details of what's been on offer, from the bare-knuckle fights upwards and the web of international companies across the world associated with Go Wild.'

'Jesus fucking Christ!' McNab said out loud.

'She also says she's spoken to a survivor discovered on the ghost ship. She hints at the suspected death of a prominent politician's son, who was on the ship to fight a girl to the death for pleasure, and asks, "Is Russia involved? Or is it a very British game?"'

Ollie took a breath. 'Finally she mentions a Police Scotland detective's capture in London and a surprise escape.'

The significance of this final piece of information wasn't lost on McNab. It wouldn't take long for someone to work out how he'd got away from his captors and who had likely helped him.

He ended the call, telling Ollie he'd be back in touch and to make sure the boss was kept fully informed.

'What is it?' Firash said, eyeing McNab anxiously via the driver's mirror.

'Just get us to the Combat address and fast,' McNab ordered.

'You have to tell me what's happening, otherwise I can't do my job,' Firash protested. He hadn't said, 'like with Mark', but it was clear that's what he meant.

McNab relented. 'Ava Clouston released the Go Wild story worldwide and she included a bit about my incarceration,' he told him. 'The guy who set me free may well be in serious trouble because of it. We need to check out Combat and then, if necessary, the place where I was held.'

He'd figured out the warehouse location with the help of Google Earth and his drugged memory of the Scottish BrewDog Clerkenwell pub which he'd visited.

Firash nodded. 'Okay, but now I think we should bring Harim, in case we need him.' When McNab didn't immediately respond, he added, 'They killed Mark. They won't hesitate to kill us too.'

Seeing his fearful expression, McNab relented and Firash made the call. McNab couldn't interpret what was being said, but it was definitely going to make something happen.

If the Kommandant was at the Combat address and this news was circulating, he would be the one in danger now, McNab thought. And if he wasn't, then, 'We check the old warehouse where they held me,' he told Firash. 'Just in case.'

Glancing out of the car window, he registered that they were back in the area of his abduction.

'How long now?' he asked, irritated at how slow the traffic was.

'According to the satnav, we're two streets away,' Firash told him.

As they slowed down for yet another red light, McNab threw open the car door and jumped out, much to Firash's dismay.

'Meet me there,' he said, closing the door, 'and make it quick,' aware that he might well need backup.

McNab realized he was now close to where he'd hung about in the rain, waiting for Cleverly. Ahead of him, the usual crowds were milling around the entrance to the Underground. Weaving among them, he emerged to see the doorway into which Cleverly had apparently darted.

Approaching, McNab noted that it was a sex shop, but the entry to the neighbouring building was via a double glass door, with the name Preston House and four buzzers to allow access, the top of which indicated it was Combat's office.

Steeling himself, he pressed the button.

Rerunning his abduction as he awaited a response, he realized that his kidnappers may well have come from these premises. Had Cleverly made his swift exit into Combat or the sex shop? Possibly something he was about to find out.

When a female voice responded to his request for entry, McNab looked up at the camera and gave his name. A few seconds later he was buzzed in.

Entering the lobby, he ignored the lift and opted for the stairs, only to discover he was out of breath by the third landing. Not a good sign. Before pushing open the door, he took a moment to compose himself.

Stepping into a carpeted area, he found it empty. Taking a quick look at the two screens on the reception desk, he spotted the one linked to the entrance webcam. So they would have seen him already, bruised face and all. But had anyone recognized the name? And where was the female who'd allowed him entry?

At that moment a dark-suited man sporting an earpiece appeared from a door behind the desk to ask him what he wanted.

McNab feigned puzzlement. 'This is Combat, isn't it?'

The man's nod was almost imperceptible.

'I'm looking to arrange a London fight,' he said, his tone verging on a threat. 'In fact, I'd like to knock the hell out of the posh fucker who did this to me recently in Glasgow.'

The guy's lips moved into something that might be

construed as a smile. He pointed to McNab's face. 'That looks like Hugo's work.'

'Is Hugo or any of his minders around?' McNab said. When the man hesitated, McNab added, 'Believe me, he'll want to hear what I have to say.'

Just then, something came in via the earpiece, which resulted in a swift change in the guy's expression. McNab wondered if he'd been rumbled.

'Okay,' the guy was saying. 'Hugo will see you now.' He unbuttoned his suit jacket and, reaching in, drew the gun from its holster. He flicked it in the direction of a fire exit, which McNab suspected led down the back of the building and to his possible grave.

A quick glance at the camera screen found no sign of Firash, or Harim.

The bodyguard might not have got here by now, but Firash should have, McNab thought.

67

The smell was back, greeting him with the tight embrace of a long-lost friend. In fact, it had roused him, not from a drugged sleep this time, but from a blow to the head.

He should be glad, McNab thought, that the gun had been used to knock him out, and not to kill him . . . yet.

The darkness hid his prison, but by smell and sound, he knew where he was. Trauma had ensured he was unlikely ever to forget.

The journey here too had been similar. He remembered entering the black van parked this time at the back of the building, the bag over the head, then the blow.

After that nothing, until now.

The last time he'd imagined Cleverly might be here, and in his drugged state had called his name, having it bounce back at him. Not something he planned to do again.

The scent of blood was fresh. The stink of warm urine even fresher. Someone had pissed nearby and recently. And – McNab quickly checked his groin – this time it hadn't been him.

He got onto his knees and attempted to follow that scent.

The body wasn't far away. In fact, in the thick darkness, he almost fell over it. But was it warm? McNab reached down, searching for the head, the face, the neck . . . and pressed, seeking a pulse.

His own heartbeat was too loud to be sure of what he felt under his fingers, until he heard the groan, weak but definitely there.

'It's me, the Jock pig,' he said, still not sure who he was touching.

There was a sound that might have been a laugh. Then, 'Fuck's sake. How often do you have to be told to fuck off home?'

'I came to tell you to get out before they saw Ava's report.'

The Kommandant began to drag himself up to a sitting position. 'Too late, I'm afraid.'

McNab felt the warmth of escaping blood against his knees. Running his hands over the man's body, McNab found the origin. The open wound was at the guy's waist and the blood was seeping rather than pumping out, but without help, soon he would likely be dead.

McNab removed his jacket and, taking off his shirt, rolled it into a tight fist and pressed it into the wound. Now to hold it there, without his hand.

Taking off his belt, he slipped it round the body, pulling it tight. He couldn't be sure, but after a few minutes he thought – or maybe just hoped – the flow of blood had lessened.

'Right,' McNab said. 'Who are you, really?'

'Since we're about to die, I might as well tell you. Name's Jack Winters and—'

'You're a Serious Crime Squad plant?'

'Yes.'

'And Cleverly?' McNab said.

'The Met were ordered to keep schtum, in view of the undercover operation. The *Orlova* hitting Orkney fucked everything up, that and the Glasgow fire. Cleverly's visit north was supposed to ease things. It clearly didn't because you appeared at the bare-knuckle fight.'

'It was your face looking down on me to check if I was still alive?' McNab said.

Now he knew why the Kommandant had seemed vaguely familiar.

'I told Hugo you were a goner to get him out of there. Then you bloody turned up down here. Just about blew my cover.'

'So there isn't a cover-up?' McNab said.

'There are some who would like one – too many prominent names involved – but there are plenty in the Met willing to fight that, just like in Police Scotland. Despite the cries from the government about national security.'

'And Cleverly?' McNab said.

'I gather you two have history?' When McNab didn't answer, Jack said, 'I have no reason as yet to doubt him.'

McNab thought of his glimpse of Cleverly before his abduction and wasn't convinced. He changed the subject.

'By the way. Who's Lily Peony?'

Jack made a strangled sound. 'How the fuck . . .'

'You popped up on her Instagram account. In the background of her photo.'

'Well, I never got any nearer to her than that.'

McNab decided it was time to spring his news. 'We have footage of the killer from the *Orlova*,' he said. 'The posh fucker's going down. He and Olivia Newton Richardson, I hope.'

There was a sigh of pleasure.

'His name's Hugo Radcliff. And I hope you're right. He's a number-one bastard. He was the one in charge of your interrogation. Not me.' There was an apology in his voice.

'Any idea why he killed Damian Charles Lloyd and his girlfriend?'

'I didn't know he was the killer until you told me.'

When he started coughing, McNab decided he'd asked him enough questions.

'Okay, Jack Winters, now I plan to get you out of here,' McNab said, hoping Winters would stay alive long enough to accomplish that.

'Good luck with that.' Groaning, he lay back down. 'But don't hang about on my account.'

McNab's mobile had gone, of course, but he still had his watch, whose illuminated dial told him he'd last seen Firash at least an hour ago.

He decided to try and locate the door. If, as he believed, he was in the same location as last time, and the door was unlocked, then they had a route out. Rising, he stuck out his right hand and walked in a straight line until he met a wall.

The last time, they'd hung him up directly opposite the door. He remembered the long shaft of light culminating at him, whenever that door was opened. Chances were they'd put Jack in the same location. If so, then the exit should be a little to the right or left of where he now stood.

He was still feeling for it when he heard the sound of someone approaching. He stopped and listened. It was said that a remembered smell was the biggest factor in revisiting trauma. That had been obvious when he'd come to, in here. But he'd heard the distinctive sound of those footsteps in that corridor before. After which his tormentors would enter to do the posh fucker's bidding.

The recall of that scenario held him in its grip, but only briefly. If it was his tormentors come back, then he knew where he should make his last stand.

As he sat down again beside Jack, he heard the voices grow louder as more footsteps approached.

Suddenly the door was flung open and a figure stood in the shaft of light.

McNab wouldn't have recognized the man as Firash, not with his head and face swathed in a scarf, with what looked like an assault rifle in his hand. Not until the figure called out his name.

'Fuck's sake, Firash! What took you so bloody long?' McNab shouted back, surprise and joy colliding.

On his answer, Firash came quickly towards him, as three more men entered, one obviously Harim.

'We need to get this man to hospital as soon as possible,' McNab said.

Pulling down his mask, Firash shouted to his backup brigade to come and carry him to their vehicle.

68

The call had come before it was light. Rhona had expected it, although she hadn't been sure when it would arrive.

'Ava,' she said quietly.

'You know I published the material?'

'I do,' Rhona said. Like everyone else, she'd devoured it. Discussed it with Bill.

'Was it a mistake to release it?'

Rhona chose her words carefully, aware of the impact they might make. 'It was what Nadia wanted.'

'But maybe it was already too late? If they're both dead.'

'There was never going to be a right time. We knew that.' She used 'we' to take some responsibility for the decision too. Bill felt the same. They'd discussed doing this and keeping Nadia in Orkney for safety. Apparently that hadn't worked out as planned.

Rhona had been involved with disappearances before. Where young people were involved, especially in a small tight-knit community such as Orphir, they usually returned, but not always. When the news was bad, the family often seemed to know that their loved one was dead before they were told.

'What's your gut feeling about Dougie?' she said.

Silence, then . . .

'He knows these waters as well as anyone. I don't think

320

they've drowned. But if the police thought I was in danger from Go Wild, then Dougie and the girl were too.'

'If they left because you were hesitating to publish as you promised, then by doing that you might bring them back.' It was what Rhona had been hoping for, as had Bill.

There was a moment's silence, as though Ava was making her mind up what she should say next.

'There's something else,' she said eventually. 'Mark gave me all his evidence. He'd told me to hold it back, when I met him in London, because he feared the police would bury it if he handed it over. I alluded to it in my piece, but there are images, videos, interviews conducted with participants in these games. It could be explosive, because of who is in there. I think that's why he was killed.' Her voice tailed off as she tried to collect herself. 'So do I wait here for Dougie to come home or come to Glasgow and hand over this evidence?'

Now Rhona knew the true nature of the call. Ava was basically asking, what job should she put first? Her professional one or the personal?

Rhona thought briefly of her own situation. How often she had put the job before her private life. Her work before her son, before Sean.

'You're asking the wrong person,' she said, in all honesty.

'I suspect I know what you would do,' Ava said. 'I'll book a flight to Glasgow as soon as possible, and let Erling know my decision.'

Rhona cut in at this point. 'If that's what you want, then you're welcome to stay here with me.'

'You would do that? I suspect, like up here, I'll have to have some sort of security.'

'I've had police minders before,' Rhona assured her. 'It occasionally comes with the job.'

'Okay, thanks,' Ava said, her voice certain again. 'I plan to ask that DS McNab does the interview. Mark trusted him and so do I.' And with that, she rang off.

Rhona went through to the kitchen, Tom following her, rubbing himself against her legs. From the window, she would watch the sunrise, because going back to bed no longer seemed an option.

She put on the coffee and made herself a bowl of cereal, pouring some of the milk into a dish for Tom, something he had been hoping for, as displayed by the joyous sounds he was now emitting.

Despite her carefully chosen answers, she'd been thrown by Ava's last question. She'd often admitted to herself how work obsessed she was, but it was more difficult to admit that to others.

She poured herself a coffee and sat on the window seat to watch the sun come up.

Their work on the items taken from the staff and visitor quarters on the ship was nearly complete. They now knew that the male who had washed ashore had slept in one of the deck containers, as had Nadia, so that part of her story was true. But it seemed the staff might have been used in other ways, for Chrissy had also found samples of Nadia's DNA in the bed used by the games' two victims. Nadia was young and pretty and, in essence, a prisoner, where her guards could demand anything of her, if the alternative was to be the victim in a killing game or thrown overboard.

If she had been working illegally, that would prove even more difficult for her, should she come in for questioning. The fact that she wanted to tell her story at all showed great courage.

Rhona watched as the first rays of the rising sun found

the resident statue of the Virgin Mary in the convent garden below, bathing her in early morning light.

Had she been religious, she would have called it a sign. In her case, Rhona just hoped it might be.

69

The water was flat calm, the two black heads of the visiting seals bobbing like corks, their eyes feasting on him as he walked the shoreline.

Nadia had wanted to return to the *Orlova*, arguing that no one would look for them there. Dougie hadn't been so sure.

Fear had driven Nadia's desire to run. He had been less keen, but he'd known that if he refused, she would have run away alone and unprotected. And he couldn't have let that happen. So he'd brought her here, knowing that eventually someone would come for them. He only hoped that it might be a friend rather than an enemy.

But how would he know the difference unless he chose them himself?

So he was planning to do that without telling her, knowing he had a limited time before his mobile and his power pack both ran to empty.

She would feel betrayed, but it had to be done, he told himself again.

He had succeeded in hiding the tent, and they'd not lit a fire. What food he'd brought was almost done. But someone would spot them eventually. And he couldn't watch the sky and the water forever.

He brought out his mobile. Now he had to decide who

to call. His guilt at not telling Ava he was alive rose again to engulf him. He'd wanted her to release the material and she'd not been sure, and Nadia wouldn't agree to wait any longer. So they'd fled, setting fire to the boathouse to cover their tracks. He was sorry about that, nearly weeping as they'd sailed away, the flames melting into the distance.

'I'll rebuild it,' he'd promised himself, 'when this is all over.'

The phone signal was poor. Walking out into the water, it grew a little stronger. Had he kept the *Fear Not*, he would have taken the boat out past the headland and called from there.

What if he'd lost his boat forever? For a moment, he considered everything he had lost in such a short time. His mum, his dad, soon his home, and now the *Fear Not*.

But not Ava, a small voice reminded him.

Thigh-high now in the water, he found a signal. Maybe just enough. He imagined he could see the house at Houton Bay, jutting out into the water. He imagined Magnus on his jetty, his dinghy tied alongside . . . and pressed the call button.

When he re-entered the tent, she was still asleep, Finn beside her as commanded. He chose not to disturb her, but silently compared her life up to now with his own.

He'd considered he'd had it bad, but it was nothing in comparison to what she had endured. While listening to the recording she'd made with Ava, he'd suspected there was more being left unsaid. Now he knew the other things she'd been forced to do on the *Orlova*.

He also knew that if the police were to be given a chance to bring some of the people involved in these crimes to justice, then they must be told the whole story. Which meant they had to be able to question Nadia properly. Get her to identify suspects.

Even identify the dead.

He thought of the body washed up on the beach at Yesnaby. She'd said it was Guido, but that couldn't be confirmed without her. And there would be others. The sea would return to land what it had been given. If they'd thrown Guido overboard, then it was likely they'd done that with the others too.

Nadia had only survived because she'd hidden. She knew everyone on that ship, and had worked on another before the MV *Orlova*. She'd viewed how many rich clients? How many famous customers?

She was stirring now, sensing perhaps that she was being observed. He watched as the fear in her eyes softened when she saw him.

'What time is it?' she said, half sitting up.

'Early,' he said.

She noticed his bare legs and feet. 'You're all wet,' she said.

'I was paddling. It's flat calm in the bay and the two seals are back.'

She'd watched them a few times, from the safety of their hideout.

'Are you hungry?' he said. 'I can mix some of the dried food with water from the burn.'

She nodded, aware that was all they had left.

He emptied some into the metal bowl and added water, watching it swell, unable at that moment to look her straight in the eye. He wasn't sure whether he should tell her that he'd called for help or, when Magnus came, pretend it was a surprise.

Handing her the dish and spoon, he urged her to eat. 'I ate something earlier.' He hadn't, but she didn't need to know that.

Yet another secret.

Her face shut down a little then and he realized she was getting better all the time at reading him, his moods, and maybe even his thoughts.

He took himself outside, just in case.

Magnus had known the bay of which he spoke and had assured Dougie he would leave immediately.

'Don't tell anyone else yet,' Dougie had implored. 'I want to speak to Ava first myself and explain.'

Magnus had readily agreed, before telling him, 'Ava has released everything online. It's all out there now, including parts of Nadia's story.'

Dougie's mix of relief and fear had almost overwhelmed him in that moment, so he'd said a quick goodbye and urged Magnus to hurry.

Why didn't I tell Nadia that? he thought. It was what she wanted.

As if on cue, she appeared behind him.

'They're still there,' she said, pointing at the bobbing black heads. 'It's as if they're on guard.'

'This is their bay,' he said. 'We're the interlopers.'

'We should leave,' she said.

He swivelled round to look at her. 'And go where?'

'Back.' She pointed across the Scapa Flow towards Orphir. 'I've decided to hand myself over to the police, on condition I'm interviewed in Glasgow by the detective Ava talked about.'

Dougie, too surprised to immediately respond, just nodded his agreement.

'So how do we get back?' she said, obviously pleased there were no arguments to be fought over it. 'Light a big fire on the beach for the coastguard?'

It was time to tell her. 'I've made a call to Magnus at Houton.' He explained who that was. 'He has a boat and is coming for us.'

He wondered how she would react, and was surprised and relieved when she just gave a little nod and slipped her hand in his.

70

'Nurse Jenny!' McNab said with a smile. 'I'm sorry I haven't come back sooner to repay my debt to you. Things got a little busy.'

Having stopped dead on spotting McNab in the waiting room, the young nurse now observed him in horror. 'What happened to you this time?'

'I'm fine,' McNab said. 'It's my mate, in there.' He gestured to the swing doors through which Jack Winters had been wheeled.

At that moment Firash appeared, thankfully carrying two coffees instead of an assault rifle.

'Firash, Nurse Jenny. My saviour last time I was here,' McNab said.

Firash offered her a devastating smile and a small bow, which almost made her blush.

'I owe Nurse Jenny money for a taxi fare,' McNab said. He indicated his empty pockets and looked to Firash to come up with the goods. 'Twenty pounds, wasn't it?'

Firash looked slightly abashed. 'I'll go and find a cashpoint. Can you direct me to one?'

Nurse Jenny smiled and gave a few concise instructions, after which Firash headed in that direction.

'So,' she said to McNab. 'What exactly is it you do?'

McNab didn't see any reason not to say. 'In Scotland I'm known as the polis,' he told her.

She nodded as though she'd expected as much. 'It was either that,' she said, 'or the Mafia.'

'Can you find out how my mate's doing?' McNab said. 'He seemed pretty bad when we brought him in.'

'If he went through there, then he's in surgery. Someone will eventually come out and tell you how that went.'

Firash came hot-footing it back and handed her a twenty-pound note. When their eyes met, McNab imagined a spark between them, probably a result of the euphoria he felt at getting Jack here at least alive.

'Firash is currently working with me at—' He gave the name of the Afghan coffee shop. 'I can recommend both the coffee and his company.'

At that moment a doctor appeared through the swing doors, as promised by Nurse Jenny.

'Detective Sergeant McNab? If you could come this way, please.'

Nurse Jenny gave him an encouraging nod. Firash, on the other hand, was wearing his serious and concerned expression again as McNab followed the doctor back through the swing doors.

On the other side, the doctor stopped and turned. 'Mr Winters survived surgery and is now in intensive care, if you would like to see him?'

When McNab nodded, the doctor added, 'He's not conscious yet and you can only stay a few minutes.'

The doctor led him down a corridor and into the IC unit. McNab had visited places like this before, in the process of doing his job, but it never got any easier.

The man who'd saved his life now lay in a bed in danger

of losing his own. Pulling up a chair, he recalled Winters's last words to him when he'd promised to get him out of there. 'Good luck with that,' he'd said before he'd closed his eyes.

McNab had wanted to question the doctor on the odds of him surviving, yet at the same time he didn't want a definitive answer on that. Better to sit here for a few moments in hope than in despair.

They had called it in to the Met shortly before Nurse Jenny had turned up. McNab had got Firash to make that call and his own name hadn't been mentioned.

His intention was to see Winters out of surgery and then leave. Get cleaned up and go back to Glasgow. He had no wish to meet Cleverly in the interim, whatever good words Winters had had to say about him.

As for the posh fucker . . .

That particular pet hate would have to wait a little longer to be satisfied. This time it would be done by the book.

Before he left, McNab took Winters's hand and, leaning close, said, 'Thanks for everything, mate. I'll buy you a pint next time we meet.'

McNab rose to go, then halted as Winters's eyes flickered open for a second. Taking heart from that, he nodded. 'See you later, mate.'

Firash appeared slightly agitated on McNab's return to the waiting room.

'What's up?'

'There's a couple of cops in reception, one in plain clothes.'

'Okay, we find an alternative route out,' McNab said.

They followed the sign for the hospital cafe, then exited and doubled back for their vehicle.

'What now?' Firash said as he pulled away.

'I catch the train north.' McNab couldn't believe how happy he was to say that.

Sometime later, cleaned up and, most importantly, fed, McNab pocketed the rest of the cash from selling Mark's stuff and yet another mobile, and proceeded to say his goodbyes.

They were all lined up: Abu-Zar, the older man who'd welcomed him into the fold; counter guy, who turned out to be called Bahnam, which according to Firash meant 'an honourable man'; Harim, the bulge of the gun still visible.

And Firash, looking bereft.

McNab thanked them all and promised to be back, although he still wasn't sure if they fully understood his Glasgow accent.

Back in the vehicle and on his way to Euston Station, he told Firash to remember to get in touch with Nurse Jenny. 'That way you can find out how Winters is doing, and let me know.'

The small smile that played on Firash's lips suggested that was perhaps already in hand.

'If the posh fucker is still here in London, I promise you we will find him.'

'When you do, remember, he's all mine,' McNab said.

They shook hands at the entrance to the station and Firash wished him well in his own language – at least, that's what McNab translated it as. He also told him there was a very good Afghan restaurant on Bridge Street in Glasgow. He should go there in honour of their friendship.

McNab promised that he would.

Picking up his ticket, he headed for the sleeper train. He'd spoken to the boss already and had told him roughly what had happened, promising the full story when he got back. In return, DI Wilson had informed him that Nadia Kowalski and Ava Clouston were due to arrive in Glasgow within the next twenty-four hours.

'You found the girl, then?' McNab had said, relieved.

'Ava's brother called Magnus and he picked them up from where they were hiding out on Hoy. She asked specifically to be interviewed by you, Sergeant.'

'Good job I'm on my way back then, sir.'

There was one thing he needed to do before he hit the sack. One thing he'd missed in his Afghan pad. Dropping what little luggage he had in his berth, he headed for the bar.

It was just as he remembered it, minus the pretty woman he'd shared it with last time. McNab ordered a double whisky, paid for it, and took it back with him.

Sitting on his bunk, he put the whisky on the fold-down shelf and opened Mark's laptop. In all the trauma he had yet to read through the material Ava had put up online. Opening Ollie's email, he found his latest update, which included a list of the online sources for him to view.

McNab settled down to study them. If he was to interview Nadia Kowalski and Ava Clouston tomorrow, then he wanted to be certain he'd read all they'd had to say.

71

Ava went outside to watch the sunset, not knowing when she might see it quite like this again. She had no plans to linger in Glasgow, but something told her that by going there she was already re-entering her previous life.

The posting of her material online had echoed this.

No longer could she hide away on Orkney, pretending to run a farm and play happy families. A decision would have to be made about the future.

She headed for the field and the kye, taking pleasure in their presence, remembering how her father seemed to know every single one of his herd, had even given them names. She wondered if Dougie would do the same. Maybe he already had.

She stopped now and again to rub a head or to admire how much a newborn calf had grown, while above her dark clouds scudded across a blue and red sky. That was the thing about Orkney, she thought, it was all sky and sea, with the land playing a lesser role, green and luscious though it might be.

When Rhona had asked her if she believed Dougie to be alive, she had realized in that moment that she did. Even stronger than that, she'd known it to be true.

She'd been twelve when he was born, and had been thrilled by his arrival. In fact, she'd always thought of him as her baby. Her teenage years had changed that, of course, when she'd gone off to the city and university, but even then, each time she'd returned, things were the same as soon as she saw him.

It had only been in the years since she'd become a world traveller that the connection between them had been broken. So when she'd returned after their parents' death, they had felt like strangers.

Dealing with the fallout from the *Orlova* and the Go Wild investigation had changed things between them. She recognized that now. Somehow, when she'd returned, she'd expected to find the small boy she'd left behind, whereas Dougie had become a man in the interim.

And had to be treated as such.

When she'd picked up what she thought was a call from Magnus, only to hear Dougie's voice, she'd thought her heart would stop. He had been so hesitant, so apologetic for making her worry.

She, on the other hand, had dismissed all of that. He was safe. She understood. She hadn't kept her promise about not revealing Nadia's presence at the farm. She had broken her word. They were safe, she'd told him. That was the important thing.

The phone had been passed back to Magnus at that point.

'I'll bring them round now,' he'd said. 'They're well, although I think a hot shower and food will be required.'

'Where were they?' she'd asked.

Magnus had described a small bay, one he used to go fishing in. 'They had a tent, well hidden. No fire. I doubt even the coastguard launch would have spotted them.'

'How's Nadia?' had been her second question.

'As keen to come back as Dougie, I gather. What are you planning to do now?'

She had told him she was going to Glasgow. 'I hope Nadia will come too,' she'd said. 'If she agrees, will you and Erling keep an eye on Dougie?'

'Of course.'

In fact, Nadia had been full of the idea on their return and more than delighted that Ava had done what she'd promised.

The day had been spent planning the trip, with Dougie saying he would have further talks with Erling's dad, Tommy, regarding the farm, while they were away.

And so it had all been arranged, the police helicopter for the flight down, plus an attempt to find spare clothes for Nadia from among her own.

'We could shop when we're there,' Ava offered, wondering how possible that would be if Nadia was under guard.

The issue of where they would stay had also come up, which she could answer.

'Dr MacLeod has offered to put us up. If the police okay that, I think we should.'

Nadia had seemed pleased by the suggestion.

Having reached the shore now, Ava walked along it, drawn as she was by the burnt-out remains of the boathouse. The *Fear Not* was already tied up by the jetty, having been returned by the coastguard.

The sooner they got the boathouse rebuilt, the better she would feel, she thought.

She stood for a moment watching the sun as it sank in the sea, knowing the likelihood would be that she would have left Orkney before the longest day. Glasgow, she realized, would be only the first stop. After that, it would be London. She would have to make arrangements for Mark's funeral. Deal with his estate, because he had, she knew, left everything to her in the event of his death 'in the field', he used to say. Even after they'd split up, that hadn't changed.

Besides, the Go Wild investigation hadn't ended with his death or her release of material. In fact, it had barely begun.

72

Stepping out of the train, McNab took a deep breath of Glasgow air. He'd always considered the countryside as his pet hate, but his trip to the Big Smoke had proved he just didn't like being *anywhere* outside his home city.

He could have arranged for a squad car to pick him up, but chose instead to get a taxi. That way he could be brought up to date with the world in general, via the driver's patter, in the fifteen minutes it took him to reach the station.

'Ah kent you were the polis as soon as you climbed in ma cab,' he was told as he paid his fare.

McNab didn't ask him how.

The desk sergeant, acting as though a welcome ghost had just walked in, informed him he was delighted to see him back.

Absence definitely did make the heart grow fonder, he thought. God, even Janice couldn't quash the smile that lit up her face when he came through the door. McNab could only hope Ellie's reaction would be the same when he finally got round to seeing her.

'So, partner,' McNab said, as he took his seat, 'what's been happening in my absence?'

'We have Steven Willis in custody.'

McNab was delighted to hear it. 'How did that happen?'

'We put his picture on Twitter and a former girlfriend

called the station. Told us where "the bastard", as she put it, was holed up. Needless to say, he wasn't pleased to see us. He denies ever having been near the scene. Didn't know the girl. Never heard of Go Wild. He's lying, but obviously terrified of repercussions if he does talk.'

'So he should be,' McNab said. 'If Go Wild get wind he's been picked up, they'll want him disposed of, and quickly. Where is he?'

'Awaiting an interview with you,' Janice told him. 'So what's your story?'

'The posh fucker's still out there. The man who set me free is in intensive care. Not sure if he'll make it.' McNab heard his voice break a little as he said the words he'd been trying to avoid even thinking.

'So the Met did have someone inside?' Janice said quietly, noting McNab's reaction.

He nodded. 'Lucky for me. Not so lucky for him, when Ava Clouston's piece went out.'

Janice, registering his anger at no forewarning, said, 'You can tell her that when you see her. She arrives shortly, or so I'm told. And you're her chosen one.'

'We come as a team,' McNab said. 'Have you read her stuff?'

'Multiple times,' Janice said, pleased at the news she was to be involved.

'The assumption is the girl's bona fide,' he said. 'At the moment we only have her word for that. Have we run a check on the name Nadia Kowalski? She says she's Polish.'

'We're on to that. Nothing back as yet,' Janice told him.

'Mark had left a memory stick for me with his Afghan friends. What's on it probably brought about his death.'

'So we've got them?' Janice's eyes lit up.

'If we're permitted to pursue it,' McNab said. 'I'm due for the boss's interrogation now. See you in the interview room.'

As he rose to leave, Janice had a last question for him. 'What happened about Cleverly?'

'I haven't changed my opinion,' McNab said. 'Despite Jack Winters's fine words.'

McNab was a full hour with the boss, aware that everything he said would also have to be written into his report.

'Hugo Radcliff? You think that's the killer's real name?' the boss said.

'According to Jack Winters, it is. Although I suspect Hugo will have numerous aliases. What his actual role is within the organization isn't clear. Nor that of his girlfriend, Ms Richardson.'

He told DI Wilson about the photograph of the two of them together in her apartment.

'Ollie suspects they may have begun the company. Hugo in charge of the games, she in charge of the locations. But Go Wild's much bigger and more international now. God help anyone trying to unravel the connections, the personnel and the money involved.'

He'd already explained the role Mark's Afghan team had played in freeing Jack and himself, although he'd missed out the bit about them carrying weapons. Now he told the boss that they were still intent on looking for Hugo.

When the disapproving look appeared, McNab added, 'They promised if they located him, they would report it to me, sir.'

'And not the Met?'

McNab shrugged. 'The Met were giving Mark a hard time because of his investigation when they should have been supporting him. His friends aren't about to forgive and forget that, sir.'

'Right,' the boss said. 'It's time you spoke to our survivor.'

'They're here?'

He nodded. 'I asked Rhona to pick them up from the heliport. Thought a friendly face might be in order. I'm pretty sure Dr MacLeod's influence has played a part in getting them here.'

Janice was already in the interview room when McNab arrived. 'How'd it go with the boss?' she said.

'Good,' he said. 'I've asked for the girl to be brought in first.'

She was small and slightly built. Pretty too. McNab could see why she would have been offered the original job with Go Wild in Ibiza. She began her story there, explaining in some detail what she thought happened at the parties. She gave the locations they were held in and names of the chief organizers, plus the fact that she'd realized after a while that the women involved had likely been trafficked.

'And you?' McNab had interrupted her at that point. 'Were you there of your own free will?'

'Initially, yes, but it became apparent after a short time that quitting the job wouldn't be easy.'

They moved then to her post on the first boat. 'It was made clear,' she said, 'that I no longer had a choice where I went.'

She gave details of the luxury yacht *Hibiscus*, which had cruised the Med, occasionally docking in the south of France or on the north coast of Africa. 'Clients were all male and very wealthy, many of them from the Middle East. Sex parties. Some of the women I saw arrive, I didn't see leave.'

She bent her head at this point, surreptitiously wiping her eyes.

Finally, they came to the *Orlova*. McNab had been in no hurry, knowing that he would have likely formed an opinion of Nadia by the time they got there. The two earlier locations could be checked to see if they were still in operation, but if deaths had happened there, it would be difficult to prove.

The *Orlova* was different.

Neither Ava nor Nadia was aware of the video footage they had of the fight and its finale. As far as Nadia knew, she was the only witness left alive to what had occurred on board that night.

'Tell us what happened on the *Orlova*,' Janice said.

Nadia gathered herself as though about to recall a nightmare. 'We were somewhere in the Atlantic when two guests came aboard. A man and a woman.'

'How were they brought to the ship?'

'By helicopter.' She hesitated. 'We were housed in containers on deck. Sometimes we would see arrivals from there.'

'Go on,' Janice said.

'There was another arrival, later on. A man, who I'd seen before. In fact, he recognized me from the *Hibiscus*. He took me to their room and introduced me.' She was looking increasingly uncomfortable.

'Why?'

'They offered us as extras, if required.'

'You took part in some of the games?'

'We had no choice.' Her face darkened.

'What was this man's name?'

'He went by the name Hugo. I don't know if that was his first or last name.'

'Tell us what happened that night.'

'It was strange. We knew something was about to happen because Hugo was there. Guido served the couple dinner. They were already dressed as Vikings by then. None of us got to watch the games, but we could hear them. The screams of the audience went all over the ship. That was how we knew something was wrong. The lights went out, the noise stopped. Then real screaming started.'

'Where were you?'

'In my hiding place.'

'Why?'

'Hugo had used me in the arena before. I didn't want it to happen again. Guido, the others . . .' She stumbled there, obviously distressed. 'When I eventually came out, there was no one there. He'd killed them all.'

'Did you go to the arena?'

She shook her head. 'Not until later. Then, when I got through the maze and saw them, I was sick. The storm had really hit by then, so I went back to my hiding place. I thought I was going to die anyway.'

'Why didn't you come out when the *Orlova* was boarded?'

'When I heard the helicopter, I thought they'd come back to clear up the bodies after the storm. I knew if I came out they would kill me too. So when Dougie broke into my room a few days later, I attacked him.'

The story had holes, but none of them pointed to the girl being involved with the deaths and they had the footage to show that.

When McNab checked with Janice, she gave a small nod indicating she too was satisfied.

They thanked Nadia and let her leave the room.

'What do you think?' McNab said.

'She's traumatized but with help and support she'll make a good witness.'

'No lies?'

'She avoided the truth on occasion. Dr MacLeod says her DNA was on the couple's bed. I think she was made to have sex with them and other guests too.'

'Hugo had the means and the opportunity to kill them,' McNab said. 'But what was the motive?'

'Pleasure? Or he was paid to do it? Or he killed them as a warning?' Janice tried.

'Or all three together,' McNab said, recalling his own brush with Hugo.

They had Ava in next. McNab hadn't laid eyes on her since their meal with Rhona. Back then she'd been concerned and still trying to decide her course of action. The woman who walked into the interview room no longer had misgivings about why she was here or what she intended doing.

Taking a seat, she reached into her pocket and drew out a memory stick. 'I should have given you this before but Mark asked me not to. I believe he was killed because of what's on here.'

'You withheld information from a police enquiry?' Janice said.

'I kept my word to Mark,' she said. 'If you want to charge me for doing that, go ahead.' Speaking directly to McNab, she asked if he had met with Mark in London prior to his death.

McNab didn't see any reason not to tell her the truth. 'He was staying where you told me he would be. With Abu-Zar and Firash.'

Her expression changed at the sound of those names. 'He was with friends then,' she said, as though that was a comfort to her.

'Before he died, he'd gone to meet someone without telling Firash,' McNab said. 'Have you any idea who that might have been?'

She thought for a while, then said, 'It could have been any of the contacts on there.'

McNab wondered if the information given to Ava would be the same as Mark had left for him.

The preliminaries now over, Janice asked her to tell them everything that had been said between herself and Nadia.

Ava took a deep breath, then began her tale.

73

Rhona and Bill had watched both interviews from the neighbouring room.

'What do you think?' Bill said when they were over.

'That Nadia's telling the truth, but not all of it. In particular, about what happened during her meeting with the dead couple. As for her being the one who was sick after the event, the tinned food she'd been eating in her hideout was present in the analysis of the vomit.'

'Could she have been involved in their deaths?'

'Forensic evidence suggests she wasn't. But she was familiar with the killer and had met him before in the other locations.'

'Which makes her an even stronger witness,' Bill said. 'One he wouldn't want to take the stand.'

'What will happen to Nadia?' she asked as they made their way back to his office.

'She'll be put under protection until we can bring this to trial.'

Which couldn't happen unless or until they took Hugo Radcliff into custody.

'Do the Met know you have her?' Rhona said.

'They do.'

'Then they'll ask that she be sent south,' Rhona said. 'Although she would be safer staying here.'

Bill nodded, indicating he too was concerned about that.

'They can't put the lid on all of this. Can they?' Rhona said.

'Jack Winters told McNab that the Met plan to continue their investigation, despite pressure from on high.'

The news outlets were still running the *Orlova* story and its association with Go Wild, but how long would that last? Especially if owners of the companies might be implicated in the fallout. The BBC had closed it down, Channel 4 had dipped in a toe, then retreated, and an army of bots were at work on social media describing it as Russian fake news.

When she repeated these thoughts to Bill, he said, 'None of that changes what we or the Met do. We pursue the criminals, regardless of what those in power say or do. Meanwhile, we have a suspect in custody for our fire death. Plus we have proof of who killed two of the victims on the *Orlova*. And a key witness to Go Wild's activities on board that ship.'

It sounded impressive, but would it be enough?

Back at Bill's office now, they found McNab and Janice waiting for them.

'You were watching, sir?' McNab said.

'We were. Nadia will make a credible witness once we catch the perpetrator.'

'That's what we wanted to talk to you about, sir,' McNab said. 'In view of the likelihood of Nadia being taken south, DS Clark and I have a proposal.'

Rhona looked from one of them to the other, wondering whether McNab was talking for himself or both of them. A quick glance from Janice told Rhona that she was fully on board.

'Go ahead, DS Clark,' Bill said.

'We know that Hugo Radcliff was in the habit of visiting Glasgow for the bare-knuckle fights. The man McNab spoke to there indicated he'd seen him before. We believe Olivia Newton Richardson may have accompanied him, perhaps even on that occasion, hence the discovery of her handbag with the fire victim.'

McNab came in at that point.

'I pissed him off that night, sir. So when he discovered that I was nosing about in London, he had me picked up. I only got away because Jack Winters, who was one of his bodyguards, risked his cover to save me. The fact that I was involved in Jack's rescue will only have made matters worse.'

He paused there, until Bill said, 'So what are you proposing, Sergeant?'

'We could try and lure him back here, sir.'

'And how exactly would you do that, Sergeant?'

74

Fear had its own particular scent, McNab thought. It was also infectious. It could permeate a crowd like a rapidly replicating virus, making them all turn and flee. Or it could be swallowed up by courage, seemingly against all the odds.

Some men felt no fear. The posh fucker was definitely one of that breed. Those not wholly psychotic in nature moved between the two states.

The man before him, McNab believed, belonged in the latter camp, because he could smell his fear from where he sat.

'Charlotte Weiner's parents couldn't identify their daughter's remains,' McNab told him. 'It's impossible to recognize someone when they've been burned to a crisp. And the smell,' he added. 'You can't rid yourself of the smell of burnt human flesh. It stays with you forever. But then you probably know that.'

He was silent for a moment.

'The thing is, some folk think that firing a body destroys all the evidence of who killed the victim.' He gave a derisory snort of laughter. 'They're wrong, of course. In fact, we have evidence of the killer all over that crime scene.'

Willis, having avoided looking at him directly, now shot him a quick glance.

'We also have the evidence collected from that room. And

349

from the female victim. We know who was in there. Who tied her up. Who raped her.'

Willis's reaction to each of these statements played out on his face and the scent of fear only grew stronger.

'As for the handbag. It didn't belong to the victim. But hey, the killer knew that when they put it beside her. Then there's the lighter used to ignite the petrol. Someone got careless there too,' McNab lied. 'Thing is, that handbag led us places. Essentially to a company specializing in providing psychopaths with their victims. A company you work for. A company that intends for you to take the blame for everything I've just described.' McNab relaxed back in his chair. 'Unless you decide otherwise.'

Willis's face twitched and twisted as he tried to gather his thoughts about all of this. Eventually he came to a decision.

'I didn't kill the girl or rape her. I rented the room out. That was all.'

'Who did you rent it to?' Janice said.

'Some bloke from the company that does the bare-knuckle fights.'

'What did he look like?'

He shook his head. 'I only spoke to him on the phone, but he was from around here. Glasgow,' he added for emphasis.

McNab glanced at Janice. This was news.

'So how come your DNA was on the girl?' Janice said.

His pent-up version of the story came rushing out now. How he'd gone to check on the flat before the storm hit and she was in there tied to the bed. He should have let her go, but thought he'd be in big trouble if he did.

'You touched her up then left her there to die?' Janice said.

'No one had said anything about killing her,' Willis said.

'If all that's true,' McNab said, standing up, 'then you might have a way out of a murder charge. If you give us what we need.'

He looked to Janice. 'Shall we grab a coffee and give Steven here time to consider his next move?'

'What d'you think?' McNab said as he waited his turn at the coffee machine.

'He might be afraid of us, but he's more afraid of them,' Janice said. 'Mark said they were everywhere. Could be he's right. What about the memory stick Ava gave you?'

'Ollie has both mine and hers for comparison purposes. He says most of the sites referenced have been closed down. We still have some images, short videos et cetera, but how to identify the people in them will take time, if it's even possible. It'll be like identifying paedophiles from just their hands. Which gives Go Wild time to close down and get rid of any of the weak links in their supply chain.'

'Like Steven Willis?' Janice said.

'If he thinks he's in danger of being dispensed with, he might agree to work with us.'

'So we give it a try?' Janice said.

McNab's attempt at a response was halted by a call to his mobile.

'How late?' McNab listened to the answer with mounting concern. 'You've tried her phone? Okay, park up and look for them inside. If they do appear they'll wait at the patrol car. I'll arrange for more officers to meet you there.'

'What is it?' Janice said as he rang off.

'Ava and Nadia are late showing up at the police car. The officer's tried Ava's mobile but it appears to be switched off.'

'How late is late?' Janice said.

'Half an hour.'

Janice didn't look as perturbed as he felt. 'Where did she drop them?'

'The Buchanan Galleries. She saw them go inside. I should have ordered her to stick with them.'

'The plan was to buy Nadia clothes. She'll be trying stuff on. Time can run away with you when you're doing that,' Janice said.

What Janice was saying was possible, even probable. The trouble was, his gut was telling a different story.

He was suddenly reliving his walk towards Cleverly, only to find himself being thrust into the back of the black van. All in broad daylight on a busy London street.

It had been that easy.

If someone had been watching them in Orkney, they would know they'd flown to Glasgow. Go Wild had folk here in the city. Steven Willis had made that plain. They could have been followed from the heliport to the police station. From the station to the shopping mall.

'You're right,' Janice said when he voiced his thoughts.

'We'll get some feet on the ground at the Galleries,' McNab said. 'If they turn up before that, all well and good. If not, the place has plenty of cameras. They're bound to have been picked up on some of them.'

'What about Willis?' Janice said.

'You organize the search party. I'll deal with Willis.'

75

Willis was staring at him as though he'd just heard an announcement of his own death.

Which, in fact, he had.

Nothing that McNab had just uttered had been a lie. The big boss, Hugo, was out there. He likely knew by now, or would find out soon, that Willis had been lifted by the police and was currently being questioned about the fire death.

He might also be aware who would be asking the questions.

'He hates me,' McNab said. 'I screwed him over. Got away when he planned to kill me. Twice. He still wants me dead.' He paused. 'Your problem is, he wants you dead too.'

Willis was chewing his lips, causing a dribble of saliva to run down his chin.

He finally mustered an answer. 'I haven't told you anything about them.'

'Hugo doesn't know that and once we put the word out that you have' – McNab swiped his hand across his throat – 'you're a goner.'

The eyes opposite him darted about like a trapped rodent looking for an escape route.

'Now, if Hugo was to be locked up, things would be different.'

'You'll never pin anything on him.' Willis gave a little laugh. 'He's too clever for that.'

'Not that clever,' McNab said.

He watched as Willis digested this.

'What are you asking me to do?'

'Give us a lead in. The guy who hired the flat. Who probably killed the girl. We take him in. You get good marks on your charge sheet.' Seeing a small but positive sheen in his eyes, McNab went on. 'You only need to make the contact. I'll do the rest.'

Janice was in with the boss when he got back. Looking through the glass door, he noted that there was a serious discussion going on inside. They both turned when he entered.

'You haven't found them?' McNab said.

'No,' Janice said. 'They're checking the CCTV footage now.'

McNab shook his head. 'They're gone. Maybe shortly after they were dropped off.'

The boss was examining him. 'You know something we don't, Sergeant?'

McNab was getting brief but sharp reminders of his last conversation with Ava.

'There's a possibility she was planning this. She knew what she wanted and wasn't giving up on it. No one is that fixated on buying clothes and toiletries.'

Okay, he was maybe thinking about himself when saying that, but a quick glance at his partner indicated she wasn't exactly disagreeing.

'We need to speak to Rhona. She was with them on the ride from the heliport. See if she picked up on anything. And Erling needs to go to the Clouston farm, right away. If all three were cooking something up together, Erling will know when he tells Dougie that we think his sister and the girl have been taken.' He thought for a moment. 'Tell him to take Magnus. If the professor of psychology is up to the job, he'll be able to spot a lie.'

'There is an alternative explanation,' Janice reminded him. 'The one you fed me when you got the call. They were tracked to the police station from Orkney and from here to the shopping precinct. And whoever wants to prevent the girl from talking picked them up from there.'

They all turned as the door opened and a voice said, 'Excuse me, sir, we have a sighting of them from the CCTV footage if you'd like to take a look.'

The Sauchiehall Street entrance was the first location. The two women entered, then stood together for a moment. After which they began walking up the concourse, passing a couple of clothes shops without pausing to even look in the windows.

Stopping again a little further in, Ava took out her mobile and read the screen. After a further short exchange, they set off in a seemingly purposeful manner.

'We lost them after that,' the officer said. 'But we haven't looked through everything yet.'

'Check all the exits and the car park cameras,' McNab told him. 'If that was a message coming in on her mobile, then they were possibly being given directions.'

'Who would they be meeting?' Janice said.

'Ava's never given up working on her story. If she got a lead, especially on Mark's death, she would follow it.'

'Can we pinpoint the last place she used her mobile?' Janice said.

'I bet when we do it's there on the concourse.' McNab pointed at the image of the two women currently on the screen. 'She then either switched it off – or someone did it for her.'

76

'What's happening?' Chrissy said as Rhona finished the call.

Rhona rarely learned something before Chrissy, and in this case she wished she hadn't.

'Ava and Nadia have gone missing,' she said.

Chrissy's expression turned swiftly from puzzlement to dismay.

'How the hell did that happen?'

Rhona repeated what McNab had just told her. 'He wanted to know what we talked about on the way from the police heliport, in case it threw any light on where they may have gone.'

'He thinks they went AWOL by choice?' Chrissy said.

'He thinks it's one possibility.'

'And did Ava indicate she might be considering such a thing?'

Thinking back, the atmosphere in the car had been tense. Rhona had assumed the decision to come to Glasgow, plus the ongoing saga of Nadia's appearance, then disappearance again with Dougie, had made the relationship between the two women strained.

And yet, in retrospect, Rhona began to wonder if that was the case.

'The first thing Ava asked me when she got in the car was whether Mark's warning about DI Cleverly had ever been properly pursued,' Rhona said.

'And?' Chrissy urged her on.

'I told her that Jack Winters, the undercover cop McNab had rescued, had vouched for Cleverly.'

Rhona recalled Ava's reaction to that, the firm set of her mouth, the steely-eyed stare out through the windscreen.

'She definitely wasn't happy that Mark's warning hadn't been taken seriously.'

'Maybe she's found out more about DI Cleverly?' Chrissy suggested.

'If she has, she didn't mention it to McNab in their interview,' Rhona said.

She began to go over every interchange she'd ever had with Ava Clouston. Their first meeting at Magnus's house for dinner the evening after she and Chrissy had arrived on Orkney. Then the very different scenario with McNab at the curry house in Glasgow. Followed by the really awkward dinner party on her second trip north, when it was obvious something was wrong. Ava's subsequent text, pleading for Rhona to come alone to the farm. And, finally, her revelation that she was harbouring Nadia and her intention not to inform the police.

Rhona had been the first person Ava had told of the girl's existence and of her fear for Nadia's safety.

Then another thought arrived. One that she should have considered before now. Mark had been more than just a journalist and colleague who'd been murdered while working on a story. She now realized Ava had been much closer to him than that.

That night in the restaurant with McNab, Ava had indicated how much faith she had in what Mark had already unearthed. Otherwise, why would she have broken her journey home to speak to them about it?

Mark believed that Cleverly couldn't be trusted. Had he been right all along? Were Jack Winters's words enough to dismiss that?

Rhona took a moment to consider the consequences if, in fact, Mark Sylvester had been correct in his suspicions. Maybe even had evidence to prove them.

That would undoubtedly have set Ava on a different path.

What if Cleverly already knew of Ava and Nadia's arrival in Glasgow and was worried about them being interviewed? Mark was dead, so any suspicions or evidence that he'd collected against Cleverly might well have gone with him.

Or maybe not . . .

'What are you thinking?' Chrissy demanded.

'McNab has two trains of thought on the women's disappearance,' Rhona told her. 'The first is that they've been taken to prevent them giving evidence about Go Wild in court. The second that Ava orchestrated their disappearance herself, but he has no idea why.'

'If she asked about Cleverly,' Chrissy said, 'it has something to do with that.'

77

Watching the car pull away, Ava allowed herself a sigh of relief.

'Let's get inside before the police officer changes her mind and decides to come shopping with us.'

'You were worried about that too?' Nadia said.

'There was always the chance DS McNab had ordered her to stay with us at all times.'

At the sound of a text arriving, Ava pulled out her mobile. 'We've to meet them in level one of the car park, opposite the lift.'

Up to that moment she hadn't known who they would send and her heart rose when she'd seen who the message was from.

Her joy was confirmed when she spotted his tall figure waiting for them.

She quickly did the introductions. 'Nadia, this is Firash, Mark's friend, who I told you about. Firash, this is Nadia.'

'Thank you so much for agreeing to come for us,' she added as Firash led them over to a sleek black car.

'My father was very happy when you called,' he said. 'We want to help you bring these people to justice.'

'We have two hours before they come looking for us,' Ava said as they were installed in the car.

'That's plenty of time to get out of Glasgow and onto the road south,' he assured her.

Ava hoped it would be. 'Are we likely to have been picked up on camera?' she said, spotting one as they approached the exit sign.

'There were none where I parked. And with the tinted windows, you wouldn't be visible once in the car.'

Ava cast her mind back to their swift walk through the shopping centre. There was no doubt that CCTV would have picked them up in the concourse. How long would it take before McNab started a search for them? How long before he figured out what had happened?

At this juncture it felt too easy, and knowing McNab's terrier-like qualities, Ava couldn't imagine him not working out how they'd departed the shopping mall.

Perhaps reading her thoughts, Firash said, 'This isn't the vehicle I used with McNab. He's never seen this one before. Plus, if he does run the plates, there's nothing in the ownership that would link it to us.'

Having navigated the exit, Firash eased his way out into the traffic.

'There's food and a flask of coffee in the bag beside you,' he called back to Nadia. 'It's our own coffee, McNab's favourite, although maybe a little cool by now.'

At the positive reminder of McNab's part in all of this, Ava felt a stab of regret at what she was doing to the man who'd done so much to help her up to now. But, she reasoned, if she had suggested this course of action to him, he would have undoubtedly forbidden and prevented it.

Her plea after the interviews that she be permitted to take Nadia to buy some much-needed clothes and toiletries had been met initially by a definite no, then an attempt at dissuasion.

'We can't let you just wander about Glasgow. You were

both in danger in Orkney. That hasn't changed,' he'd said. It was then she'd pointed out that the identity of the *Orlova* witness hadn't been made public. Neither was it known that they'd both given statements to Police Scotland or that Nadia was even in Glasgow.

After that, McNab had reluctantly agreed to their outing, but ordered that they shouldn't leave the shopping centre. 'We can't be certain news of you being here isn't already out there,' had been his final words.

Ava, accepting a coffee from Nadia, changed the subject. 'Did you drive through the night?'

Firash nodded. 'I've done the journey many times. We have relatives who have a restaurant in Glasgow. I'll take you there sometime when this is all over.'

When this is all over.

Ava welcomed those words, even though she wasn't sure if they would ever be realized.

Her heart began to slow as they eventually departed the city centre, then its outskirts, finally joining the main road heading south. Knowing they were definitely on their way, she relaxed and, closing her eyes, eventually drifted off, to dream she was back on Orkney with her parents still alive.

In the dream, her father was asking what she planned to do about Dougie and the farm, and she was telling him about Tommy Flett and how everything would come out all right in the end.

When she resurfaced, Firash had Afghan music playing and he and Nadia were having an animated conversation about it. To hear Nadia laugh was a wondrous thing, Ava thought, and closed her eyes again so that she might listen to their chat, but leave them free not to include her in it.

Eventually, as silence fell, she roused herself and asked Firash where they were.

'Passing Oxford,' Firash told her. 'Not long now.'

'Have you been in touch with McNab since he left London?'

'He asked that I keep him posted on Jack Winters, so I've messaged him a couple of times,' Firash told her.

'Is he likely to contact you when he realizes we've gone?'

Firash shrugged. 'It's a possibility. If he does, I'll at least find out what he's thinking about your disappearance.'

'We won't be able to keep him in the dark for long,' she said.

'We'll tell him where you are as soon as possible,' he promised, then hesitated. 'McNab knows they couldn't have kept you in Scotland for long. You were always going to go south because of the suggested threat to national security. McNab or his boss couldn't have prevented that.'

Knowing Firash was right, Ava moved her thoughts to Dougie.

As soon as Erling learned she and Nadia were missing, he would go and see Dougie. How would her brother react?

He had a teenager's ability to blank out bad news, showing no emotion at all, or else be very angry. If he accused Police Scotland of not keeping them safe, that would probably work with Erling.

Though perhaps not with Magnus.

She felt a surge of guilt about deceiving both men, but reminded herself that it wouldn't be for long. Glancing behind her, she saw that Nadia had fallen asleep, which would allow her to talk to Firash in private.

'How is the police officer?' she said quietly.

'Nurse Jenny says he has regained consciousness and has

been able to talk a little. He is guarded round the clock. No visitors are permitted, but Nurse Jenny gave him my message.'

'Will he agree to see you?'

'I helped save his life. I think he will agree.'

78

'You're sure you want to go ahead with this?'

Janice fired him a pointed look. 'Do you think he set that girl on fire? Or that he rented the flat to the man who did do it?'

McNab could tell by Janice's expression that she was playing devil's advocate on this. Plus he didn't need to remind her that the only real evidence they had on Willis was the print on the credit card and his DNA on the handle of the bag. Both of which could have been put there when he claimed he visited the room. He could just see Willis considering stealing both items, then thinking the better of it.

'And the semen?' Janice checked. 'It's definitely not his?'

'Rhona's confirmed that now. She's running a profile through the database just in case it finds a match.'

'You lied to him about us finding the lighter.' Janice waved a finger at him. 'Naughty.'

'You could tell from his face when I said it that he hadn't touched a lighter. And we now know Willis has a Go Wild contact, here in Glasgow.'

'Or who happens to sound Glaswegian,' she corrected him.

'And I thought you were the positive one in this partnership,' McNab said with an attempt at humour.

'What if they know he's been lifted?'

'That's a chance he says he's willing to take, to get himself off the hook for murder.'

'If they can pinpoint where he's calling them from . . .' Janice said.

'We plan to let him go and keep a tail on him.'

'We could lose our only suspect in a murder case?' she queried.

'True. However, I've talked it over with the boss and he's agreed to amend our original suggestion to go for Hugo and replace it with Willis's contact,' he said. 'Provided surveillance have him well covered at all times.'

McNab had already had all these arguments with himself. With the boss and, to a lesser extent, with Willis.

A spell alone after McNab had left the interview room had apparently persuaded Willis that he didn't have much to lose, but a lot to gain, if he did what was asked of him.

Janice still didn't look convinced. 'If we hadn't already misplaced our key witness . . .'

McNab didn't want to discuss it any more. The need to do something was, he accepted, too strong to simply wait and hope they might get a lead on the whereabouts of the two women.

'I'm going to talk to Ollie about the memory stick Ava gave us,' he told her. 'Can you find out what happened about the Combat offices? The Met were supposed to be checking them. I'm particularly interested in any footage from the entry door camera. I know I'll be on it, but I still don't know if Cleverly went into the sex shop the first time I was taken or whether he was heading into the Combat offices, where I'm pretty sure my abductors came from.'

In an attempt at normality, McNab went to the cafe first and bought two coffees and two cakes. If Ollie had forsaken the doughnuts again, he would just eat them both himself. He definitely required a sugar rush along with the top-up of caffeine.

He tried to remember when he'd last sat down to eat properly, and couldn't. That thought reminded him that no decision had yet been made on the elusive dinner party, which meant he hadn't contacted Ellie again since he'd got back from London.

Calling her before a date was settled on felt odd. At least that's what he'd told himself. After all, they were no longer officially a couple. That thought reminded him of the existence of Baldy in their story. He'd told Ellie he was a stalker, which wasn't actually true, although he was on the system for something along those lines. Baldy's claim to fame had been for cyber flashing. Sending dick pics via AirDrop to unsuspecting nearby females, usually when on public transport.

Maybe I should have told her the truth, McNab thought. *Maybe I still will*, he decided as he entered the IT suite in fighting mode.

For a brief moment he thought it must be over between Ollie and the lovely Maria due to the alacrity of Ollie's acceptance of the paper bag.

'Maria says if *you* bring me something, then that's okay. I think she's a fan,' Ollie told him. 'Anyway, I need the energy.'

'You and me both,' McNab said, helping himself. 'So what do we have?' he asked, catching a scent of Ollie's excitement.

'The two memory sticks hold essentially the same material, but not quite. As you are probably aware, most of the sites Mark gave a link to have been shut down already. Checking on dates, this started happening from the night he disappeared.'

So Ava was right when she'd maintained that the contents of the memory stick were the reason Mark had died.

'There is one difference between the two sets of data,' Ollie said.

'What's that?'

'There's a hidden list of contacts embedded in the final material given to you. Together with dates and times when Mark spoke to someone either online or in person.'

'I never spotted that,' McNab said.

'It wasn't obvious. In fact, it took me until now, and having access to both drives, to discover it.'

McNab knew better than to rush Ollie by demanding to be told what this hidden diary had revealed. Eventually Ollie was ready with his declaration. 'Mark had a meeting arranged the night he died.'

'We know that already,' McNab couldn't stop himself from saying.

'That meeting, I suspect, was arranged after he'd met with both you and Ava. However, he did make a note of it on the memory stick he'd left with Abu-Zar to give to you . . . should anything happen to him.'

Which suggested that Mark didn't trust the person he'd arranged to meet.

'Who was it?' McNab said.

Ollie's expression was a mix of concern and distaste. 'He says it was a Met officer.'

'The name?' McNab demanded.

'That's just it. There isn't one. Just a time and a location.'

79

Sitting in here, Ava could still feel the power of Mark's presence. It was as though he had merely left the room to fetch a refill of coffee or select a favourite sweet cake from the cafe counter.

It reminded her too of their apartment in Kabul. Above her, in the main household, food was being prepared, the scents of which transported her back to their time in Afghanistan.

Then, danger had been always present, heightening their desire to live, and to love.

Firash had taken Nadia upstairs. As well as the aromatic scents wafting down, there was also the sound of music, chatter and laughter. It was difficult to imagine how long a time it had been since Nadia had been free to enjoy such things.

Extracting her laptop from her bag, Ava set up her own centre of operations where Mark's had been. Her mobile she kept switched off; a sequence of burner phones would be what she would use from now, until she'd deemed the job complete.

Her first task was to speak to her brother. By now Erling would have visited Dougie to tell him of their disappearance. Dougie would be anxious to know if they'd arrived safely at their destination.

A text would have sufficed when they'd finally got here, but Ava wanted to hear his voice, and for him to hear hers.

After all, they only had each other now.

She'd arranged that her call from an unknown number would stop after a couple of rings. When she rang again shortly after, he would know it was her.

She imagined him sitting in the kitchen, Finn at his side, waiting to answer. When he finally did, she could hear the catch of relief in his voice.

'You got there?' he said.

'Safe and sound,' she told him, trying to sound normal. 'I slept a lot of the way. So did Nadia. She's upstairs now with the family. There's laughter and chat and an excellent smell wafting down.' She hesitated before asking if Erling had been.

He told her yes. 'He brought Magnus Pirie with him.'

So, she'd been right about that, suggesting McNab hadn't completely bought her story regarding the shopping trip.

'How did it go?' she said.

'I played fearful and angry,' he told her in a worried tone. 'I think. I hoped it worked.'

Magnus would have smelt fear, or the lack of it, but Ava didn't mention that because she could hear the worry in Dougie's voice, even now, when he knew they were safe.

For the moment.

They chatted briefly about farm matters before she confirmed she'd call again with any developments.

At this point, Firash popped his head round the door. 'We're ready to eat. It's all set up in the cafe. Afterwards we can talk with my father.'

'Is there any news from the hospital?' she said.

'He will see me tomorrow.'

Ava allowed herself a small sigh of relief.

They were all there, the people who had taken Mark and her under their wing in Kabul. Looking round at the welcoming faces of Abu-Zar's extended family, Ava could only think of the one that was missing.

When the meal was over, Abu-Zar indicated that he and Ava should go with Harim and Firash to Mark's room to talk.

'You,' he told Nadia, 'will go to bed. This part of the story is ours alone.'

Nadia conceded without argument, heading upstairs to her room.

'I asked Firash not to reveal this until we brought you here,' Abu-Zar said. 'When Mark went out to meet someone the night he was killed, he did not tell us where he was going or whom he was seeing. As you know, the police took most of his things, but not everything. He left a memory stick in our safe to be given to the Scottish detective if anything should happen to him. We passed that on as promised.'

'McNab never told me that,' Ava said, thinking about her recent interview. 'Even when I gave him the one I had from Mark.'

Abu-Zar looked serious. 'Mark trusted the Scottish detective. I believe his aim is to do his job and to keep you from harm.'

Like Mark, was left unsaid.

Abu-Zar turned to Firash now and asked him to explain what they'd discovered about the night Mark had died.

'When he didn't come back, we tried to look for him, but we had no way of knowing where he had gone. After he was found in the river, we began to receive news of sightings of him from people in the community. None of this we reported to the police because we knew that they'd been trying to prevent him from doing his job. Anyway, we believe we now know where he went that night. We also believe he met with a police officer.'

'Who was Mark meeting? Was his name Cleverly?' she demanded when Firash didn't immediately answer.

He shook his head. 'We believe it was the man in the hospital. The man McNab rescued.'

'You think Jack Winters killed Mark?' Ava couldn't believe what she was saying.

'Mark believed he was going to meet Jack Winters that night. We need to find out if that was true.'

It would have been the perfect set-up. If Mark thought he was meeting a police plant inside Go Wild, he would have gone without a moment's hesitation. It was also why he wouldn't have revealed his possible source to anyone, even Firash.

Had Winters been playing both sides? Or was he just being used? If so, by which side in the game?

There was another name in all of this. A name Firash had acknowledged but not spoken about as yet.

'Mark distrusted DI Cleverly. Do you know why?'

Firash nodded. 'DI Cleverly has a son, who Mark believed was connected to Go Wild in some way. He thinks the policeman was trying to cover for him.'

80

Ava glanced at the large clock in the hospital entrance hall, aware that Firash had been gone for at least half an hour.

Surely that meant he'd been allowed in to speak with Jack Winters?

The presence of two armed officers on patrol in the main concourse suggested that the police were taking security seriously. Swallowing a mouthful of cold coffee, she averted her eyes as they made yet another circuit, while chiding herself that it only made her look suspicious.

Had she forgotten everything Mark had taught her about being undercover?

The officers having now passed her by, she attempted a quick scan of the crowd, only to find Firash at her side.

'He's gone,' he said as he took a seat at her table.

'What do you mean, gone? Gone where?'

'They wouldn't say.'

Firash had caught sight of the police patrol and gently angled his chair round to face towards the queue at the cafe counter.

Ava voiced the unthinkable. 'Might he have died?'

'It's possible,' Firash said quietly. 'Or they've moved him elsewhere in the hospital. I texted Jenny to ask if she knows what's happened to him.'

Ava's heart was bumping so loudly, she thought the armed duo now en route past the cafe must be able to hear it.

'How long do we sit here and wait?' she said.

Firash, his face drawn, indicated he didn't know. At that moment his phone rang. Glancing at the screen, he nodded to Ava and mouthed 'Jenny' before answering.

The interchange was brief and, by the look on Firash's face, positive.

'He's been moved, Jenny says. She's not sure where, but he left a message for her with the ward sister. It's the phone number we can reach him on.'

'What if it's a trap?' Ava said.

'Why would he want to harm the man who rescued him?' Firash said.

Ava had been in too many situations where people were playing multiple sides. Sometimes they survived; sometimes, like Mark, they didn't.

'What do you want to do?' he said, studying her expression.

'We'll call from my burner phone,' she said. 'You'll open the conversation then hand the phone to me.' She thought for a moment. 'Would you recognize his voice?'

'He was barely conscious by the time we got there, so no, I wouldn't.'

If McNab had been here, it would have been easy. Maybe it was time to call him? *No*, she thought, *I'm not ready for that yet*.

'Is there a question you could ask that only he would know the answer to?' she said.

Firash considered this. 'I know what McNab did to save his life. And since there was only the two of them there at that point . . .'

Once out of the hospital grounds, Firash chose a spot and drew the car over.

'Okay?' he said.

When Ava nodded, he accepted her phone and dialled the number, switching it to speaker.

The phone rang three times before a male voice answered, 'Yes?', without giving a name.

Ava nodded to Firash to ask the question they'd agreed on.

There was a short silence before the voice responded. 'I assume I'm talking to Firash, one of the men who rescued me. The answer to your question is that McNab plugged the hole in my stomach with his rolled-up shirt and fastened his belt around me. That's the reason I stayed alive long enough for you to get me to a hospital.'

As he spoke these words, Ava felt a weight lift from her shoulders. Taking the mobile, she said, 'Mark Sylvester had a meeting with you the night he was murdered.'

'Not me,' the voice said.

'It's in his diary.'

Silence, then, 'He wasn't meeting me. Whoever arranged it must have said it was.'

'Then that person killed him.'

'Very probably,' he said, his tone serious. 'How was this meeting arranged?'

Firash shook his head at Ava, indicating he didn't know.

'The police seized his possessions from his workplace, including his laptop and phone. If they're doing their job properly, they would be able to find that out.'

Winters's breathing sounded laboured as he answered. 'You're Ava Clouston, aren't you? You broke the story that almost got me killed.'

'You told McNab he could trust DI Cleverly, when Mark

had warned him not to. And Mark was killed. Doesn't that strike you as odd?'

'Does McNab know you've contacted me?'

She didn't answer his question. Instead, she said, 'Mark discovered that Cleverly has a son, who is involved with Go Wild.'

Ava could taste the thick silence that now fell between them.

'The Met weren't investigating Mark,' she said. 'DI Cleverly was, because he'd found out that Mark had something on his son.'

'You have proof of this?'

'It was in the material taken by the Met.'

'Can I get back to you on this number?'

Ava told him he could, and ended the call.

Entering the cafe, they found Nadia helping Bahnam behind the counter.

'How did it go?' she said, her face lighting up when she saw them.

'Okay,' Ava told her, knowing she would have to eventually explain this part of the story to the girl, but only when it was safe to do so.

'Are you sure she should be out here?' she said to Firash as they went behind the curtain.

'She's hiding in plain sight. Plus Bahnam's been telling everyone that she's my current girlfriend.' Firash smiled at that.

'And is she?' Ava said.

'We're friends, supporting one another in extremity,' he told her with a serious expression. 'I too know what it's like to be a refugee, who no one will take responsibility for.'

When they reached Mark's office, he said, 'What do you plan to do now?'

'I have some calls to make,' Ava told him.

81

McNab knew that the only thing to do now was wait.

It was the aspect of the job he hated most. There were other tasks he disliked, even hated, like the endless reports always waiting to be written.

But even those paled beside the waiting game.

Everything now depended on other people, instead of him. The momentum that had swept him to this point was no more. All he had left was fear of things going wrong. Of failure in his plans. Of the wrong ending.

Having reached his destination, he looked up, seeking a light at a window and finding one.

So, she was home, but was she on her own?

There was only one way to find out, he thought, pressing the buzzer. When the door was released at the mention of his name, his heart lifted a little, hoping she was in fact alone.

The door to her flat stood ajar and, as he crossed the threshold, he heard no voices from the kitchen. As he closed the door behind him, the cat appeared like a flash to accompany him.

She was seated at the kitchen table, a pizza box and glass of wine alongside her open laptop.

'If you're not on duty, there's beer in the fridge. Or,' she said, reading his expression, 'whisky in the usual place. Plus there's pizza left. I always order enough for two.'

She went back to studying her screen while he helped himself to a slice of pizza. Eventually she shut the laptop down.

'I was planning on giving you a call,' Rhona said.

'That makes me feel better about the intrusion. Thought I might be interrupting your evening.'

'There's no one here but Tom and me.'

Many of their exchanges over the years had been fractious, sometimes outright furious, especially if or when they'd strayed from work and into their private lives. He wondered which of the two her proposed call had been about.

'Bill checked in about the forensic material we had on Steven Willis,' she said. 'We can put him in the room, and we have evidence of him on the handle of the bag and the credit card. The semen retrieved from the victim is not a match. I understand Willis has given you a lead on the Go Wild man who rented the flat from him?'

McNab nodded. 'That's why the boss let us set up the sting for later tonight.'

'So that's not why you're here?' she said, meeting his eye.

He indicated it wasn't. 'It's about Ava Clouston.'

'I thought it might be.' She fell silent for a moment, then said abruptly, 'Why didn't you pursue Mark's warning about Cleverly? And don't say it was because of what Jack Winters told you. You didn't trust Cleverly before, and with good reason. Why would anything Winters have said change your mind?'

Stung by that interpretation of events, he came back at her. 'It didn't. Mark was killed because of what he unearthed, and that included what he'd found out about Cleverly.'

She nodded, as though accepting his response. 'Ava called me shortly before your arrival,' she said. 'They're both well and staying with Firash's family at the cafe.'

Relief threatened to swamp him, revealing, even to him, how truly worried he had been.

'Ava said that Mark's diary indicated he was meeting with a police officer the evening he was murdered,' she told him.

'I know,' he blurted out. 'I just don't know who.'

'She believes it was DI Cleverly. I recorded what she said.'

McNab listened as Ava's voice rang out, strong and determined, ending with, *'Cleverly has a son who's involved with Go Wild. That's who he's covering for.'*

He began to absorb the significance of this as the pieces of the jigsaw started fitting together.

'Cleverly said when he was younger he'd had a girlfriend up here. Came to Glasgow all the time, until she chucked him out. Maybe they had a son together?'

Cleverly, he registered, had come to Glasgow determined to find out everything they had on the fire death; on the victim, on possible suspects. He'd even given old Jimmy a bad time. Accused him of being an unreliable witness when Jimmy mentioned he'd seen a male figure at the entrance to the back court.

He'd thought all that was down to the Met wanting to control anything linked to Go Wild, because it messed with their own investigation. Maybe tonight would prove him wrong.

He rose from the table.

'Where are you going?' Rhona said.

'It's time to pick up this guy and find out who he is.'

82

'What took you so long?' Janice said as he slid in beside her.

'I needed to speak to Dr MacLeod about Steven Willis. Turns out she'd just had a conversation with Ava. She and Nadia are in London staying with Firash's family.'

'God, that's a relief.'

'Ava had a lot to say about DI Cleverly in particular.' He gave his partner a quick summary.

'You're saying Cleverly's bent? But I thought you said Jack Winters vouched for him?'

He told her what Ollie had found on the memory stick Mark had left for him.

'Mark believed he was going out to meet a police officer. My bet's on Mark thinking he was meeting an undercover cop, like Winters. That's why he didn't reveal a name.'

'And he met Cleverly instead?' Janice said.

He nodded. 'If we're right, you're about to meet Cleverly's son.'

'It's almost time,' Janice said, checking her watch.

'You ready for this?'

McNab had a sudden fear that he'd put her in danger, when in fact she was the one who'd insisted on it.

'How do I look?' she said, trying a red-lipped smile.

McNab couldn't bear to tell her. 'Stay safe,' he said instead.

As she sashayed away from the car, he found himself

holding his breath. Why had he agreed to this? *Because she volunteered and she's a police officer.*

There were two bouncers on the door to the dive she was heading for. The red light above the entrance illuminated her painted face as she talked her way successfully inside.

A couple of minutes later, her male minders appeared. Seeing the two young cops dressed for a night out clubbing, McNab was reminded of his own age, plus the fact he couldn't be the one keeping watch on his partner. Something he hated, but as he'd been told, he – unlike a tarted-up Janice – was a well-kent face in Glasgow.

One of the two undercover officers turned briefly towards his vehicle, indicating they were about to head inside.

Don't mess this up, McNab said in his head.

Now he truly was in the waiting game, when anything and everything could go wrong, and he, on the outside, could do nothing about it but wait.

His own gear switched on, he spoke to the comms van, parked round the corner and out of sight.

'All good, sir. It's noisy in there, but we're picking up DS Clark and the guys okay.'

He could have gone to sit in the van with them, but he felt compelled to keep his eyes on that door.

A gang of females were now on approach. High and drunk, they skittered along the pavement on shoes that would never permit them to run from trouble. By the end of the night no doubt some of them would be sitting weeping barefoot on the pavement, their fun turned swiftly to misery.

Suddenly there was a skirmish at the door when one of the bouncers put his hands on one of the women, only to discover that the pack had claws and weren't willing to be manhandled.

McNab's estimation of the women rose. Maybe they weren't as out of their heads as he'd imagined.

The tiff over, the women went inside, leaving the pavement bare again.

In the sudden silence, time slowly drifted past him and he began to fill the emptiness with small, insignificant details. The rumble of a corporation bus passing in the distance. One of the bouncers lighting up a cigarette and beginning a conversation with his mate.

It was the car winding its way much too slowly past him, blocking his view of the entrance, that snapped him back to life.

'What's happening?' he checked with the van.

'Clark's at the bar with DC Martin.'

'And Willis?' McNab said.

'He's with a guy, dark hair, bearded, mid-twenties. They're in an alcove, talking. DC Sanders believes that's our mark, sir.'

McNab felt his heart rate quicken. The plan was for Willis to introduce Janice to the mark. Let them get acquainted. Janice had been well up for that, but his own gut had rebelled. He hadn't wanted his partner anywhere near a man who could rape and torture a woman, then set her alight.

There was a pause, then, 'Willis is beckoning Clark over, sir.'

McNab reminded himself it was what they wanted. Despite this, he felt his chest tighten, knowing he should be in there with her.

'What's happening?' he demanded.

'Talking, sir, just talking. And laughing.'

'Fuck's sake,' McNab said. 'Do we still have eyes on Willis?'

A moment's silence, then a slightly worried voice, 'Currently in the Gents. Sanders checking.'

Which meant only one pair of eyes on Clark and the mark. McNab's guts twisted. Two minders weren't enough. They should have had another one inside. He should be in there.

As he made to exit the car, intent on bringing this sting to completion, his mobile rang. Glancing at the screen, he saw Jack Winters's name come up.

What a fucking time to call. He hesitated before pressing the dismiss button. Whatever Winters had to say, it could wait until he got Janice out of there.

Suddenly the worried voice was back in his ear. 'Sir, Willis is no longer in view. I repeat, we have lost Willis.'

McNab cursed under his breath.

So Willis was making a run for it, but not, it seemed, via the front door.

Reconnaissance had indicated the back exit from the club led onto a narrow alley with only one way out, and that was directly across from where he had chosen to park.

He got back on the comms. 'Tell them to stay with Clark. Repeat, stay with Clark. I'm coming in.'

McNab jumped out of the vehicle and, walking casually, crossed the road as though he was bound for the entrance before ducking into the side alley. Narrow, a stone wall forming the outside, only a corner light broke the darkness.

Breaking into a run, he reached the corner and made the ninety-degree turn to find Willis leaning against the wall next to the fire exit, apparently having a leisurely fag.

McNab hesitated. It didn't look as though Willis had any intention of running.

Spotting McNab's figure under the light, Willis nodded,

evidently unfazed by his sudden arrival, maybe even pleased by his appearance. 'Evening, DS McNab.'

McNab's brain was racing. What the hell was going on here? Even as he tried to work the scenario out, a voice in his ear demanded to be told what to do.

'Get DS Clark out and arrest the mark. I have Willis. Repeat, I have Willis.'

As he completed his command, he realized a figure had emerged alongside Willis.

Yards away now, McNab stopped in his tracks when he saw who it was. Only a psycho fucker would have put themselves in this position, he thought.

So that makes two of us.

The earpiece had gone silent, no doubt because his orders were being carried out, but the man before him wouldn't have come alone, which meant the likelihood was that the team inside was already outnumbered.

'Told you he was too clever for you,' Willis said, his eyes shining with glee.

Hugo had sidestepped Willis and was walking towards McNab. He was fully clothed this time, no tanned torso gleaming with sweat, but the expression on his face was the one McNab remembered.

Even in the poor light, McNab could smell the eagerness to kill.

He could stand and fight, or he could flee.

As he fought himself over which to choose, he thought of his partner inside, hardly recognizable in those clothes, painted up like he'd never seen her before.

Without help she would likely pay the price for his mess.

The boss's words rang in his ears. *If some other mad bastard challenges you to a fight . . . get out of there, and fast, Sergeant.*

His retreat through the alley was twice as fast as his entry, his intention being to get inside the front door by whatever means and make sure Janice was okay. Behind him he heard his opponent roar his fury as he swiftly followed.

McNab exited seconds ahead, crashing into what he thought would be Hugo's rearguard.

Lucky for him, it wasn't. Pushed to one side, he watched, gasping for breath, as Hugo ran into a roadblock of waiting officers, backed up by a couple of police vans.

Standing next to his own vehicle, the door hanging open, was the boss.

'Clark?' McNab said, still fighting for breath.

'Fine, and we have our mark. And Willis too.'

'I fucked up, sir. Judgement on how we dealt with this—'

DI Wilson held up his hand to stop him. 'You missed a call from DI Winters?'

McNab looked at his mobile, still lying on the passenger seat where he'd cast it as he'd taken off.

'He'd already called me to warn us that they'd had a tip-off Hugo Radcliff was headed for Glasgow. It didn't take much to wonder if word had got through to Radcliff about all of this.'

'Willis had a direct line to him after all?' McNab said.

'Maybe Willis thought Hugo was a better bet to save him, or else he just wanted to give him a prize. That prize being you. I've a feeling Willis will be keener to talk now.'

'What about our mark?' McNab said.

'The suspect's name is, we believe, Joe Hill. As for who fathered him, that's yet to be established.'

'Are the Met talking to Cleverly?' McNab demanded.

'According to DI Winters, he's gone missing.'

'Some bastard tipped him off,' McNab said angrily, then apologized for swearing.

DI Wilson dismissed his apology. 'Exactly what I was thinking myself, Sergeant.'

'So what now?'

'You go home and get some well-earned sleep, and we discuss this further tomorrow.'

'Not before I speak to my partner, sir,' said McNab, seeing the painted version of Janice emerge from the crowd and come towards him.

83

Janice handed Rhona her phone.

'This is what I looked like last night,' she said. 'You should have seen McNab's face when he got into the car and saw me.'

'Who did your make-up? Those lips, and the eyebrows!' Rhona said, both impressed and slightly horrified at the same time.

'Paula. An ace job, don't you think? It's surprising how getting tarted up changes your mindset. It's a bit like when I was in uniform. Somehow wearing it made me braver.'

'Is McNab in yet?' Rhona said, indicating his empty desk.

'He was here when I arrived. Not sure he got much, if any, sleep. He's in with the boss. A confab before the meeting. You all set?'

Rhona nodded.

'Okay, shall we go in together?'

The atmosphere in the room had changed dramatically since she'd last been here. Getting a result always had that effect. Like winning the lottery, it lifted everyone's spirits.

Rhona had already had a brief résumé from Chrissy about what had gone down last night. Her forensic assistant had been agog with it over their joint breakfast.

Once she'd told Rhona her version, Rhona had been able to fill her in on Ava's phone call and McNab's visit.

Chrissy had given her a knowing look at that point.

'What?' Rhona had remonstrated with her.

'Nothing . . . just that when he's worried about something, you're always his first port of call.'

Maybe in the past, she'd insisted, when McNab was playing the maverick game, but less so now that he'd been partnered with Janice.

'Aye, right,' had been Chrissy's closing retort.

That riposte sprang to mind as McNab climbed on stage to a round of applause and made a point of checking out the audience until his gaze found her, which resulted in a smile.

'He told me you gave him a hard time about Ava,' Janice said. 'Looks like you're forgiven.'

'McNab infuriates me most of the time,' Rhona said.

'You and me both.' Janice gave a wry smile. 'But I also know he always has my back.'

And mine, Rhona thought.

Calling them to order, Bill said, 'As you are no doubt aware, last night's operation was a success. We now have three suspects in custody. Hugo Radcliff, known to most of you by DS McNab's nickname of the posh fucker . . .' He paused as the laughter erupted, then, silencing it, continued. 'As you may also recall, this is the man who knocked out DS McNab earlier in this case. What you might not know is that he tried to do it again last night. Fortunately, on this occasion, the detective sergeant took my advice and ran away to fight another day.'

More laughter as Bill gave McNab a pat on the back. The highest of praise indeed.

'On a more serious note, our prime suspect, Radcliff, is being held in connection with the murder of the recently identified Damian Lloyd and Penny Addington on board the MV *Orlova*. His motive for that is still to be determined. He could simply enjoy killing. He may have been paid to do it. Or it was done as a warning. We cannot ignore the fact that Damian Lloyd's father is a cabinet minister and that Go Wild has links to powerful people.

'Joe Hill is our suspect in the death of fire victim Charlotte Weiner, and Steven Willis as an accomplice in that murder. Exactly what happened that night is still unclear. Willis admits to sexually assaulting Charlotte and handling the bag and the credit cards inside, but not to raping her or killing her. Hill denies ever being there. However, the semen sample retrieved from Charlotte is his. Only recently we also discovered the missing petrol can. It had been dumped nearby and a motorist had picked it up and put it in his boot. It too held Hill's fingerprints. Well done, DS Neville, on discovering that evidence.

'We think Charlotte was cut loose and taken down by Hill in the storm, together with the bag, and set alight. Why was Olivia Newton Richardson's bag used? We can only assume it was to make us think she was the victim. Perhaps she needed to disappear? Something which is still to be determined. We think Hill's motive for raping and killing Charlotte was that he wanted to, and used Go Wild to allow him to do that.'

He paused there for a moment to allow them to digest all of that.

'The sting designed to capture Joe Hill, which resulted in our success, was the work of DS Clark, who volunteered to be the guinea pig, used as bait for Hill, with Steven Willis as the go-between.'

At this point it was Janice who got the round of applause.

'We also have to thank investigative reporter Ava Clouston,

who discovered material collected by her dead colleague, Mark Sylvester, which pointed to the probability that DI Cleverly was working on his own behalf, rather than the Metropolitan Police, when he visited us recently.

'DI Jack Winters, who had been deeply embedded in Go Wild, initially vouched for DS Cleverly to DS McNab, then, after listening to Ava, acted on that knowledge.

'Much of this was made possible by all of your in-depth work on Go Wild, and I fear we have only just scratched the surface of what this company has been involved in worldwide. It has been used by powerful people who will do whatever it takes to stop us from bringing those involved to justice. And, by Hugo Radcliff's demeanour when he was brought in last night, he expects to be back out on bail almost immediately. What he doesn't know is that we retrieved the video of the killings and that our key witness is alive and well, despite apparent plans to add her life to the ones already taken.'

He turned their attention to the screen.

'DI Winters asked if he might join us today to speak to you all.'

The figure visible now on the main screen was sitting up in a hospital bed, his face stitched, his body still heavily bandaged.

'I wanted to thank you all personally, firstly for sending DS McNab down to spy on us. He is, as you all must know, a regular pain in the neck. He is also the most dogged officer I've ever had the pleasure, or misfortune, to work with. We'd offer him a job with the Met, but we know he'd just laugh at us.

'Your forensic identification of Willis, and then the opportunity you gave him to make contact with Joe Hill, led him to head higher up the ladder. Radcliff hates being outsmarted by a cop. McNab's escape, followed by his rescue of me, rankled. Especially because I – an inside witness to what has been going on in Go Wild – survived. So he grabbed the chance to come to Glasgow, something we luckily got wind of. The rest, as you know, is history. As for DI Cleverly, we are still currently trying to locate him.'

Winters waited for the negative response on that to recede before he spoke again.

'I'd just like to finish by assuring you that the Met are fully committed to cooperation with Police Scotland on the continuing investigation, and we are also in touch with both Interpol and the FBI.

'This is a long road we have to travel, but your investigation on both the fire death and the MV *Orlova* have produced the first results we all needed and wanted to see.'

McNab's face throughout Jack Winters's speech told its own tale. Whatever the two men had endured together in captivity, Rhona thought, would never be spoken about, unless it was to one another.

As the boss dismissed the team, he reminded McNab that he had a backlog of reports to write and that he was expecting them on his desk by the end of the day.

It didn't wipe the smile off McNab's face.

'Can I get a decent coffee first?' he suggested to Janice. 'I could bring you back a cake?' When her expression didn't change, he added, 'They have rather good doughnuts, which are a big hit with Ollie?'

Rhona watched as he accompanied this request with his signature smile. Surprisingly, it seemed to work on Janice.

'Why don't you accompany me, Dr MacLeod? I have a couple of forensic questions I'd like to ask you. About fathers and sons.'

Rhona realized she too wasn't averse to that look of his, which was now turned on her.

'Just go,' Janice told her. 'It's sometimes easier to fulfil an occasional wish. Oh,' she went on, 'and while I remember, our dinner party can now be scheduled for Friday evening. D'you think you and Sean might be able to join us?'

Rhona smiled her thanks. 'I'll check with his music time-table and get back to you.'

'Time to call Ellie, McNab,' Janice reminded him. 'Eight o'clock at our place. No excuses.'

'What is it you need to forensically know about?' Rhona said as she and McNab made their way to the cafeteria.

'Did you do anything with the information I fed you last night about Cleverly possibly having a son in Glasgow?'

'I did,' she told him.

He was waiting to hear what exactly it was.

'Cleverly's DNA is on NDNAD as a police officer for elimination purposes,' she reminded him. 'So I ran a familial check on the semen sample taken from the dead girl.'

When McNab looked slightly puzzled, she expanded, 'I'm checking to see if Cleverly and Joe Hill are related.'

He gave her a big, satisfied grin. 'Anything back as yet?'

'If I can get back to my lab, I could find that out.'

'You, Dr MacLeod, can take away two iced doughnuts with sprinkles. The second, of course, being for my name-sake's wonderful mum.'

84

McNab, watching as Rhona left with her doughnut bag, was aware that report writing wasn't the only job he should be doing.

The one he had delayed for even longer now seemed verging on the impossible.

When in doubt, do nothing, a small voice told him.

In his job, he wasn't known for procrastination. His personal life was a different matter.

The situation with Ellie had freaked him so much, he wondered now if he wanted to be back in it again. Plus there was the question of sharing her with someone else. Even if Baldy was eventually cast aside, there would likely be someone to replace him.

He'd had his own one-night – or half-night – stand on the train south, and didn't feel guilty about it, he tried to tell himself. There had also been the skirmish with Mary. Maybe that was the way to go. See Ellie on her terms and do what he liked as well.

None of these thoughts made him feel any better.

It was pretty obvious, even to him, that he got his main kicks from the job, and the messier it was, the better.

He suspected Dr MacLeod suffered from much the same condition.

His work partner, Janice, not so much. She apparently

knew how to balance home life and work, and looked very happy on it.

Plus Sean Maguire was laid-back enough to make a good fit for Rhona, he had to admit that if only to himself.

Jeez, even Ollie had found a match with Maria. Despite the fact she had him on a diet, he still appeared happy.

With that thought, he set off for IT, really as a further displacement activity, but ostensibly to discover if Ollie had anything further of interest to report.

As it turned out, it was a wise move.

Ollie appeared very pleased to see him, which, he thought, wasn't only about the paper bag he was carrying.

'I've been checking out Joe Hill. A swab taken after he was lifted had no direct match on the database, so our Joe Hill hasn't as yet been convicted of a crime in Scotland. However, that doesn't mean he didn't leave a trail behind him somewhere else. I went back to the gamers on the dark web and located him there, under a pseudonym. From where I pieced together more about him: date of birth, mother's name Sheila Hill, father not named on the birth certificate. Looks like he went into care at fourteen, when his mother died.'

'Any obvious relationship with Cleverly?'

'That I haven't established yet.'

When McNab looked disappointed, Ollie said, 'That'll be down to Dr MacLeod, I think.'

Just then, McNab's mobile buzzed with his partner's name on the screen. Indicating his thanks to Ollie, he took himself outside the room to answer the call.

He had started to say he was on his way back when Janice interrupted him. 'Jimmy Donaldson's been on the phone asking for you, but fortunately he agreed to talk to your partner, the *lassie*.'

'And?'

'He wants you over there. Seems he's found what he believes is a piece of evidence.'

'Did he say what?'

'No. He wants to reveal that to you.'

'So you don't want to come along?' McNab tried.

'Have my reports to write. Oh, and remember you promised him a blanket to replace the one he used to put out the fire.'

McNab had a sudden thought. 'Can you send the mugshots of Joe Hill and Steven Willis through to my phone?'

'Sure thing. Where do you plan to get the blanket?' she said sweetly.

McNab had no idea, but didn't like to expose his inadequacy.

'Check with the custody suite,' she offered. 'I'm sure they can spare you one.'

Suitably supplied with blanket and photos, McNab drew up outside the infamous close where this had all begun.

A little net curtain twitching suggested Jimmy had been on the lookout for him via his front window. The main question now was whether Lucifer was at home too.

He had barely banged the knocker when the door was opened.

'Come away in, son. I've been hoping you got my message. The nice lassie police officer said she would pass it on.' At this point he spotted the plastic bag McNab was carrying.

McNab handed it to him. 'As promised, Jimmy, a replacement blanket for the one you lost.'

'Oh my, that's kind of you, son. With the summer almost here I won't be needing it for a couple of months, but I thank you all the same.' He smiled as they entered the back room. 'Good for a mug of coffee, son?'

McNab had hoped to be there and away again, but it appeared that Jimmy had other plans.

'That'd be good, thanks, Jimmy.'

He'd already checked the window ledge for Lucifer and, thankfully, had found it empty. He didn't regret not having those yellow eyes watching his every move, just waiting to pounce and scratch his own eyes out.

Jimmy brought in the pair of Old Firm mugs and handed McNab the Celtic one with a smile. He didn't seem in a hurry to tell McNab why he'd been asked to come here, so he decided to show him the photos on the off-chance Jimmy had taken note of either men in the close.

Jimmy seemed mightily glad to be asked to give his opinion, and studied the images diligently.

'Right,' he finally said, pointing to Steven Willis. 'I've definitely seen this bloke. Remember I said I thought the place might be an Airbnb? He was up and down the stairs a fair bit, so I guessed he had something to do with the place. The other bloke, though. What height is he?'

'Same as me, but stockier.'

'It's the beard. I don't recognize the beard,' Jimmy said, as though he seriously wanted to.

'No worries,' McNab said. 'What about this evidence you wanted to show me?'

Jimmy looked awkward and, for a moment, McNab thought he'd been brought there on false pretences.

'It's just that the cat has this habit of bringing back stuff. He's a hoarder. It's weird, but there it is. He pisses on the stairs and brings back stuff. Thinks he's a dog.'

McNab found himself unsurprised by this new aspect of the devil cat.

'I thought he was outside or up peeing on the stairs, so

I went looking for him. Couldn't find him, so came back and discovered him under my bed with his wee stash. A dead bird, a half-eaten mouse, a sock and this.' He handed McNab a plastic bag. Inside was a cheap throwaway lighter.

'It's not mine,' Jimmy immediately said. 'I don't smoke and the cooker and fire are electric.' He stared at McNab, wide-eyed. 'You lot were looking for a lighter out there, weren't you? D'you think that's it?'

A couple of thoughts ran through McNab's head, one of which was that Jimmy had had the lighter from the beginning. The second was that he'd picked it up off the street as a way of enticing the police to visit again.

Looking at the old man's apologetic face, he tried not to show his suspicions.

'Don't clean under your bed very often, Jimmy?'

'Once a month, Sergeant, without fail. Wish I'd done it sooner though, if it's any help to you.'

'Right. I'll take this in and have forensic take a look. Did you handle it yourself?'

'No, sir. I swept the stuff out with the floor brush. Lucifer was fair spitting at me for doing that. I already had on my Marigolds. I don't like touching the dead stuff he brings in.'

'The cat could have picked it up out front on the road.'

'Maybe, but unlikely. Lucifer's patch is the close and the back court, including the bins. He doesn't like the cars on the road and the main door's mostly closed anyway. He tried out front once when he was younger and got stuck there. You should have heard the racket he made. Would have wakened the dead. That's why I ended up calling him Lucifer.'

'Thanks, Jimmy.'

'Nae bother, son, hope it's what you think and you get the bastard that burned the lassie.'

McNab could have told him there and then that they believed they already had the killer, but thought he would save it for another day. If the lighter did turn out to be evidence in the case, that would be a better story for Jimmy to tell.

'Maybe you'd come back and let me know if it's useful, son?' Jimmy said as he let McNab out.

Getting back in the car, McNab spotted Jimmy's face at the window, watching him leave. Thinking on the lonely old man inside, and how he might end up like that one day, prompted McNab to finally make the long-postponed call.

When Ellie answered, he realized how sweet it was to hear her voice.

He explained about Friday in a tentative manner. 'We're meeting at the jazz club around seven and getting a joint taxi from there. If you still fancy coming,' he added.

There was a short pause, which worried him, before she said, 'Great. See you then.'

85

Cross-border turf wars weren't uncommon. The lawyers and the cops could insist, or resist, all they liked. At the end of the day, it was the prosecuting authorities who decided, DI Wilson told his assembled team.

In general, the jurisdiction of the most serious crime would prevail. Since Police Scotland had video evidence of a double murder being executed on board the MV *Orlova* and had apprehended the perpetrator while he was on Scottish soil, they should have precedence.

However, politics also played a role in all of this. Radcliff had been apprehended here in Glasgow because the Met had given them their intel that he was coming here.

'Plus they believe they have evidence which links him to the death of Mark Sylvester.'

'So he's headed south?' McNab asked the question they all wanted the answer to.

DI Wilson indicated that that would be the case.

'Both Joe Hill and Steven Willis, however, will stand trial here in Glasgow,' he told them. 'And the most recent forensic evidence from Dr MacLeod and her team is, I believe, sufficient to have them both charged with kidnapping, assault and, in Joe Hill's case, rape and murder.'

Janice was the one who now asked about Cleverly.

The news of his death, currently unsubstantiated, had

been running through the station like wildfire since early that morning.

'As you're all aware, DI Cleverly had been picked up and was in custody pending an investigation into his conduct. After a call south by DCI Sutherland, I can now confirm that former DI Cleverly was found dead in his cell at 1.30 a.m. The cause of his death is as yet unknown.'

McNab wasn't surprised by Cleverly's demise. After all, if he'd reached court, his trial would have been damaging to the reputation of the Met, as well as anything he would have to say about those who'd made use of Go Wild.

Neither Nadia's testimony nor Ava's exposé held the same danger for the organization as the bent cop, who'd been working with them . . . for how long?

Thinking back to the Kalinin case, McNab wondered if Cleverly had been in the Russians' pay even back then.

'You were right about Cleverly all along,' Janice said as they settled at their desks. 'Sorry I didn't believe you. I assume someone will tell Joe Hill about his father?'

That had been the really weird thing about the recorded interviews with Hill. He hadn't seemed to have a clue about his link with the police inspector. Claimed never to have known his father.

McNab recalled his own feelings during the initial interview. Thinking how, when you finally got to meet a killer, it was always a let-down. Simply because the person who'd invaded your thoughts for so long invariably turned out to be ordinary.

Joe Hill had fallen into that mould.

Dark-haired, with a beard covering most of his face, only his eyes had been truly noticeable. McNab had tried to find Cleverly somewhere in those eyes . . . and couldn't.

Yet Cleverly had sired the man who'd sat opposite McNab and, despite the apparent fact that he'd had nothing to do with him from birth until now, had attempted to cover up his crime.

Had Cleverly just been worried that any DNA left at the scene might find a familial link with himself?

'If Cleverly hadn't come up here that time,' Janice broke in on his thoughts, 'we may never have discovered the connection.'

In the end, McNab decided his money was on the two men being aware of one another. Which one had made the first move, they were unlikely ever to find out. Especially now that Cleverly was dead.

'Did you ever try to find your father?' Janice suddenly said.

'Never,' McNab said. 'My mother insinuated he was dead. Maybe she did that to make me feel better about never meeting him.'

'Would you have liked to meet him?'

'Sadly,' McNab said, honestly, 'I fear he would be too much like me.'

86

'So tonight's the big night?' Chrissy said.

'I wouldn't call it big. More like – interesting,' Rhona said.

'God, I'd love to be a fly on the wall at this one. Could you record the proceedings for me?' Chrissy asked with an innocent air.

'No photos, no videos. You'll just have to rely on what I tell you, or what Janice does. What about your plans for the weekend?'

'Well, Mum and her man are staying in, so I can go out.' Chrissy smiled. 'Go on, ask me who with?'

Normally Rhona couldn't really keep up with Chrissy's string of boyfriends, but recently things had been slower, with the absence of a babysitter. She decided to take a wild guess. 'What about the helicopter guy. Is it him?'

Chrissy's face fell. 'How did you know?' she said, mystified.

'He spent a lot of time up in the air talking about you, which kept my mind off the fact that I was actually up in the air.'

'His name's Angus Neil and I don't know where we're going or what we're doing.' She looked quite happy about that.

'I have a feeling your evening will be more relaxing than mine,' Rhona said.

Drinks after work with colleagues was fine, when you could always find a reason to head for home. Couples-themed dinner parties could be harder work, depending on how the couples were actually getting along.

Paula and Janice were okay, she thought. She and Sean could be all right, depending on the topic of conversation. McNab and Ellie . . . well, she had no idea how that would go.

At this point in her thoughts, Chrissy came back in.

'The three of you will end up talking about work and piss off Paula, Ellie and Sean.'

Sean hadn't looked too keen when she'd told him about the invite. 'Won't it be all shop talk?' had been his exact words.

Rhona had responded with 'You and McNab have been doing quite a lot of that yourselves recently.'

'Not any more,' Sean had said.

'Are you going to tell me what it was all about?'

Sean had given her a thoughtful look. 'Are you really interested?'

'About as interested as you are in my shop talk.'

'That's why we go so well together,' he'd said. 'If it puts your mind at rest, McNab checked out a guy who was giving me grief about a loan I took out on the club. Turns out he's not bona fide. McNab had a word with him regarding harassment. So all is well.'

Chrissy broke into Rhona's thoughts once more. 'Shall we take bets on whether McNab and Ellie will be a couple again by the end of tonight?'

Rhona shook her head. 'There's no winning that one.'

*

Recalling that conversation as she gazed around the dinner table, Rhona was a little surprised at how well it was going. Maybe it was the excellent food and the copious amount of wine that was being drunk, but she was actually enjoying herself.

Then began a brief foray into work topics, which Paula allowed. One of which was McNab's tale of Lucifer the devil cat, and the surprise discovery of the lighter used to start the fire.

'The lighter Dr MacLeod forensically linked to the perpetrator,' he said with a congratulatory look at Rhona.

At that point the amusing aspects of the story – the cat as hoarder, the dead mouse, the bird, the sock and the lighter stashed under an old man's bed – suddenly ceased to be amusing because they all led inevitably to what the lighter had been used to do.

As silence fell like a stone and Rhona caught the shadow crossing McNab's face, she registered again what she'd always known.

It wasn't what a detective did in a case. It was what the case did to them.

Seeing Ellie's expression at this point showed just how hard it would be for her to stick with McNab. She wanted to, Rhona thought, but probably couldn't.

Rhona wondered if McNab already knew that.

Sean eventually saved the day, as he was often wont to do, by using an Irish tale to make them all laugh, and suddenly life was light again. However briefly.

The evening ended well enough. Sean had decided on a break-out phrase, to be used if required.

In fact, it was Rhona who used it first, but Sean happily obliged by standing up and agreeing with their need to go home *because of her cat, Tom, having been shut out on the roof.*

As they climbed into the taxi and therefore out of earshot of their hosts, he said, 'You're a terrible liar, Dr MacLeod. Sure, not a soul in there believed you. Especially McNab. They just thought you wanted home to have sex with me.'

'And they were right,' Rhona said.

Six weeks later

Fast approaching midsummer, sunrise and sunset on Orkney were currently over eighteen hours apart. Ask Dougie and he would recite the rise and fall of the sun to the exact minute.

All Ava knew was that her curtains weren't thick enough to keep out the light, either at night or in the early morning. She didn't care.

She had promised herself that if they were successful in their efforts to bring Nadia's persecutor to justice, she would bring the girl back here to Orkney for the summer. After which, Nadia could decide what she wanted to do and where she wanted to go in the future.

Already she had made Polish friends in Stromness and was able to use her own language again. She had also been offered work, and had accepted a job in a local hotel.

Her stay at the farm would end soon, when she would move into the accommodation that went with the job.

Ava would miss the person she had become. Gone was the traumatized girl Dougie had rescued from the *Orlova*. In her place was a girl who would not give up in her attempts to catch the man who had been responsible for the death of her friends.

For that was what had driven her on, despite her fears. Not the deaths of the two people who had chosen to be on the ship, but the deaths of Guido and the others, whose names she had reeled off to DS McNab in her interview.

Standing now by the edge of the water, where the boat-house was already rising from its ashes and the *Fear Not* tied up nearby, Ava was thankful that the ship that had haunted their lives had finally left Scapa Flow, bound for the scrap-ping yard.

Crowds had apparently gathered at Houton Pier to watch. Magnus had asked her to join him there, but she hadn't wanted to, preferring to wait until it had truly gone, that she might stand here and look on Hoy without its monstrous presence spoiling the view.

Since its removal, the world had taken on a different hue.

Dougie and Tommy Flett had come to an arrangement with the farm, which seemed to be working well. As the elder sibling, she was still ultimately financially responsible, but Dougie's eighteenth birthday had placed him firmly in the adult category and he was living up to her expectations of that.

They had finally visited their parents' graves in Stromness cemetery together, something, until now, he'd refused to do. They were both healing, as was Nadia.

Her own still-open wound was the loss of Mark. Their plan, Nadia and she, in going to London, had been twofold. To bring Hugo Radcliff to justice and to identify Mark's killer.

They had succeeded in the first instance, but not yet the second. Something Ava was unwilling to accept. Neither was she going to stop her investigation into Go Wild.

So many doors had closed when the police had brought in Radcliff, and despite all their efforts, he had made bail. The issue of jurisdiction had of course arisen. Whether he should be prosecuted under Scottish or English Law. As they'd known, he had proved to have important friends in high places, who did not want his crimes, or theirs, to be revealed.

For that to be controlled, it was better for them to have him down in London.

In previous cases like this, the accused had often taken their own life. Or, at least, appeared to. As for Radcliff, he was still very much alive and well. As was his female counterpart, who Interpol had not yet located.

With the number of Go Wild ships still operating in the Mediterranean and other exotic places around the world, Olivia Newton Richardson could be anywhere at sea or on land. Working to rebuild the company.

Tonight would be Ava's last Orkney sunset for a while. London beckoned her. Mark still needed her to try to expose what had cost him his life.

It was her job, after all.

Acknowledgements

When we first moved to Orkney from Glasgow many years ago, we stayed with the Piries on their Orakirk farm in Orphir, which became the inspiration for Ava Clouston's home in *The Killing Tide*. Their kindness and hospitality, plus Geordie's great storytelling, inspired both this story and an enduring love of Orkney.

Thanks must also go to . . .

Dr Jennifer Miller, Associate Professor of Forensic Science at Nottingham Trent University, who I first met when I did the Diploma in Forensic Medical Science at Glasgow University, and who continues to be an inspiration.

Professor Niamh Nic Daeid, Director of the Leverhulme Research Centre for Forensic Science at the University of Dundee, for her help with fire forensics.

Emeritus Professor of Forensic Pathology James Grieve, who was happy, as always, to discuss weapons and their resultant injuries.

Finally Professor Lorna Dawson at the James Hutton Institute, who is always on hand to answer any soil forensic questions I might have.

Without the real experts, Dr Rhona MacLeod would be unable to solve the crimes I create for her, and of course any errors are entirely my own.

I'd also like to give thanks to Donald Findlay QC, who

advised me on the intricacies of cross border cooperation and jurisdiction.

Last but not least, a big thank you to my excellent editor Alex Saunders, my desk editor Samantha Fletcher for her eagle eye, and all at Pan Macmillan, who continue to champion the Dr Rhona MacLeod series.

OUT NOW

DRIFTNET

Go back to where it all began with the thrilling
first novel in the Rhona MacLeod series.

OUT IN AUGUST 2022

THE PARTY HOUSE

By Lin Anderson

The village of Blackrig in the Scottish Highlands was shocked when seventeen-year-old Ailsa Cummings went missing five years ago. And a recent pandemic has stirred up old tensions and sparked an animosity towards outsiders in the small community.

After a local estate decides to reopen its luxury 'party house' to tourists, an angry mob causes damage to the property's hot tub, only to unearth the buried body of the missing girl in its foundations. The discovery reignites old suspicions among the villagers, especially the men, who'd known Ailsa.

Men like Greg, who has invited Joanne to stay with him having met her on a recent business trip in London. When questioned about the girl, he angrily refuses to discuss the case. Joanne, disturbed by his reaction, questions how well she knows this new man in her life. Then again, he's not the only one with secrets in their volatile relationship.

When a police team arrives to excavate the remains, they find a close-knit community who would prefer the past to stay buried . . .

Turn the page to read a teaser now.

Ailsa

Before

Eleven o'clock and the sky was still light. In Glasgow it would be dark by now, she thought.

She hadn't wanted to come here, to this dead-end village in the Highlands, but here she was.

You could have run away again, a small voice reminded her.

No, I made a deal. Come here, stay clean. Go to art college in September.

She'd hated it at first. Folk looking at her as though she'd just dropped in from outer space. They were friendly enough, she had to admit that, especially the local boys, who'd fought for her attention from the outset.

She smiled, remembering the fun she'd had with that, playing them off one against the other. It was a game that had kept her sane at the beginning. Made her feel good about herself. She'd even tasted some of the wares on offer, and found a few to her liking.

Especially when they took place here in the heart of the woods.

She ran her eyes over the circle of carvings that stood sentinel among the trees, thinking again how beautiful they were. The birds fashioned from stripped pine, some in flight,

1

others resting quietly on a branch. Her favourite was the owl sitting watching her from atop a tree trunk pedestal.

He was so real that she often found herself talking to him.

Then the woodland creatures . . . A roe deer, she could imagine taking off to bound away through the trees. A pair of majestic wolves nearby which might pursue it. Even imagining this didn't worry her, because she had no doubt who would win that particular race.

Her eyes were now drawn to the centre of the circle and the father and mother of all the carvings . . . literally. The green woman of the woods, together with the green man.

Until it was explained to her that they were a symbol of rebirth, she'd had no idea what the green faces staring out of the leaves and twigs were. Initially, she'd found them rather spooky. Once she knew they represented the cycle of new growth that occurred with every spring, her attitude to them had changed.

She'd starting bringing her sketch pad here and, sitting on this tree trunk, she'd drawn all of the carvings, then added a few imaginary ones of her own.

It was here she'd first encountered him. In fact, it was he who'd explained the carvings to her.

She was startled from her reverie by a burst of music escaping from the distant village hall as someone opened the back exit. Raucous shouts followed from the guys who were hanging about on the steps, drinking and smoking.

She'd already run that particular gauntlet when she'd left the ceilidh, with plenty of offers to walk her home. All the way to her family's cottage, Forrigan.

The familiar faces of Josh Huntly and his assorted mates had met her at the door. She'd already danced with Josh and a couple of the others, including the shy Finn Campbell, but hadn't taken anyone up on their offer, knowing full well a walk wasn't what they had in mind.

Been there. Done that. No longer interested.

She checked her phone, but the waited-for message hadn't arrived . . . yet.

She took a deep breath of the night air, filled with the scent of pine. The June weather had been warm and dry. Even here, the normally boggy ground and its three amber peaty pools had partially dried out.

The rain will come, everyone said. Hopefully soon enough to prevent a fire in the pinewoods or the moor.

She tried to imagine such a fire . . . the crackling of the bone-dry heather, the whoosh as the pine needles flared up, the hot sweet smell of smouldering peat.

It should have frightened her, but it didn't. Not until she thought of the green woman and man ablaze. The leaves and winding branches that made up their bodies a mass of fire. Like back when they'd burned women as witches. That was an image she didn't like.

The crack of a twig underfoot caused her to turn in anticipation.

She rose to greet him, hearing his footsteps cross the needle-strewn forest floor, feeling a surge of desire.

Her smile, at first warm and welcoming, slowly shifted to something very different as she realized the footsteps were multiple, and none of them were likely to be his.

Greg

Now

Blood hit the mirror in a fine spray.

Cursing, he grabbed a towel and wiped his face, his hand and then the mirror.

So much blood for such a small cut.

He was examining the damage when a sleepy Joanne appeared beside him to kiss the wound.

'There,' she said. 'All better.' She laughed. 'For a man who can cleanly butcher a deer, you seem a little careless with your own face.'

There was a smear of blood on her lips. He put his mouth on hers, tasting it. This is what it had been like since the moment they'd met in London. This gnawing hunger for her, which had never abated.

Taking her in his arms, he lifted her on to the surface. She laughed as he moved to position himself between her legs.

Later, when he was finally dressed, she asked if he might pick up a few things in the local shop for her.

He assumed an amused smile. 'I'm out on the hill all day. You could take a walk down yourself?'

She didn't look keen to do that. 'Caroline doesn't like me,' she said with a wry smile.

'I told you, it's not personal. Besides, you don't strike me as a big fearty.'

'What's a big fearty?' she demanded.

'Something you're not.' He kissed her firmly. 'There are venison steaks in the fridge. I'll cook them when I get back.'

He headed out to the Land Rover, releasing his two labs, Cal and Sasha, from their kennels to jump into the back.

In the glen below, where Blackrig nestled, the morning sun had burned off most of the mist, although faint spirals of it still rose from the surrounding pinewoods like spirits escaping the dawn.

Settled now in the Land Rover, he glanced in the rear-view mirror to find Joanne, still in a state of undress, observing his departure. He hooted the horn in response to her wave, and thought back to the moment they'd first met.